ST. MARTIN'S
MINOTAUR
MYSTERIES

EXTRAORDINARY ACCLAIM FOR

STEVEN SAYLOR

"Saylor offers rich history with great imagination."

—*Seattle Times*

"Gordianus has wisdom and prudence; Saylor has intelligence, wit, and insight. Saylor has acquired the information of a historian but he enjoys the gifts of a born novelist."

—*The Boston Globe*

ARMS OF NEMESIS

"Captivating descriptions of Roman customs and mythologies, and interesting characters, enlivened from the pages of history."

—*San Francisco Sentinel*

"Sensuously written . . . Richly detailed bacchanalian feasts and mesmerizing visits to the Sybil at Cumae lead to the spellbinding conclusion."

—*Publishers Weekly*

"Really excellent . . . an enthralling recreation of time and place, fascinating storytelling."

—Derek Jacobi, star of BBC's *I, Claudius*

"A most intriguing mystery . . . highly researched and authentic historical background . . . characters all of whom are realistic flesh-and-blood people."

—*The Southbridge Massachusetts News*

"Fine mystery, great history, this novel is crammed with vivid details of patrician and slave life. After reading the below decks description of a time you'll thank your lucky stars you're not a galley slave."

—*Omnibus*

ROMAN BLOOD

"Saylor's evocation of ancient Rome is vivid and realistic. Within its compelling story, one tours Roman life from bottom to top in what is both good history and good mystery . . . A novelist whose future work will be well worth reading." —*Austin Chronicle*

"Gripping . . . a combination of Hitchcock-style suspense and vivid historical detail." —*Pittsburgh Post-Gazette*

"Engrossing . . . An entertaining mystery [which] also provides a view of life in ancient Rome. Highly recommended."
—*Booklist*

"Capturing the time and place brilliantly, this is one of the best historical mysteries I've read." —*The Armchair Detective*

"Saylor visits all the strata of Roman life and gives a vivid picture of ancient society to go with the complex puzzle . . . A remarkable achievement."
—*Ellery Queen's Mystery Magazine*

THE HOUSE OF THE VESTALS

"Entertainment of the first order."
—*The Washington Post Book World*

"As usual, Saylor does a superb job of seamlessly incorporating the tumultuous history of the Roman Republic into the narrative flow. A welcome addition to the ever fascinating chronicles of Gordianus the Finder." —*Booklist*

"Remarkable . . . A stirring blend of history and mystery, well seasoned with conspiracy, passion and intrigue. A classic historical mystery in every sense." —*Publishers Weekly*

"Fans of Gordianus the Finder, rejoice! . . . Working with a scholar's knowledge of period detail and a born story-teller's genius, Saylor both instructs and entertains." —*Anniston Star*

ST. MARTIN'S PAPERBACKS TITLES BY STEVEN SAYLOR

ROMAN BLOOD
THE HOUSE OF THE VESTALS
ARMS OF NEMESIS
THE VENUS THROW
A MURDER ON THE APPIAN WAY
RUBICON

ARMS OF NEMESIS

STEVEN SAYLOR

St. Martin's Paperbacks

ARMS OF NEMESIS

Library of Congress Catalog Card Number: 92-25221

ISBN: 0-312-97832-4

Printed in the United States of America

St. Martin's Press hardcover edition 1992
St. Martin's Paperbacks edition / February 2001

St. Martin's Paperbacks are published by St. Martin's Press, 175 Fifth Avenue, New York, N.Y. 10010.

10 9 8 7 6 5 4 3 2 1

To Penni Kimmel,
helluo librorum et litterarum studiosus

CONTENTS

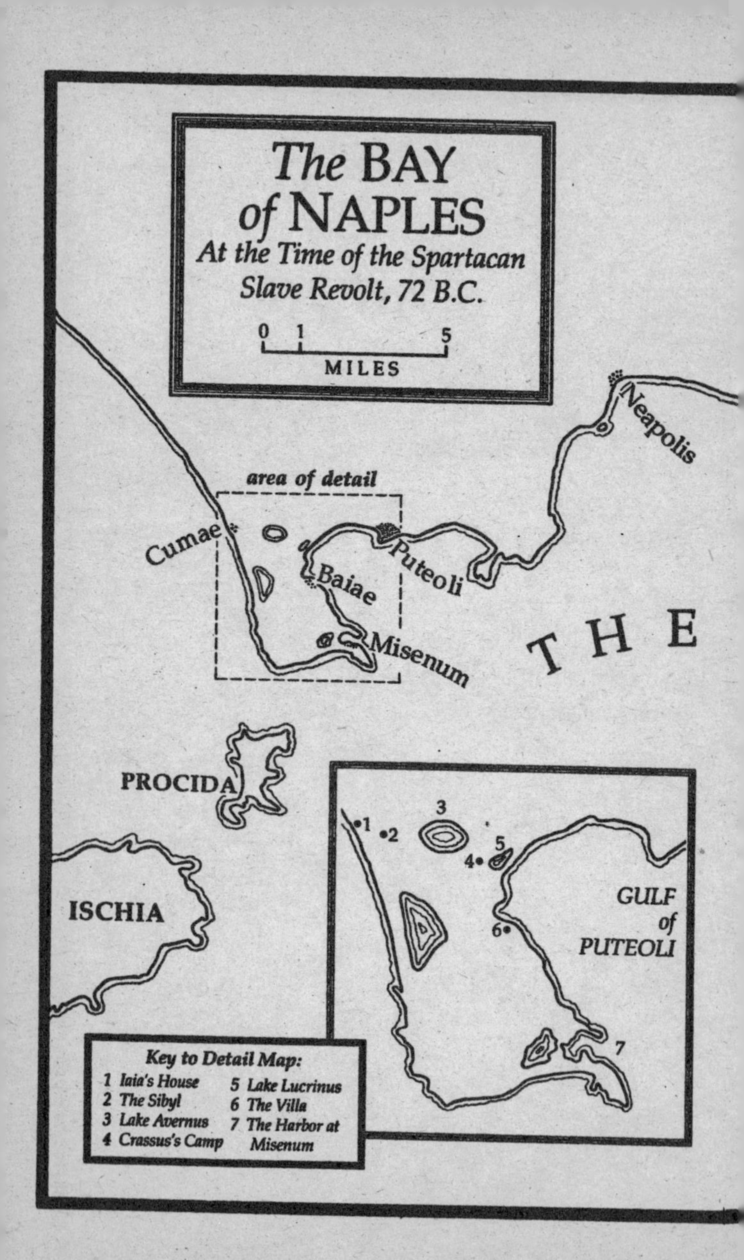
The BAY of NAPLES
At the Time of the Spartacan Slave Revolt, 72 B.C.
0 1 5
MILES
area of detail
Neapolis
Cumae
Puteoli
Baiae
Misenum
THE
PROCIDA
ISCHIA
1
2
3
4
5
6
7
GULF of PUTEOLI
Key to Detail Map:
1 Iaia's House
2 The Sibyl
3 Lake Avernus
4 Crassus's Camp
5 Lake Lucrinus
6 The Villa
7 The Harbor at Misenum

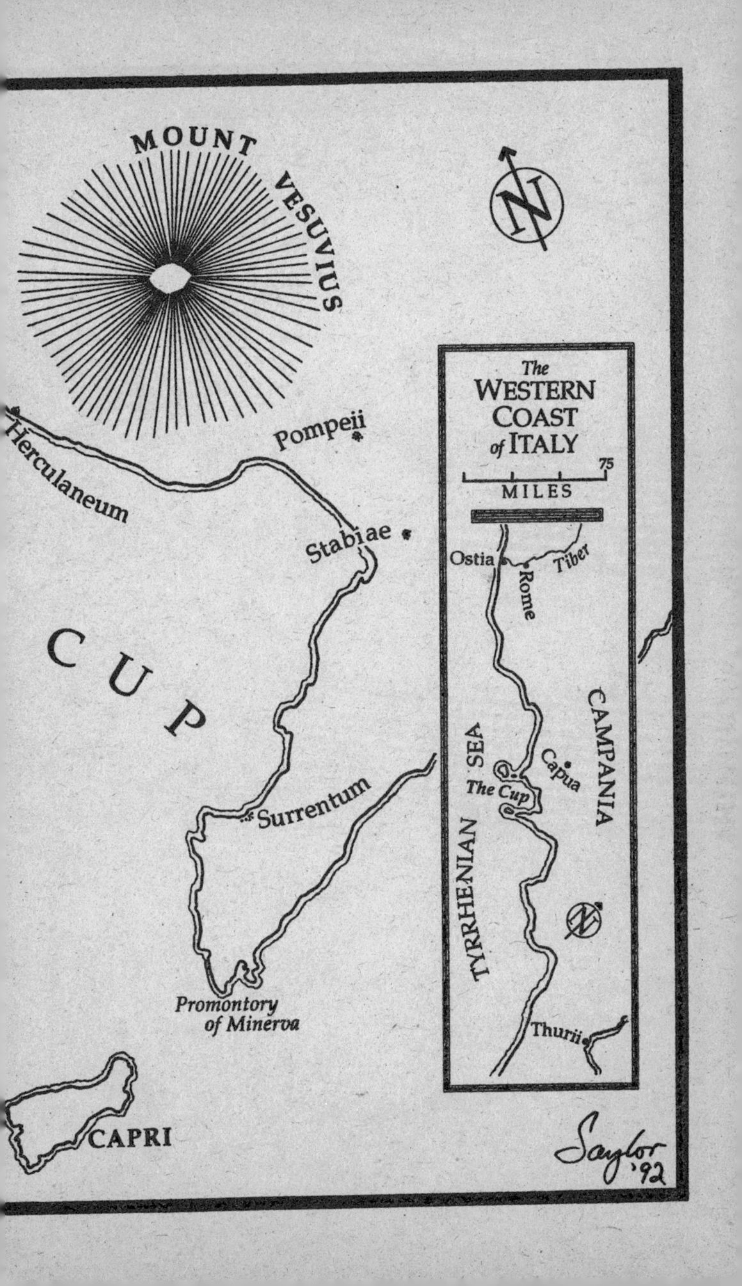

MOUNT VESUVIUS
Herculaneum
Pompeii
Stabiae
CUP
Surrentum
Promontory
of Minerva
CAPRI
The
WESTERN
COAST
of ITALY
75
MILES
Ostia
Rome
Tiber
TYRRHENIAN SEA
CAMPANIA
Capua
The Cup
Thurii
Saylor
'92

PART ONE

Corpses, Living and Dead

ONE

FOR all his fine qualities—his honesty and devotion, his cleverness, his uncanny agility—Eco was not well suited for answering the door. Eco was mute.

But he was not and has never been deaf. He has, in fact, the sharpest ears of anyone I've ever known. He is also a light sleeper, a habit held over from the wretched, watchful days of his childhood, before his mother abandoned him and I took him in from the street and finally adopted him. Not surprisingly, it was Eco who heard the knock at the door in the second hour after nightfall, when everyone in the household had gone to bed. It was Eco who greeted my nocturnal visitor, but was unable to send him away, short of shooing at him the way a farmer shoos an errant goose from his doorway.

Therefore, what else could Eco have done? He might have roused Belbo, my strongarmer. Hulking and reeking of garlic and stupidly rubbing the sleep from his eyes, Belbo might have intimidated my visitor, but I doubt that he could have gotten rid of him; the stranger was persistent and twice as clever as Belbo is strong. So Eco did what he had to do; he made a sign for my visitor to wait in the doorway and came rapping gently at my door. Rapping having failed to rouse me—generous helpings of Bethesda's fish and barley soup washed down with white wine had sent me fast asleep—Eco gingerly opened the door, tiptoed into the room, and shook my shoulder.

Beside me Bethesda stirred and sighed. A mass of black hair had somehow settled across my face and neck. The shifting strands tickled my nose and lips. The odor of her perfumed henna sent a quiver of erotic tingling below my waist. I reached for her, making my lips into a kiss, running my hands over her body. How was it possible, I wondered, that she could reach all the way over and around me to tug at my shoulder from behind?

Eco never liked to make those grunting, half-animal noises eked out by the speechless, finding such measures degrading and embarrassing. He preferred to remain austerely silent, like the Sphinx, and to let his hands speak for him. He gripped my shoulder harder and shook it just a bit more firmly. I recognized his touch then, as surely as one knows a familiar voice. I could even understand what he was saying.

"Someone at the door?" I mumbled, clearing my throat and keeping my eyes shut for a moment longer.

Eco gave my shoulder a little slap of assent, his way of saying "yes" in the dark.

I snuggled against Bethesda, who had turned her back on the disturbance. I touched my lips to her shoulder. She let out a breath, something between a coo and a sigh. In all my travels from the Pillars of Hercules to the Parthian border, I have never met a more responsive woman. Like an exquisitely crafted lyre, I thought to myself, perfectly tuned and polished, growing finer with the years; what a lucky man you are, Gordianus the Finder, what a find you made in that slave market in Alexandria fifteen years ago.

Somewhere under the sheets the kitten was stirring. Egyptian to her core, Bethesda has always kept cats and even invites them into our bed. This one was traversing the valley between our bodies, picking a path from thigh to thigh. So far it had kept its claws hidden; a good thing, since in the last few moments my most vulnerable part had grown conspicuously more vulnerable and the kitten seemed to be heading straight for it, perhaps thinking it was a serpent to play with. I snuggled against Bethesda for protection. She sighed. I remembered a rainy night at least ten years ago, before Eco joined us—a different cat, a different bed, but the very same house, the house that my father left me, and the two of us, Bethesda and myself, younger but not so very different from today. I dozed, nearly dreaming.

Two sharp slaps landed on my shoulder.

Two slaps was Eco's way of saying "no," like shaking his head. No, he would not or could not send my visitor away.

He tapped me again, twice sharply on the shoulder. "All right, all right!" I muttered. Bethesda rolled aggressively away, dragging the sheet with her and exposing me to the dank September air. The kitten tumbled toward me, sticking out its claws as it flailed for balance.

"Numa's balls!" I snapped, though it wasn't fabled King Numa who found himself wounded by a single tiny claw. Eco discreetly ignored my yelp of pain. Bethesda laughed sleepily in the darkness.

I snapped out of bed and fumbled for my tunic. Eco was already holding it ready for me to crawl into.

"This had better be important!" I said.

It was important, just how important I had no way of knowing that night, and not for some time after. If the emissary waiting in my vestibule had made himself clear, if he had been frank about why and for whom he had come, I would have bent to his wishes without the least hesitation. Such a case and such a client as fell into my lap that night are few and far between; I would have fought for the chance to take on the job. Instead, the man, who curtly introduced himself as Marcus Mummius, affected an air of portentous secrecy and treated me with a suspicion that bordered on contempt.

He told me that my services were needed, without delay, for a job that would take me away from Rome for several days. "Are you in some sort of trouble?" I asked.

"Not me!" he bellowed. He seemed incapable of talking in a tone of voice reasonable for a sleeping household. His words came out in a series of grunts and barks, the way that one speaks to an unruly slave or a bad dog. There is no language as ugly as Latin when it is spoken in such a fashion—barracks-fashion, I mean, for as sleepy as I was and as numbed with the evening's wine, I was beginning to make certain deductions about my uninvited guest. Disguised behind his well-trimmed beard, his austere but expensive-looking black tunic, his finely made boots and plush woolen cloak, I saw a soldier, a man used to giving orders and being instantly obeyed.

"Well," he said, looking me up and down as if I were a lazy recruit fresh out of bed and dragging my feet before the day's march. "Are you coming or not?"

Eco, offended at such rudeness, put his hands on his hips and glowered. Mummius threw back his head and snorted in a fit of impatience.

I cleared my throat. "Eco," I said, "fetch me a cup of wine, please. Warmed, if you can; see if the embers are still glowing in the kitchen. And a cup for you as well, Marcus Mummius?" My guest scowled and shook his head sharply, like a good legionnaire on guard duty.

"Some warm cider, perhaps? No, I insist, Marcus Mummius. The night is cool. Come, follow me into my study. Look, Eco has already lit the lamps for us; he anticipates all my needs. Here, sit—no, I insist. Now, Marcus Mummius, I take it you've come here offering me work."

In the brighter light of the study I could see that Mummius looked worn and tired, as if he had not slept properly for some time. He fidgeted in his chair and held his eyes open with an unnatural alertness. After a moment he sprang up and began pacing, and when Eco came with his warm cider he refused to take it. Thus does a soldier on a long watch refuse to make himself comfortable for fear that sleep will come against his will.

"Yes," he finally said. "I have come to summon you—"

"Summon me? No one *summons* Gordianus the Finder. I am a citizen, no man's slave or freedman, and at last report Rome was still a Republic, amazingly enough, and not a dictatorship. Other citizens come to consult me, to ask for my services, to *hire* me. And they usually come during daylight. At least the honest ones do."

Mummius appeared to be working hard to contain his exasperation. "This is ridiculous," he said. "You'll be paid, of course, if that's what you're worried about. In fact, I'm authorized to offer you five times your regular daily pay, considering the inconvenience and the . . . travel," he said cautiously. "Five days of guaranteed pay, plus all your lodging and expenses."

He had my full attention. From the corner of my eye I saw Eco raise an eyebrow, counseling me to be shrewd; children of the streets grow up to be hard bargainers. "Very generous, Marcus Mummius, very generous," I said. "Of course you may not realize that I had to raise my rates only last month. Prices in Rome keep shooting up, what with this slave revolt and the invincible Spartacus rampaging through the countryside, spreading chaos—"

"Invincible?" Mummius seemed personally offended. "Spartacus invincible? We'll soon see about that."

"Invincible when confronted by a Roman army, I mean. The Spartacans have beaten every contingent sent against them; they've even sent two Roman consuls running home in disgrace. I suppose that when Pompey—"

"Pompey!" Mummius spat the name.

"Yes, I suppose that when Pompey finally manages to bring back his troops from Spain, the revolt will be quickly disposed of. . . ." I rambled on only because the topic seemed to irritate my guest, and I wanted to keep him distracted while I drove up my price.

Mummius cooperated gloriously, pacing, gnashing his teeth, glowering. But it seemed he would not descend to gossiping about a subject as important as the slave revolt. "We'll see about that," was all he would mutter, trying feebly to interrupt me. Finally he raised his voice to command level and effectively cut me off. "We'll soon see about *Spartacus*! Now, then, you were saying something about your rates."

I cleared my throat and took a sip of warm wine. "Yes. Well, as I was saying, with prices wildly out of control—"

"Yes, yes—"

"Well, I don't know what you or your employer may have heard about my rates. I don't know how you obtained my name or who recommended me."

"Never mind that."

"All right. Though you did say five times . . ."

"Yes, five times your daily pay!"

"It might be rather steep, considering that my normal price . . ." Eco had moved behind the man and was gesturing *up, up, up* with his thumb. "Eighty sesterces a day," I said, wildly choosing a number from nowhere—about twice the monthly pay of a regular legionnaire.

Mummius looked at me oddly, and for a moment I thought I had gone too far. Ah, well, if he turned and stamped out of the house without another word, at least I could return to my warm bed and Bethesda. He was probably luring me on a fool's errand, anyway.

Then he burst out laughing.

Even Eco was taken aback. I watched him over Mummius's shoulder, wrinkling his eyebrows. "Eighty sesterces a day," I said, as serenely as I could, trying not to mirror Eco's confusion. "You do understand?"

"Oh, yes," Mummius said, his barking barracks laughter reduced to a smirk.

"And five times that—"

"Four hundred a day!" he snapped. "I know my figures." Then he snorted, with such sincere contempt that I knew I could have demanded much more.

My work frequently brings me into contact with the wealthy classes of Rome. The rich need lawyers in their battles against each other; lawyers need information; obtaining information is my specialty. I have accepted fees from advocates like Hortensius and Cicero, and sometimes directly from clients as distinguished as the great Metelli and Messalli families. But even they might balk at the idea of paying Gordianus the Finder a daily fee of four hundred sesterces. Just how wealthy was the client whom Marcus Mummius represented?

There was no question now that I would take the job. The money assured it—Bethesda would coo with delight to see so much silver pour into the household coffers, and certain creditors might start greeting me with smiles again instead of unleashed dogs. But curiosity was the real trap. I wanted to know who had sent Marcus Mummius to my door. Still, I didn't want him to see that he had won me over quite yet.

"This investigation must be rather important," I said

blandly, trying to sound professionally cool while fountains of silver coins splashed in my head. Four hundred sesterces a day, multiplied by five guaranteed days of work, equaled two thousand sesterces. At last I could have the back wall of the house repaired, have new tiles laid to replace the cracked ones in the atrium, perhaps even afford a new slave girl to help Bethesda with her duties. . . .

Mummius nodded gravely. "It's as important a case as you're ever likely to be called for."

"And sensitive, I take it."

"Extremely."

"Requiring discretion."

"Great discretion," he agreed.

"I assume that more than mere property is at stake. Honor, then?"

"More than honor," said Mummius gravely, with a haunted look in his eyes.

"A life, then? A life at stake?" From the look on his face I knew that we were talking about a case of murder. A fat fee, a mysterious client, a murder—I had no resistance left. I did my best to make my face a blank.

Mummius looked very grave—the way that men look on a battlefield, not in the rush of excitement before the killing, but afterward, amid the carnage and despair. "Not a life," he said slowly, "not merely a single life at stake, but many lives. Scores of lives—men, women, children—all hang in the balance. Unless something is done to stop it, blood will flow like water, and the wailing of babies will be heard in the very Jaws of Hades."

I finished my wine and set it aside. "Marcus Mummius, will you not tell me outright who sent you, and what it is you want me to do?"

He shook his head. "I've said too much as it is. Perhaps, by the time we arrive, the crisis will be over, the problem solved, and there'll be no need for you after all. In that case, it's best that you know nothing, now or ever."

"No explanation?"

"None. But you'll be paid, no matter what."

I nodded. "How long will we be away from Rome?"

"Five days, as I said before."

"You seem very sure."

"Five days," he assured me, "and then you can return to Rome. Unless it's sooner. But no longer than that. In five days all will be finished, one way or another, for better . . . or for worse."

"I see," I said, not seeing at all. "And where exactly are we going?"

Mummius pressed his lips tightly shut.

"Because," I said, "I'm not at all sure that I care to be traipsing about the countryside just now, without even an idea of where I'm headed. There's a little slave revolt going on; I believe we were discussing it only a moment ago. My sources in the countryside tell me that unnecessary travel is highly inadvisable."

"You'll be safe," Mummius snapped with authority.

"Then I have your word as a soldier—or is it ex-soldier?—that I won't be placed in tactical jeopardy?"

Mummius narrowed his eyes. "I said you'll be safe."

"Very well. Then I think I shall leave Belbo here, for Bethesda's protection; I'm sure your employer can supply me with a bodyguard if I require it. But I shall want to bring Eco with me. I take it your employer's generosity will extend to feeding him and giving him a place to sleep?"

He looked over his shoulder at Eco with a skeptical gleam in his eye. "He's only a boy."

"Eco is eighteen; he put on his first manly toga over two years ago."

"Mute, isn't he?"

"Yes. Ideal for a soldier, I should think."

Mummius grunted. "I suppose you can take him."

"When do we leave?" I asked.

"As soon as you're ready."

"In the morning, then?"

He looked at me as if I were a lazy legionnaire asking for a nap before a battle. The commander's edge returned to his voice. "No, as soon as you're ready! We've wasted enough time as it is!"

"Very well," I yawned. "I'll just tell Bethesda to gather up a few of my things—"

"That won't be necessary." Mummius pulled himself up to his full height, still weary-looking but happy to be in charge at last. "Anything you need will be supplied to you."

Of course; a client willing to pay four hundred sesterces a day could certainly supply mere necessities like a change of clothing or a comb or a slave to carry my things. "Then I'll take only a moment to say good-bye to Bethesda."

I was stepping out of the room when Mummius cleared his throat. "Just to be sure," he said, looking at me and Eco in turn, "I don't suppose either one of you has a problem with seasickness?"

TWO

BUT where is the man taking you?" Bethesda demanded to know. (Yes, "demanded"; never mind her status as a slave. If her impertinence seems unlikely, that is because you have not met Bethesda.) "Who is he? What makes you think he can be trusted? What if he's been sent by one of your old enemies, just to lure you away from the city where he can slit your throat with no one to see?"

"Bethesda, if someone cared to slit my throat, they could go to far less trouble and do the job right here in the Subura. They could hire an assassin on any street corner."

"Yes, and that's why you have Belbo to protect you. Why aren't you taking him with you?"

"Because I would rather he stayed here to protect you and the other slaves in my absence, so that I won't have to worry about you while I'm gone."

Even roused from sleep in the middle of the night, Bethesda was spectacular. Her hair, black with strands of silver, tumbled about her face in unkempt glory. Even pouting, she maintained that same air of unshakable dignity that had first drawn me to her in the slave market at Alexandria fifteen years ago. I felt a shiver of doubt, as I always do at parting with her. The world is an unsafe and uncertain place, and the life I have chosen often courts danger. I learned long ago not to show my doubts. Bethesda did the opposite.

"It's a great deal of money," I told her.

She snorted. "If he tells the truth."

"I think he does. A man doesn't survive in a city like Rome for as long as I have without gaining a grain of judgment. Marcus Mummius is honest, insofar as he can be. Not very forthcoming, I'll admit—"

"But he won't even tell you who sent him!"

"Indeed, he won't tell me, but he openly admits that he won't. In other words, he tells the truth."

Bethesda made a rude noise with her lips. "You sound like one of those orators you're always working for, like that ridiculous Cicero, saying truth is a lie and a lie is the truth, however it happens to suit you."

I bit my tongue and took a deep breath. "Trust me, Bethesda. I've stayed alive until now, haven't I?" I looked into her eyes and thought I saw a slight warmth amid the cold fire. I laid my hand on her shoulder. She shrugged it off and turned away. So it always goes.

I stepped closer and put my hands on the back of her neck, sliding them under the cascades of her hair. She had no right to refuse me, and did not draw away, but she stiffened at my touch and held her head high, even when I bent to kiss her ear. "I will come back," I said. "After five days I return. So the man promises."

I saw her cheeks tighten and her jaw tremble. She blinked rapidly, and I noticed the fan of wrinkles that time had gathered at the outer corner of her eye. She stared at the blank wall before her. "It would be different if I knew where you were going."

I smiled. Bethesda had known only two cities in her life, Alexandria and Rome, and except for the voyage between has never ventured a mile outside either one. What could it matter to her whether I was going to Cumae or Carthage?

"Well," I sighed, "if it will give you any comfort, I suspect that Eco and I will be spending the next few days somewhere in the vicinity of Baiae. You've heard of it, haven't you?"

She nodded.

"It's a beautiful little region down the coast," I said, "inside the Cape of Misenum, situated on the bay which the locals call the Cup, across the water from Puteoli and Pompeii. They say the views of Capri and Vesuvius are quite splendid. The richest of the rich build fine homes on the seashore and bathe in hot mud."

"But how do you know where you're going if the man won't tell you?"

"It's only a guess."

Bethesda softened beneath my touch. She sighed, and I knew that she was reconciled to my going, and to the prospect of being the mistress of the house for a few days, having sole command over the other slaves. From previous experience, I knew that in my absence she was a thoroughly ruthless tyrant. I only hoped that Belbo would be able to bear up under her harsh rule. The thought made me smile.

I turned and saw that Eco waited in the doorway. For an instant his face held an expression of intense fascination; then he crossed his arms and rolled his eyes, as if to deny any interest or sympathy with the moment of tenderness he had interrupted. I quickly kissed Bethesda's cheek and turned to go.

Marcus Mummius was pacing in the vestibule, looking weary and impatient. He threw up his hands when I appeared and hurried out the door, not even waiting for me to catch up, only giving me a look over his shoulder that showed what he thought of wasting so much time to say good-bye to a woman, and a slave at that.

We hurried down the steep path that descends the Esquiline hill, watching for pitfalls by the light of Eco's torch. Where the path ended, spilling into the Subura Way, four horses and two men awaited us.

Mummius's men looked and acted like legionnaires out of uniform. Beneath their light woolen cloaks I caught the glint of knives, which made me feel safer at the prospect of venturing through Roman streets after dark. I reached inside my cloak and touched my own dagger. Mummius had said that all my needs would be supplied, but I preferred to bring my own weapon.

Mummius had not counted on Eco, so I was given the strongest mount and he rode behind me, clutching my waist. Where my body is broad and thick through the shoulders and chest (and in recent years, through the middle as well), Eco's is thin and wiry; his added weight was hardly enough for the beast to notice.

The evening was mild, with only a faint early-autumn chill in the air, but the streets were nearly deserted. In times of trouble, Romans shun the darkness and lock up their houses at sundown, leaving the streets to pimps, drunks, and thrill seekers. So it was in the turmoil of the civil wars and the gloomy years of Sulla's dictatorship; so it was again now that the revolt of the Spartacans was on everyone's lips. Terrifying stories were told in the Forum about whole villages where citizens had been overwhelmed and roasted alive by slaves who ate their former masters for dinner. After sundown Romans refused party invitations and vacated the streets. They locked their bedchamber doors to keep out even their most trusted slaves while they slept, and they woke up from nightmares, drenched in sweat. Chaos was loose in the world again, and his name was Spartacus.

We clattered through the Subura past alleys that stank of urine and rotting garbage. Our way was lit here and there by the glow from open windows along the overhanging upper stories; snatches of music and drunken laughter wafted over our heads and faded behind us. Above us, the stars looked very far away and very cold, a sign of a frosty winter to come. It would be warmer down in Baiae, I thought, where summer lingers in Vesuvius's shadow.

The Subura Way emptied at last into the Forum, where the hooves of our horses echoed unnaturally loud about the deserted squares and temples. We skirted the more sacred areas, where horses are not allowed even by night, and headed south across the narrow valley between the Capitoline and Palatine hills. The smell of straw and dung predominated as we passed by the great cattle market of the Forum Boarium, quiet except for the occasional lowing of the beasts in their pens. The enormous bronze ox on its pedestal loomed above us, a great horned silhouette against the starry sky, like a giant minotaur poised on a ledge.

I tapped Eco's leg and he leaned forward, bringing his ear

to my lips. "It's as I thought," I whispered. "We make for the Tiber. Are you sleepy?"

He tapped me emphatically twice.

"Good." I laughed. "Then you keep watch while we drift downriver to Ostia."

More of Mummius's men waited on the riverbank, ready to take our horses as we dismounted. At the end of the longest pier our boat was ready. If in my sleepiness I had pictured a slow, casual journey down the Tiber to the coast, I was mistaken. The boat was not the tiny skiff I had imagined, but a small barge oared by a dozen slaves with a helmsman at the rear and a canopy amidships, a vessel built for speed and strength. Mummius wasted no time in ushering us aboard. His two bodyguards followed, and we cast off immediately.

"You can sleep if you care to," he said, indicating the space beneath the canopy, where a mound of blankets had been haphazardly tossed. "Not very luxurious, and there's no slave woman to keep you warm, but there are no lice. Unless they've crawled off one of this lot." He gave a sharp kick to the shoulder of one of the rowers. "Row!" he bellowed. "And you'd better keep sharper time than you did on the journey upriver, or I'll have the lot of you moved onto the big ship for good." He laughed without mirth. Back in his element, Mummius was beginning to show a more jovial personality, and I was not sure I liked what I saw. He placed one of his men in charge and crawled under the blankets.

"Wake me if you need to," I whispered to Eco, squeezing his hand to make sure I had his attention. "Or sleep if you can; I doubt there's danger." Then I joined Mummius beneath the tent, nestling against its farther edge and trying hard not to think of my own bed and the warmth of Bethesda's body.

I tried to sleep, but without much success. The creaking of manacles, the sluicing of the oars through the water, and the unending churning of the river against the bottom of the barge finally lulled me into fitful half-sleep, from which I woke over and over, always to the sound of Marcus Mummius's snoring. The fourth time I awoke to the raucous noise I poked my foot from under my blankets and gave him a gentle kick. He stopped for a moment and then resumed, making noises like a man slowly being strangled to death. I heard low chuckles of laughter and rose on my elbows to see his two guardsmen smiling back at me from the prow. They stood close together, talking quietly, wide awake. I looked behind and saw the helmsman at his station, a bearded giant who seemed to see and hear nothing but the river. Eco crouched nearby, gazing over the low bulwark into the water, looking like a statue of Narcissus contemplating his reflection beneath the starry sky.

Eventually Mummius's snoring quieted and blended with the slapping of water on wood and the steady, rhythmic breathing of the rowers, but still the deep, healing embrace of Morpheus eluded me. I tossed and turned uneasily inside the blankets, too hot and then too cold, my thoughts straying down blind alleys and doubling back on themselves. Dozing brought sluggishness without rest, stillness without refreshment; when we at last reached Ostia and the sea, I was a duller man than the one Marcus Mummius had lured from his bed some hours before. In the strange disjuncture of time and space that clouded my mind I imagined that the night would never end and we would journey in darkness forever.

Mummius ushered us from the barge onto a pier. The bodyguards came with us, but the rowers were left behind, gasping and bent double over their oars in exhaustion. I glanced back for a moment at their broad naked backs heaving and glinting with sweat in the starlight. One of them leaned over the bow and began to vomit. At some point during the journey I had stopped hearing their ragged breathing and the steady grating of the oars; I had forgotten them completely as one forgets the wheels of a grinding machine. Who notices a wheel until it needs oiling, or a slave until he turns sick or hungry or violent? I shivered and pulled the blanket around my shoulders to shut out the chilly sea air.

Mummius led us along the riverfront. Beneath the boardwalk I heard the soft lapping of waves against the wooden posts. To our right were clustered a fleet of small riverboats chained to the docks. To our left ran a low stone wall with crates and baskets piled against it in a wild confusion of shadows. Beyond the wall was the sleeping town of Ostia. Here and there I glimpsed the lit window of an upper story, and at intervals there were lamps set into the city wall, but other than ourselves not a living person was stirring. The light played strange tricks; I imagined I saw a family of beggars huddled in a corner, then saw a rat come racing from the heap, which before my eyes resolved itself into nothing more than a pile of rags.

I tripped against a loose plank. Eco grabbed my shoulder to steady me, then Mummius almost knocked me down with a slap across the back. "Didn't you sleep well enough?" he barked in his barracks voice. "I can manage on two hours a day. In the army you learn to sleep standing up, even marching, if you have to."

I nodded dully. We walked past warehouses and jetties, through shut-down markets and shipyards. The smell of salt grew stronger on the air, and the vague hissing of the sea joined with the steady lapping of the river. We came to the end of the docks, where the Tiber abruptly broadens and empties into the sea. The city wall swung away to the south, and a vast, starlit prospect of calm waters opened before us. Here another, larger boat awaited us. Mummius ushered us down the steps and into the hold. He barked at the overseer and the boat cast off.

The dock receded. The waves began to swell around us. Eco looked alarmed and clutched my sleeve. "Don't worry," I told him. "We won't be on this boat for long."

A moment later, as we navigated around a shallow, rocky promontory, the vessel came in sight. "A trireme!" I whispered.

"The *Fury*, she's called," said Mummius, seeing my surprise and smiling proudly.

I had expected a large ship, but nothing as large as this one. Three masts, their sails cowled, rose from the deck. Three rows of oars projected from her belly. It hardly seemed possible that such a hulking monster had been dispatched merely to fetch a single man. Mummius lit a torch and waved it over his head. A torch was lit on deck and waved back at us. As we drew nearer, men suddenly swarmed about the deck and up the masts, as quiet as ghosts in the starlight. The oars, retracted from the water, stirred like the quivering legs of a centipede and dipped downward. Sails unfurled and snapped taut in the soft breeze. Mummius wet his finger and held it aloft. "Not much of a wind, but steady to the south. Good!"

We drew abreast. A rope ladder was lowered. Eco scrambled up first and I followed. Marcus Mummius came last and pulled up the ladder behind him. The smaller boat drew away, back toward Ostia. Mummius walked quickly up and down the length of the ship, giving orders. The *Fury* heaved and swung about. The steady rhythm of oarsmen groaning in unison rose up through the boards, and on either side there was a great splash as the first stroke sliced into the waves. I looked back at Ostia, at the narrow beach that fronted the city's shoreward side and the tiled rooftops that rose above the walls. The town receded with stunning speed; the walls dwindled, the gulf of dark water grew greater and greater. Rome suddenly seemed very far away.

Marcus Mummius, busy with the crew, ignored us. Eco and I found a quiet spot and did our best to sleep, leaning against each other and huddling in our blankets to shut out the chill of the open sea.

Suddenly Mummius was shaking me awake.

"What are you doing on deck? A pampered city dweller like you will take a fever and die from this damp air. Come on, both of you, there's a room for you at the stern."

We followed him, stumbling over coils of rope and hidden hatches. The first rays of dawn were breaking over the dark hills to the east. Mummius led us down a short flight of steps and into a tiny room with two pallets, side by side. I fell onto the nearer one and shuddered at the pleasant shock of feeling myself submerged in a thick mattress of the finest goose down. Eco took the other and began to yawn and stretch like a cat. I pulled my blanket up around my neck, already half-asleep, and vaguely wondered if Mummius had allowed us to take his own accommodations.

I opened my eyes and saw him standing with his arms crossed, leaning against the wall in the hall outside. His face was barely visible in the pale light of dawn, but there could be no doubt, from the gentle flutter of his eyelids and the slackness of his jaw, that Marcus Mummius, an honest soldier and no boaster, was fast asleep and dreaming, standing up.

THREE

I woke with a start, wondering where I was. It must have been morning, because even at my most dissolute I seldom sleep until noon, and yet the bright sunlight streaming into the window above my head had the soft quality of afternoon light in early autumn. The earth seemed to shudder, but not with the sudden convulsion of an earthquake. The house creaked and groaned all about me, and when I started to rise I felt my elbows sink into a vast, bottomless pillow of down.

A vaguely familiar voice drifted in from the porthole above my head, a gruff soldier's voice shouting orders, and I remembered all at once.

Next to me Eco groaned and blinked open his eyes. I managed to pull myself up and sat on the edge of the bed, which seemed to be trying to pull me back into the soft, forgetful haze of that luxurious mountain of down. I shook my head to clear it. A ewer of water was hooked into a bracket on the wall. I picked it up by both handles and drank a long draft, then scooped my hands full of water to splash my face.

"Don't waste it," a voice barked. "That's fresh water from the Tiber. For drinking, not washing." I looked up to see Marcus Mummius standing in the doorway with his arms crossed, looking bright and alert and flashing the superior smile of an early riser. He had changed into military garb, a tunic of red linen and red leather beneath a coat of mail armor.

"What time is it?"

"Two hours past noon. Or as they say on land, the ninth hour of the day. You've done nothing but sleep and snore since you fell into that bed last night." He shook his head.

"A real Roman shouldn't be able to sleep on a bed that soft. Leave that kind of nonsense to fancy Egyptians, I say. I thought you'd taken ill, but I'm told that dying men never snore, so I decided it couldn't be too serious." He laughed, and I enjoyed the grim fantasy of imagining him suddenly spitted on a fancy Egyptian spear.

I shook my head again. "How much longer? On this ship, I mean?"

He wrinkled his brow. "That would be telling, wouldn't it?"

I sighed. "Let me ask you this way: How much longer until we reach Baiae?"

Mummius looked suddenly seasick. "I never said—"

"Indeed you did not. You're a good soldier, Marcus Mummius, and you divulged nothing to me that you were sworn to conceal. Still, I'm curious to know when we'll come to Baiae."

"What makes you think—"

"I *think*, Marcus Mummius; exactly. I would hardly be the man your employer was seeking if I couldn't figure out a simple riddle such as our destination. First, we are most assuredly heading south; I'm not much of a sailor, but I do know the sun rises in the east and sets in the west, and since the afternoon sun is on our right and the coast on our left, I deduce we must be sailing south. Given the fact that you promise that my work will be done in five days, we can hardly be going beyond Italy. Where else, then, but a town on the southern coast, and most likely on the Cup? Oh, perhaps I'm wrong in choosing Baiae; it could be Puteoli, or Neapolis or even Pompeii, but I think not. Anyone as wealthy as your employer—able to pay five times my fee without a qualm, able to send a ship such as this on what seems to be a whim—anyone that rich is going to have a house at Baiae, because Baiae is where any Roman who can afford it builds a summer villa. Besides, yesterday you said something about the Jaws of Hades."

"I never—"

"Yes, you said many lives were at stake, and you spoke of babies wailing in the Jaws of Hades. Now, you could have been speaking in metaphors, like a poet, but I suspect there is a conspicuous absence of poetry in your soul, Marcus Mummius. You carry a sword, not a lyre, and when you said 'Jaws of Hades' you meant the words literally. I've never seen it for myself, but the Greek colonists who originally settled around the Cup believed they had located an entrance to the underworld in a sulphurous crater called Lake Avernus—also known as the Jaws of Hades, Hades being the Greeks' word for the underworld, which old-fashioned Romans still call Orcus. The place is only a brisk walk, I hear, from the finest homes in Baiae."

Mummius looked at me shrewdly. "You are a sharp one," he finally said. "Maybe you'll be worth your fee, after all." I heard no sarcasm in his voice. Instead there was a kind of sadness, as if he truly hoped I would succeed at my task, but expected me to fail.

An instant later Mummius was swaggering out the door and bellowing over his shoulder. "I suppose you'll be hungry, after snoring all day. There's food in the mess cabin amidships, probably better than what you're used to at home. Too rich for me—I prefer a skin of watery wine and a hard crust of bread—but the owner always stocks the best, or what the merchants tell him is best, which means whatever is most expensive. After you eat you can take a long nap." He laughed. "Might as well, you'll only get in the way if you're awake. Passengers are pretty useless on a ship. Not much for them to do. Might as well pretend you're a bag of grain and find a spot to gather mold. Follow me."

By changing the subject, Marcus Mummius had avoided admitting that Baiae was our destination. There was no point in pressing the matter; I already knew where we were going, and now a greater matter weighed on my thoughts, for I was beginning to suspect that I knew the identity of my mysterious new employer. Who could have afforded so ostentatious a means of transport for a mere hireling, and a barely reputable one like Gordianus the Finder, at that? Pompey, perhaps, could muster such resources on a private whim, but Pompey was in Spain. Who then but the man reputed to be the richest Roman alive, indeed the richest Roman who had ever lived—but what could Marcus Licinius Crassus want of me, when he owned whole cities of slaves and could afford the services of any free man he desired?

I might have badgered Mummius with more questions, but decided I had taxed his patience enough. I followed him into the afternoon sunlight and caught a whiff of roasted lamb on the bracing sea breeze. My stomach roared like a lion, and I abandoned curiosity to satisfy a more pressing appetite.

Mummius was wrong to think that I would be bored with nothing to do on the *Fury*, at least as long as the sun was up. The ever-changing vista of the coast of Italy, the wheeling gulls overhead, the work of the sailors, the play of sunlight on water, the schools of fish that darted below the surface, the crisp, tangy air of a day that was no longer summer but not quite autumn—all this was more than enough to occupy me until the sun went down.

Eco was even more entranced. Everything fascinated him. A pair of dolphins joined us at twilight and swam alongside the ship until long after darkness had fallen, darting in and out of the splashing wake. At times they seemed to laugh like men, and Eco mimicked the sound in return, as if he shared a secret language with them. When at last they disappeared beneath the foam and did not return, he went smiling to his bed and fell fast asleep.

I was not so lucky. Having slept most of the day, I faced a sleepless night. For a while the shadowy coast and the sparkle of stars on the water charmed me quite as much as had the luminous afternoon, but then the night grew colder, and I took to my bed. Marcus Mummius was right: The bed was too soft, or else the blanket was too rough, or the faint starlight through the porthole was too distracting, or the noises Eco made in his sleep, mimicking the dolphins' laughter, grated on my ears. I could not sleep.

Then I heard the drum. It came from somewhere below, a hollow, throbbing beat slower than my own pulse but just as steady. I had been so exhausted the night before that I had not heard it; now I found it impossible to ignore. It was the beat that drove the slaves at their oars below deck, setting the rhythm that carried the ship closer and closer to Baiae. The more I tried not to hear it, the louder it seemed to rise up through the planks, beating, beating, beating. The longer I tossed and turned, the further sleep seemed to recede.

I found myself trying to recollect the face of Marcus Crassus, the richest man in Rome. I had seen him a hundred times in the Forum, but his visage escaped me. I counted money in my head, imagining the soft jingle of coins in a purse, and spent my fee a dozen times over. I thought of Bethesda; I imagined her sleeping alone with the kitten curled up between her breasts, and I traced a path by memory from room to room through my house in Rome, like an invisible phantom standing guard. Abruptly an image rose unbidden in my mind, of Belbo lying across my portal in a drunken stupor, with the door wide open for any thief or assassin to step inside. . . .

I gave a start and sat upright. Eco turned in his sleep and made a chattering noise. I strapped on my shoes, wrapped the blanket around me like a cloak, and returned to the deck.

Here and there sailors lay huddled together in sleep. A few strolled the deck, watchful and alert for any danger from the sea or shore. A steady breeze blew from the north, filling the sail and raising gooseflesh wherever the blanket did not cover my arms and legs. I strolled once about the deck, then found myself drawn toward the portal amidships that led down into the galley.

It is curious that a man can sail upon many ships in his life and never wonder at the hidden motive power that drives them, yet this is how most people live their lives every day—men eat and dress and go about their business, and never give a thought to all the sweat of all the slaves who labored to grind the grain and spin the cloth and pave the roads, wondering about these things no more than they wonder about the blood that heats their bodies or the mucus that cradles their brains.

I stepped through the portal and down the steps. Instantly a wave of heat struck my face, warm and stifling like rising steam. I heard the dull, throbbing boom of the drum and the shuffling of many men. I smelled them before I saw them.

All the odors that the human body can produce were concentrated in that airless space, rising up like the breath of demons from a sulphurous pit. I took another step downward into a world of living corpses, thinking that the Jaws of Hades could hardly lead to a more terrible netherworld than this.

The place was like a long, narrow cavern. Here and there lamps suspended from the ceiling cast a lurid glow across the pale naked bodies of the oarsmen. At first, in the dimness, I saw only an impression of rippling movements everywhere around me, like the writhing of maggots. As my eyes adjusted I slowly made out the details.

Down the center ran a narrow aisle, like a suspended bridge. On each side slaves were stationed in tiers, three-deep. Those against the hull were able to sit at their stations, expending the least effort to power their shorter oars. Those in the middle were seated higher and had to brace themselves against a footrest with each backward pull, then rise from their seats to push the oars forward. Those on the aisle were the unlucky ones. They ran the catwalk, shuffling back and forth to push their oars in a great circle, stretching onto their toes at full extension, then kneeling and lurching forward to lift the oars out of the water. Each slave was manacled to his oar by a rusted link of chain around one wrist.

There were hundreds of them packed tightly together, rubbing against one another as they pushed and pulled and strained. I thought of cattle or goats pressed together in a pen, but animals move without purpose. Here each man was like a tiny wheel in a vast, constantly moving machine. The drumbeat drove them.

I turned and saw the drummer at the stern, on a low bench that must have been just below my bed. His legs were spread wide apart. His knees grasped the rim of a low, broad drum. Thongs were wrapped around each hand, and at the end of each thong was a leather ball. One by one he lifted the balls in the air and brought them down upon the skin of the drum, sending out a low pulse that throbbed through the dense, warm air. He sat with his eyes closed and a faint smile on his face as if he were dreaming, but the rhythm never faltered.

Beside him stood another man, dressed like a soldier and holding a long whip in his right hand. He glowered when he saw me, then snapped his whip in the air as if to impress me. The slaves nearest him shuddered and some of them groaned, as if a wave of pain passed over them.

I pressed the blanket over my mouth and nose to filter the stench. Where the lamplight penetrated through the maze of catwalks and manacled feet, I saw that the bilge was awash with a mixture of feces and urine and vomit and bits of rotting food. How could they bear it? Did they grow used to it over time, the way men grow accustomed to the clasp of manacles? Or did it never cease to nauseate them, just as it sickened me?

There are religious sects in the East which postulate abodes of eternal punishment for the shades of the wicked. Their gods are not content to see a man suffer in this world, but will pursue him with fire and torment into the next. Of this I know nothing, but I do know that if a place of damnation exists here on earth, it is surely within the bowels of a Roman galley, where men are forced to work their bodies to ruination amid the stench of their own sweat and vomit and excreta, playing out their anguish against the maniacal, never-ending pulse of the drum. To become mere fuel, to be consumed, drained and discarded with hardly a thought, is surely as horrible a damnation as any god could contrive.

They say most men die after three or four years in the galleys; the lucky ones die before that. A captive prisoner or a slave guilty of theft, if given the choice, will go to the mines or become a gladiator before he will serve in the galleys. Of all the cruel sentences of death that can be meted out to a man, slavery in the galley is considered by all to be the cruelest. Death comes, but not before the last measure of strength has been squeezed from a man's body and the last of his dignity has been annihilated by suffering and despair.

Men become monsters in the galleys. Some ship captains never rotate the positions of the slaves; a man who rows for day after day, month after month on the same side, especially if he runs the catwalk, develops great muscles on one side of his body out of all proportion to the other. At the same time his flesh grows pale as a fish from lack of sunlight. If such a man escapes, he is easily detected by his deformity. Once in the Subura I saw a troop of private guards dragging such a man from a brothel, naked and screaming. Eco, then only a boy, had been horrified by the slave's appearance, and then, after I had explained it, had begun to weep.

Men become gods in the galley, as well. Crassus, if indeed he was the owner of this ship, took care to rotate his rowers, or else used them up more quickly than most, for I saw no lopsided monsters among them. Instead I saw young men with deep chests and great shoulders and arms, and among them a few older survivors with even more massive physiques, like a crew of bearded Apollos sprinkled with a hoary Hercules here and there, at least from the neck down. Above the neck their faces were all too human, wretched with care and suffering.

As I looked from face to face, most of them averted their eyes, as if my gaze could hurt them as surely as the whipmaster's lash. But a few of them dared to look back at me. I saw eyes dulled by endless labor and monotony; eyes envious of a man who possessed the simple freedom to walk about at will, to wipe the sweat from his face, to clean himself after defecating. In some eyes I saw lurking fear and hatred, and in others a kind of fascination, almost a lust, the kind of naked stare that a starving man might cast on a glutton.

A kind of fever seized me, warm and trancelike, as I walked down the long central aisle between the naked slaves, my nostrils filled with the smell of their flesh, my skin awash in the humid heat of their straining bodies, my eyes roving among the great congregation of suffering constantly asway in the darkness. I was a man in a dream watching other men in a nightmare.

Away from the drumbeater's platform and the central stairway, the lamps grew fewer, but here and there a bit of moonlight found its way into the dim hold, shining silver-blue on the sweat-glazed arms and shoulders of the rowers, glinting upon the manacles that kept their hands locked in place upon the oars. The dull beat of the drum grew softer as it receded behind me, but continued slow and steady, setting an easy nocturnal pace, its constant rhythm as hypnotic as the hissing murmur of the waves sluicing against the prow.

I reached the end of the walkway. I turned and looked back, over the laboring multitude. Suddenly I had seen enough; I hurried toward the exit. Ahead of me, illuminated by lamplight as if on a stage, I saw the whipmaster look toward me and nod knowingly. Even at a distance I could see the disdain on his face. This was his domain; I was an intruder, a curiosity seeker, too soft and too pampered for such a place. He cracked his whip over his head for my benefit and smiled at the wave of groans that passed through the slaves at his feet.

I put one foot upon the stair and would have followed with the other, but a face in the lamplight stopped me. The boy must have reminded me of Eco, and that was why I noticed his face among all the others. His place was in the highest tier along the aisle. When he turned to look at me a beam of moonlight fell upon one cheek, casting his face half in moonlight, half in lamplight, split between pale blue and orange. Despite his massive shoulders and chest, he was hardly more than a child. Along with the filth that smudged his cheeks and the suffering in his eyes, there was a strange look of innocence about him. His dark features were strikingly handsome, his prominent nose and mouth and wide dark eyes suggestive of the East. As I studied him in the moonlight, he dared to look back at me and then actually smiled—a sad, pathetic smile, tentative and fearful.

I thought of how easily Eco might have ended up in such a place if I had not found him and taken him home that day long ago—a boy with a strong body without a tongue or a family to defend himself might easily be waylaid and sold at auction. I looked back at the slave boy. I tried to smile in return, but could not.

Suddenly a man descended the stairs and pushed roughly past me, then hurried toward the stern. He shouted something and the drumbeat abruptly accelerated to twice its tempo. There was a great lurch as the ship bolted forward. I fell against the rail of the stairs. The increase in speed was astounding.

The drum boomed louder and louder, faster and faster. The messenger pushed past me again, heading up to the deck. I grabbed the sleeve of his tunic. "Pirates!" he said, with a theatrical lilt in his voice. "Two ships slipped out of a hidden cove as we passed. They're after us now." His face was grim, but as he tore himself from my grip, astonishingly enough, I thought I saw him laughing.

I began to follow him, then stopped, arrested by the sudden spectacle all around me. The drum boomed faster. The rowers groaned and followed the tempo. The whipmaster swaggered up the aisle. He cracked his whip in the air, loosening his arm. The rowers cringed.

The beat grew faster. The rowers at the outer edges of the ship were able to stay in their seats, but those along the aisle were abruptly driven to their toes by the heightened motion of the oars, scrambling to keep up, stretching their arms high in the air to keep the gyrating oars under control. Manacled to the wood, they had no choice.

The beat accelerated even more. The vast machine was at full throttle. The oars moved in great circles at a mad tempo. The slaves pumped with all their might. Horrified but unable to look away, I studied their grinning faces—jaws clenched, eyes burning with fear and confusion.

There was a loud snap and a crack, as if one of the great oars had suddenly split asunder, so close that I covered my face. In the same instant the boy who had smiled at me threw back his head. His mouth wrenched open in a silent howl.

The whipmaster raised his arm again. The lash slithered through the air. The boy shrieked as if he had been scalded. I saw the lash slither across his naked shoulders. He faltered against the oar, tripping on the catwalk. For a long moment he hung suspended from the manacles around his wrists as he was dragged forward, backward and up again. As he hung from the highest point, desperately trying to find his balance, the whip lashed against his thighs.

The boy screamed, convulsed and fell again. The oar carried him for another revolution. He somehow found his grip and joined in the effort, every muscle straining. The lash struck again. The drumbeat boomed. The whip rose and fell. Squealing and gasping from the pain, the boy danced like a spastic. His broad shoulders convulsed at the whipmaster's rhythm, out of time with the great machine. His face contorted in agony. He cried like a child. The whipmaster struck him again and again.

I looked at the man's face. He smiled grimly back at me, showing a mouth full of rotten teeth, then turned and spat across the shoulders of one of the straining slaves. He looked me in the eye and he raised his whip again, as if daring me to interfere. With a single voice the rowers groaned, like a tragic chorus. I looked at the boy, who never ceased rowing. He looked back at me and moved his lips, unable to speak.

Suddenly I heard footsteps from above. The messenger returned, holding up his open hand as a signal to the drumbeater. "All clear! All clear!" he shouted.

The drumbeat abruptly ceased. The oars were still. The sudden quiet was broken only by the lapping of waves against the ship, the creaking of wood, and the hoarse, gasping breath of the rowers. At my feet, the boy lay collapsed atop his oar, wracked with sobbing. I looked down at his broad, muscle-scalloped back, livid with welts. The fresh wounds lay atop an accumulation of older scars; this was not the first time the whipmaster had singled him out.

Suddenly I saw nothing, heard nothing; the smell of the place overwhelmed me, as if the sweat of so many close-packed bodies had turned the fetid air to poison. I pushed the messenger aside and hurried up the steps, into the fresh air. Beneath the stars I leaned over the bulwark and emptied my stomach.

Afterward I looked about, disoriented, weak, disgusted. The men on deck were busy taking down the auxiliary sail from the second mast. The water was calm, the shore dark and silent.

Marcus Mummius saw me and approached. He was in high spirits.

"Lost your dinner, eh? It can happen when we rush to full speed and you've got a full belly. I told the owner not to stock such rich provisions. I'd rather throw up a bellyful of bread and water any day than a stomach full of half-chewed flesh and bile."

I wiped my chin. "We outran them, then? The danger's over?"

Mummius shrugged. "In a manner of speaking."

"What do you mean?" I looked toward the stern. The sea behind us was empty. "How many were there? Where did they go?"

"Oh, there were a thousand ships at least, all flying pirate banners. And now they've gone back to Hades, where they belong." He saw the look on my face and laughed. "Phantom pirates," he explained. "Sea spirits."

"What? I don't understand." Men at sea are superstitious, but I could hardly believe that Mummius would half kill the galley slaves to outrun a few sea vapors or a stray whale.

But Mummius was not mad; it was worse than that. "A drill," he finally said, shaking his head and slapping me on the back, as if it were a joke I was too stupid to grasp.

"A drill?"

"Yes! A drill, an exercise. You have to have them every so often, especially on a nonmilitary ship like the *Fury*, to make sure everyone's on his toes. At least that's the way we run things under—" He began to say a name, then caught himself. "Under my commander," he finished. "Really catches the slaves off their guard when you do it at night!"

"A drill?" I repeated stupidly. "You mean there were no pirates? It was all unnecessary? But the slaves below are run ragged. . . ."

"Good!" Mummius said, thrusting his jaw in the air. " 'The slaves of a Roman master must be always ready, always strong. Or else what good are they?' " The words were not his own; he was quoting someone. What manner of man commanded Marcus Mummius and could afford to be so profligate with his human tools?

I looked down at the oars that projected from the *Fury*, suspended motionless above the waves. A moment later the oars stirred and dipped into the waves. The slaves had been given a brief respite and now were at work once again.

I hung my head and took a deep breath of salty air and wished I were back in Rome, asleep in Bethesda's arms.

FOUR

I was awakened by a poke in the ribs. Eco stood over me, gesturing for me to get up.

Sunlight was streaming through the porthole. I rose to my knees on the mattress and looked out to see land nearby with here and there a habitation set among the rocky cliffs. The buildings lower down, nearest the water, were ramshackle affairs, humble dwellings pieced together with driftwood, festooned with nets and surrounded by little shipyards. The buildings higher up were markedly different—sprawling villas with white columns and grapevine trellises.

I stood up to stretch as best I could within the cramped quarters. I splashed my face with water and sucked in a mouthful, swished it to clean my tongue and spat it out the porthole. Eco had already set out my better tunic. While I dressed he combed my hair and then played barber. When the ship gave a tiny pitch I held my breath, but he did not nick me once.

Eco fetched bread and apples, and we fed ourselves on the deck, contemplating the view as Marcus Mummius guided the ship into the great bay which Romans have always called the Cup, likening it to a vast bowl of water with villages all about its rim. The ancient Greeks who first colonized the region called it the Bay of Neapolis, I think, after their chief settlement. My sometimes-client Cicero calls it the Bay of Luxury, with a derisive tone of voice; he himself does not own a villa there—yet.

We entered the Cup from the north, skirting the narrows between the Cape of Misenum and the small island of Procida. Directly before us, at the far side of the bay, loomed the larger island of Capri, like a craggy finger pointing skyward. The sun was high, the day was fine and clear without a touch of haze on the water. Between us and the opposite strait that separates Capri from the Promontory of Minerva the water was spangled with the multicolored sails of fishing boats and the bigger sails of the trading ships and ferries that circle the bay, carrying goods and passengers from Surrentum and Pompeii on the south side to Neapolis and Puteoli on the north.

We rounded the headland, and the entire bay opened before us, glittering beneath the sun. At its apex, looming above the little village of Herculaneum, rose Vesuvius. The sight always impresses me. The mountain towers on the horizon like a great pyramid flattened at the top. With its fertile slopes covered by meadows and vineyards, Vesuvius presides over the Cup like a bounteous, benevolent god, an emblem of steadfastness and serenity. For a while, in the early days of slave revolt, Spartacus and his men took refuge on the higher slopes.

The *Fury* stayed close to the land, circling the Cape of Misenum and then turning her back on Vesuvius to glide majestically into the hidden harbor. The sails were furled; sailors ran about the deck securing ropes and tackles. I pulled Eco out of the way, fearing that without a voice to protect himself he might be stepped on or tangled in the swinging ropes. He gently shrugged my hand from his shoulder and rolled his eyes. *I'm not a boy any longer,* he seemed to be saying, but it was with a boy's excitement that he turned his head this way and that, trying to observe everything at once, craning his neck and skittering about with a look of awe on his face. His eye missed nothing; in the rush of confusion he grabbed my arm and pointed toward the skiff that had pushed off from the docks and was making its way toward the *Fury*.

The boat pulled alongside. Marcus Mummius leaned over the bulwark, shouting a question. After he heard the reply he threw back his head and let out a sigh—whether of relief or regret I could not tell.

He looked up and scowled at my approach. "Nothing was

resolved in my absence,'' he sighed. ''You'll be needed after all. At least the journey wasn't wasted.''

''Then you can tell me officially now that my employer is Marcus Crassus?''

Mummius looked at me ruefully. ''You think you're awfully clever, don't you? I only hope you'll be half that clever when the need comes. Now off with you—down the ladder!''

''And you?''

''I'll follow later, after I've seen to the ship. For now you're in the hands of Faustus Fabius. He'll take you to the villa at Baiae and see to matters there.''

Eco and I descended to the skiff, where a tall redheaded man in a dark blue tunic stood waiting to greet us. His face was young, but I saw the lines of age at the corners of his cat-green eyes; he was probably in his middle thirties, about the same age as Mummius. He clasped my hand, and I saw the flash of a patrician ring on his finger, but a gold ring was hardly necessary to show that he came from an old family. The Fabii are as old as the Cornelii or Aemilii, older than the Claudii. But even without the ring and without the name I would have known him for a patrician. Only a Roman noble of the most venerable ancestry can pull back his shoulders quite so stiffly and hold his chin so rigidly upright—even in a small, rocking boat—without looking either pompous or ridiculous.

''You're the one they call the Finder?'' His voice was smooth and deep. As he spoke he arched one eyebrow, such a typical patrician gesture that I sometimes wonder if the old nobility have an extra muscle in their foreheads for just this purpose.

''Gordianus, from Rome,'' I said.

''Good, good. Here, we'd better sit, unless you're an excellent swimmer.''

''I'm hardly a swimmer at all,'' I confessed.

Faustus Fabius nodded. ''This is your assistant?''

''My son, Eco.''

''I see. It's good that you've arrived. Gelina will be relieved. For some reason she took it into her head that Mummius might be able to get back by late last night. We all told her that was impossible; even under the very best conditions the ship couldn't return before this afternoon. But she wouldn't listen. Before she went to bed she arranged to have messengers descend to the harbor, one every hour, to see if the ship had arrived. The household is in chaos, as you can imagine."

He saw the blank look on my face. "Ah, but Mummius has told you next to nothing, I suppose. Yes, those were his instructions. Never fear, all shall be made clear to you." He turned his face to the breeze and took a deep breath, letting his unfashionably long hair flutter in the wind like a red mane.

I looked about the harbor. The *Fury* was by far the largest vessel. The rest were small fishing boats and pleasure craft. Misenum has never been a particularly busy port; most of the trade that flows into and out of the Cup is channeled through Puteoli, the busiest port in all Italy. Yet it seemed to me that Misenum was more quiet than it should be, considering its proximity to the luxurious district of Baiae and its famous mineral springs. I said as much to Faustus Fabius.

"So you've been here before?" he asked.

"A few times."

"Well acquainted with trading vessels and business on the Campanian coast, are you?"

I shrugged. "Business has brought me to the Cup now and again over the years. I'm no expert on sea traffic, but am I wrong to say that the harbor appears rather empty?"

He made a slight grimace. "Not wrong at all. Between the pirates at sea and Spartacus inland, trade everywhere in Campania had come to a standstill. Hardly anything moves on the roads or the sea lanes—which makes it all the more amazing that Marcus was willing to send the *Fury* after you."

"By Marcus you mean Marcus Mummius?"

"Of course not; Mummius doesn't own a trireme! I mean Marcus Crassus." Fabius smiled thinly. "Oh, but you weren't supposed to know that, were you, at least not until you landed? Well, here we are. Hold on for the jolt—these clumsy rowers, you'd think they were trying to ram an enemy vessel. A stint on the *Fury* might do them some good." I saw the slaves at the oars cower, or pretend to.

As we stepped onto the dock I looked back again at the harbor. "You mean to say there's no trade at all these days?"

Fabius shrugged. I ascribed his grimace to the patricians' traditional disdain for all matters of commerce. "Sailboats and skiffs shuttle back and forth across the Cup, of course, exchanging goods and passengers between the villages," he said. "But it's a rarer and rarer occurrence to see a big ship from Egypt or Africa or even Spain come in from the sea headed for the big docks at Puteoli. Of course, in another few weeks travel by sea will stop altogether for the winter. As for goods from inland, all of the south of Italy is under the shadow of Spartacus now. He's made his winter stronghold in the mountains around Thurii, after spending all summer terrorizing the region east of Vesuvius. Crops were destroyed, farms and villas were burned to the ground. The markets are empty. It's a good thing the locals needn't live off bread; no one around here will starve so long as there are fish in the Cup or oysters in Lake Lucrinus."

He turned and led us across the dock. "I don't suppose there are any shortages in Rome, despite the troubles? Shortages are not allowed in Rome."

" 'The people fear, but suffer not,' " I quoted from a recent speech I had heard in the Forum.

Fabius snorted. "It's just like the Senate. They'll go to any lengths to see that the rabble in Rome remains comfortable. Meanwhile, they can't manage to send a decent commander against either Spartacus or the pirates. What a congregation of incompetents! Rome has never been the same since Sulla opened the doors of the Senate as a reward to all his rich cronies; now trinket salesmen and olive oil merchants line up to give speeches, while gladiators rape the countryside. It's only luck that Spartacus has so far lacked either the brains or the nerve to march on Rome itself."

"That possibility is discussed daily."

"I'm sure it is. What else do Romans have to talk about these days, between plates of caviar and stuffed quail?"

"Pompey is always a popular subject for gossip," I offered. "They say he's almost put down the rebels in Spain. Popular opinion looks to Pompey to hurry back and put an end to Spartacus."

"Pompey!" Faustus Fabius infused the name with almost as much disdain as had Marcus Mummius. "Not that he doesn't come from a good family, of course, and no one can discount his military achievements. But for once Pompey is not the right man in the right place at the right time."

"And who is?"

Fabius smiled and dilated his broad nostrils. "You'll be meeting him shortly."

Horses awaited us. Accompanied by Fabius's bodyguard, we rode through the village of Misenum and then headed north on a stone-paved road beside the broad, muddy beach. At length the road turned inland from the beach and ascended a low wooded ridge. On either side, through the trees, I began to glimpse great houses, set far apart with cultivated gardens and patches of wilderness between them. Eco widened his eyes. At my side he had met wealthy men and had occasionally been allowed in their homes, but such ostentation as that which thrives on the Cup was new to him. The city houses of the wealthy, set close together with plain facades, do not impose as do their country villas. Away from the jealous eyes of the urban masses, in settings where no one but slaves or visitors as wealthy as themselves are likely to come knocking, the great Romans show no fear in advertising their taste and their ability to pay for it. Old-fashioned orators in the Forum say that wealth did not flaunt itself in earlier days, but in my lifetime gold has never been afraid to show its face, especially on the Bay of Luxury.

Faustus Fabius set a leisurely pace. If this errand was urgent, he did not show it. There seems to be something in the very air of the Campanian coast that relaxes even the most harried of city dwellers from the north. I sensed it myself—a crispness in the pine-scented air spiced with sea spray, a special clarity of sunlight charging the sky and reflected from the vast bowl of the bay, a feeling of harmony with the gods of earth, air, fire, and water. Such contentment loosens tongues, and I found it easy to open up Faustus Fabius by exclaiming at the views and asking a few questions about the topography and the local cuisine. He was a Roman through and through, but clearly he visited the region often enough to have a thorough knowledge of the coastal Campanians and their old Greek customs.

"I must say, Faustus Fabius, my host on land is certainly more informative than the one I had at sea." He acknowledged the comment with a thin smile and a knowing nod; I could see he had little affection for Marcus Mummius. "Tell me," I went on, "just who is this Mummius?"

Fabius raised his eyebrow. "I thought you would have known that. Mummius was one of Crassus's protégés in the civil wars; since then he's become Crassus's right-hand man in military affairs. The Mummii aren't a particularly distinguished family, but like most Roman families that survive long enough, they do possess at least one famous ancestor. Unfortunately, the fame goes hand in hand with a taint of scandal. Marcus Mummius's great-grandfather was a consul back in the days of the Gracchi; he won triumphs for his campaigns in Spain and Greece. You never heard of Mad Mummius, also known as the Barbarian?"

I shrugged. The minds of patricians are surely different from those of us ordinary men; how else can they effortlessly catalogue so much glory and gossip and scandal about so many ancestors, not just their own but everyone else's? At the least prompting they can recount picayune details of life after life, going all the way back to King Numa and beyond.

Fabius smiled. "It's unlikely, but if the matter should happen to come up around Marcus, be careful what you say; he's surprisingly sensitive about his ancestor's reputation. Well, then: Many years ago this Mad Mummius was commissioned by the Senate to put down the revolt of the Achaean League in Greece. Mummius destroyed them completely, and then systematically looted Corinth before leveling the city and enslaving the populace by senatorial decree."

"Another glorious chapter in the history of our empire. Surely an ancestor any Roman should be proud of."

"Indeed," said Fabius, his teeth slightly clenched at the irony in my voice.

"And his butchery earned him the name Mad Mummius?"

"Oh, by Hercules, no. It wasn't his bloodthirstiness or his cruelty. It was the indiscriminate way he handled the works of art he shipped back to Rome. Priceless statuary arrived in pieces, filigreed urns were scarred and scraped, jewels were torn from caskets, precious glassware was shattered. They say the man couldn't tell a Polyclitus from a Polydorus!"

"Imagine that!"

"No, really! They say a Juno by Polyclitus and a Venus by Polydorus each lost her head in transit, and when Mad Mummius was having them reassembled he ordered the workmen to attach the wrong heads to the wrong statues. The error was evident to any fool with two eyes. One of the Corinthian captives, outraged by the blasphemy, advised Mad Mummius of the error, whereupon the general had the old man soundly whipped and sold to the mines. Then he ordered his men to leave the statues exactly as they were, saying he thought they looked better that way." Fabius shook his head in disgust; to a patrician, a scandal a hundred years ago is still a scandal this morning. "Old Mummius became known as Mad Mummius, the Barbarian, given that his sensibilities were no better than those of a Thracian or a Gaul. The family has never quite shaken the embarrassment. A pity, since our Marcus Mummius idolized his ancestor for his military skills, and rightly so."

"And Crassus recognizes the skills of Marcus Mummius?"

"His right hand, as I said."

I nodded. "And who are you, Faustus Fabius?"

I looked at him steadily, trying to pierce his feline countenance, but he rewarded my scrutiny with a bland expression that seemed to be a smile on one side and a frown on the other. "I suppose that would make me the *left* hand of Crassus," he said.

The road grew level as we gained the summit of the ridge. Through the trees to the right I caught occasional glimpses of water below and, far away across the inlet, the clay rooftops of Puteoli, shimmering like tiny red beads. For some time I had seen no houses on either side; it seemed that we were passing through a single large estate. We passed grape arbors and cultivated fields, but I saw no slaves at work. I remarked on the absence of any signs of life. Thinking Fabius had not heard me over the clatter of our horses, I repeated my remark more loudly, but he only looked straight ahead and did not answer.

At last a smaller road branched off to the right. There was no gate, but two pylons flanked the road. Each red-stained column was surmounted by the bronze head of a bull with a ring through its nose.

The land on either side of the road was wild and forested. The way wound gradually downward toward the coast. Through the trees I could see blue water flecked with faraway sails, and again the roofs of Puteoli across the water. Then the way took a sharp turn around a large boulder. The trees and thickets abruptly drew back, revealing the massive facade of the villa.

The roof was of clay tiles which blazed fiery red in the sunlight. The walls were stained saffron. The central mass was two stories high, flanked by wings that projected to the north and south. We halted in the gravel courtyard, where a pair of slaves ran to help us dismount and to lead the horses to the nearby stables. Eco dusted his tunic and looked about, wide-eyed, as Faustus Fabius escorted us to the entrance. Funeral wreaths of cypress and fir adorned the high oak doors.

Fabius knocked. The door opened just enough for a blinking eye to peer out, and then was pulled wide open by an unseen slave who cowered behind it. Fabius raised his hand in a gesture that invited us to follow and at the same time demanded silence. My eyes were used to the sunlight, so that the hallway seemed quite dark. I saw the wax masks of the household ancestors in their niches only as vague shadows on either side of us, like ghosts without bodies peering from little windows.

The dark hallway opened into an atrium. The space was

square, surrounded by a colonnaded portico on the ground floor and a narrow walkway on the floor above. Cobblestone pathways meandered through a low garden. There was a small fountain at the center, where a bronze faun threw back his head in delight as tiny jets of water splashed from his pipes. The workmanship was exquisite. The creature seemed to be alive, ready to leap and dance; the sound of bubbling water was almost like laughter. At our approach, two yellow birds who were bathing themselves in the tiny pool flew in a startled circle about the faun's prancing hooves, then upward to perch nervously on the balustrade that circled the upper story, and then upward again into the blue sky.

I watched them ascend, then lowered my eyes to the garden again. That was when I saw the great funeral bier at the far end of the atrium, and the body that lay upon it.

Fabius walked through the garden, where he paused to dip his fingers into the basin at the faun's feet and then touch them to his forehead. Eco and I followed his example and joined him before the body. "Lucius Licinius," said Fabius in a low voice.

In life, the dead man had possessed great wealth; either that or his funeral arrangements were being provided by someone with a remarkable purse. Even very wealthy families are usually content to lay their deceased upon a wooden bed with ivory legs and perhaps some decorative ivory inlays. This elegantly carved bed was entirely overlaid with ivory, from head to foot. I had heard of such lavishness, but had never before seen an example. The precious substance glowed with a waxen paleness almost as smooth and colorless as the flesh of the dead man himself.

Purple blankets embroidered with gold lay upon the bed, along with adornments of asters and evergreen branches. The corpse was dressed in a white toga with elegant green and white embroidery. The feet were clad in freshly oiled sandals and pointed toward the door of the house, as prescribed by tradition.

Eco wrinkled his nose. An instant later I did the same. Despite the perfumes and unguents with which the body had been anointed, and the pan of incense set above a low brazier nearby, there was a decided odor of decay in the air. Eco moved to cover his nose with the hem of his sleeve; I batted his hand away and frowned at his rudeness.

Fabius said in a low voice, "This is the fifth day." It would be two more days until the funeral then, to allow the seven days of public mourning. The body would be quite pungent by then. With such an ostentatious display of wealth, surely the family had paid for the best anointers to be found in Baiae, or more likely had brought them over from bustling Puteoli, but their skill had not been good enough. There was an added irony in the carelessness with which the deceased was displayed; a few stray tendrils of ivy had fallen over his head, obscuring not only half his face but any laurel crown that he might have been wearing in remembrance of some earthly honor.

"This ivy," I said, "looks almost as if it had been placed over his face on purpose. . . ."

Fabius did not stop me as I gently lifted the green tendrils that had been so skillfully arranged to hide the dead man's scalp. The wound beneath was of the sort that makes anointers of the dead throw up their hands in despair—almost impossible to purify and seal, too large to be hidden in any subtle way, too deep and ugly to be looked at for long. Eco made an involuntary sound of disgust and turned his face away, then leaned back to take a closer look.

"Hideous, isn't it?" whispered Fabius, averting his face. "And Lucius Licinius was such a vain man. A pity he can't look his best in death."

I steeled myself to look at the dead man's face. A sharp, heavy blow or blows had destroyed the upper right quadrant of his face, tearing the ear, smashing the cheekbone and jaw and ruining the eye, which despite any efforts to close it after death remained narrowly opened and clotted with blood. I studied what remained of the face and was able to imagine a handsome man of middle age, graying slightly at the temples, with a strong nose and chin. The lips were slightly parted, showing the gold coin that had been placed on his tongue by the anointers—the fee for the boatman Charon to ferry him across the river Styx.

"His death was not an accident?" I offered.

"Hardly."

"An altercation that came to blows?"

"Possibly. It happened late at night. His body was found here in the atrium the next morning. The circumstances were obvious."

"Yes?"

"A runaway slave—some fool following the example of Spartacus, it appears. Someone else will explain the matter to you in more detail."

"This was done by an escaped slave? I am not a slave hunter, Faustus Fabius. Why was I brought here?"

He glanced at the dead man, then at the bubbling faun. "Someone else will explain."

"Very well. The victim—what did you call him?"

"Lucius Licinius."

"He was the master of the house?"

"More or less," said Fabius.

"No riddles, please."

Fabius pursed his lips. "This should have been Mummius's job, not mine. I agreed to escort you to the villa, but I never agreed to explain the matter to you once you arrived."

"Marcus Mummius isn't here. But I am, and so is the corpse of a murdered man."

Fabius grimaced. Patrician or not, he struck me as a man used to being stuck with unpleasant jobs, and he did not like it. What had he called himself—the left hand of Crassus? "Very well," he finally said. "This is the way things were with Lucius Licinius. He and Crassus were cousins, closely linked by blood. I gather they hardly knew one another growing up, but that changed when they became men. Many of the Licinii were wiped out in the civil wars; once things got back to normal under Sulla's dictatorship, Crassus and Lucius formed a closer relationship."

"Not a friendship?"

"It was more in the nature of a business partnership." Fabius smiled. "But then everything is business with Marcus Crassus. Anyway, in any relationship there must be a stronger and a weaker partner. I think you must know enough about Crassus, if only by hearsay, to imagine which of them was subservient.''

''Lucius Licinius.''

''Yes. Lucius was a poor man to start with, and he would have stayed that way without Crassus's help. Lucius had so little imagination; he wasn't the sort to see an opportunity and seize it, unless he was pushed. Meanwhile, Crassus was busy making his millions in real estate up in Rome—you must know the legend.''

I nodded. When the dictator Sulla finally triumphed in the civil wars, he destroyed his enemies by seizing their property and rewarded his supporters, Pompey and Crassus among them, with villas and farms; thus had Crassus begun his ascent, driven by an apparently boundless appetite for property. Once in the streets of Rome I had come upon a burning building, and there was Crassus bidding on the tenement next to it. The owner, confused and desperate and believing he was about to lose his property to the spreading flames, sold it to Crassus on the spot for a song, whereupon the millionaire called out his private fire brigades to put out the flames. Such tales about Crassus were commonplace in Rome.

''Everything Crassus touched seemed to turn to gold,'' Fabius explained. ''His cousin Lucius, on the other hand, muddled about trying to make a living off the land, like all good, old-fashioned plebeians. He lost and lost until he was bankrupt. Finally he begged Crassus to save him, and Crassus did. He made Lucius a kind of factotum, a representative to look after some of Crassus's business enterprises on the Cup. In a good year—without pirates or Spartacus—there's a great deal of business transacted on the Cup; it's not all luxurious villas and oyster farms. Crassus owns mines in Spain, and a fleet of ships that bring the ore to Puteoli. He owns metalworkers in Neapolis and Pompeii who turn the ore into utensils and weapons and finished works of art. He owns ships that transport slaves from Alexandria to Puteoli. He owns farms and vineyards all over Campania, and supplies the hordes of slaves that are needed to work them. Crassus can't oversee all these small details himself; his interests extend from Spain to Egypt. He delegated responsibility for local business here on the Cup to Lucius, who oversaw Crassus's investments and enterprises in a plodding but adequate manner."

"The running of this house, for example?"

"Actually, Crassus himself owns the house and all the land around it. He has no need for villas; he scoffs at the idea of retreating to the countryside or the coast to relax and read poetry. And yet somehow he keeps acquiring them, dozens of villas by now. He can't keep empty houses all over Italy, so he prefers to rent them to his family and his factotums. Then, when he travels, he can reside in them when and as he needs to, a guest and yet more than a guest."

"And the household slaves?"

"They are also the property of Crassus."

"And the *Fury*, the trireme in the harbor that brought me from Ostia?"

"That belongs to Crassus, too, although it was Lucius who oversaw its use."

"And the deserted vineyards and fields we rode through on the way from Misenum?"

"Property of Crassus. Along with numerous other properties and manufactories and gladiator schools and farms in the region, from here to Surrentum."

"Then to call Lucius Licinius the master of this house—"

"Licinius gave the orders and acted independently in his own home, to be sure. But he was nothing more than Crassus's creature. A servant, really, if a privileged and very pampered one."

"I see. Is there a widow?"

"Her name is Gelina."

"And children?"

"Their marriage was barren."

"No heir?"

"Crassus, as his cousin and patron, will inherit Licinius's debts and possessions."

"And Gelina?"

"She now becomes Crassus's dependent."

"From the way you speak, Faustus Fabius, it seems that Crassus owns the whole world."

"I sometimes think he does. Or will," he said, raising an eyebrow.

FIVE

THERE was a loud booming at the door. A slave hurried to answer it. The door swung ponderously open, illuminating the dim hallway with a wedge of muted sunlight that framed a stocky, broad-shouldered silhouette in the flowing red cape of a military officer. Marcus Mummius marched toward us through the little garden, trampling on a bed of herbs and banging his elbow against the delicate faun.

He stopped before the body and scowled at the sight of the exposed wound. "You've already seen it, then," he said, reaching out to replace the camouflage of ivy and making a mess of it. "Poor Lucius Licinius. I suppose Fabius has explained everything to you."

"Not at all," I said.

"Good! Because it's not his job to brief you. I wouldn't have thought he could keep his lips sealed around a stranger, but perhaps we'll make a soldier of him yet." Mummius smiled broadly.

Fabius gave him a withering look. "You seem to be in high spirits."

"I raced my men all the way up from Misenum. A swift ride to loosen the joints after a few days at sea—that and the air of the Cup should put any man in high spirits."

"Still, you might lower your voice just a little, in deference to the dead."

Mummius's smile disappeared in his beard. "Sorry," he muttered, and returned to the fountain to dab at the water and touch his moistened fingers to his bowed forehead. He looked uneasily at the body, and then at each of us, waiting for any notice of his impiety to the shade of Lucius Licinius to pass.

"Perhaps we should call on Gelina," he finally said.

"Without me," Fabius said. "I have business to attend to in Puteoli, and not much time if I'm to get there and back before sundown."

"And where is Crassus?" Mummius called after him.

"In Puteoli as well, on business of his own. He left this morning with word that Gelina should not expect him back before dinner this evening." The door opened for him, pulled by an invisible slave in the shadows so that it seemed to open by magic at his approach. He stepped into the light and disappeared.

"What a prig," Mummius muttered under his breath. "And for all his high-flown attitude, they say his family could barely afford to buy him a decent tutor. Good blood, but one of his ancestors emptied the family coffers and no one ever filled them up again. Crassus took him on as a lieutenant only as a favor to Fabius's father; he hasn't turned out to have much talent as a military man, either. I could name a few plebeian families who've made more of a mark in the last hundred years or so." He smiled a bit smugly, then called to a little slave boy who was crossing the atrium: "You there, Meto, go and find your mistress and tell her I've arrived with her guest from Rome. As soon as we've refreshed ourselves in the baths, we shall call on her."

"Is that necessary?" I asked. "After the insane rush to get me here, do you really think we should spend time in a tub of water?"

"Nonsense. You can't meet Gelina smelling like a sea horse." He laughed at his own joke and put a hand on my shoulder to lead me away from the corpse. "Besides, taking the waters is the first thing anyone does when he arrives in Baiae. It's like praying to Neptune before setting out to sea. The waters here are alive, you know. Homage must be paid."

It seemed that the relaxing airs of the Cup could loosen even Mummius's staid and stodgy discipline. I put my arm around Eco's shoulders and followed our host, shaking my head in wonder.

* * *

What Mummius had casually referred to as the baths was in fact an impressive installation within the house that seemed to have been built over a natural terrace on the side of the hill, facing the bay. A great coffered dome lacquered with gold paint arched over the space, pierced by a round hole at the summit that admitted a beam of pure white light. Beneath this was a round pool with concentric steps leading into its depths, its surface obscured by roiling masses of sulphurous steam. An archway on the eastern side opened onto a terrace furnished with tables and chairs, with a view of the bay. A series of doors around the pool defined a semicircular arcade; the doors were of wood painted dark red, the handles were of gold in the shape of fish with their heads and tails attached to the wood. The first door led into a heated changing room; the other rooms, so Mummius explained as we shed our tunics, contained pools of various sizes and shapes, filled with water of various temperatures.

"Built by the famous Sergius Orata himself," Mummius boasted. "You've heard of him?"

"No."

"The most famous Puteolian of all, the man who made Baiae what it is today. He started the oyster farms on Lake Lucrinus—that earned him his first fortune. Then he turned out to be a master engineer at building pools and fish ponds, and villa owners all around the Cup showered him with commissions. This house contained a modest bath when Crassus acquired the estate. With Crassus's permission, not to mention Crassus's money, Lucius Licinius added an upper story here, a new wing there, and had the baths completely rebuilt, employing Sergius Orata himself to draw up and execute the plans. I'd prefer a little grotto in the woods or a common city pool myself—this kind of luxury is rather absurd, isn't it? Impressive but excessive, as the philosophers say."

Mummius stepped up to a brass hook cast as the heads of Cerberus and mounted in the wall. He hooked his shoes over two of the heads and hung his belt in the open jaws of the third. He pulled the heavy chain mail over his head and set about unbuckling leather straps. "But you have to admire such feats of plumbing. There's a natural hot spring that comes out of the earth at just this spot; that's why the first owner chose to build here—that, and the view. When Orata rebuilt, he designed the pipes so that some of the pools are piping hot, while others are mixed with cool water from a different spring up the hill. You can pass from the coolest to the hottest and back again. In winter some of the rooms in the house are even heated by water from the hot spring, piped under the floors. This changing room, for example, is kept warm all year long."

"Most impressive," I agreed, pulling my undertunic over my head. I started to place it in one of the coffers in the wall but Mummius intervened. He called to an old, stooped slave who stood at a discreet distance across the room. "Here, take these and have them washed," he said, indicating my things and Eco's and pulling his own tunic over his shoulders. "Bring back something suitable for an audience with your mistress." The slave gathered up the garments and studied us for a moment, estimating our sizes, then slunk from the room.

Naked, Marcus Mummius looked something like a bear, with big shoulders, a broad middle and dense swirls of black hair all over his body, except where he was marked by scars. Eco seemed particularly intrigued by a long slash that ran across his left pectoral like a cleared furrow in a forest.

"Battle of the Colline Gate," Mummius said proudly, looking down and pointing to the scar. "Crassus's proudest moment, and mine. That was the day we retook Rome for Sulla; the dictator never forgot what we did for him. I was wounded early in the day, but fortunately it was on the left side, which allowed me to go on using my sword arm." He mimed the action, bolting forward and swinging his right arm, causing the rather stout sword between his legs to swing heavily back and forth as well. "In the pitch of battle I hardly noticed the wound, just a dull burning. It wasn't until late that night when I went to deliver a message to Crassus that I passed clear out. They say I was as white as marble and didn't wake up for two days. Oh, but that was over ten years ago, I was just a boy, really—couldn't have been that much older than you,'' he said, punching Eco on the shoulder.

Eco smiled back at him crookedly and curiously examined Mummius for more scars, of which there was no shortage. Tiny nicks and plugs were scattered all over his limbs and torso like badges, easily discernible where they interrupted the general hairiness of his flesh.

He gathered a towel about his waist and gestured for us to do likewise, then led us from the changing room back into the great domed vault with the circular pool. The day was beginning to cool and the steam rose in great clouds from the water, hissing and smelling strongly of sulphur.

''Apollonius!'' Mummius smiled broadly and strode to the far side of the pool, where a young slave in a green tunic stood at the water's edge, obscured by the mist.

As we drew closer, I was impressed by the slave's extraordinary beauty. His hair was thick and almost blue-black, the color of the sky on a moonless night. His eyes were a vibrant blue. His forehead, nose, cheeks, and chin were perfectly smooth and followed the serene proportions from which the Greeks defined perfection. His full, bow-shaped lips seemed to hover on the edge of a smile. He was not tall, but beneath the loose folds of his tunic he clearly had an athlete's physique.

''Apollonius!'' Mummius said again. He looked back at me over his shoulder. ''I shall begin with the hottest pool,'' he announced, pointing at a door across the way, ''followed by a vigorous massage from Apollonius. And you?''

''I think I'll test these waters first,'' I said, dipping my foot into the main pool and quickly drawing it back. ''Or perhaps one a little less scalding.''

''Try that one, it's the coolest,'' said Mummius, indicating a chamber next to the changing room. He strode away with his hand on the slave's shoulder, humming a boisterous marching tune.

We sweated and scraped ourselves clean with ivory strigils; we immersed ourselves in one pool and then in another, going from cool to hot and back again, and when we were done with our ablutions Marcus Mummius rejoined us in the heated dressing room, where fresh undergarments and tunics had been laid out for us. Mine was of dark blue wool with a simple black border, befitting a guest in a household in mourning. The old slave had a sharp eye; it was a perfect fit, not even tight across my shoulders, as I often find borrowed garments to be. Mummius dressed in the plain but well-tailored black tunic he had worn on the night he summoned me.

Eco was less pleased with his costume. The slave, apparently thinking him younger than he was, or else too good-looking to be seen bare-limbed about the house, had brought him a long-sleeved blue tunic that reached to his knees. It was so modest that it would have been more suitable for a boy or girl of thirteen. I told Eco he should be flattered if the old slave found him so dazzling that he should hide himself. Mummius laughed; Eco blushed and would have none of it. He refused to dress until the slave brought him a tunic that matched mine. It was not quite as good a fit, but Eco made do by tightening the black woolen belt about his waist and seemed happy to be dressed in a more manly garment that showed his arms and legs.

Mummius guided us down long hallways where slaves bowed their heads and stepped meekly out of the way, down one flight of stairs and up another, through rooms decorated with exquisite statues and sumptuous wall paintings, across gardens breathing the last sweet breath of summer. At last we came to a semicircular room at the northern end of the house, set above a crag of rock overlooking the bay. A slave girl announced us and then departed.

The room was shaped like a theater. Where the stage would have been, steps led up to a colonnaded gallery. It opened onto a spectacular vista of sparkling water below and the port of Puteoli in the distance, and far away to the right an unimpeded view of Mount Vesuvius on the horizon and the towns of Herculaneum and Pompeii at its feet.

The interior of the room was so dark and the light from outside so dazzling that I could see the woman who reclined on the terrace only as a stark silhouette. She sat with her legs extended and her back upright on a low divan beside a small table set with a ewer and cups. She stared out at the bay and made no reaction as we entered; she might have been another statue, except that a gentle breeze wafted through the colonnade and caused the hanging folds of her gown to sway in the air.

She turned toward us. I could not yet distinguish her features, but there was a warm smile in her voice. "Marcus," she said, extending her right arm across her body in a gesture of welcome.

Mummius stepped onto the terrace, took her hand and bowed. "Your guest has arrived."

"So I see. Two of them, in fact. You must be Gordianus, the one they call the Finder."

"Yes."

"And this one?"

"My son, called Eco. He does not speak, but he hears."

She nodded and gestured for us to sit. As my eyes adjusted to the light, I began to make out the austere, rather stark features of her face—a strong jaw, high cheekbones, a high forehead—softened by the lush blackness of her eyebrows and eyelashes and the softness of her gray eyes. In deference to her widowhood, her black hair, touched with gray at the temples, was not dressed or arranged but simply brushed back from her face. From her neck to her ankles she was wrapped in a black stola loosely belted beneath her breasts and again at her waist. Her face was like the vista behind her, more lofty than lovely, animated and yet serenely detached. She spoke in even, measured tones and seemed to weigh each thought before she spoke it.

"My name is Gelina. My father was Gaius Gelinus. My mother was of the Cornelii, distantly related to the dictator Sulla. The Gelinii came to Rome long ago from inland Campania. In recent years many died in the civil wars, fighting Cinna and Marius on behalf of Sulla. We are an old and proud family, but neither wealthy nor particularly prolific. There are not many of the Gelinii left."

She paused to take a sip from the silver cup on the table

beside her. The wine was almost black. It gave her lips a vivid magenta stain. She gestured to the cups on the table, which had already been filled for us.

"Having no dowry to offer," she went on, "I was very lucky to marry a man like Lucius Licinius. The marriage was our own choice, not a family arrangement. You must understand, this was before Sulla's dictatorship, during the wars; times were cruel and the future was very uncertain. Our families were equally impoverished and unenthusiastic about the march, but they acquiesced. I am sorry to say that in twenty years of marriage we had no children, nor was my husband as wealthy as you might think from the evidence of this house. But in our way we prospered."

She began idly to rearrange the folds of the gown about her knee, as if to signal a change of subject. "You must wonder how I know of you, Gordianus. I learned of you from our mutual friend, Marcus Tullius Cicero. He speaks of you highly."

"Does he?"

"He does. I myself met Cicero only last winter, when Lucius and I happened to be seated at the divan next to his at a dinner in Rome. He was a most charming man."

"That is a word some people use in describing Cicero," I agreed.

"I asked him about his career in the law courts—men are always happy to talk about their careers," said Gelina. "Usually I only half listen, but something in his manner compelled me to pay attention."

"They say he is a most compelling speaker."

"Oh, he is, most certainly. Surely you've heard him yourself, speaking from the Rostra in the Forum?"

"Often enough."

Gelina narrowed her eyes in recollection, as serene as the profile of Vesuvius just above her head. "I found myself quite enthralled by his tale of Sextus Roscius, a wealthy farmer accused of murdering his own father, who called upon Cicero for legal counsel when no one else in Rome would come to his aid. It was Cicero's first murder case; I understand it made his reputation. Cicero told me he was assisted by a man named Gordianus, called the Finder. You were absolutely invaluable to him—as brave as an eagle and as stubborn as a mule, he said."

"Did he? Yes, well, that was eight years ago. I was still a young man, and Cicero was even younger."

"Since then he has ascended like a comet. The most talked-about advocate in Rome—quite a feat, for a man from such an obscure family. I understand that he has called upon your services a number of times."

I nodded. "There was, of course, the matter of the woman of Arretium, only shortly after the trial of Sextus Roscius, while Sulla was still alive. And various murder trials, cases of extortion, and property disagreements over the years, not to mention a few private affairs concerning which I cannot mention names."

"It must be very rewarding to work for such a man."

Sometimes I wish I were mute like Eco, so that I would not have to bite my tongue. I have fallen out and made up with Cicero so many times I am weary of it. Is he an honest man or a crass opportunist? A principled man of the people or an apologist for the rich nobility? If he were clearly one thing or the other, like most men, I would know what to think of him. Instead, he is the most exasperating man in Rome. His conceit and superior attitude, no matter how well deserved, do nothing to endear him to me; neither does his propensity for telling only half the truth, even when his purpose may be honorable. Cicero gives me a headache.

Gelina sipped her wine. "When this matter arose and I asked myself on whom I could call—someone trustworthy and discreet, someone from beyond the Cup, a man who would be dogged in pursuit of the truth and unafraid—brave as an eagle, Cicero said . . ."

"And stubborn as a mule."

"And clever. Above all, clever . . ." Gelina sighed and looked out at the water. She seemed to be gathering strength. "You have seen the body of my husband?"

"Yes."

"He was murdered."

"Yes."

"Brutally murdered. It happened five days ago, on the Nones of September—although his body was not discovered until the next morning . . ." Her serenity suddenly departed; her voice quavered and she looked away.

Mummius moved closer to her and took her hand. "Strength," he whispered to her. Gelina nodded and caught her breath. She gripped his hand tightly, then released him.

"If I am to help you," I said quietly, "I must know everything."

For a long moment Gelina studied the view. When she looked back at me, her face had recomposed itself, as if she were able to absorb the serene detachment of the panorama by gazing upon it. Her voice was steady and calm as she continued.

"He was discovered, as I said, early the next morning."

"Discovered where? By whom?"

"In the front atrium, not far from where his body lies at this moment. It was one of the slaves who found him—Meto, the little boy who carries messages and wakes the other slaves to begin their morning duties. It was still dark; not a cock had crowed, the boy said, and the whole world seemed as still as death."

"What was the exact disposition of the body? Perhaps we should summon this Meto—"

"No, I can tell you myself. Meto came to fetch me right away, and nothing was touched before I arrived. Lucius lay on his back, his eyes still open."

"Flat on his back?"

"Yes."

"And his arms and legs, were they crumpled about his body? Was he clutching his head?"

"No. His legs were straight, and his arms were above his head."

"Like Atlas, holding up the world?"

"I suppose."

"And the weapon that was used to kill him, was it nearby?"

"It was never found."

"No? Surely there was a stone with blood on it, or a piece of metal. If not in the house, then perhaps in the courtyard."

"No. But there was a piece of cloth." She shuddered. Mummius sat up in his chair; this was apparently a detail that was new to him.

"Cloth?" I said.

"A man's cloak, soaked with blood. It was found only yesterday, not in the courtyard, but about half a mile up the road that heads northward, toward Cumae and Puteoli. One of the slaves going to market happened to see it among the brush and brought it to me."

"Was it your husband's cloak?"

Gelina frowned. "I don't know. It's hard to tell what it must have looked like; you would hardly know it was a cloak at all without examining it—all rumpled and stiff with blood, you understand?" She took a deep breath. "It's simple wool, dyed a dark brown, almost black. It might have belonged to Lucius; he owned many cloaks. It could be anyone's."

"Surely not. Was it the cloak of a rich man, or a slave? Was it new or old, well made or tawdry?"

Gelina shrugged. "I can't say."

"I'll need to see it."

"Of course. Ask Meto, later; I couldn't bear to look at it now."

"I understand. But tell me this: Was there much blood on the floor, beneath the wound? Or was there little blood?"

"I think—only a little. Yes, I remember wondering how such a terrible wound could have bled so little."

"Then perhaps we can assume that the blood on this cloak came from Lucius Licinius. What else can you tell me?"

Gelina paused for a long moment. I could see she was faced with a disagreeable but unavoidable declaration. "On the morning that Lucius was found dead, there were two slaves missing from the household. They've been missing ever since. But I cannot believe that either of them could possibly have murdered Lucius."

"Who are these slaves?"

"Their names are Zeno and Alexandros. Zeno is—was—my husband's accountant and secretary. He wrote letters, balanced accounts, managed this and that. He had been with Lucius for almost six years, ever since Crassus began to favor us and our fortunes changed. An educated Greek slave, quiet and soft-spoken, very gentle, with a white beard and a frail body. I had always hoped, if we ever had a son, that Zeno could be his first tutor. It is simply not conceivable that he could have murdered Lucius. The idea that he could murder anyone is preposterous."

"And the other slave?"

"A young Thracian called Alexandros. We bought him four months ago at the market in Puteoli, to work in the stables. He has a marvelous way with horses. He could read and do simple sums, as well. Zeno used him sometimes in my husband's library, to add figures or copy letters. Alexandros is very quick to learn, very clever. He never showed any signs of discontent. On the contrary, it seemed to me that he was one of the happiest slaves in the household. I can't believe that he murdered Lucius."

"And yet both these slaves disappeared on the night your husband was murdered?"

"Yes. I can't explain it."

Mummius, who until then had been silent, cleared his throat. "There is more to the story. The most damning evidence of all." Gelina looked away, then nodded in resignation. She gestured for him to continue. "On the floor at Lucius's feet, someone used a knife to carve out six letters. They're crude and shallow, hastily done, but you can read them clearly enough."

"What do they spell?" I asked.

"The name of a famous village in Greece," said Mummius grimly. "Although someone as clever as you might presume that whoever did the scrawling simply didn't have the time to finish the job."

"What village? I don't understand."

Mummius dipped his finger into his goblet and wrote the

letters in blood-red wine on the marble table, all straight lines and sharp points:

SPARTA

"Yes, I see," I said. "A village in Greece." Either that, or a hurried, interrupted homage to the king of runaway slaves, the murderer of Roman slave owners, the escaped Thracian gladiator: Spartacus.

SIX

THAT night no one heard anything, saw anything?"

"No," said Gelina.

"And yet, if the name Spartacus was left incomplete, that would seem to indicate that whoever carved it was disturbed and fled; very odd."

"Perhaps they simply panicked," said Mummius.

"Perhaps. The next morning, what else was discovered missing from the household, besides the two slaves?"

Gelina thought for a moment, then shook her head. "Nothing."

"Nothing? No coins? No weapons? Knives from the kitchen? I should think that escaping slaves would loot the house for silver and weapons."

"Unless, as you say, they were disturbed," said Mummius.

"What about horses?"

"Yes," said Gelina, "two horses *were* gone the next morning, but in the confusion no one even noticed until they both came wandering back that afternoon."

"Without horses they couldn't have gone far," I muttered.

Gelina shook her head. "You're already assuming what everyone else assumes—that Zeno and Alexandros murdered Lucius and set out to join Spartacus."

"What else can I assume? The head of the household is found murdered in the atrium of his home; two slaves are missing, having evidently escaped on horseback. And one of the slaves is a young Thracian, like Spartacus—so proud of his infamous countryman he's insolently carved the name at his dead master's feet. You hardly need my skills to figure it out for yourself. It's a story that's been repeated all over Italy with many variations in the past months. What do you need me for? As I told Faustus Fabius earlier today, I don't track down escaped slaves. I regret the absurd efforts that were squandered on my coming here, but I cannot imagine what you want from me."

"The truth!" said Gelina desperately. "Cicero said you have a nose for it, like a boar for truffles."

"Ah, now I understand why Cicero has treated me so shabbily over the years. I'm a menagerie, not a man!"

Gelina's eyes flashed. Mummius scowled darkly, and from the corner of my eye I saw Eco give a twitch. Unseen beneath the table I gave his foot a tap with mine to let him know that all was under control; he glanced at me and gave a conspiratorial sigh of relief. I have been through many interviews with wealthy clients, under many circumstances. Even those who most need and sincerely want my help are often maddeningly slow to come to the point. I much prefer conferring with common merchants or simple shopkeepers, men who will say right out what they want from you. The rich seem to think I should surmise their needs without being told. Sometimes abruptness or a feigned bit of rudeness will speed them along.

"You don't understand," said Gelina hopelessly.

"No, I do not. What is it you want from me? Why did you have me brought here so mysteriously, and in such an extravagant manner? What is this strange game, Gelina?"

The animation left her face. Like a pliable mask, her serenity changed to simple resignation, dulled by a bit too much red wine. "I've said all I can say. I don't have the strength to explain it all to you. But unless someone can uncover the truth—" She stopped short and bit her lip. "They will all die, every one of them," she whispered hoarsely. "The suffering, the waste—I cannot bear it. . . ."

"What do you mean? Who will die?"

"The slaves," said Mummius. "Every slave in the household."

I felt a sudden chill. Eco shuddered, and I saw that he felt it as well, even though the air was mild and calm.

"Explain, Marcus Mummius."

He drew himself up stiffly, like a commander briefing his lieutenant. "You know that Marcus Licinius Crassus is the actual owner of this household?"

"So I gathered."

"Very well. It so happens that on the night of the murder, Crassus and his retinue, including Fabius and myself, had just come down from Rome. We were busy setting up camp on the plain beside Lake Lucrinus, only a few miles up the road, along with our recruits."

"Recruits?"

"Soldiers, many of them veterans who served under Crassus in the civil wars."

"How many soldiers?"

"Six hundred."

"A whole cohort?"

Mummius looked at me dubiously. "You might as well know. Certain events are transpiring in Rome; Marcus Crassus has begun to lobby for a special commission from the Senate that will allow him to raise his own army and march against Spartacus."

"But that's the job of praetors and consuls, elected officials—"

"The elected officials have failed, disgracefully. Crassus has the military skill and the financial means to dispose of the rebels once and for all. He came down from Rome to muster recruits and to consolidate his political and financial support here on the Cup. When he's ready, he'll prod the Senate in Rome to vote him the special commission."

"Just what the Republic needs," I said, "another warlord with his own private army."

"*Exactly* what Rome needs!" said Mummius. "Or would you rather have slaves marauding across the countryside?"

"And what does this have to do with the murder of Crassus's cousin, or with my being here?"

"I'll tell you. On the night that Lucius Licinius was killed, we were camped at Lake Lucrinus. The next morning Crassus assembled his staff and we headed for Baiae. We arrived here at the villa only hours after Lucius had been found dead.

Crassus was outraged, naturally. I myself organized teams of men to search for the missing slaves; in my absence the hunt has continued, but the escaped slaves are still missing." He sighed. "And now we come to the crux of the problem. The funeral of Lucius Licinius will take place on the seventh day of mourning—that's the day after tomorrow. On the day after that, Crassus has decreed there will be funeral games with gladiators, in keeping with ancient tradition. That will be the Ides of September, the date of the full moon; a propitious date for sacred games."

"And after the gladiators have fought their matches?" I said, suspecting what the answer would be.

"Every slave in this household will be publicly executed."

"Can you imagine?" murmured Gelina. "Even the old and the innocent; all of them will be killed. Have you ever heard of such a law?"

"Oh, yes," I said, "a very ancient and venerated law, handed down by our forefathers: If a slave kills his master, all the slaves in the household must die. Such harsh measures keep slaves in their place, and there are those who would argue that having seen another slave murder their master, even the meekest slave is contaminated by the knowledge and can never be trusted again. These days the application of the law is a matter of discretion. The slaying of a master by a slave is a rare atrocity, or was, before Spartacus. Faced with a choice of killing every slave in a household or punishing only the miscreants, most heirs would choose to preserve their property. Crassus has a great reputation for greed; why would he choose to sacrifice every slave on the estate?"

"He wants to make a point," said Mummius.

"But it means the death of children and old women," protested Gelina.

"Let me explain it so that you will understand, Gordianus." Mummius looked like a glum commander addressing his troops before a dubious battle. "Crassus has come to Campania and the Cup gathering support for his bid to be awarded the military command against Spartacus. The Senate's campaign has been one long disaster—Roman armies defeated, generals humiliated and sent home in disgrace, consuls forced out of office by public outrage, the state left leaderless. So much havoc, wrought by a ragtag army of escaped criminals and slaves! All of Italy quakes with fear and outrage.

"Crassus is a fine commander; he proved that under Sulla. With his wealth—and the defeat of Spartacus to his credit—he's well on his way to the consulship. While lesser men are fleeing from the job, Crassus sees the command as an opportunity. The Roman who stops Spartacus will be a hero. Crassus intends to be that man."

"Because otherwise that man will be Pompey."

Mummius made a face. "Probably. Half the Senators in Rome have run off to their villas to try to save their own property, while the other half bite their nails and wait for Pompey to return from Spain, praying the state can survive that long. As if Pompey were another Alexander! A qualified commander is all that's needed to put an end to Spartacus. Crassus can do it in a matter of months if the Senate will only give him the nod. He can gather up the remnants of the surviving legions here in Italy, add to them his own private army raised largely from his clients here in the south, and make himself the savior of the Republic overnight."

I looked out at the bay and Vesuvius beyond. "I see. That's why the murder of Lucius Licinius is more than just a tragedy."

"It's an incredible embarrassment, that's what it is!" said Mummius. "To have slaves murdering and running free from one of his own households, even as he's asking the Senate to hand him a sword to punish Spartacus—in the Forum, they'll laugh until they weep. That's why he feels compelled to exact the sternest judgment possible, to fall back on tradition and ancient law, the harsher the better."

"To turn an embarrassment into a political boon, you mean."

"Exactly. What might have been a disaster could turn into just the sort of propaganda victory he needs. 'Crassus, soft on runaway slaves? Hardly! The man slew a whole household of them down in Baiae, men, women, and children, showed no mercy at all, made a public spectacle of it, a feast day—

just the sort of man we can trust to take on Spartacus and his murderous rabble!' That's what people will say."

"Yes. I see."

"But Zeno and Alexandros are innocent," said Gelina wearily. "I know they are. Someone else must have murdered Lucius. None of the slaves should be punished, yet Crassus refuses to listen. Thank the gods for Marcus Mummius, who understands. Together we convinced Crassus to at least let me summon you from Rome. There was no other way to get you here in time, except to send the *Fury*; Crassus made a great show of his generosity in allowing me to use it. He offered to pay for your services as well, just to humor me. I can ask no more favors of him, no postponements. We have so little time. Only three days until the funeral games, and then—"

"How many slaves are there in all, not counting Zeno and Alexandros?" I asked.

"I lay awake last night counting them: Ninety-nine. There were a hundred and one, counting Zeno and Alexandros."

"So many, for a villa?"

"There are vineyards to the north and south," she said vaguely, "and of course the olive orchards, the stables, the boathouse . . ."

"Do the slaves know?" I asked.

Mummius looked at Gelina, who looked at me with her eyebrows raised high. "Most of the slaves are being kept under guard in the annex on the far side of the stables," she said quietly. "Crassus won't allow the field slaves to go out, and he's let me have only the essential slaves here in the house. They're in custody, they know that, but no one has told them the whole truth. Certainly you must not tell them. Who knows what might transpire if the slaves suspected . . ."

I nodded, but I saw no point in secrecy. Except for young Apollonius in the baths, I had hardly glimpsed the face of a single slave in the household, only a succession of bowed heads and averted eyes. Even if they had not been told, somehow they knew.

* * *

We took our leave of Gelina. The interview had exhausted her. As we left the semicircular room, I glanced back to see her silhouette reaching for the ewer to replenish her cup with wine.

Mummius led us back to the atrium and showed me where the letters SPARTA had been scrawled into the flagstones. Each letter was as tall as my finger. As Mummius had said, they appeared to have been hastily made, crudely scraped rather than chiseled. I had stepped right over them without noticing when Faustus Fabius had first shown us into the house. In the dim light of the hallway they were easily overlooked. How strange the hallway and atrium suddenly seemed, with the death masks of the ancestors staring from their niches, the piping faun prancing in his fountain, the dead man on his ivory bier, and the name of the most dreaded and despised man in all of Italy half-scrawled on the floor.

The light in the atrium was beginning to grow soft and hazy; it would soon be time to light the lamps, but there was still enough sunlight before dinner to ride out and see where the bloodied cloak had been found. Mummius summoned the boy Meto, who fetched the cloak and the slave who had found it, and we rode out past the pylons onto the northern road.

The cloak was as nondescript as Gelina had indicated, a dark, muddy-colored garment neither tattered nor new. There was no decoration or embroidery to indicate whether it might be locally made or from far away, the cloak of a rich man or a poor one. The bloodstain covered a great deal of it, not just in one place but spattered and smeared all about. One corner appeared to have been cut away—to eradicate an identifying insignia or seal?

The slave had found it along a secluded, narrow section of road that clung to a steep cliff above the bay. Someone must have cast it from the cliff's edge, trying to throw it into the water below; the crumpled cloak had been caught on a scraggly tree that projected from the rocky hillside, several feet below the road. A man on foot or horseback could not have seen it without stepping to the edge of the cliff and peering over; the slave, mounted atop a high wagon, had barely glimpsed it on his way to market, and indeed had left it there until his return from Puteoli, when he took a closer look and realized that it might be important.

"The fool says that he wasn't going to bother getting it, because he could see it had blood on it," said Mummius under his breath. "He figured it was ruined and of no use to him; then it occurred to him that the blood might have come from his master."

"Or from Zeno or Alexandros," I said. "Tell me, who else knows that this cloak was found?"

"Only the slave who found it, Gelina, and the boy, Meto. And now yourself, Eco, and I."

"Good. I think, Marcus Mummius, that there may be some cause for hope."

"Yes?" His eyes lit up. For a hardened military man who could treat his galley slaves so harshly, he seemed oddly eager to save the slaves of Gelina's household.

"I say this not because I have any solution, but because things as they stand are more convoluted than they should be. For instance, though it has not been found, it appears that the killer used a bludgeon of some sort to murder Lucius Licinius. Why, when a knife was at hand?"

"A knife?"

"The killer must have used some sort of blade to scrape the letters. And why was the body dragged into position instead of being left where it fell?"

"Why do you think it was dragged at all?"

"Because of the posture Gelina described. Think: legs straight, arms above the head—not likely to be the pose of a man who collapses to the ground after being struck in the head, but exactly the posture of a body that has been dragged feetfirst across a floor. Dragged from where, and for what reason? Then there is the matter of this cloak."

"Yes?"

"There is no way of knowing whose blood is on it, but for now, and because there is so much blood, we shall assume that it came from the dead man. Gelina told us that there was not much blood on the floor beneath the wound, and yet Lucius must have bled profusely; it seems likely this cloak was used to absorb the blood. And yet this garment could hardly have belonged to Lucius himself; having seen the extravagant sort of house he lived in, I can hardly believe that he would choose such a drab garment. No, this is the very best cloak that a common man might own, or the sort of common cloak that a rich man with pretensions to old-fashioned Roman virtue might affect to wear, or simply the sort of dark, common cloak that a man or woman might choose so as to move about unseen at night—an assassin's cloak.

"Somehow, this cloak must be incriminating. Otherwise, why carry it away from the scene of the crime, and why attempt to cast it into the sea? And why cut away a corner of it? If the escaped slaves did indeed kill Lucius, they were evidently bold enough to brag about it by inscribing the name of Spartacus on the floor; why would they bother to hide the cloak after so brazenly proclaiming their allegiance? Why wouldn't they leave it behind for all to look at in horror? I think we must be very careful to see that no one else discovers this cloak has been found. The true killer must continue to think that it was successfully cast into the water. I shall take it and hide it among my own things."

Eco, who had been listening intently, tugged on my tunic. At his insistence, I handed him the bloodstained cloak, whereupon he pointed to the various patches of blood, and mimed a series of motions with his open palm.

Mummius looked on, baffled. "What is he saying?"

"Eco makes an excellent point! See here, where the blood is most concentrated, roughly in a circle—as if it had been placed under a gushing wound to catch the blood? While elsewhere the blood is smeared in swaths about the width of a man's hand—as if it had been used to wipe up blood, perhaps from a floor."

Eco pantomimed again, lying backward and putting his hands behind his head, then extending both arms as if dragging a heavy object, all done so enthusiastically that I feared he might fall from his horse.

"And what is all that about?" said Mummius.

"Eco points out the possibility that the cloak was first placed under the dying man's head, so as to catch the blood while his body was dragged across the floor. Then the murderer might have used the clean portion of the cloth to wipe up the spatters of blood from the room where the blows were actually delivered, as well as whatever had gotten onto the floor in transit."

Mummius crossed his arms. "Is he really that eloquent?"

"I scarcely do him justice. So much for the cloak. Most disturbing of all is the fact that the two missing horses returned to the stable the next day. Surely Zeno and Alexandros would not have relinquished them willingly—unless they obtained horses elsewhere."

Mummius shook his head. "My men made inquiries. No horses have been stolen in the area."

"Then Zeno and Alexandros would have been reduced to traveling on foot. In an area as civilized as this, with so much traffic on the roads, so much suspicion and fear of escaped slaves among the populace, and with your men actively searching, it seems hardly possible that they could have escaped."

Eco intersected one hand with the other in pantomime of a sail on the sea. Mummius looked puzzled for a moment, then glowered. "Of course we inquired among the ship owners. None of the ferries to Pompeii or Herculaneum would have taken two runaway slaves, and there have been no stolen vessels. Neither of them would have known the first thing about sailing a boat, anyway."

"Then what possibilities remain?" I said.

Mummius shrugged. "They're still somewhere in the area, hiding."

"Or else, more likely, they are both dead." The light had begun to fade rapidly. The cliff cast a long shadow onto the water. I looked back toward the villa, and above the trees could see only a few tiles of the rooftop and some plumes of smoke; the evening fires were being stoked. I turned my horse around.

"Tell me, Mummius, who currently resides in the villa?"

"Besides Gelina, only a handful of people. This is the end

of the holiday season in Baiae. There weren't that many visitors this year even in the spring. I was here myself in May, along with Crassus and Fabius and a few others. Baiae seemed a shadow of itself. Between Spartacus and the pirates, everyone is afraid to leave Rome."

"Yes, but who is staying here *now*?"

"Let me think. Gelina, of course. And Dionysius, her philosopher in residence—calls himself a polymath, writes plays and histories and pretends to make witty conversation, but he puts me right to sleep. Then there's Iaia, the painter."

"Iaia? A woman?"

He nodded. "Originally from Cyzicus. Crassus says she was all the rage when he was a boy, with paintings in the best houses in Rome and all around the Cup. Specialized in portraits, mainly women. Never married, but seems to have made quite a success on her own. She's retired now and paints for pleasure, together with a young assistant she's instructing. They're here doing some project as a favor for Gelina, painting an anteroom in the women's baths."

"And who is Iaia's assistant?"

"Olympias, originally from Neapolis across the bay."

"A girl?" I asked.

"A very beautiful girl," Mummius assured me, at which Eco's eyes lit up. "Iaia treats her like a daughter. They have their own small villa on the seacoast up in Cumae, but they often stay here for days at a time, working in the mornings and keeping Gelina company at night."

"Were they in the house on the night Lucius was killed?"

"Actually, no. They were up in Cumae."

"Is that far?"

"Not very; an hour away on foot, closer on horseback."

"Besides the philosopher and the painters, are there any guests in the house?"

Mummius thought. "Yes, two."

"And they were here on the night of the murder?"

"Yes," Mummius said slowly, "but neither of them could possibly be suspected of murder."

"Even so . . ."

"Very well, the first is Sergius Orata. I mentioned him to

you before, the builder of the baths in the south wing. He comes from Puteoli and has villas all around the Cup, but as often as not you'll find him staying in other people's houses; that's the way they do it here, the rich move about playing guest in each other's villas. Gelina says he was here talking business with Lucius when word came that Crassus was on his way from Rome and wanted to consult with them both. Orata decided to stay on, so that the three of them could transact their business together in one place. He was here on the night of the murder and is still here, staying in a suite of rooms in the north wing."

"And the other houseguest?"

"Metrobius, up from his villa across the bay in Pompeii."

"Metrobius? The name sounds familiar."

"Famous from the stage, once the best-loved female impersonator in Rome. A favorite of Sulla's. That's how he got his villa, back when Sulla was dictator and was handing out the confiscated property of his enemies like party favors to his inner circle."

"Ah, yes, I did once see Metrobius perform."

"I never had the privilege," Mummius said, with a sarcastic edge in his voice. "Doing Plautus, or some creation of his own?"

"Neither. He was performing a rather lewd mock homage to Sulla at a private party in the house of Chrysogonus, years ago."

"And you were there?" Mummius seemed skeptical that I could have moved in such rarefied and debauched circles.

"I was an uninvited guest. Very uninvited. But what is Metrobius doing here?"

"He's a great friend of Gelina's. The two of them can carry on for hours, trading local gossip. Or so I'm told. Between us, I can't stand to spend more than a few minutes in a room with him."

"You dislike Metrobius?"

"I have my reasons."

"But you don't suspect him of murder."

Mummius snorted. "Let me tell you something, Gordianus. I have killed more than my share of men, always honorably and in battle, you understand, but killing is killing. I've killed with a sword, I've killed with a bludgeon, I've even killed with my bare hands. I know something of what it takes to snuff out the life of another man. Believe me, Metrobius hasn't the mettle to have bashed in Lucius's skull, even if he did have a reason."

"What about Zeno, or Alexandros, the two slaves?"

"It hardly seems likely."

"But not impossible?"

He shrugged.

"So," I said, "we know that these people were in the house on the night of the murder: Dionysius the resident polymath, the Puteolian businessman Sergius Orata, and the retired actor Metrobius. Iaia the painter and her assistant Olympias are often here, but not on that night."

"So far as I know. Of those who were here, each was alone and asleep in his or her own private bed, or so they say. None of them heard anything, which is perfectly possible, given the distance between rooms. None of the slaves claims to have heard anything either, which also seems plausible, since they sleep in their own quarters out by the stables."

"Surely at least one slave has the duty to keep watch through the night," I said.

"Yes, but on the grounds, not in the house. He's supposed to make a circuit, keeping one eye on the road in front of the house and another on the coast behind. Pirates have been known to attack private villas on the coast, though never in Baiae, so far as I know. When the slaves made their escape the watchman must have been out back. He saw nothing."

"Is there anyone you suspect? Any of the residents or guests in Gelina's house who seem more likely to have killed Lucius than the slaves?"

In answer he only shrugged and scowled.

"Which makes me wonder, Mummius, why you've expended so much of your own time and energy to help Gelina prove that the slaves are innocent."

"I have my reasons," he said curtly, thrusting out his jaw and staring straight ahead. He spurred his horse to a gallop and raced on to the villa alone.

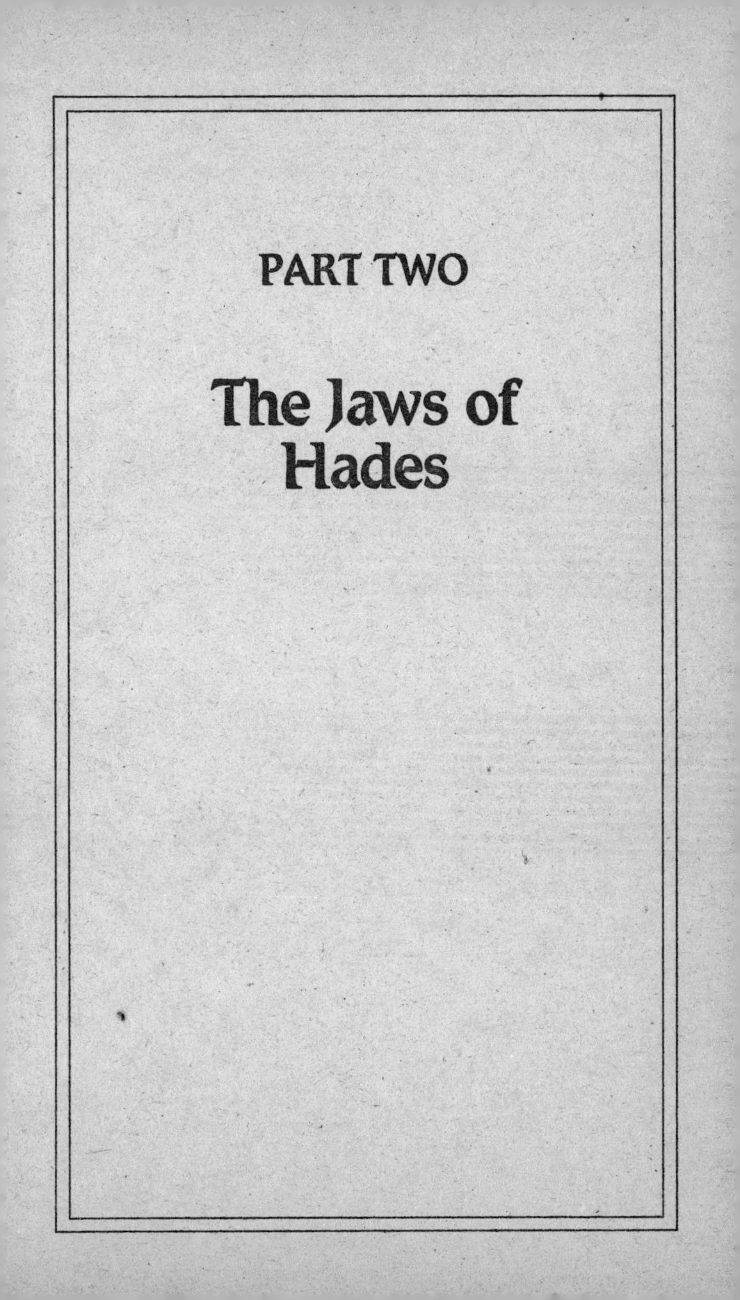

PART TWO

The Jaws of Hades

SEVEN

DINNER began at the twelfth hour of the day, just after sundown, in a modestly appointed room in the southeast corner of the upper floor. Windows opened onto views of Puteoli to the east and Vesuvius farther south. A coterie of slaves unobtrusively hurried about the room and the adjoining hallways, lighting braziers against the slight chill in the air and illuminating the richly colored walls with an array of hanging lamps. The air was windless, empty of bird song or the noise of any other living thing; the only sound from the world outside was the vague murmur of the sea, like a distant sighing. Looking out the southern window, I saw a single star glimmering above Vesuvius in a sky of darkest blue. A sensation of hushed luxury descended upon the villa, that special feeling of comfort and sumptuous privilege peculiar to the homes of the rich at twilight.

Gelina, already reclining on her divan, welcomed her guests as they arrived separately or in pairs, all dressed in somber dark blue or black. There were places for eleven people in all, an awkward number for a dinner, but Gelina managed it by placing the company in a square with three divans on each of three sides and two on the last, one for herself and another reserved for Crassus. The small tables before each divan were already set with cups of honeyed wine, white and black olives, and an appetizer of sea urchins in a cumin sauce.

The painter Iaia and her protégée Olympias, along with the polymath Dionysius, sat opposite Gelina; Marcus Mummius, Faustus Fabius, and Sergius Orata sat to her right; Eco and I were to her left, along with the actor Metrobius. Gelina introduced us simply as Gordianus of Rome and his son, with no further explanation. From their expressions, I gathered that Gelina's guests already had some idea of my purpose in being there. In their eyes I saw varying degrees of skepticism, suspicion, and disinterest.

Iaia, striking in her jet-black stola, silver jewelry, and voluminously coiffed magenta hair (surely dyed), had clearly been a great beauty in her day; now she exuded that mellow, self-confident appeal of women who have lost their youth but kept their charm. Her high cheekbones were generously rouged, her eyebrows shaved and penciled.

While Iaia gave me cool glances, her young protégée, a dazzling blonde, stared at me brazenly as if my presence were some sort of affront. Olympias could afford to be careless with her beauty; her undressed hair was like a mane of spun gold and silver in the lamplight, her eyes an almost purple shade of blue that would have made the least trace of makeup, had she bothered to use it, look pale and tawdry on her perfect flesh. Her sleeveless, dark blue stola was absolutely plain, even plainer than the tunics Eco and I wore, having no embroidery or border. She wore no jewelry. I noticed traces of pigment on her fingers, and a few dabs of paint near the bottom hem of her gown.

Dionysius, a gaunt graybeard with a supercilious expression, gave me shifty-eyed glances between dabbing at his olives with the fingers of his left hand. He was almost silent during the first part of the evening, as if holding his words in reserve for later use. He looked to me like a man with a secret, but perhaps that was only due to the appearance of smug sagacity which he affected, like so many other philosophers.

Dionysius's reserved, sour countenance offered a striking contrast to that of the local businessman and engineer, Orata, who shared the polymath's corner. Almost bald except for a fringe of orange hair like a victory wreath, Orata had the portly build of a man grown fat on his successes. His plump, bemused face seemed out of place amid the general gloom. When he happened to look my way, I could not tell whether he liked me at first sight or was craftily smiling to conceal some other reaction. For the most part he seemed to take little notice of me at all as he busily ordered the table slaves assigned to his divan to slice the pits from his olives and fetch more cumin sauce.

The elderly actor Metrobius, who reclined at my right, gave me a nod as I was introduced and then immediately turned his attention to Gelina. He reclined on his right side, she on her left, so that their heads were together. They spoke to each other in hushed voices, and occasionally Metrobius would reach out and clasp her hand reassuringly. His long, flowing robe covered him from head to foot; the finely spun linen appeared funereal black at first glance, but upon closer inspection I saw it was actually a very dark purple. He wore gold around his neck and wrists, and a great jewel-encrusted ring on his left hand, which flashed in the light whenever he lifted his cup. Metrobius had been Sulla's great love, it was said, the dictator's companion and friend throughout his life, outlasting all of Sulla's many marriages and liaisons. Whatever physical allure he had possessed in youth was long gone, but there was an assertive dignity in his great mane of white hair and a kind of robust beauty in the weathered wrinkles of his face. I recalled the night ten years ago when I had seen him perform for Sulla, and remembered the spell cast by his presence. Even with his attentions directed toward Gelina, I could feel the charismatic power he exuded, as palpable as the smell of myrrh and roses that spiced his clothing. His every movement was accomplished with an unstudied grace, and the low, calm murmur of his voice had a soothing quality like the drumming of rain on a summer night or the soughing of wind in treetops.

Except for Eco and myself, it seemed a typical dinnertime gathering for a Baian villa—a military man and a patrician, a painter and her protégée, a polymath and a builder, an actor, and their hostess. The host was missing—or more precisely, laid to rest on an ivory bier down in the atrium—but to take his place we would have the richest man in Rome. So far, however, Marcus Crassus had not deigned to appear.

Given such a sparkling gathering, the conversation was surprisingly desultory. Mummius and Faustus quietly discussed the day's business and the provisions for Crassus's camp on Lake Lucrinus; Iaia and Olympias exchanged inaudible whispers; the philosopher brooded over his food while the businessman relished each bite; Gelina and Metrobius seemed oblivious of everything but each other. At length the slave boy Meto entered and whispered in Gelina's ear. She nodded and sent him off. "I fear that Marcus Crassus will not be joining us tonight," she announced. I had thought that the vague tension in the room was due to my presence, or to the air of death in the house, but in that instant the gathered household seemed to give a collective sigh of relief.

"Detained by his business in Puteoli, is he?" asked Mummius through a mouthful of sea urchin.

"Yes. He sends word that he will make provision for his own supper and ride back afterward. So we need not wait any longer." She signaled to the slaves, who cleared away the appetizers and served the main dishes—a sweet citron ragout of ham and apples, seafood dumplings spiced with lovage and pepper, and fish fillets with leeks and coriander, all served on silver platters, along with a barley soup with cabbage and lentils that we sipped from tiny clay pots.

As the meal progressed the conversation grew more animated. The principal subject was food. Death and impending disaster, political ambition and the threat of Spartacus were ignored in favor of the relative merits of hare and pork. Beef was debated, and roundly declared inedible. Faustus Fabius declared that cattle were useless except for their hides, but the philosopher Dionysius, who spoke in a lecturing tone, claimed that the barbarians of the North actually preferred the milk of cows to that of goats.

Sergius Orata seemed to be something of an expert on trading spices and other delicacies with the East. Once he had traveled as far as Parthia investigating the potentials of the market, and on the Euphrates had been induced by good manners to drink a local beverage made of fermented barley, which the Parthians preferred to wine. "It was the exact color of urine," he laughed, "and tasted like it!"

"But how would you know? Are you in the habit of drinking urine?" asked Olympias, who demurely lowered her face so that a strand of blond hair fell over one eye. Iaia looked at her sidelong, suppressing a smile. Orata's bald pate blushed pink. Mummius laughed raucously.

"Better urine than beans!" exclaimed Dionysius. "You know the advice of Plato: One must set forth for the realm of dreams each night with a pure spirit."

"And what does that have to do with beans?" asked Fabius.

"Surely you know the opinion of the Pythagoreans? Beans produce great flatulence, which induces a condition at war with a soul in search of truth."

"Really, as if it were the soul and not the belly that gets filled with wind!" exclaimed Metrobius, who leaned toward me and lowered his voice. "These philosophers—no idea is too absurd for them. This one is certainly a windbag, but I think it all comes out his mouth and not the other end!"

Gelina seemed immune to both wit and crudity and ate in silence, picking restlessly at her food and calling for fresh wine in her cup more often than any of her guests.

Metrobius began to enlighten me about the differences between Roman and Baian cuisine. "There is a greater variety of fresh seafood in the markets here, of course, and many maritime specialties unknown in Rome, but the distinctions are more subtle than that. For instance, any cook will tell you that the best cooking pots are made from a special clay found only in the vicinity of Cumae. In Rome such pots are precious and hard to replace, but here even the lowliest fisherman owns one, and so we have all sorts of peasant dishes that are as sublime as they are simple—this barley soup, for instance. Then there are the famous Baian green beans, more tender and sweet than those grown anywhere else. Gelina's cook makes a dish with green beans, coriander, and chopped chives, fit for a Bacchanalia. Ah, but the slaves have begun to clear away the main dishes, which means the second course must be on its way."

Slaves entered bearing silver trays that flashed in the lamplight, bringing baked pears stuffed with cinnamon, roasted chestnuts, and cheese seasoned in fermented berry juice. Outside, the sky darkened from deep blue to black spangled with bright stars. Gelina shivered and ordered the braziers to be brought nearer. The leaping flames were reflected in the silver platters, so that the delicacies on each table seemed to float upon pools of fire.

"A pity Marcus Crassus is not here to enjoy such a feast," said Metrobius, picking up a stuffed pear and breathing in its aroma. "Of course, with Crassus here, the discussion would have turned on nothing but politics, politics, politics."

Mummius glowered at him. "About which some people know less than nothing. A good political discussion might keep certain people quiet for a change." He popped a chestnut into his mouth and smacked his lips.

"The table manners of a barbarian," Metrobius muttered to me under his breath.

"What did you say?" Mummius bolted forward.

"I said you have the able manner of an agrarian. Your family still farms, do they not?"

Mummius sat back slowly, looking skeptical.

"Perhaps we should discuss something we all have in common," suggested Metrobius. "What about art? Iaia and Olympias create it, Dionysius contemplates it, Orata buys it. Is it true, Sergius, that you've contracted to construct and decorate a new fish pond for one of the Cornelii down in Misenum?"

"True," said Sergius Orata.

"Ah, these villa owners on the Cup and their love of a decorative fish pond. How they cherish each and every bearded mullet! I've heard of senators who give each fish a name and feed them by hand from infancy, and when the mullets are grown they cannot bear to eat them."

Gelina finally smiled. "Oh, stop, Metrobius. No one is that silly."

"Oh, yes, they are. I hear the Cornelii insist on surrounding their new pond with all sorts of pretty statues—not for the enjoyment of their human guests, but for the edification of their fish."

"Nonsense!" Gelina giggled and drained her cup, then held it up for a slave to refill it.

Metrobius looked utterly serious. "Of course, the problem is that the mullets—well, I hate to pass on such vicious gossip—but they say that the mullets of the Cornelii are so stupid that they can't even tell the difference between a Polyclitus and a Polydorus. You could switch the head of Juno and Venus and they wouldn't know. Imagine that!" Amid the general laughter Metrobius wagged his finger at Orata. "So be careful, Sergius, what kind of statuary you bring over for the Cornelii's new pond! No need to spend a fortune on a Mad Mullet who won't appreciate the difference."

Orata blushed amiably. Mummius looked apoplectic. Faustus Fabius, I noticed, had one restraining hand on Mummius's thigh, clutching hard enough to whiten his knuckles, while with his left hand he raised his cup to his lips to hide his smile.

Gelina was suddenly talkative. "If you wish to discuss art, we should talk about Iaia's project downstairs, in the anteroom to the women's baths. It's delightful! From the floor to the ceiling on all four walls, octopi and squid and dolphins all cavorting beneath the skylight. It makes me feel so serene and protected, as if I were at the bottom of the sea. Such shades of blue—dark blue and pale azure and blue-green seaweed. I love blue, don't you?" she said tipsily, smiling at Olympias. "Such a lovely blue color you're wearing tonight, so lovely with your lovely blond hair. What talent you both have!"

Iaia pursed her lips. "Thank you, Gelina, but I think everyone here has already seen the work in progress."

"No!" Gelina said. "Gordianus hasn't, nor has his charming boy, Eco. They must be shown everything. Do you understand? We must conceal nothing from them, nothing at all. That's why they're here. To see, to observe. He has a sharp eye, they say. Not the eye of a connoisseur, I mean, but the eye of a hunter. Or a Finder, that's what you call yourself, isn't it? Perhaps tomorrow, Iaia, you can show him your work, and let him contemplate the wonder of your flying fish and terrible squids. Yes, I don't see why not, as long as there are no women in the women's baths, no women bathing, that is. Why not? I'm sure Gordianus appreciates art as much as any of us."

Olympias cocked one eyebrow and looked at me coolly, then at Eco, who fidgeted under her gaze. Iaia, imperturbable, smiled and nodded. "Certainly, Gelina, I'll be happy to give Gordianus a look at our work. Perhaps in the morning, when the light is at its best. But as long as we're speaking of art, I know that Dionysius has a new play in progress, and we've hardly heard a thing about it."

"That because Crassus always shuts him up," Metrobius whispered in my ear.

"Actually, I've set aside my comedy for the time being." Dionysius's thin lips compressed into a smile. "The events of the last few months, and especially of the last few days, have turned my thoughts to more serious matters. I am engrossed in a new work, a treatise with a timely subject—an examination of previous slave revolts, with some observations on how best to avoid such disruptions in the future."

"Previous revolts?" Gelina said. "You mean such things happened before Spartacus?"

"Oh, yes. The first that we know of was about a hundred and twenty years ago, after the war with Hannibal. Rome's victory resulted in a great capture of Carthaginians, who were held as hostages and prisoners of war. The slaves of these Carthaginians were captured as well, and were sold as booty. It happened that a large number of these hostages and slaves came to be concentrated in the town of Setia, near Rome. The hostages contrived a plot to free themselves, and in this enterprise they embroiled their former slaves, promising them their freedom if they should rise up against their new Roman masters and help their former masters return to Carthage. Gladiator games were to be held in a few days' time at Setia; the plan was to rise up then and to slaughter the unsuspecting populace. Fortunately, two of the slaves betrayed the conspiracy to the praetor in Rome, who gathered a force of two thousand men and rushed to Setia. The leaders of the conspiracy were arrested, but there was a great flight of slaves from the town. Eventually they were all recaptured or slaughtered, but not before spreading terror through the vicinity. The two slaves who had wisely informed on their fellows were rewarded with twenty-five thousand pieces of bronze and given their freedom."

"Ah!" Gelina, who had been listening, wide-eyed, nodded approvingly. "I like a story with a happy ending."

"The only thing more boring than politics is history," said Metrobius with a yawn. "In times of great crisis, such as we live in now, it seems to me that Dionysius would be doing the world a far greater service by producing a decent comedy instead of rehashing the dead past."

"What on earth did a man like Sulla ever find to talk about with a man like you?" muttered Mummius.

Metrobius looked at him balefully. "I might ask the same question about you and your—"

"Please, no unpleasantness after the meal," insisted Gelina. "It disturbs the digestion. Dionysius, do go on. How did you ever discover such a fascinating tale?"

"I have often given thanks to Minerva and to the shade of Herodotus for the magnificent library so assiduously collected by your late husband," said Dionysius delicately. "For a man such as myself, to reside in a house full of knowledge is almost as great an inspiration as to reside in a house full of beauty. Here in this villa, happily, I have never had to choose between the two."

Gelina smiled, and there was a general murmur of approval at such a pretty compliment.

"But to continue: The aborted uprising at Setia was the first instance I can find of a general revolt or attempted escape by a large, organized body of slaves. There followed a few other, similar occurrences over the years, in Italy and elsewhere, but I can find only scanty documentation of them. And they are of no account compared to the two Sicilian slave wars, the first of which began about sixty years ago—in the year of my birth, in fact. I often heard tales of it when I was growing up.

"It seems that in those days the landowners of Sicily first began to accumulate great wealth and to amass vast numbers of slaves. Their wealth made the Sicilians arrogant; the constant influx of slaves from captured provinces in Africa and the East made them treat their slaves with little regard, for a slave crippled by overwork or malnutrition was easily replaced. Indeed, many landowners would send out slaves to work as shepherds without proper clothing or even food. When those slaves complained of their nakedness and hunger, their masters would tell them to steal clothes and food from travelers on the road! For all its wealth, Sicily degenerated into a lawless and desperate place.

"There was one landowner, Antigenes by name, who was known to everyone for his excessive cruelty. He was the first man on the island to brand his slaves for identification, and the practice soon spread all over Sicily. Slaves who came to him begging for food or clothing were beaten, chained, and put on humiliating display before being sent back to their tasks, as naked and hungry as before.

"This Antigenes did have a favorite slave whom he delighted in both coddling and humiliating, a Syrian called Eunus, who fancied himself a wizard and wonder-worker. This Eunus would tell of dreams in which the gods had spoken to him. People always like to hear such stories, even from a slave. Soon Eunus began to see the gods, or pretend that he did, in broad daylight, and to converse with them in strange tongues while others looked on in wonder. He could also spit fire from his mouth."

"Fire?" Gelina was aghast.

"An old theatrical trick," Metrobius explained. "You bore holes into either end of a walnut or something similar, stuff it with fuel, light it and pop it into your mouth, then blow flames and sparks. Any conjurer in the Subura can do it."

"Ah, but it was Eunus who first brought the trick from Syria," said Dionysius. "His master Antigenes would display him at dinner parties, where Eunus would fall into his trance, spit fire, and afterward reveal the future. The more outlandish the tale, the better it was received. For instance, he told Antigenes and his guests that a Syrian goddess had appeared to him promising that he, a slave, would become king of all Sicily, but that they should not fear him, for he would have a very tolerant policy toward the slave owners. Antigenes' guests found this highly amusing and rewarded Eunus with delicacies from the table, telling him to remember their kindness when he became king. Little did they realize the dark course of the future.

"It came about that the slaves of Antigenes decided to revolt against their master, but first they consulted Eunus, asking him if the gods would favor their enterprise. Eunus told them that their revolt would be successful, but only if they struck brutally and without hesitation. The slaves, about four hundred of them, held a ceremony in an open field that night, exchanging oaths and performing rites and sacrifices as Eunus instructed. They worked themselves into a murderous frenzy and then broke into the city, killing free men, raping women, even slaughtering babies. Antigenes was captured, stripped, beaten, and beheaded. The slaves dressed Eunus in rich garments and a crown of gold leaf and proclaimed him their king.

"News of their rebellion spread like wildfire across the island, inciting other slaves to revolt. Rival groups of rebel slaves rose up, and it was hoped they would turn against one another. Instead, they banded together, taking into their army all sorts of bandits and outlaws. Word of their success spread beyond Sicily and encouraged widespread unrest—a hundred and fifty slaves conspired to revolt in Rome, more than a thousand rose up in Athens, and there were similar disturbances all over Italy and Greece. All these were quickly suppressed, but the situation in Sicily deteriorated into utter chaos.

"Sicily was overwhelmed by rebelling slaves, all proclaiming Eunus their king. The common folk, in an access of hatred against the rich, actually sided with the slaves. For all its madness, the revolt was conducted with a certain intelligence, for while many a landowner was tortured and killed, the slaves took thought for the future and avoided destroying harvests and property that would be useful to them."

"How did it end?" asked Gelina.

"Armies were sent from Rome. There was a series of battles all over Sicily, and for a time it seemed that the slaves were invincible, until at last the Roman governor, Publius Rupilius, managed to trap them in the city of Tauromenium.

The siege continued until the insurgents were reduced to conditions of unspeakable hunger, and finally cannibalism. They began by eating their children, then their women, and at last each other."

"Oh! And the wizard?" Gelina whispered.

"He escaped from Tauromenium and hid himself in a cave, until at last Rupilius flushed him out. Just as the slaves had consumed one another, so the king of the slaves was discovered half-eaten by worms—yes, just such worms as were said to have plagued the great Sulla in his last years here on the Cup, before his death from apoplexy, which demonstrates that these devouring worms, like the lower grade of humans, will take sustenance from any leader, high or low. Eunus was dragged from his cave, screaming and clawing at his own flesh, and put in a dungeon at Morgantina. The wizard continued to see visions, which became more and more horrible; at the end he was raving. At last the worms consumed him, and so the first of the great slave revolts came to its miserable end."

There was a deep silence. The faces of Gelina's guests were impassive, except for Eco, who sat wide-eyed, and young Olympias, who seemed to have a tear in her eye. Mummius fidgeted on his couch. The silence was broken by the soft shuffling footsteps of a slave retreating toward the kitchens with an empty platter. I looked about the room at the faces of the table slaves, who stood rigidly at their posts behind the guests. None of them would meet my eyes, nor would they look at one another; instead they stared at the floor.

"You see," said Metrobius, his voice sounding unnaturally loud after the stillness, "you have all the elements for a divine comedy right at your fingertips, Dionysius! Call it 'Eunus of Sicily' and let me direct it for you!"

"Metrobius, really!" protested Gelina.

"I'm serious. All you need to do is cast it with the standard roles. Let me see: a bumbling Sicilian landowner and his son, who of course will be love-struck by a neighbor's daughter; add to that the son's tutor, a good slave who will be tempted to join in this slave revolt but will choose virtue instead and save his young master from the mob. We can bring this Eunus onto the stage for a few grotesque comedy turns, spitting fire and babbling nonsense. Introduce the general Rupilius as a bombastic braggart; he mistakes the good slave, the tutor, for Eunus, and wants to crucify him; at the last instant the young master saves his tutor from death and thus repays him for saving his own life. The revolt is suppressed offstage, and all ends with a happy song! Really, Plautus himself never came up with a better plot."

"I believe you're half-serious," said Iaia shrewdly.

"It all sounds a bit distasteful," complained Orata, "considering current circumstances."

"Oh, dear, you might be right," admitted Metrobius. "Perhaps I've been away from the stage too long. Go on, then, Dionysius. I only hope your next account of past atrocities will be as amusing as that last one."

The philosopher cleared his throat. "I fear you will be disappointed, Metrobius. Since Eunus there have been a number of slave revolts in Sicily; something about the island seems to encourage depravity among the rich and insurrection among the slaves. The last and greatest of these revolts was centered in Syracuse, in the days when Marius was consul, thirty-five years ago. Its scale was as great as the first uprising under Eunus, but I fear that the story is not nearly as colorful."

"No fire-breathing wizards?" said Metrobius.

"No," said Dionysius. "Only thousands of dangerous slaves rampaging across the countryside, raping and pillaging, crowning false kings and defying the power of Rome, and in the end a general comes to crucify the ringleaders and put the rest in chains, and law and order are restored."

"So it shall always be," said Faustus Fabius darkly, "as long as slaves are foolish enough to upset the natural order." At either side of him, Orata and Mummius nodded sagely in agreement.

"Enough of this gloominess," said Gelina abruptly. "Let's move to another subject. I think it's time we had an amusement. Metrobius, a recitation?" The actor shook his white head. Gelina did not press him. "Then perhaps a song. Yes, a song is what we need to lift everyone's spirits. Meto . . . Meto! Meto, fetch that boy who sings so divinely, you know the one. Yes, the handsome Greek with the sweet smile and the black curls."

I saw a strange expression cross Mummius's face. While we awaited the slave's arrival, Gelina drank a fresh cup of wine and insisted that we all follow her example. Only Dionysius declined; instead, a slave brought him a frothy green concoction in a silver cup.

"What in Hercules' name is that?" I asked.

Olympia laughed. "Dionysius drinks it twice a day, before his midday meal and after his dinner, and he's tried to convince the rest of us to do likewise. An awful-looking potion, isn't it? But of course, if Orata can drink urine . . ."

"It wasn't urine, it was fermented barley. I only said it *looked* like urine."

Dionysius laughed. "This contains nothing as exotic—or should I say as common?—as urine." He drank from the cup and then lowered it, revealing green-stained lips. "Nor is it a potion; there's nothing magical about it. It's a simple puree of watercress and grape leaves, together with my own blend of medicinal herbs—rue for sharp eyes, silphium for strong lungs, garlic for stamina . . ."

"Which explains," said Faustus Fabius affably, "how Dionysius can read for hours, talk for days, and never feel faint—even if his audience does!"

There was a round of laughter, and then the young Greek arrived carrying a lyre. It was Apollonius, the slave who had attended Marcus Mummius in the baths. I glanced at Mummius. He yawned and showed little interest, but his yawn seemed too elaborate and his vacant gaze was uneasy. The lamps were lowered, casting the room in shadow. Gelina requested a song with a Greek name—"a happy song," she assured us—and the boy began to play.

Apollonius sang in a Greek dialect, of which I could apprehend only scattered words and phrases. Perhaps it was a shepherd's song, for I heard him sing of green fields and great mountains of fleecy clouds, or perhaps it was a legend, for I heard his golden voice shape the name of Apollo and sing of sunlight on the shimmering waters of the Cyclades—"like pebbles of lapis in a sea of gold," he sang, "like the eyes of the goddess in the face of the moon." Perhaps it was a love song, for I heard him sing of jet-black hair and a glance that pierced like arrows. Perhaps it was a song of loss, for in each refrain he sang, "Never again, never again, never again."

Whatever else it was, I would not have called it a happy song. Perhaps it was not the song that Gelina had expected. She listened with a sober intensity, and slowly her expression became as despondent as when I had met her that afternoon. There were no smiles among the guests; even Metrobius listened with a kind of reverence, his eyes half-shut. Strangely, for so sad a tune so soulfully sung, there was only one tear in the room. I watched it descend the grizzled cheek of Marcus Mummius, a glistening track of crystal in the lamplight that quickly disappeared into his beard and was as quickly followed by another.

I looked at Apollonius, at his trembling lips parted to sing a perfect note full of all the heartbreak and hopelessness of the world. I shivered; my skin prickled and turned to gooseflesh, not from the pathos of his song or from the sudden chill breath of the sea that blew into the room. I realized that in three days he would be dead along with all the other slaves, never to sing again.

Across from me, hidden by shadows, Mummius covered his face and silently wept.

EIGHT

OUR accommodations were generous: a small room in the south wing with two sumptuously padded couches and a thick rug on the floor. A door, facing east, opened onto a small terrace with a view of the dome above the baths. Eco complained that we couldn't see the bay. I told him we were lucky that Gelina hadn't put us in the stables.

He stripped down to his undertunic and tested his bed, bouncing up and down on it until I slapped him on the forehead. "So what do you think, Eco? How do we stand?"

He stared for a moment at the ceiling above, then swung his open palm flat against his nose.

"Yes, I'm inclined to agree. We're up against a brick wall this time. I suppose I'll be paid no matter what, but how much can the woman expect me to do in three days? Only two days, really, tomorrow and the funeral day; then comes the game day and, if Crassus has his way, the execution of the slaves. Only one day, if you think about it, because how much can we hope to accomplish on the funeral day? So, Eco, did you see any murderers at the meal?"

Eco indicated the long tresses of Olympias. "The painter's protégée? You can't be serious." He smiled and made his fingers into an arrow piercing his heart.

I laughed softly and pulled the dark tunic over my shoulders. "At least one of us will have pleasant dreams tonight."

I put out the lamps and sat for a long time on my bed with my bare feet on the rug. I looked out the window at the cold stars and the waxing moon. Beside the window there was a small trunk, in which I had hidden the bloodstained tunic and had stored our things, including the daggers we had brought from Rome. Above the trunk a polished mirror was hung on the wall. I rose and stepped toward the starkly moonlit reflection of my face.

I saw a man of thirty-eight years, surprisingly healthy considering his many journeys and his dangerous occupation, with broad shoulders and a wide middle and streaks of gray amid his black curls—not a young man, but not an old man either. Not a particularly handsome face, but not an ugly one, with a flat, slightly hooked nose, a broad jaw, and staid brown eyes. A very lucky man, I thought, not fawned over by Fortune but not despised by her either. A man with a house in Rome, steady work, a beautiful woman to share his bed and run his household, and a son to carry his name. No matter that the house was a ramshackle affair handed down from his father, or that his work was often disreputable and frequently dangerous, or that the woman was a slave, not a wife, or that the son was not of his blood and stricken with muteness—still, a very lucky man, all in all.

I thought of the slaves on the *Fury*—the vile stench of their bodies, the haunted misery in their eyes, the utter hopelessness of their desperation—property of a man who would never see their faces or know their names, who would not even know if they lived or died until a secretary handed him a requisition asking for more slaves to replace them. I thought of the boy who had reminded me of Eco, the one the whipmaster had singled out for punishment and humiliation, and the way he had looked at me with his pathetic smile, as if I somehow had the power to help him, as if, merely by being a free man, I was somehow like a god.

I was weary, but sleep seemed far away. I pulled up a chair from the corner and sat staring at my own face. I thought of the young slave Apollonius. The strains of his song echoed through my head. I remembered the philosopher's tale of the wizard-slave Eunus, who belched fire and roused his companions into a mad revolt. At some point I must have begun to dream, for I thought I could see Eunus in the mirror beside me, hissing, wearing a crown of fire with little wisps of flame leaking from his nostrils and between his teeth. Over my other shoulder the face of Lucius Licinius loomed up, one eye half-shut and matted with blood, a corpse and yet able to speak in a vague murmur too low for me to understand. He rapped on the floor, as if in a code. I shook my head, perplexed, and told him to speak up, but instead he began to dribble blood from his lips. Some of it fell over my shoulder, onto my lap. I looked down to see a bloody cloak. It writhed and hissed. The thing was crawling with thousands of worms, the same worms that had eaten a dictator and a slave-king. I tried to cast the cloak aside, but I could not move.

Then there was a strong, heavy hand on my shoulder—not a dream, but real. I opened my eyes with a start. In the mirror I saw the face of a man abruptly roused from a deep dream, his jaw slack and his eyes heavy with sleep. I blinked at the reflected glare of a lamp held aloft behind me. In the mirror I saw a looming giant dressed like a soldier. His face was smudged with dirt, ugly and stupid looking, like a mask in a comedy. A bodyguard—a trained killer, I thought, instantly recognizing the type. It seemed cruelly unfair that someone in the household had already sent an assassin to murder me before I had even begun to make trouble.

"Did I wake you?" His voice was hoarse but surprisingly gentle. "I knocked and could have sworn I heard you answer, so I came in. With you sitting up in the chair like that, I thought you must be awake."

He cocked an eyebrow at me. I stared back at him dumbly, no longer quite sure I was awake and wondering how he had stumbled into my dream. "What are you doing here?" I finally said.

The soldier's ugly face opened in an ingratiating smile. "Marcus Crassus requests your presence in the library downstairs. If you're not too busy, that is."

It took only a moment to slip into my sandals. I began searching in the lamplight for a suitable tunic, but the bodyguard told me to come as I was. Eco softly snored through the whole exchange. The day had worn him out, and his sleep was uncommonly deep.

A long straight hallway took us to the central atrium; winding stairs led down to the open garden, where the light of tiny lamps on the floor cast strange shadows across the corpse of Lucius Licinius. The library was a short walk up a hallway into the north wing. The guard indicated a door to our right as we passed and put a finger to his lips. "The lady Gelina is asleep," he explained. A few steps farther on he pushed open a door on our left and ushered me inside.

"Gordianus of Rome," he announced.

A cloaked figure sat at a square table across the room, his back to us. Another bodyguard stood nearby. The figure turned a bit in his backless chair, just enough to give me a glimpse of one eye, then turned back to his business and gestured for both guards to leave the room.

After a long moment he stood, tossed aside the simple cloak he wore—a Greek chlamys, such as Romans often adopt when they visit the Cup—and turned to greet me. He wore a plain tunic of durable fabric and simple cut. He looked slightly disheveled, as if he had been riding. His smile was weary but not insincere.

"So you are Gordianus," he said, leaning back against the table, which was strewn with documents. "I suppose you know who I am."

"Yes, Marcus Crassus." He was only slightly older than myself, but considerably grayer—not surprising, considering the hardships and tragedies of his early life, including his flight to Spain after the suicide of his father and the assassination of his brother by anti-Sullan forces. I had seen him often in the Forum delivering speeches or overseeing his interests at the markets, always attended by a large coterie of secretaries and sycophants. It was a little unnerving to see him on so intimate a scale—his hair untidy, his eyes tired, his hands unwashed and stained from handling a rein. He was quite human, after all, despite his fabulous wealth. "Crassus, Crassus, rich as Croesus," went the ditty, and the popular imagination at Rome pictured him as a man of excessive habits. But those powerful enough to move in his circle painted a different image, which was borne out by his unpretentious appearance; Crassus's craving for wealth was not for the luxuries that gold could buy, but for the power it could harness.

"It's a wonder we've never met before," he said in his smooth orator's voice. "I know of you, certainly. There was that affair of the Vestal Virgins last year; you played some part in saving Catilina's hide, I understand. I've also heard Cicero praise your work, if in a somewhat backhanded way. Hortensius, too. I do recognize your face, from the Forum I suspect. Generally I don't hire free agents such as yourself. I prefer to use men I own."

"Or to own the men you use?"

"You understand me exactly. If I want, say, to build a new villa, it's much more efficient to purchase an educated slave, or to educate a bright slave I already own, rather than to hire whatever architect happens to be fashionable, at some exorbitant rate. I buy an architect rather than an architect's services; that way I can use him again and again at no extra cost."

"Some of the skills I offer are beyond the capacities of a slave," I said.

"Yes, I suppose they are. For instance, a slave could hardly have been invited to join Gelina's dinner guests and to question them at will. Have you learned anything of value since you arrived?"

"As a matter of fact, I have."

"Yes? Speak up. After all, I'm the man who's hired you."

"I thought it was Gelina who sent for me."

"But it was my ship that brought you, and it's my purse that will pay your fee. That makes me your employer."

"Still, if you would permit, I should prefer to keep my discoveries to myself for a time. Sometimes information is like the pressed juice of the grape; it needs to ferment in a dark and quiet place away from probing eyes."

"I see. Well, I shall not press you. Frankly, I think your presence here is a waste of my money and your time. But Gelina insisted, and as it was her husband who was murdered, I decided to indulge her."

"You're not curious yourself about the murder of Lucius Licinius? I understand he was your cousin, and a steward of your property for many years."

Crassus shrugged. "Is there really any question at all about who killed him? Surely Gelina has told you about the missing slaves, and the letters scrawled at Lucius's feet? That such a thing should happen to one of my kinsmen, in one of my own villas, is outrageous. It cannot be overlooked."

"And yet there may be reasons to believe that the slaves are innocent of the crime."

"What reasons? Ah, I forgot, your head is some sort of dark casket where the truth slowly ferments." He smiled grimly. "Metrobius could no doubt come up with more puns on the same theme, but I'm too tired to make them. Ah, these accounting ledgers are a scandal." He turned away from me to study the scrolls laid out on the table, apparently no longer interested in my reason for being there. "I had no idea Lucius had become so careless. With the slave Zeno gone there's no making sense of these documents at all. . . ."

"Are you done with me, Marcus Crassus?"

He was absorbed in the ledgers and seemed not to hear me. I looked about the room. The floor was covered with a thick carpet with a geometric design in red and black. The walls on the left and right were covered with shelves full of scrolls, some of them stacked together and others neatly stored in pigeonholes. The wall opposite the door was pierced by two narrow windows that faced the courtyard in front of the house, shuttered against the cold and covered by dark red draperies.

Between the windows, above the table where Crassus labored, was a painting of Gelina. It was a portrait of rare distinction, touched with life, as the Greeks say. In the background loomed Vesuvius, with blue sky above and green sea below; in the foreground the image of Gelina seemed to radiate a sense of profound equanimity and grace. The portraitist was evidently quite proud of her work, for in the lower right-hand corner was printed IAIA CYZICENA. She made the letter "A" with an eccentric flourish, tilting the crossbar sharply downward toward the right.

On either side of the table stood squat pedestals supporting small bronze statues, each about the height of a man's forearm. The statue on the left I could not see, for it was covered by Crassus's carelessly discarded chlamys. The one on the right was of Hercules bearing a club across his shoulders, naked except for a lionskin cloak, with the lion's head for a hood and its paws clasped at his throat. It was an odd choice for a library, but the workmanship could not be faulted. The tufts of the lion's fur had been scrupulously modeled; the texture of fur contrasted with the smooth muscularity of the demigod's flesh. Lucius Licinius had been as careless of his art as of his ledgers, I thought, for it appeared that the scalloped fur of the lion's head had somehow begun to rust.

"Marcus Crassus . . ." I began again.

He sighed and waved me aside without looking up. "Yes, go now. I suppose I've made it clear that I have no enthusiasm for your project, but I will support you in whatever you need. Go to Fabius or Mummius first. If you cannot find satisfaction on some point, come to me directly, although I can't guarantee you'll be able to find me. I have a great deal of business to transact before I return to Rome, and not much time. The important thing is that when this matter is done, no man will be able to say that the truth was not sought or that justice did not prevail." He at last turned his head, only to give me a weary and insincere smile of dismissal.

I stepped into the hall and closed the door behind me. The guard offered to show me the way to my room, but I told him that I was quite awake. I paused for a moment in the central atrium to look again at the corpse of Lucius Licinius. More incense had been put out, but the smell of decay, like the odor of roses, seemed to grow stronger at night. I was halfway to my room before I turned abruptly back.

The guard was surprised and a little suspicious. He insisted on entering the library first and consulted with Crassus before allowing me to enter. He stepped into the hall and shut the door, leaving us alone once more.

Crassus was still poring over the ledgers. He now sat in his undertunic, having stripped off his riding tunic and thrown it over the Hercules. In the few moments I had been gone, one of the slaves had delivered a tray with a steaming cup from which he sipped. The infusion of hot water and mint filled the room with its smell.

"Yes?" He cocked one eyebrow impatiently. "Was there some point I neglected to discuss?"

"It's a small thing, Marcus Crassus. Perhaps I'm entirely mistaken," I said, as I lifted his tunic from the Hercules. The cloth was still warm from his body. Crassus looked at me darkly. Clearly he was not used to having his personal things touched by people he did not own.

"A very interesting statue," I remarked, looking down on the Hercules from above.

"I suppose. It's a copy of an original I have in my villa at Falerii. Lucius admired it once on a visit, so I had one made for him."

"How ironic, then, that it should have been used to murder him."

"What?"

"I think we're both sufficiently acquainted with the sight of blood to know it when we see it, Marcus Crassus. What do you make of this rusty substance trapped in the crevices of the lion's fur?"

He rose from his chair and peered down, then picked up the statue with both hands and held it beneath a hanging lamp. At length he set it down on the table and looked at me soberly. "You have very sharp eyes, Gordianus. But it seems quite unlikely that such a cumbersome bludgeon should have been carried all the way down the hall to the atrium for the purpose of murdering my cousin Lucius, and then carried back again."

"It was not the statue that was moved," I said, "but the body."

Crassus looked doubtful.

"Consider the posture of the corpse as it was found, like that of a man who had been dragged. Certainly from this room to the atrium is not too far for a strong man to drag a body."

"Easier for two men," he said, and I saw he meant the missing slaves. "But where is the rest of the blood? Surely there must have been more on the statue, and a dragged body would have left a trail."

"Not if a cloth was placed beneath the head, and the same cloth was used to clean whatever blood was left behind."

"Was such a cloth found?"

I hesitated. "Marcus Crassus, forgive my presumption when I ask that you share this knowledge with no one else. Gelina, Mummius, and two of the slaves already know. Yes, such a cloth was found, soaked with blood, down the road where someone attempted to fling it into the sea."

He looked at me shrewdly. "This bloodstained cloth was one of the discoveries you mentioned earlier, the secrets you prefer to withhold from me while the evidence ferments in your head?"

"Yes." I squatted down and looked for traces of blood on the floor. A cloak would hardly have been adequate to clean blood from the dark carpet, but in the dim light it was impossible to see any stains.

"But why should the assassins have moved his body?" He picked up the statue with his left hand and fingered the encrusted blood with his right, then set it on the table with a grimace.

"You say assassins, not assassin, Marcus Crassus."

"The slaves—"

"Perhaps the body was moved and the name of Spartacus carved precisely to implicate the slaves and distract us from the truth."

"Or perhaps the slaves moved his body to the most public part of the house precisely to make their point, where all would be sure to see it and the name they carved."

To that I had no answer. One doubt led to another. "It does seem unlikely that the killing could have occurred in this room without anyone hearing, especially if it followed an argument, or if Lucius was able to make any noise at all. Gelina sleeps just across the hall; surely the noise would have awakened her."

Crassus smiled at me sardonically. "Gelina need not figure in your calculations."

"No?"

"Gelina sleeps like the dead. Perhaps you've noticed her liberal consumption of wine? It's not a new habit. Dancing girls with cymbals could parade down the hallway and Gelina wouldn't stir."

"Then the question must be: Why was Lucius murdered here in his library?"

"No, Gordianus, the question is the same as it always was: Where are the two escaped slaves? That Zeno, his secretary, should have murdered Lucius here in the room where they often worked together is hardly surprising. The young stableman Alexandros may have been here with them; I understand he could read and do figures, and Zeno used him sometimes as a helper. Perhaps it was this Alexandros who committed the crime; a stableman would have had the strength to drag Lucius down the hall, and a Thracian would have had the gall to scrawl his countryman's name on the floor. Something interrupted him in the act and he fled before he could write the whole name."

"But no one interrupted them. The body wasn't discovered until morning."

Crassus shrugged. "An owl hooted, or a cat stirred a pebble. Or perhaps this Thracian slave simply hadn't yet learned the letter C and was stumped," he said facetiously, rubbing his eyes with his forefinger and thumb. "Forgive me, Gordianus, but I think I've had enough for tonight. Even Marcus Mummius has gone to bed, and we should do the same." He picked up the Hercules from the table and replaced it on its pedestal. "I suppose this is another of your secrets that needs fermenting? I shall mention it only to Morpheus in my dreams."

The lamp that illuminated the hallway had grown dim. I stepped past Gelina's door, treading lightly despite Crassus's assertion that nothing could wake her. In the darkness an eerie sensation crept over me; this was the very route by which Lucius's lifeless or dying body had been dragged. I glanced over my shoulder, almost wishing that I had accepted the bodyguard's offer to escort me back to my room.

In the moonlit atrium I paused for a long moment. The place was still, but not entirely quiet. The fountain continued to splash; the sound echoed in the well-like atrium, and was certainly loud enough to cover the incidental noises made by a man moving with intentional stealth. But would it have concealed the high-pitched screeching of a knife carving letters on a hard flagstone? The very idea of the noise set my teeth on edge.

From the corner of my eye I saw a strange shape like a white veil floating beside the funeral bier. I started back, my heart pounding, and then realized it was only a plume of smoke from the incense, captured for a moment in a beam of blue moonlight. I shivered, and blamed it on the clammy night air.

I ascended the stairway to the upper story. I must have turned down the wrong hallway and somehow lost my way. Tiny lamps lit the passages at intervals, and windows let in shafts of moonlight, but still I found myself confused. I tried to determine the direction of the bay by listening, and instead found myself hearing the faint gurgling of hot water through Orata's much-esteemed pipes where they were invisibly laid beneath the floor and along the walls. I passed a closed door and thought I heard faint laughter within—the deep voice of Marcus Mummius, I was almost certain, and another, softer voice replying. I walked on and came to an open doorway from which came a steady, raucous snoring. I took a step inside, squinting in the darkness, and saw what appeared to be the bulbous profile of Sergius Orata reclining on a wide couch with a gauzy canopy. I returned to the hall and pressed on until I came to the semicircular room where Gelina had greeted us earlier.

"Gordianus the Finder" you call yourself, I thought with disgust, thanking the gods that no one was there to laugh at me. I had come to the northern end of the house, having turned in exactly the wrong direction after I ascended the stairway in the atrium. I was about to turn back, when I decided to step onto the terrace for a breath of air to clear my head.

Beneath a waxing moon, the bay was a vast expanse of silver scalloped with tiny black waves and circled by black mountains pierced here and there with a point of yellow light to indicate a distant lamp within a distant house. The sky above was rent by a few ragged clouds aglow from the moon, but otherwise was full of stars. Entranced by the view, I almost failed to catch the tiny glimmer of a lamp on the shore below, where the land steeply descended to meet the water.

Gelina had mentioned a boathouse. An outcropping of rock and the tops of tall trees obscured the view, but almost directly below me I could see a bit of roof and what must have been a pier projecting into the water, very small in the distance. I could also see at intervals a tiny flash of flame, coming and going. I listened more closely, and it seemed that each appearance of the lamp coincided with a soft splashing noise, as if something were being quietly dropped into the water.

I looked around trying to locate a stairway, and saw that a broad, descending path began at one end of the terrace on which I stood. I stepped carefully forward.

The path began as a paved ramp that doubled back on itself, then narrowed to a steep stairway that joined with another flight of stairs descending from elsewhere in the villa. The stairs narrowed into a trail paved with cobblestones that wound back and forth down the hillside beneath a canopy of high shrubs and trees. I quickly lost sight of the villa above and for a while could not see the boathouse below.

At last I rounded a corner and saw below me the roof, and beyond it the far end of the pier projecting into the water. A lamp flashed on the pier; there was a splash, and the lamp as quickly disappeared. In the same instant I felt my feet slip from beneath me and found myself skidding down the pathway, setting loose a spray of gravel that rained like hail onto the roof of the boathouse below.

I sat stock-still in the silence that followed, catching my breath and listening, wishing I had brought my dagger. The light did not reappear, but I heard a sudden loud splash followed by silence, then a noise in the underbrush below like the leaping of a frightened deer. I scrambled up and trotted down the pathway until it ended. Between the foot of the path and the boathouse there was a deeply shadowed patch of almost impenetrable darkness overhung by trees and vines. I stepped forward slowly, listening to the magnified sound of my own footsteps on the grass and the gentle lapping of water against the pier.

Beyond the circle of shadow, the boathouse and the pier were illuminated by full moonlight. The pier projected perhaps fifty feet into the water; it had no rail but was studded along either side with mooring posts. No boats were moored to it, and the pier was deserted. The boathouse was a simple, square building with a single door that opened onto the pier. The door stood open.

I stepped into the moonlight, toward the open door. I peered inside, listening intently, hearing nothing. A window high up in the wall admitted enough light to show me the coils of rope that lay on the floor, a few oars stacked beside the door, and the obscure implements that were hung on the opposite wall. Deep shadows filled the corners of the room. In the utter stillness I could hear my own breathing, but no one else's. I withdrew and stepped onto the pier.

I walked to the end, where the disk of the moon seemed to hover on the water just beyond the pier. The curving shore on either side was dotted with the lights of distant villas, and far away across the great flat water the lamps of Puteoli were like stars. I looked over the side of the pier, but there was nothing to see in the black water except the reflection of my own scowling face. I turned back.

The blow seemed to come from nowhere, like an invisible mallet swung from a black abyss. It struck my forehead and sent me staggering backward. I felt no pain, only a sudden overwhelming dizziness. The invisible mallet swung out of the darkness again, but this time I saw it—a short, stout oar. I avoided the second blow by accident as much as by design—a staggering man makes an uncertain target. Flashes of color swam before my eyes, but beyond the oar I glimpsed the dark, hooded figure who swung it.

Then I was in the water. Men who hire me sometimes ask if I can swim. I usually tell them I can, which is a lie. I shouted. I splashed. I somehow stayed afloat and desperately reached for the pier, even though the hooded figure waited there with the oar uplifted.

I reached for one of the mooring posts. My fingers slipped on the green moss. The oar swung down to strike my hand, but somehow I caught it in my grasp. I pulled hard, more to lift myself out of the water than to pull him into it, but the result was that my attacker lost his balance. An instant later, with a great splash, he joined me in the black water.

He came up beside me, struck me in the chest with his flailing elbow, and reached for the pier. I grabbed onto his cloak, frantically trying to climb over him onto the pier. Together we thrashed and struggled. Salt stung my eyes. I opened my mouth and sucked in a burning draft of saltwater. I lashed out at him blindly.

I think he knew that if he struggled with me I would only kill us both. He broke away and swam away from the pier, toward the overgrown shore beyond the boathouse. I clung to the slippery mooring post and watched him retreat like a ponderous sea monster, weighted down by his drenched clothing. His hooded head bobbed and retreated, bobbed and retreated. When he was safely far away I struggled onto the pier and lay gasping for breath. He disappeared into the shadows beyond the boathouse. I heard him climb out of the water, slipping and splashing, and then tearing through the underbrush.

The world was quiet again, except for the noise of my own labored breathing. I stood up. I touched my forehead and hissed at the stinging pain, but I felt no blood. I staggered forward, my legs trembling but my head clear.

I should never have come to the boathouse by night, alone and weaponless; I should have brought Eco with me, and a lamp, and a good, sharp knife, but it was too late for that. I fished the oar from the water to use as a weapon and hurried to the foot of the pathway. The way was hard and steep, but I ran all the way to the top, staring into every dark patch and swinging the oar at the invisible assassin who might be lurking there. The trail became stairs, the stairs became a ramp, the ramp opened onto the terrace, where at last I felt safe. I paused for a long moment to catch my breath. I began to feel the cold through my wet tunic. I hurried through the darkened house, shivering and still carrying the oar. I came at last to my room.

I stepped inside and closed the door behind me. Eco was peacefully snoring. I reached down and touched the soft shock of hair across his forehead, feeling a sudden welling of tenderness for him and a longing to protect him—but from whom, and what? Most of all I felt cold and wet, and so weary I could hardly take another step or think another thought. I stripped off my sodden tunic and dried myself as best I could with a blanket, then pulled back the coverlet on my bed and fell onto my back, desperate for sleep.

Something hard and sharp stabbed my back. I jumped to my feet. The night's surprises were not over.

I stared down and could only see a dark shape on the cushion. I bolted naked from the room to fetch a lamp from the hall. By its lurid glow I studied the thing that someone had left in my bed. It was a figurine the size of my hand carved in porous black stone, a grotesque creature with a hideous face. Its eyes were set with tiny shards of red glass that glinted in the light. It was the sharp, beaked nose that had stabbed me.

"Have you ever seen anything uglier?" I muttered. Eco made a noise in his throat and rolled toward the wall, sound asleep. Like Gelina, he would have slept through a train of dancing girls with cymbals. I set the little monster on the windowsill, not knowing what else to do with it and too weary to think about it.

I set the lamp on a table and left it burning, not because I trusted the light's protection but because I was too tired to put it out. I fell into my bed and was almost instantly asleep. Just before Morpheus claimed me, I realized with a shiver why the thing in my bed had been put there. Friendly or not—gift, warning, or curse—it was an act of sorcery. We had come to the region of the Cup, where the earth breathes sulphur and steam, where the ancient inhabitants practiced earth magic and the colonizing Greeks brought new gods and oracles. That knowledge unsettled my dreams and clouded my sleep, but nothing, not even dancing girls in the hallway, could have kept me awake an instant longer.

NINE

I winced at a sharp pain in my head, as if someone were poking me with a nettle, and opened my eyes to see Eco peering down at me, pursing his lips thoughtfully. He was reaching out to tap at a spot on my forehead just below the scalp. I grunted and pushed his hand away. He winced sympathetically and drew back, shaking his head.

"Is it that bad?" I said, swinging my feet onto the floor and leaning forward to look into the mirror. Even by the gray light of dawn the bump was quite evident, a raised red knob that looked more painful than it felt. Eco held up my still-damp tunic with one hand and the oar with the other. He looked at me disapprovingly, demanding an explanation.

I began with my interview with Crassus—the bloodstains on the statue of Hercules, the evidence that Lucius Licinius was killed in his library, our employer's determined disinterest. I told him about the moving lamp at the boathouse, the periodic splashing as of something being dropped into the water, the steep descent, the deserted pier and boathouse, the oar swung against my head, the struggle in the water.

Eco shook his head at me angrily and stamped his foot.

"Yes, Eco, I was a fool, and a lucky one at that. I should have fetched you out of bed to come with me instead of rushing down to investigate. Or better yet, I should have brought Belbo along to play bodyguard and left you in Rome to look after Bethesda." That suggestion riled him even more.

"I have no idea who struck me. As for the boathouse and the pier, there was nothing to be seen, at least not by night. How I hate the water!" I remembered the burning draft of saltwater in my throat, the struggling and thrashing; my hands were suddenly shaky and I had to struggle for breath. Eco's anger vanished and his arm was around me, holding me tight. I caught my breath and patted his hand.

"And if my adventure at the boathouse was not enough, I came back to find this in my bed." I stepped to the window and picked up the figurine. The black, porous stone seemed clammy to the touch. I had kept waking up during the night to see it staring down at me from the windowsill, its ugly face weirdly illuminated by the lamplight, its red eyes shining. At one point I actually thought I saw it moving, undulating in a kind of dance—but that was only a dream, of course.

"What does it remind you of?"

Eco shrugged.

"I've seen something like it before; it reminds me of an Egyptian household god of pleasure, Bes they call him, an ugly little fellow who brings bliss and frivolity into the house. So hideous, if you didn't know he was friendly you might be frightened of him—a huge, gaping mouth, staring eyes, a pointed nose. But this isn't Bes; it's an hermaphrodite, for one thing—see the tiny round breasts, and the little penis? Moreover, the workmanship is not Egyptian. It seems to have been made from local stone, that soft, porous black stuff one finds on the slopes of Vesuvius. Not an easy medium to work in, I imagine, too crumbly, so it's hard to say whether the workmanship is crude or simply rushed. Who could have fashioned such a thing, and why was it put in my bed?

"The practice of sorcery is very popular here on the Cup, much more so than in Rome. There's a great deal of indigenous magic among those whose families have always lived here, whose race predates the Romans in these parts. Then the Greeks settled here, bringing their oracles with them. Even so, this strikes me as a thing someone from the East might carve, and more likely a woman than a man. What do you think, Eco—is one of the household slaves trying to cast a spell on me? Or could it be—"

Eco clapped and gestured toward the door behind me, where the little slave boy Meto stood waiting expectantly, bearing a tray of bread and fruit. I saw his eyes dart nervously about the room. I hid the figurine from sight while I turned, so that when I faced him I held it behind my back. I smiled at him. He smiled back. Then I produced the figurine and thrust it onto the tray.

He let out a little gasp.

"You've seen this thing before?" I said accusingly.

"No!" he whispered. That might be literally true, given the frantic way he averted his eyes.

"But you know what it is, and where it comes from?"

He was silent, biting his lip. The tray trembled. An apple pitched onto its side and rolled into a bunch of figs. I took the tray from him and set it on the bed, picked up the statuette and thrust it against his nose. He peered at it, cross-eyed, and then shut his eyes tightly. "Well?" I pressed.

"Please, if I tell you, it may not work . . ."

"What? Speak clearly."

"If I explain it to you, the test may come to nothing."

"Do you hear that, Eco? Someone is testing me. I wonder who, and why."

Meto quailed under my glare. "Please, I don't really understand it all myself, it's just something I happened to overhear."

"Overhear? When?"

"Last night."

"Here in the house?"

"Yes."

"I suppose you must overhear many things, coming and going as you do."

"Sometimes, but never on purpose."

"And whom did you overhear last night?"

"Please!"

I looked at him for a long moment, then stepped back and let the sternness fall from my face. "You understand why I'm here, don't you, Meto?"

He nodded. "I think so."

"I'm here because you and many others are in very grave danger. I want to help you if I can."

He looked at me skeptically. "If I could be sure of that . . ." he whispered in a very small voice.

"Be sure of it, Meto. I think you know how great the danger is." He was only a little boy, far too young to be facing the prospect Crassus had planned for him. Had he ever seen a man put to death? Was he old enough to really understand? "Trust me, Meto. Tell me where this statue came from."

He stared at me for a long moment, then looked unflinchingly at the grotesque in my hands. "I can't tell you that," he finally said. Eco moved toward him in exasperation; I blocked him with my arm. "But I *can* tell you . . ."

"Yes, Meto?"

"That you must show the figurine to no one else. And you must tell no one about it. And . . ."

"Yes?"

He bit his lower lip. "When you leave this room, don't take it with you. Leave it here. But not on the table or the windowsill . . ."

"Where, then? Where I found it?"

He looked relieved, as if his honor were less compromised if I spoke the words instead of him. "Yes, only . . ."

"Meto, speak up!"

"Only leave it opposite of how you found it!"

"Face-down, you mean?"

"Yes, and . . ."

"With its feet toward the wall?"

He nodded, then quickly looked at the statue. He clapped his hand over his mouth and cringed. "Look how it stares at me! Oh, what have I done?"

"You've done the right thing," I assured him, placing the statue out of his sight. "Here, I have an errand for you: return this oar to the boathouse. Now go, and tell no one that we talked. No one! Stop trembling, people will notice. You've done the right thing," I said again, closing the door behind him, and then added, "I hope!"

After a hurried breakfast we made our way to the library. The slaves were up and about, sweeping and carrying and spreading baking smells from the kitchens, but no one else seemed to be stirring. A few lamps still burned in the hallways, and shadows lurked in the more remote corners, but most of the house was suffused with a soft blue light. We passed by a long window that faced eastward; the sun, not yet risen behind Vesuvius, cast a halo of pale gold about the mountain's shoulders. It was the first hour of the day, when most Romans would be up and about. The denizens of the Cup keep a more leisurely schedule.

The library was unguarded and empty. I opened the shutters to let in as much light as possible. Eco stepped to the right of the table and studied the dried residue of blood on the Hercules statue to confirm what I had told him, then shivered at the early-morning chill that crept in through the windows from the graveled courtyard outside. He picked up the chlamys that Crassus had draped over the other statue, which turned out to be a centaur, and wrapped it around his shoulders.

"I wouldn't borrow that particular cloak if I were you, Eco. I'm not sure how a man like Crassus would react to people of our ilk handling his personal things."

Eco only shrugged and walked slowly around the room, gazing at the multitude of scrolls. Most of them were neatly rolled and inserted into long jackets of cloth or leather and identified by little tags. It appeared that the more literary works intended for pleasure or instruction—philosophical treatises, quaint Greek novels, plays, histories—had been given red or green tags, and were rather haphazardly catalogued, heaped atop one another in tall, narrow shelves. Documents relating to business transactions were more fastidiously arranged in individual pigeonholes and given blue or yellow tags. All in all, there were hundreds of scrolls, filling two walls from floor to ceiling.

Eco let out a low whistle. "Yes, quite impressive," I agreed. "I don't think I've ever seen so many scrolls in one place, not even in Cicero's house. But for now I'd rather you directed your eyes downward, to the floor. If ever a carpet was designed to hide a bloodstain it must be this one, all dark red and black. Still, if Lucius bled on the floor and the assassin used only a cloak to wipe it up, there should be some sign of the stain."

Eco joined me in peering down at the geometric pattern. The morning light grew stronger moment by moment, but the longer we studied it the more baffling the dark pattern seemed to become. Together we crossed the carpet step by step. Eco eventually dropped to his hands and knees like a hound, but to no avail. If there had ever been a drop of blood on the carpet, some god must have turned it to dust and blown it away.

The tile floor, where it showed beyond the carpet's edge, was no more revealing. I lifted the edge of the carpet and folded it back, thinking it might have been moved to cover a bit of bloodstain, but I found nothing.

"Perhaps Lucius wasn't killed in this room, after all." I sighed. "He must have bled somewhere, and there's nowhere to bleed except on the floor. Unless . . ." I stepped toward the table. "Unless he was standing here, where he naturally would be standing in his library, in front of the table. The blow was to the front of his head, not the back, so he must have been facing his assailant. And the blow was on the right, not the left, so he must have been facing north, with his left side toward the table and his right side exposed. To strike the right temple head-on, the assailant must have used his left hand; that could be very important, Eco—anyone who picked up a heavy statue to use as a bludgeon would use the arm he favored. We assume the killer was left-handed, then. Lucius would have been knocked sidelong onto the table. . . ."

Eco obligingly pitched himself onto the table amid the clutter of documents Crassus had been studying the night before. He fell face-down with one arm beneath him and the other outstretched.

"In which case the blood might well have been spattered above the table, onto the wall—where it might as easily have been wiped away. I see no blood there now. Unless it spattered even higher. . . ." I climbed onto my knees on the table. Eco pushed himself up to join me in studying the painting of Gelina. "Encaustic on canvas, set in a frame of black wood with mother-of-pearl inlay—easy to wipe clean—and encased in the wall. Had any blood landed on the painting itself, I doubt the murderer would have dared to scrub the wax too vigorously for fear of damaging it, if indeed he saw the blood among all these pigments. Amazing, isn't it, how many colors there are in a painting when you see it this close? At this distance Iaia's signature is certainly large enough, done in red, but more likely cinnabar than blood. The folds of Gelina's stola are a mottled red and black; no doubt she chose these carpets to match her gown in the painting. Red here, black there, and—Eco, do you see it?''

Eco anxiously nodded. Dribbled across a patch of green background, where no painter would have been so careless as to spill it, was a spray of red-black drops the color of dried blood. Eco peered closer and then began pointing out more drops—on the background, on the stola, everywhere across the bottom of the painting, even a smear across the first letter of Iaia's signature. The more we looked, the more we saw. In the growing morning light the drops seemed to blossom before our eyes, as if the painting itself wept blood. Eco made a face, and I grimaced in agreement: What a grisly blow must have been struck across the head of Lucius Licinius to have scattered so much gore. I drew back from the painting, repulsed.

''Ironic,'' I whispered, ''that Lucius should have polluted with his own blood the painting of the wife he married for love, and ended here, a corpse, prostrate before her image. A jealous lover, Eco? Did someone intentionally murder him here, in front of the painting? It must have made quite a tableau, the dead husband crumpled lifeless before the serene image of his wife. But if someone intended it that way, then why was the body moved, and the specter of Spartacus invoked?''

I stepped off the table, followed by Eco. ''There must have been blood on the table, easily wiped clean. Which means there must have been no documents lying here, as there are now, or else they would have been bloodied as well, and impossible to clean; blood will wipe off lacquered wood, but not parchment or papyrus. I wonder, though . . . here, help me pull the table from the wall.''

It was easier said than done. The table was heavy, too

heavy perhaps for one man alone to lift it. Even with one of us at either end the job was awkward; we knocked over the chair, bunched the carpet and caused a loud screech as one table leg scraped across the tiled floor. Our reward was blood: on both the wall and the back edge of the table, trapped where no cloth could have reached it, there were patches of a gummy, red-brown residue. Lucius's blood had run across the table and pooled in the narrow space between table and wall, leaving its trace on both.

Eco wrinkled his nose. "More proof that Lucius was murdered here, if we needed it," I said. "But what does that tell us? It makes no sense that the missing slaves would have wiped up the blood, especially if they were proud of the crime; still, it will take stronger proof than that to shake Crassus from his intention. Here, Eco, help me replace the table as it was. I hear footsteps in the hall."

Just as I was picking up the chair and Eco was straightening the carpet, an inquiring face peered around the corner.

"Meto! Just the one I wanted to see. Step inside, and shut the door behind you."

He did as I ordered, but not without hesitating. "Are you sure we should be in this room?" he whispered.

"Meto, your mistress made it clear that I should have access to any part of the house, did she not?"

"I suppose. But no one was ever allowed in this room without the master's permission."

"No one? Not even the scrub maids?"

"Only when the master would let them in, and even then he usually wanted himself or Zeno to be in the room."

"But there's nothing here for a slave to pilfer—no small coins, no jewelry or trinkets."

"Even so—once I snuck in, just because I wanted to have a closer look at the horse—"

"Horse? Ah, the centaur statue."

"Yes, and the master himself walked in on me. He was angry in an instant, and the master wasn't normally an angry man. But his face turned all red and he shouted at me till I thought I would die from the pounding in my chest." Meto's eyes opened wide at the memory. He puffed out his cheeks and shook his head, like a man trying to recover from a terrible dream. "He called in Alexandros and ordered him to give me a beating, right here. Normally it would have been Clito, who also works in the stables and likes to give beatings, but I was lucky because Clito was working in Puteoli that day. I had to bend over and touch the floor while Alex gave me ten blows with a cane. He only did it because the master made him. He could have hit me a lot harder, I'm sure, but it still made me cry."

"I see. You like this Alexandros?"

The boy's eyes sparkled. "Of course. Everyone likes Alex."

"And what about Zeno, did you like him, too?"

He shrugged. "Nobody liked Zeno. But not because he's cruel or a bully, like Clito. He's haughty and speaks languages and thinks he's so much better than any of the other slaves. And he farts a lot."

"He sounds thoroughly disagreeable. Tell me, on the night your master was killed, was anyone up and about? You, perhaps, or some other slave?"

He shook his head.

"You're sure? No one heard anything, saw anything?"

"Everyone's been talking about it, of course. But no one knows what happened. The mistress told us the next day that if anyone knew anything, he must go directly to Master Crassus, or to Mummius or Fabius. If anyone had seen or heard what happened, they would tell, I'm sure."

"And among the slaves themselves, there are no rumors, no whispers?"

"Nothing. And if anyone had said anything at all, even in secret, I'm the one who's most likely to have overheard. Not that I eavesdrop—"

"I understand. Your duties take you all over the house, from room to room, dawn to dusk, while the cooks and stablemen and cleaners stay in one place all day and gossip to each other. Hearing things and seeing things is nothing to be ashamed of, Meto. I do it for a living. When I first saw you, I could tell right away that you are the very eyes and ears of this house."

He looked at me in wonderment, and then cautiously smiled, as if no one had ever perceived his true worth before.

"Tell me, Meto, on that night, might Zeno have been in this room with your master?"

"It's possible. They often came here and worked together after dark, sometimes very late, especially if a ship had just arrived or was about to leave from Puteoli, or if Master Crassus was on his way."

"And might Alexandros have been here as well?"

"Possibly."

"But on that night you saw no one going in or out of this room? Heard nothing from the stables or the atrium?"

"I sleep in a little room with some of the others," he said slowly, "over in the east wing of the house, behind the stables. Usually I'm the last one in bed. Alex laughs and says he's never seen a boy who needed less sleep. On any other night I might have been up and about. I might have seen whatever it is you want to know. But that night I was so tired from running so many errands and carrying so many messages all day . . ." His voice began to quaver. "I'm sorry."

I put my hands on his thin shoulders. "You have nothing to be sorry for, Meto. But answer one more question. Last night, were you up late wandering about the house?"

He looked thoughtful. "Yesterday was so busy, with you and Mummius arriving on the *Fury*, and the extra work for the dinner last night . . ."

"So you went to sleep early?"

"Yes."

"Then you saw nothing unusual, heard no one wandering in the hallways or going down the hillside to the boathouse?"

He shrugged helplessly and bit his lip, sad to disappoint me. I looked at him gravely and nodded. "It's all right, I only thought you might know something I don't. But here, before you go, I want you to see something."

I guided him with a hand on his shoulder until we stood beside the centaur statue. "Look at it all you want. Touch it, if you'd like." He looked at me for reassurance, then reached out with trembling fingers and a glow in his eyes, then abruptly pulled back and bit his lip.

"No, no, it's all right," I said. "I won't let anyone punish you."

And I will not let Marcus Crassus destroy you, I thought, though I dared not speak aloud so rash a pledge. Fortune herself might hear, and smite me for making promises even a god could not be sure of keeping.

TEN

"WHEN I was a girl, I would never have stooped to painting a fresco. One painted in encaustic on panels of canvas or wood, using an easel, and never, never in fresco on a wall; so my mentor taught me. 'Wall painters are mere workmen,' he would say, 'while an easel painter, ah, an easel painter is treated like the very hand of Apollo! Easel painters receive all the glory, and the gold. Make your reputation on the easel and they will flock to you like pigeons to the Forum.' My, that's a nasty bump on your forehead."

Iaia looked very different than she had the night before at dinner. Gone were the jewelry and the elegant gown; instead she was dressed in a shapeless long-sleeved garment that reached to the floor. It was made of coarse linen and spattered all over with dabs of color. Her young assistant was similarly dressed, and even more remarkably beautiful by the light of day. Together they looked like priestesses of some strange cult of women who wore their paints upon their clothing rather than their faces.

The skylight above filled the little circular anteroom with a cone of yellow light, around which swirled a vortex of underwater blues and greens populated by silvery wisps of fish and weird monsters of the deep. The figures were remarkably fluid and superbly shaded, and the rendering of the water itself produced illusions of impossible depth; Eco and I together with arms outstretched could have reached from wall to wall, but in places the murky depths appeared to recede forever. Had it not been for the jumble of scaffolding and drop cloths, the scene might have been almost frighteningly real, like a dream of death by drowning.

"Of course, these days, I'm long past scrambling for commissions," Iaia continued. "I made my fortune back in the good old days. Did you know that in my prime I was better paid than even Sopolis? It's true. Every rich matron in Rome wanted her portrait painted by the strange young lady from Cyzicus. Now I paint what I want and when I want. This project is just a favor for Gelina. One day we were leaving the baths, feeling all fresh and relaxed, and she complained about how plain this room was. Suddenly I had a vision of fish, fish, fish everywhere! Fish flying above our heads and octopi coiling at our feet. And dolphins, darting through the seaweed. What do you think?"

"Astounding," I said. Eco gazed about the room and shook out his hands as if he were sopping wet.

Iaia laughed. "It's almost finished now. There's no real painting left to be done. We're at the stage of sealing the watercolors with an encaustic varnish, which is why these slaves are helping. There's no real skill to the job, just smoothing on the varnish with a brush, but I have to watch them to be sure nothing's damaged. Olympias, nudge that one over there, on the top scaffold. He's putting it on too thick—the colors will never show through."

Olympias looked down from above our heads and smiled. I secretly pinched Eco, whose slack-jawed stare was not in response to the artwork around us.

"Ah, yes, in the good old days I could never have taken on a project like this one," Iaia went on. "My mentor wouldn't have allowed it. I can just imagine his reaction. 'Too vulgar,' he'd have said, 'too *merely* decorative. Painting histories or fables with a moral point is one thing, but painting fish? Portraits are your strong point, Iaia, and portraits of women, at that; no man can paint a woman half so well as you can. But one look at these staring fish heads and no Roman matron will ever allow you to paint her! She'd be looking for traces of satire in every brush-stroke!' Well, that's what my old mentor would have said. But now, if I wish to paint fish, by Neptune, I'll paint fish. I think they're lovely."

She seemed quite enraptured by her own skill, an immodesty perhaps forgivable in an artist in the final stages of an almost-done creation. "I can see why you became renowned for your portraits," I said. "I saw your picture of Gelina in the library."

Her smile wavered. "Yes, I did that only a year ago. Gelina wanted it for a birthday present, for Lucius. We spent weeks working on it, out on her private terrace at the north end of the house, in her room where Lucius never went, so it would be a surprise."

"Didn't he like it?"

"Frankly, no. It was done especially to fit the wall above his table in the library. Well, he made it quite plain that he didn't want it there. If you've seen the room, you've seen his taste—those awful statues of Hercules and Chiron. The painting above his table was even worse, a horrible thing that purported to show the Argonauts attacked by harpies, such a hideous embarrassment I can't imagine how he dared to allow visitors in the room. A really terrible painting done by some unknown hack in Neapolis, a mishmash of naked breasts and flailing claws and stiffly painted warriors brandishing swords. Words cannot exaggerate how awful it was. Am I not right, Olympias?"

The girl looked down from her work and laughed. "It was a very bad painting, Iaia."

"In the end Lucius acquiesced and had the thing removed so that we could mount Gelina's portrait into the wall, but he was most ungracious. Gelina had ordered a rug to match, and he complained endlessly about the expense. She was in tears more than once, thanks to that episode. Of course, misery about money was an old story in this house. What a failure Lucius was! What an impostor! What's the point of living in a villa like this if you have to count every sesterce before you spend it?"

There was a sudden tension in the room. Olympias no longer smiled. One of the slaves knocked over a pot of varnish and cursed. Even the fish seemed to quiver with unease. Iaia lowered her voice. "Let's step into the baths. The rooms are all empty, and the light at this time of day is quite delightful. Let the boy stay here and watch Olympias work."

The plan of the women's baths mirrored that of the men's,

except for the scale, which was considerably smaller. Across the open terrace the view was much the same; beneath the rising sun the bay shone with thousands of tiny points of silver light. We walked around the circular pool, which billowed with steam in the crisp morning air. Beneath the high dome our hushed voices echoed strangely.

"I thought that Lucius and Gelina were a happy couple," I said.

"Does she seem happy to you?"

"Her husband died a horrible death only days ago. I hardly expect to find her smiling."

"Her mood now is little changed from before. She was miserable then, thanks to him, and she is miserable now, thanks again to him and his messy death."

"She doesn't look miserable in the painting. Does the image lie?"

"The image captures her just as she was. And why does she seem so happy and at peace in the portrait? Consider that it was posed for and painted in the one room in the house where Lucius never set foot."

"I was told they married for love."

"So they did, and you see what comes of that sort of match. I knew Gelina when she was a girl, before she married. Her mother and I were about the same age and great friends. When Gelina married Lucius it was hardly my place to criticize, but I knew that only sorrow would come of it."

"How could you be so sure? Was he such a wicked character?"

She was silent for a long moment. "I don't claim to be a great judge of character, Gordianus, at least not when it comes to men. Do you know what they called me in the good old days? Iaia Cyzicena, Always Virgin, they called me, and not without reason. When it comes to men, I have little experience and I claim no special insight. I'm sure my judgment of a man's character is less reliable than most women's. But judgment based on experience goes only so far. There are other, surer ways of foreseeing the future." She gazed into the swirling mists above the water.

"Yes? And what does the future hold for this house and its inhabitants?"

"Something dark and dreadful, no matter what." She shivered. "But to answer your question: No, Lucius was not wicked, only weak. A man of no vision, no energy, no ambition. Were it not for Crassus, he and Gelina would have starved long ago."

"A villa and a hundred slaves are far from starvation."

"But Lucius himself owned not a bit of it! From what I gather, his income was entirely consumed in running this palace and maintaining a facade of great wealth. Given his connection to Crassus, any other man would have made himself independently wealthy long before now. Not Lucius; he was content to amble along, taking what was given him and asking for no more, like a pampered dog begging for scraps from his master's table. To be sure, the same hand that lifted him up held him down; Crassus seemed determined that Lucius should always be the cringing, ever-thankful kinsman, never an equal or a rival, and Crassus has ways of seeing that people stay in their places. Well, Gelina deserved better than that. Now she's completely at the mercy of Crassus, not even able to say whether her own household slaves should live or die."

"And if that should come to pass?"

Iaia stared deeply into the mist and did not answer. We circled the pool in silence.

"No matter what their differences, I think that Gelina has suffered greatly from the death of her husband," I said quietly. "She will suffer even more if Crassus proceeds with this terrible scheme of his."

"Yes," said Iaia in a dull, faraway voice. "And she will not be alone in her suffering."

"Surely, if it was someone here in the house who murdered Lucius, that person cannot stand by and see so many people slaughtered in his stead."

"Not people," she corrected, "slaves."

"Still—"

"And for slaves to die, even ninety-nine slaves, for the

benefit of a great and wealthy man—is that not the Roman way?"

To that, I had no answer. I left her standing by the pool, staring into its sulphurous depths.

In the anteroom Eco stood on the scaffold holding a horsehair brush, while Olympias hovered behind him, her hand laid gently atop his to guide his strokes. "A single sweeping motion," she was saying. "Lay it on in a thin, even coat."

"Really, Eco," I called up to him, "I had no idea you had a gift for painting."

He gave a start. Olympias looked over her shoulder with a cheerful smile. "He has a very steady hand," she said.

"I'm sure he does. But I think we will take our leave. Come, Eco." He scrambled nimbly down, looking flushed and slightly disoriented and glancing awkwardly over his shoulder as we stepped into the portico outside.

"Did you press your attentions on her, Eco, or was it Olympias who suggested that you join her on the scaffold?" Eco indicated the latter. "Ah, it was she who stepped so close, putting her arm around you?" He nodded dreamily, then frowned at the way I pursed my lips. "I would not be entirely trusting of that young woman's friendliness, Eco. No, don't be silly; I'm not jealous of you. There's something about the way she smiles that makes me uncomfortable."

A voice hailed us from behind, and I turned to see Metrobius and Sergius Orata, each attended by a slave. "Are you on your way to the baths, too?" asked the businessman with a yawn that indicated he had just gotten out of bed.

"Yes," I said. Why not?

While Orata and Eco relaxed in the hot pool, I accepted an offer from Metrobius to share his masseur. We stripped and reclined side by side on pallets in the changing room. The slave went back and forth between us, kneading our shoulders and poking at our spines. The slave was a tall, wizened man with extraordinarily strong hands.

"If I were rich," I grunted, "I think I would have this done to me every day."

"I am rich," said Metrobius, "and I do. How did you ever get that awful bump on your head?"

"Oh, it's nothing. A doorway was shorter than I expected. Oh! That's good! Yes, there, that spot below my shoulder. . . . These baths are quite wonderful, aren't they? Eco and I came here yesterday, after we first arrived. Mummius wanted to show off the plumbing. He had a massage from the boy who sang last night, Apollonius I think he's called. But I doubt that Apollonius could be half as skillful as your man."

"I wouldn't know," said Metrobius cautiously, lying on his side with his head propped on one hand and looking at me with sudden suspicion.

"No? You're such a frequent houseguest, I thought you might have taken the opportunity to use this Apollonius yourself."

Metrobius hummed and raised an eyebrow. "Only Mollio here massages me. He was a gift from Sulla, years ago. Knows every aching muscle and cracked bone in this tired old body. A callow youth like Apollonius would probably give me a sprain."

"Yes, I suppose Mummius can take that risk. He's not exactly delicate. Tough as an ox, by the looks of him."

"And nearly as smart."

"Oh! Could you do that again, Mollio? For some reason, Metrobius, I don't believe you like Marcus Mummius."

"I'm indifferent to him."

"You detest him."

"I confess. Here, Mollio, attend to me. Gordianus has had enough for the moment."

I lay in a state of bliss, as limp as pummeled dough. I closed my eyes and saw visions of starfish and octopi, attended by strange gasping noises. It was Metrobius's turn to grunt and wheeze.

"Why does the grudge run so deep?" I asked.

"I never liked Mummius, from the first moment I met him."

"But there must have been some incident, some offense."

"Oh, very well." He sighed. "This was ten years ago,

just after Sulla was made dictator. You remember that Sulla set up the proscription lists and posted them in the Forum, offering rewards to whoever would bring him the heads of his enemies?''

''I remember it well.''

''It was an ugly process, but unavoidable. The Republic had to be purged. For Sulla to restore order and put an end to years of civil war, the opposition had to be eliminated. Otherwise the conflicts and vendettas would have gone on endlessly.''

''And what does this have to do with your feud with Mummius?''

''The estates of Sulla's enemies were made property of the state and sold at public auction. I need not tell you that the first people in line at these so-called public auctions were usually Sulla's close friends and associates. How else could a mere actor like myself end up with a villa on the Cup? But there were others in line ahead of me.''

''Including Mummius?''

''Yes. Crassus was much in favor then, almost as important as Pompey. Eventually he overstepped himself and embarrassed Sulla; you may remember a certain scandal involving an innocent man added to Sulla's lists just so Crassus could obtain the poor man's property.''

''There was more than one such scandal.''

''Yes, but Crassus was a Roman of good birth, a general, the hero of the Colline Gate, thought to be above such grubbiness. Even so, Sulla only slapped his wrists for that offense. But before the scandal, Crassus came first in all things, just behind Pompey. And Crassus's men were to be pampered and coddled, even above many of Sulla's oldest friends and supporters.''

''Like yourself.''

''Yes.''

''I take it Mummius got the best of you in something, and Sulla took his side.''

''There was a certain property we both coveted.''

''Real estate, or a human?''

''A slave.''

"I see."

"No, you don't. The boy had been the property of a certain senator in Rome. Once I heard him sing at a dinner party. He came from my own hometown in Etruria. He sang in the dialect I learned as a child. To hear him made me weep. When I learned that he was being sold in a lot with the rest of the household slaves, I rushed down to the Forum. The auctioneer happened to be a friend of Crassus's. It turned out that Mummius desired the boy as well, and not for his singing. The auctioneer ignored my bids, and Marcus Mummius was awarded the entire lot of slaves for the price of a used tunic. How smug he was when he passed by me to collect his receipt. We exchanged threats. I drew a knife. The crowd was packed with Crassus's men, and I had to flee for my life while they jeered after me. I went to Sulla, demanding justice, but he refused to intervene. Mummius was too close to Crassus, he said, and at that moment he could not afford to offend Crassus."

"So Mummius bested you over a boy."

"That wasn't the end of it. It took him only two years to tire of the slave. Mummius decided to get rid of him, but he refused to sell him to me, purely out of spite. By then, Sulla was dead and I had no influence at Rome. I wrote a letter to Mummius and asked him as humbly as I could to let me buy the boy. Do you know what he did? He passed the letter around at a dinner party and made a joke of it. And then he passed the boy around. He made sure I heard all about it."

"And the boy?"

"Mummius sold him to a slave trader bound for Alexandria. The boy disappeared forever. Mollio!" he snapped. "Your hands are useless this morning!"

"Patience, master," cooed the wizened slave. "Your spine is as stiff as wood. Your shoulders are like rusty hinges."

The door opened. A rush of cool air brought with it the high, piping voice of Sergius Orata. "And more ducts run under this floor and along both of these walls," he was saying. "You can see the vents that release the hot air, spaced evenly apart.'' Eco followed him, nodding without much enthusiasm. Orata was naked except for a very large towel wrapped around his middle. Clouds of steam rose from his plump pink flesh.

''Gordianus, your son is an apt pupil. A better listener I've never encountered. I do believe the boy may have some talent for engineering.''

''Really?'' I glanced over the fat man's shoulder at Eco, who looked quite bored. No doubt his thoughts were in a more briny milieu, floating across the seascape of the women's anteroom with Olympias. ''I've always thought so myself, Sergius Orata. No doubt he finds it difficult to pose complicated questions, but I seem to remember yesterday that he was most curious about how the waters were disposed of after circulating through the pools. I told him I assumed some system of pipes led down to the bay, but my explanation failed to satisfy him.''

''Oh, yes?'' Orata looked pleased. Eco stared at me, perplexed, then perceived the wink I gave him when Orata's back was turned. ''Then I shall have to explain it to him in detail, and leave nothing out. Come along, young man.'' Orata disappeared through the door, and Eco trudged after him.

Metrobius laughed, then grunted as the slave Mollio recommenced pinching and pounding his flesh. ''Sergius Orata isn't quite the simple soul he pretends to be,'' he said with a wry smile. ''There's quite a head on those shoulders, always calculating and counting his profits. He's certainly rich enough, and rumors allude to a weakness for gambling and dancing girls. Still, in this house he must seem a paragon of virtue—neither as greedy as Crassus nor as wicked as Mummius, not by a long shot.''

''About Crassus I know very little,'' I confessed, ''only what they say behind his back in the Forum.''

''Believe every word. Really, I'm surprised he hasn't stolen the coin from the corpse's mouth.''

''As for Mummius—''

''The swine.''

''He seems an odd mix of a man to me. I'll grant you that

there's a harsh side to him. I saw an example of it on the journey here. For a drill, he ordered the galley slaves driven to the maximum—as frightening a spectacle as I've ever witnessed."

"That sounds like Mummius, with his stupid military discipline. Discipline is a god he uses to excuse any act of wickedness, no matter how vile, just as Crassus can justify any crime for the sake of acquisition. They're two faces of a coin, opposites in many ways but essentially alike." Such criticism struck me as odd, coming from a man who had been so closely allied with Sulla. But as the Etruscans say, love turns a blind eye to corruption, while jealousy sees every vice.

"And yet," I said, "I think I glimpse in both of them a certain weakness, a softness that shows through their armor. Mummius's armor is of steel, Crassus's is of silver, but why does any man cover himself with armor except to shield his vulnerability?"

Metrobius raised an eyebrow and looked at me shrewdly. "Well, Gordianus of Rome, you may be more perceptive than I thought. What are these weaknesses evinced by Crassus and his lieutenant?"

I shrugged. "I don't yet know enough about either of them to say."

Metrobius nodded. "Search and you may find, Finder. But enough about those two." He rolled over and allowed the slave to stretch his arms above his head. "Let's change the subject."

"Perhaps you could tell me something about Lucius and Gelina. I understand that you and Gelina are very close friends."

"We are."

"And Lucius?"

"Didn't you just come from viewing Iaia's painted room?"

"Yes."

"Then you must have seen his portrait."

"Oh?"

"The jellyfish, just above the door."

"What? Oh, I see, you're joking."

"I'm not. Have a good look at it the next chance you get. The body is that of a jellyfish, but the face is quite unmistakably Lucius. It's in the eyes. A brilliant piece of satire, all the more satisfying because Lucius himself would never have gotten the joke. It elevates the whole mural to the level of high art. Iaia was once called the finest portraitist in Rome, and for good reason."

"Then Lucius was a jellyfish?"

He snorted. "A more useless man I never met. A mere footrest for Crassus, though a footrest might have had more personality. He's better off dead than alive."

"Yet Gelina loved him."

"Did she? Yes, I suppose she did. 'Love turns a blind eye,' as the Etruscans say."

"I was just thinking of that proverb myself. But I suppose Gelina is by nature an emotional woman. She certainly seems distraught about the fate of her slaves."

He shrugged. "If Crassus insists on killing them, it's a stupid waste, but I'm sure he'll give her others. Crassus owns more slaves than there are fish in the sea."

"It impresses me that Gelina was able to convince Crassus to send a ship for me."

"Gelina?" Metrobius smiled oddly. "Yes, it was Gelina who first mentioned your name, but by herself I doubt that she could have talked Crassus into going to so much effort and expense on account of mere slaves."

"What do you mean?"

"I thought you knew. There is another who longs to see these slaves plucked from the jaws of death."

"Whom do you mean?"

"Who journeyed all the way to Rome just to fetch you?"

"Marcus Mummius? A man who would drive a whole ship of slaves to the point of death on a mere whim? Why would he lift a finger to save Gelina's slaves, especially in defiance of Crassus's will?"

Metrobius looked at me oddly. "I thought surely you knew. When you spoke of Mummius having a weakness . . ." He frowned. "You disappoint me, Finder. I think perhaps you *are* as dense as I originally thought. You were sitting beside me at dinner last night. You saw as clearly as I did the tears that sprang from Mummius's eyes when the slave boy sang. Do you think he wept for cheap sentiment? A man like Mummius weeps only because his heart is breaking."

"You mean—"

"The other day, when Crassus made up his mind that the slaves should die, they argued and argued. Mummius was practically on his knees, begging Crassus to make an exception. But Crassus insists that they shall all be punished, including the beautiful Apollonius, no matter how harmless or innocent the boy may be, and no matter how much Mummius desires him. And so, the day after the funeral, Marcus Mummius will have to watch as his own men herd the boy into the arena and put him to death along with the rest of the household slaves. I wonder if they'll behead them one by one? Surely not, it would take all afternoon, and even a jaded Baian audience would start to fidget. Perhaps they'll have the gladiators do the dirty work, trapping the slaves under nets and rushing at them with spears. . . ."

"Then Mummius wishes to save them all, simply for the sake of Apollonius?"

"Of course. He's quite willing to make a fool of himself on the boy's behalf. It all began on his last visit here with Crassus, back in the spring. Mummius was instantly smitten, like a stag struck with an arrow between the eyes. During the summer he actually wrote the boy a letter from Rome. Lucius intercepted it and was quite disgusted."

"Because the letter was pornographic?"

"Pornography, from Mummius? Please, I'm sure he has neither the imagination nor the literary skill. On the contrary, it was quite chaste and cautious, rather like an epistle from Plato to one of his students, full of pious praise for Apollonius's spiritual wisdom and his transcendent beauty, that sort of thing."

"But Lucius married for love. I should think he might have sympathized."

"It was the impropriety of it that scandalized Lucius. A citizen consorting with one of his own slaves is one thing; it need never be known. But a citizen writing letters to another man's slave is an embarrassment to everyone. Lucius complained to Crassus, who must have said something to Mummius, since there was never a second letter. But Mummius remained smitten. He wanted to buy Apollonius for himself, but to do that required going through both Lucius and Crassus. One or the other refused to sell—perhaps Lucius, to spite Mummius, or perhaps Crassus, wanting to avoid further embarrassments from his lieutenant."

"And now Mummius finds himself awaiting the slave's destruction."

"Yes. He's tried to hide his anguish from Faustus Fabius and the rest of Crassus's retinue, and most of all from the men under his command, but everyone knows. Rumors spread very quickly in a small, private army. It was quite a spectacle to hear him prostrating himself before Crassus in the library the other day, scrambling to come up with the most ludicrous arguments to save Apollonius—"

"This was behind closed doors, I assume?"

"Can I help it if I could hear every word through the windows that face the courtyard? Mummius pleaded for the boy's life; Crassus invoked the stern majesty of Roman law. Mummius argued for an exception; Crassus told him to stop playing the fool. I believe he even called Mummius 'unRoman' at one point, the direst insult a stolid soldier like Mummius can receive from his commander. If you think Gelina is distraught, you should have heard Mummius that day. I can't imagine how he will react when a Roman blade cuts into the tender young flesh of Apollonius and the pretty slave begins to bleed . . ." Metrobius slowly shut his eyes, and a strange expression settled on his face.

"You're smiling," I whispered.

"And why not? Mollio gives the finest massage on the Cup. I feel quite delicious, and am ready for my bath."

Metrobius stood and held his arms aloft while the slave wound the long towel around him. I sat up and mopped my perspiring forehead. "Do I only imagine it," I said quietly, "or are there those in this house who actually look forward to seeing the slaves executed? A Roman seeks justice, not vengeance."

Metrobius did not answer, but slowly turned and left the room.

"A pity you're no better at swimming than I am," I said to Eco as we left the baths. He gave me a pained look but did not dispute the fact. "Our next task must be to have a look at the waters around the boathouse. What was being dumped from the pier last night, and why?" I looked down from the terrace outside the baths. From where we stood I could see the boathouse and most of the pier. There was no one about. The coastline was dotted with craggy rocks, and the water looked sufficiently deep to be daunting. "I wonder if that boy Meto is a swimmer? He probably grew up here on the Cup; aren't all the local boys divers and swimmers, even the slaves? If we can find him quickly, perhaps we can explore the boathouse and its environs before time for the midday meal." We found him on the upper floor. When he saw us he smiled and came running.

I began to speak, but he seized my hand and tugged at it. "You must go back to your room," he whispered. I tried to make him explain, but he only shook his head and repeated himself. Eco and I followed while he ran ahead.

The room was flooded with sunlight. No one had come to tidy our beds yet, but I sensed that someone had been in the room. I looked sidelong at Meto, who peeked back at me from behind the door. I pulled back the coverlet on my bed.

The ugly little figurine was gone. In its place was a piece of parchment with a message in red letters:

CONSULT THE SIBYL AT CUMAE
GO QUICKLY

"Well, Eco, this changes our plans. No swimming this morning. Someone has arranged for us to receive a message directly from the gods."

Eco looked at the scrap of parchment, then handed it back

to me. He seemed not to notice, as I had, that wherever the letter "A" occurred it was given an eccentric flourish, with the crossbar tilted sharply down to the right.

ELEVEN

WHEN I asked Meto if he could show us the way to the Sibyl's cave, or at least to Cumae, he stepped back, shaking his head. When I pressed him, his face turned pale. "Not me," he whispered. "I'm afraid of the Sibyl. But I know who could show you."

"Yes?"

"Olympias goes to Cumae every day at about this time, to fetch things from Iaia's house and to look after the place."

"How convenient for us," I said. "Does a wagon take her, or does Olympias prefer the luxury of a litter?"

"Oh, no, she rides a horse, as well as any man. She's probably in the stable now. If you hurry—"

"Come along, Eco," I started to say, but he was already out the door ahead of me.

I half expected to find Olympias waiting for us, but she seemed genuinely surprised when I called to her from the courtyard. She was already setting out from the stable mounted on a small white horse. She had changed her long, shapeless painter's gown for a short stola that allowed her to sit astraddle the horse. The garment left her legs completely naked from the knees down. Eco pretended to study the horse with admiration while darting glances at the perfect curvature of the girl's tawny calves pressed against the animal's flanks.

Olympias agreed to accompany us to Cumae, but only after some hesitation. When I told her that we were seeking the Sibyl, she looked alarmed at first, then skeptical. Her confusion surprised me. I had thought she must have some part in this shadowy plan to lure me to Cumae, yet she seemed to resent the imposition. She waited while Eco and I borrowed horses from the stable keeper, and then the three of us set out together.

"The boy Meto says you make this journey every day. Isn't it a long ride there and back?"

"I know a shortcut," she said.

We passed between the bull-headed pylons and onto the public road, then turned right, as Mummius and I had done the day before when the slave showed us where the bloody tunic had been found. We quickly passed that place and proceeded north. The hills on our left were covered with orchards of olive trees, their branches heavy with an early crop; there were no slaves to be seen. After the orchards there came a vineyard, then scattered patches of cultivated farmland, then a patch of woodland. "The land all around the Cup is remarkable for its fertility," I said.

"And for stranger things," Olympias remarked.

The road began to wind downward. Through the trees I saw ahead what had to be Lake Lucrinus, a long lagoon separated from the bay by a narrow stretch of beach. "That's where Sergius Orata made his fortune," I said to Eco. "Farming oysters and selling them to the rich. If only he were here with us, I'm sure he'd want to treat you to an extensive tour and lecture." Eco rolled his eyes and made an exaggerated shudder.

The prospect widened and ahead I was able to see the course of the road as it followed the strand between the lake and the bay and then curved away toward the east, where it passed through a series of low hills before descending again into the town of Puteoli. I saw many docks there, but as Faustus Fabius had said, few big ships.

Olympias looked over her shoulder. "If we were to take the road all the way, we'd pass Lake Lucrinus and go halfway to Puteoli before turning back toward Cumae. But that's for wagons and litters and others who need a paved road. This is the way I go." She turned off the road onto a narrow path that cut through low bushes. We passed through a stand of trees onto a bald ridge, following a narrow track that looked like a goat path. There were rolling hills on our left, but on our right, toward Lake Lucrinus, the land fell steeply away. Far below us, on the broad, low plain surrounding the lake, the private army of Crassus was encamped.

Tents had been pitched all about the shore. Little plumes of smoke rose from cooking fires. Mounted horsemen cantered on the plain, throwing up clouds of dust. Soldiers drilled in marching formation, or practiced swordplay in groups of two. The sound of swords banging shields echoed up from the valley, along with a deep bellowing voice that was too indistinct to understand but impossible not to recognize. Marcus Mummius was shouting instructions at a group of soldiers who stood in rigid formation. Nearby, before the largest of the tents, stood Faustus Fabius, recognizable from his mane of red hair; he was leaning over and speaking to Crassus, who sat in a backless folding chair. He was dressed in full military regalia, his silver accoutrements glinting in the sun, his great red cape as vivid as a drop of blood on the dusty landscape.

"They say he's getting ready to press for the command against Spartacus," said Olympias, gazing down at the spectacle with a moody look on her face. "The Senate has its own armies, of course, but the ranks have been devastated by the defeats of the spring and summer. So Crassus is raising his own army. Fabius tells me there are six hundred men at Lake Lucrinus. Crassus has already raised five times that many at a camp outside Rome, and can raise many more once the Senate approves. Crassus says no man can really call himself rich unless he can afford his own army."

While we watched, a cymbal was beaten and the soldiers began to congregate for their midday meal. Slaves hurried to and fro among the boiling pots. "Do you recognize the tunics? Those kitchen slaves are from Gelina's house," Olympias said. "Scurrying to feed the same men who in two days' time will be cutting their throats."

Eco touched my arm and pointed to the far side of the plain, where bare earth gave way to woods. A great swath of felled trees had been cleared from the forest, and a team of soldiers was building a temporary arena from the raw wood. A deep bowl had been dug in the earth and stamped flat, and around it the soldiers were constructing a high wall surrounded by tiers of seats. I squinted and was barely able to make out the groups of helmeted men within the ring who practiced mock combat with swords, tridents, and nets. "For the funeral games," I muttered. "The gladiators must have already arrived. That's where they'll fight on the day after tomorrow in honor of Lucius Licinius. That must also be where . . ."

"Yes," said Olympias. "Where the slaves will be put to death." Her face became hard. "Crassus's men shouldn't have used those trees. They belong to the forest of Lake Avernus, farther north. No man owns them. The Avernine wood is a holy wood. To have cut down even a few of them for any purpose is a great impiety. To have cut down so many to satisfy his own ambitious schemes is a terrible act of hubris for Marcus Crassus. No good will come of it. You'll see. If you don't believe me, ask the Sibyl when you see her."

We continued in silence along the ridge, then entered the forest again and began a gradual descent. The woods became thicker. The trees themselves changed character. Their leaves were no longer green, but almost black; great shaggy trees loomed all about, fingering the air with convoluted branches. The understory grew dense with thorny bushes and hanging tufts of mossy lichen. Mushrooms sprouted underfoot. The goat path disappeared, and it seemed to me that Olympias was finding her way by instinct through the woods. A heavy silence enfolded us, broken only by the footfall of our horses and the faraway cry of a strange bird.

"You travel this route alone?" I said. "Such a lonely place, I should think you would feel unsafe."

"What could harm me in these woods? Bandits, brigands, runaway slaves?" Olympias looked straight ahead, so that I could not see her face. "These woods are consecrated to the goddess Diana; these woods have been Diana's for a thousand years, before even the Greeks came. Diana carries a great bow with which to guard her domain. When she takes aim, no beating heart can escape her arrow. I feel no more fear here than if I were a doe or a hawk. Only the man who enters these woods with evil intent faces any danger. Outlaws know this in their hearts and do not enter. Do you feel fear, Gordianus?"

A cloud obscured the sun. The patches of sunlight faded, and a gray chill spread through the forest. A strange illusion gripped me: night reigned within the woods, the hidden sun was replaced by the moon, and darkness seeped out of the hollow bowls of dying trees and from the deep shadows under fallen branches. All was silent except for the footfall of the horses; even that seemed muffled, as if the moist earth swallowed the sound of each step. An odd drowsiness descended on me, not as if I fell asleep but as if I slowly wakened into a realm where all my senses were slightly askew.

"Do you feel fear, Gordianus?"

I stared at the back of her head, at the soft golden mane of her hair. I imagined the strangest thing—that if she were to turn suddenly I would see not her own beautiful face, but a visage too terrible to look at, a harsh, grinning mask with cruel eyes, the face of an angry goddess. "No, I feel no fear," I whispered hoarsely.

"Good. Then you have a right to be here, and you will be safe." She turned and it was only the harmless, smiling face of Olympias that looked back at me. I sighed with relief.

The woods grew darker. A heavy, clinging mist spread through the forest. The smell of sea spray mingled with the dank odors of rotting leaves and moldering bark. Then another smell assaulted us, the stench of boiling sulphur.

Olympias pointed to a clearing on our right. We rode onto a lip of bare rock. Above us loomed the tattered edge of a fog bank rolling in from the sea. Below us opened a great gulf of space. A vast bowl of vapor swirled below, ringed by dark, brooding trees. Through the vapors I could barely discern the surface of a great roiling cesspit that bubbled and seethed and spat.

"The Jaws of Hades," I whispered.

Olympias nodded. "Some say that it was here that Pluto pulled Proserpina into the Underworld. They say that beneath this pool of sputtering sulphurous mud, deep in the restless bowels of the earth, there run a host of subterranean rivers that separate the realm of the living from the realm of the dead. There is Acheron, the river of woe, and Cocytus, the river of lamentation. There is Phlegethon, the river of fire, and Lethe, the river of forgetfulness. Together they converge into the great river Styx, across which the ferryman Charon carries the spirits of the dead to the bleak wastelands of Tartarus. They say that Pluto's watchdog Cerberus escapes his bonds every so often and flees to the upper world. I spoke once to a farmer in Cumae who had heard the monster in the Avernine woods, all three heads howling together under the light of the full moon. On the other nights the dreaded lemures escape from Lake Avernus, malicious spirits of the dead who haunt the woods and inhabit the bodies of wolves. Still, Pluto always draws them back by morning. No one escapes his realm for long." She turned her face from the ghastly vista below to glance at Eco, who stared back at her, wide-eyed.

"Strange, isn't it," she said, "to think that all of this exists so near to the civility and comfort of Baiae and its villas? At Gelina's house the world seems to be a place made of sunlight dancing on water, and fresh salty air; it's easy to forget the gods who live under dank stones and the lemures that dwell beneath the sulphurous pits. Lake Avernus was here before the Romans, before the Greeks. These woods were here, and so were all the steaming fumaroles and the boiling pits filled with stench that circle the Cup. This is the place where the Underworld comes closest to the world of the living. All the beautiful houses and bright lights that ring the Cup are like a mask, a charade, as insubstantial as the skin of a bubble; beneath them the sulphur rumbles and boils, as it has forever. Long after the pretty houses rot and the lights grow dim, the belching Jaws of Hades will still be gaping open to receive the shades of the dead."

I looked at her in wonder, bewildered that such words could come from the lips of a creature so young and full of life. She met my eyes for an instant and smiled her cryptic smile, then spun her horse around. "It's not good to look too long at the face of Avernus, or to breath the fumes."

Our course began gradually to descend. At length we left

the woods for a grassy landscape of low hills pierced by jagged white rocks. The hills became more and more windswept and barren as we neared the sea; the fog lifted and hung above our heads in tatters. The rocks grew as big as houses and lay scattered about us like the broken and weathered bones of giants. They took on fantastic shapes, bristling with sharp edges and shot through with swirling tunnels and wormholes.

We passed through the maze of rocks for a time, until we came to a hidden hollow set into a steep hillside, like the crook of an elbow. The narrow defile was strewn with tumbled rocks and trees weirdly sculpted by the wind.

"This is where I leave you," said Olympias. "Find a place to tie your horse, and wait. The priestess will come for you."

"But where is the temple?"

"The priestess will take you to the temple."

"But I thought there was a great temple to mark the site of the Sibyl's shrine."

Olympias nodded. "You mean the temple that Daedalus built when he came to earth on this spot after his long flight. Daedalus built it in honor of Apollo, and decorated it with panels all in hammered gold and covered it with a golden roof. So they say in the village of Cumae. But the golden temple is only a legend, or else the earth swallowed it up long ago. That happens here sometimes—the earth gapes open and devours whole houses. Nowadays the temple is in a hidden, rocky place near the mouth of the Sibyl's cave. Don't worry, the priestess will come. You brought a token gift of gold or silver?"

"I brought the few coins I had with me in my room."

"It will be enough. Now I leave you." She tugged impatiently at the reins of her horse.

"But wait! How shall we find you again?"

"Why must you find me at all?" There was an unpleasant edge in her voice. "I brought you here, as you asked. Can't you find your own way back?"

I looked at the maze of rocks. The descending fog swirled overhead and a low wind moaned amid the stones. I shrugged uncertainly.

"Very well," she said, "when the Sibyl is done with you, ride on a short distance toward the sea. Over the crest of a grassy hill you'll come upon the village of Cumae. Iaia's house is at the far end of the village. One of the slaves will let you in, if"—she paused uncertainly—"if I'm not there. Wait for me."

"And where else would you be?"

She rode away without answering, and quickly vanished amid the boulders.

"What vital business draws her to Cumae every day?" I said to myself. "And why is she so eager to be rid of us? Well, Eco, what do you think of this place?"

Eco clutched himself and shivered, not from the cold.

"I agree. There is something here that sets my teeth on edge." I looked at the maze of rocks all around us. The wind moaned and whistled through the wormholes. "You can't see farther than a few feet in any direction, thanks to all these jagged boulders. A whole army could be hidden out of sight, an assassin behind every rock."

We dismounted and led the horses deeper into the crook of the hill. A bald band had been worn into a twisted branch, showing where many others before us had tethered their horses. I secured the beasts, then felt Eco tugging urgently at my sleeve.

"Yes, what do you—"

I stopped short. From nowhere, it seemed, a figure passed between two nearby stones, following the same path that Olympias had taken. The descending fog swallowed all noise of his horse's footfalls, so that the figure passed by as silently as a phantom. He was visible for only an instant, draped in a dark hooded cloak. "What do you make of that?" I whispered.

Eco leaped to the tallest of the nearby rocks and scrambled atop it, finding holds for his fingers amid the wormholes. He peered into the middle distance. For an instant his face lit up and then darkened again. He waved to me but kept his eyes on the maze of rocks. By way of signal, he pinched his chin and drew his fingers away to a point.

"A long beard?" I said. Eco nodded. "Do you mean the

rider is Dionysius, the philosopher?" He nodded again. "How peculiar. Can you still see him?" Eco frowned and shook his head. Then he brightened again. He pointed his finger as the arrow flies, in an arc that ascended and then fell, indicating something farther afield. He made his sign for Olympias's tresses. "You can see the girl?" He nodded yes, then no as she passed from sight. "And does it seem that the philosopher follows her?" Eco watched for a moment longer, then looked down at me with an expression of grave concern and slowly nodded.

"How odd. How very odd. If you can see no more, come down." Eco watched for a moment longer, then sat on the rock and pushed himself off, landing with a grunt. He hurried to the horses and indicated the knotted tethers.

"Ride after them? Don't be ridiculous. There's no reason to assume that Dionysius means her any harm. Perhaps he isn't following her at all." Eco put his hands on his hips and looked at me the way that Bethesda so often does, as if I were a foolish child. "Very well, I'll admit it's odd that he should pass by on the same obscure path only moments behind us, unless he has some secret reason. Perhaps it was us he was following, and not Olympias, in which case we've given him the slip."

Eco was not satisfied. He crossed his arms and fretted. "No," I said firmly. "We are not going after them. And no, you are not going off on your own. By now Olympias is probably already in Cumae. Besides, I doubt that a young woman as strong and capable as Olympias is in need of protection from an old graybeard like Dionysius."

Eco wrinkled his brow and kicked at a stone. With his arms still crossed he began to walk toward the tall rock, as if he meant to climb it again. An instant later he froze and spun around, as did I.

The voice was strange and unnerving—gruff, wheezing, barely recognizable as that of a woman. Its owner wore a blood-red hooded cloak and stood with her hands joined within the voluminous sleeves so that no part of her body was visible. From the deep shadow that hid her face the voice issued like the moaning of a phantom from the Jaws of Hades.

"Come back, young man! The girl is safe. You, on the other hand, are an intruder here, and in constant danger until the god sees your naked face and judges whether to blast you with lightning or open your ears to the voice of the Sibyl. Both of you, gather your courage and follow me. Now!"

TWELVE

VERY long ago there was a king of the Romans called Tarquinius the Proud. One day a sorceress came up to Rome from her cave at Cumae and offered to Tarquinius nine books of occult knowledge. These books were made of palm leaves and were not bound as a scroll, so that the pages could be put in any order. This Tarquinius found very strange. They were also written in Greek, not Latin, but the sorceress claimed that the books foretold the entire future of Rome. Those who studied them, she said, would comprehend all those strange phenomena by which the gods make known their will on earth, as when geese are seen flying north in winter, or water ignites into flame, or cocks are heard crowing at noon.

Tarquinius considered her offer, but the sum of gold she demanded was too great. He sent her away, saying that King Numa a hundred years before had established the priesthoods, cults, and rituals of the Romans, and these institutions had always sufficed to discern the will of the gods.

That night three balls of fire were seen hovering above the horizon. The people were alarmed. Tarquinius called upon the priests to explain the phenomenon, but to their great chagrin no explanation could be found.

The next day the sorceress visited Tarquinius again, saying she had six books of knowledge for sale. She asked the same price she had asked for nine books the previous day. Tarquinius demanded to know what had become of the other three books, and the witch said she had burned them during the night. Tarquinius, insulted that the sorceress demanded for six books what he had refused to pay for nine, sent her away.

That night three convoluted columns of smoke rose above the horizon, blown by the wind and illuminated by the moon so that they took on a grotesque and foreboding aspect. Again the people were alarmed, thinking it must be a sign from an angry god. Tarquinius summoned the priests. Again they were baffled.

The next day the sorceress came to visit the king again. She had burned three more books the night before, she said, and now offered him the remaining three, for the same price she had originally asked for all nine. Though it vexed him greatly, Tarquinius paid the woman the sum she demanded.

And so, because Tarquinius hesitated, the Sibylline Books were received in only fragmentary fashion. The future of Rome could be discerned only imperfectly, and the reading of auspices and auguries was not always precise. Tarquinius was both revered for obtaining the sacred texts and derided for not acquiring them all. The Sibyl of Cumae gained a legendary reputation for her wisdom. She was respected both as a great sorceress and a shrewd bargainer, having obtained the price of nine books for only three.

The Sibylline Books became objects of awesome veneration. They outlasted the kings of Rome and became the most sacred property of the Roman people. The Senate decreed that they should be kept in a stone chest deep underground in the temple of Jupiter on the Capitoline Hill, above the Forum. The books were consulted in times of great calamities or when inexplicable omens appeared. Those priests who were specially charged to study the books were constrained under penalty of death to keep their contents secret, even from the Senate. One curious fact about the verses became commonly known, however. They were written in acrostic; together, the initial letters of each line spelled out the subject of each verse. Such cleverness as would have driven a mortal to distraction must have been child's play for the divine will.

Because the books remained so mysterious, very few persons know exactly what was lost when, ten years ago in the final convulsions of the civil wars, a great fire swept the

Capitoline and consumed the Temple of Jupiter, penetrating the stone chest and reducing the Sibylline Books to ash. Sulla blamed his enemies for the fire, his enemies blamed Sulla; in any case it was not an auspicious beginning for the dictator's three-year reign. Without the Sibylline Books to foretell it, did Rome have a future? The Senate sent special envoys all over Greece and Asia to search for sacred texts to replace the lost Sibylline Books. Officially, this has been done to the full satisfaction of the priesthood and the Senate. For those respectful of divine will, but skeptical of human institutions, the opportunities for fraud and bamboozlement offered by such a scavenger hunt are too staggering to contemplate.

It is no small indication of the depths to which the Sibyl of Cumae has fallen in public esteem, at least in Rome, that no envoy was sent to her when the original books were lost. Surely it would make sense to go back to the source in order to replace the arcane books—or did the Senate balk at the prospect of being gotten the better of in a second bargain with the Sibyl of Cumae?

Around the Cup, the Sibyl is still venerated, especially by denizens of the old Greek towns, where the chlamys is worn instead of the toga and Greek is spoken more often than Latin, not only in the markets but in the temples and law courts as well. The Sibyl is an oracle in the Eastern sense; she, or more precisely *it*, is a mediating force between the human and divine, able to touch both worlds. When the Sibyl enters one of her priestesses, that priestess is able to speak with the voice of Apollo himself. Such oracles have existed since the dawn of time, from Persia to Greece and in the far-flung Greek colonies of old, like Cumae, but they have never been wholly embraced by the Romans, who prefer that inspired individuals should interpret the will of the gods by watching puffs of smoke or rattling beans in a gourd rather than uttering the divine message directly. The Sibyl of Cumae is still venerated by the local villagers, who bring her gifts of livestock and coins, but she is not favored by the fashionable elite of Rome who inhabit the great seaside villas; they prefer to seek wisdom from visiting philosophers and to bestow their patronage on the respectable temples of

Jupiter and Fortune in the forums of Puteoli, Neapolis, and Pompeii.

I was not surprised to find the temple of Apollo attached to the Sibyl's shrine to be in a state of some decay. It had never been a grandiose structure, notwithstanding tales of Daedalus and his golden embellishments. It was not even built of stone but of wood, with a bronze statue of Apollo upon a marble pedestal at the center. Painted columns of red, green, and saffron were surmounted by a circular roof, the underside of which was segmented into triangles and painted with images of Apollo overseeing various acts in the tale of Theseus: the lusting of Pasiphaë for a bull and the birth of the Minotaur of Crete; the casting of lots for the yearly sacrifice of seven Athenian sons to the beast; the construction of the great maze by Daedalus; the sorrow of Ariadne; the slaying of the monster by Theseus; the winged flight of Daedalus and his doomed son Icarus. Some of the paintings looked very old and were so faded that they could hardly be discerned; others had been recently repainted and glowed with vivid color. A restoration was in progress, and I suspected that I knew the woman responsible.

The temple was situated in a nook of land hemmed in on three sides by walls of jagged stone. It was the only flat surface on the steep hillside, which otherwise was strewn with boulders; the great stones seemed to have frozen in mid-avalanche and were overgrown with twisted trees that looked as if their flailing limbs were outstretched to save themselves from falling. The priestess walked ahead of us with a serene and unfailing sense of balance, never setting a foot wrong, while Eco and I followed, slipping and sliding after her, sending bits of gravel flying down the hill as we grabbed branches for support.

The spot was secluded from sight and protected from the wind. A quiet hush reigned over us. Above our heads the fog struggled to push itself over the hilltop and emerged in tatters, casting the place into a weird, dappled mixture of darkness and sunlight.

Within the temple the priestess turned to face us. Beneath her hood her features remained hidden in darkness. Her voice emerged as strange as before, the way that Aesop says that animals would speak if they could, forcing their inhuman throats to make human noises. "Obviously," she said, "you didn't bring a cow."

"No."

"Nor a goat."

"No."

"Only your horses, which are not a suitable sacrifice to the god. You have money, then, to purchase a beast for sacrifice?"

"Yes."

She named a sum that did not seem outrageous; the Sibyl of Cumae was apparently not the hard bargainer she once had been. I pulled the money from my purse and wondered if Crassus would accept the expense as an addendum to my fee.

I saw her right hand for just an instant as she accepted the coins from me. It was an old woman's hand, as I would have expected, with prominent bones and patches of discolored flesh. No rings adorned her fingers, and there was no bracelet on her wrist. There was, however, a smudge of blue-green paint on her thumb, just such a hue as Iaia might have been using that morning to touch up a bit of her mosaic.

Perhaps she saw the smudge of paint herself. Either that or she was eager for the money, for she clutched the coins and snatched her hand away, hiding it again within the sleeves of her robe. I noticed also that the hems of her sleeves were a darker red than the rest of her garment, stained by blood.

"Damon!" she called. "Fetch a lamb!"

From nowhere a child appeared, a little boy who thrust his head from between two columns and then as quickly vanished. A few moments later he reappeared carrying a bleating lamb over his shoulders. The beast was not farm stock, but a pampered temple animal fattened for ritual sacrifice, kept clean and carefully groomed and brushed. The boy swung it over his shoulders onto a short altar before the statue of Apollo. The creature bleated at the touch of cold marble, but the boy managed to calm it with soft strokes and whispers in its ear even as he deftly trussed its legs.

He ran swiftly away and then returned, bearing in his outstretched hands a long silver blade with a handle encrusted with lapis and garnets. The priestess took it from him and stood over the lamb with her back toward us, holding the blade aloft and muttering incantations. I expected a longer ceremony and perhaps a series of questions, as many oracles required from their supplicants, and so I was a little startled when the blade suddenly flashed and descended.

The priestess possessed skill, and more strength than I would have thought. The blade must have gone straight to the heart of the beast, killing it instantly. There were a few convulsions and a spattering of blood, but not a sound, not even the least whimper of protest as it gave up its life to the god. Would the slaves down in Baiae die as easily? In that moment a chill descended upon the place, though the air was still. Eco felt it as well, for I saw him shiver beside me.

The priestess slit open the lamb's underside from its breast to its belly, then reached inside. I saw how the hems of her sleeves had become so dark with bloodstains. She searched for a moment, then found what she was seeking. She turned toward us, bearing in her hands the lamb's quivering heart and a portion of its entrails. We followed her a short distance to the side of the temple, where a rude brazier had been hewn from the stone wall. The boy had already prepared the fire.

The priestess cast the organs upon the hot stone. There was a loud sizzling and a small explosion of steam. The vapor issued outward and then was sucked back toward the rock wall, drawn into fissures in the stone like smoke pulled into a flue. The priestess stirred the hissing entrails with a stick. The smell of seared flesh reminded me that we had neglected to eat at midday. My stomach growled. She cast a handful of something onto the heated stone, producing another cloud of smoke. A strange, aromatic scent like burning hemp filled the air, making me dizzy. Beside me, Eco swayed so violently that I reached to hold him up, but when I gripped his shoulder he looked at me oddly, as if it were I who had stumbled. I saw a movement from the corner of my eye and looked at the great wall of stone above and before us, where peculiar faces had begun to appear amid the fissures and shadows.

Such apparitions are not unknown at sacred shrines. I had witnessed them before. Still, there is always a sudden stirring of dread and doubt in that instant when the world changes and the powers of the unseen begin to manifest themselves.

Though I could not see her shadowed face, I knew that the priestess was watching me. She saw that I was ready. Again we followed her up a steep, stony path that traversed the slope, then descended into a dark, ever deepening ravine. The way seemed very far. The path was so difficult that I found myself stooped over, scrambling on my hands and feet. I glanced behind to see that Eco did the same. Strangely, the priestess was able to walk upright, striding forward with perfectly measured steps.

We came to the mouth of a cave. As we stepped inside, a cold, clammy wind rushed over my face, carrying a strange smell like the breath of many flowers in decay. I looked up to see that the cave was not a tunnel but a high, airy chamber, pierced all about by tiny holes and jagged fissures. These openings admitted a twilight glimmer, and the rush of the wind sighing through them created an ever changing cacophony that was sometimes like music, sometimes like a great chorus of moaning. Sometimes a singular sound would rise above all the others and then fade away—a trilling of notes like a satyr playing his pipes, or the bellowing voice of a famous actor I heard once as a boy, or the sigh that Bethesda makes before she wakes in the morning.

We descended deeper into the cave, to a place where the walls narrowed. The darkness deepened and the chorus of voices receded. The priestess raised her arm to signal that we should stop. In the dimness her blood-red robe had become jet black, so dark that it seemed to be a gaping hole that moved about in the gray gloom. She stepped onto a low shelf of stone, like a stage, and for a moment I thought that she danced. The black robe spun and twisted and seemed to fold in on itself. There was a long, wailing shriek that made my hair stand on end. The contortions were not a dance but the convulsions of the priestess as her body was possessed by the Sibyl.

The black robe fluttered to the ground, becoming nothing more than a great lump of cloth. Eco stepped forward to touch it, but I restrained him. In the next instant the robe began to fill again and rise up. Before our eyes the Sibyl of Cumae began to take shape. She seemed taller than the priestess, larger than life. She lifted her hands and pushed the cowl from her head.

Her face was barely discernible in the darkness, and yet it seemed that I could make out her features with a kind of supernatural clarity. I chided myself for ever imagining that the priestess was Iaia. This was the face of an old woman, to be sure, and in some superficial regards it resembled Iaia; the mouth might have been the same, and the high, gaunt cheekbones, and the proud forehead—but no mortal voice ever uttered such noises, and no mortal woman ever possessed such eyes, flashing as brightly as the light through the fissures in the cave.

She began to speak, then clutched herself. Her breast heaved, and a rattling sound issued from her throat as the god began to breathe through her. A sudden wind blew up from behind us and scattered her hair like flailing tendrils. She struggled, not yet submissive to the god and trying to shake him from her brain, like a horse trying to unseat its rider. Her mouth foamed. Noises came from her throat like wind in a cavern, and then like the gurgling of water in a pipe. Little by little the god mastered her and then calmed her. She hid her face in her hands, then slowly drew herself erect.

"The god is with me," she said, in a voice that was neither male nor female. The Sibyl seemed merely to mouth words that issued from some other source. I glanced at Eco. His forehead was beaded with sweat, his eyes were wide open, his nostrils were dilated. I clutched his hand to give him strength in the darkness.

"Why do you come?" the Sibyl asked.

I started to speak, but my throat was too thick. I swallowed and tried again. "We were told . . . to come." Even my own voice sounded unnatural to my ears.

"What do you seek?"

"We come . . . seeking knowledge . . . of certain events . . . in Baiae."

She nodded. "You come from the house of the dead man, Lucius Licinius."

"Yes."

"You seek the answer to a riddle."

"We seek to know how he died . . . and by whose hand."

"Not by the hand of those who stand accused," said the Sibyl emphatically.

"And yet I have no proof of that. Unless I can show who murdered Licinius . . . every slave in the household will be put to death. The man who seeks to do this thinks only of his own advancement . . . not of justice. It will be a cruel tragedy. Can you tell me the name of the man who killed Licinius?"

The Sibyl was silent.

"Can you show me his face in a dream?"

The Sibyl set her eyes upon me. An icy shiver ran through my bones. She shook her head.

"But this is what I must know," I protested. "This is the knowledge I seek."

Again the Sibyl shook her head. "If a general came to me and asked me to strike his enemies dead, would I not refuse? If a physician came and asked me to heal his patient, would I not send him away? The oracle does not exist to do the work of men for them. Yet if these men came to me seeking only knowledge, I would give it. If it were the will of the god, I would tell the doctor where his hidden enemy lurked, and I would tell the doctor where he might find the herb that could save his patient. The rest would be up to them.

"What shall I do with you, then, Gordianus of Rome? To find knowledge is your work, but I will not do your work for you. If I give you the answer you seek, I will rob you of the very means by which you may achieve your end. If you go to Crassus with nothing but a name, he will merely laugh at you or punish you for false accusations. Unless you acquire it on your own, using your skills, the knowledge you seek will be meaningless. That which you assert you must be able to prove. It is the will of the god that I assist you, but I will not do your work for you."

I shook my head. Of what use was the Sibyl if she refused to utter a simple name? Could it be that she did not know? I cringed at playing host to such impious thoughts, but at the same time it seemed that a veil was being slowly lifted from my eyes and the Sibyl once more began to look suspiciously like Iaia.

Eco touched my sleeve, demanding my attention. With one hand he held up two fingers, and with the other hand turned two fingers down, his sign for a man: *two men*. He wrapped one hand around the wrist of the other, symbolizing a shackle, his sign for a slave: *two slaves*.

I turned back to the Sibyl. "The two missing slaves, Zeno and Alexandros—are they living or dead? Where can I find them?"

The Sibyl nodded in stern approval. "You ask wisely. I will tell you that one of them is hidden, and the other is in plain sight."

"Yes?"

"I will tell you that after they fled from Baiae, this was their first destination."

"Here? They came to your cave?"

"They came to seek the guidance of the Sibyl. They came to me as innocent men, not guilty ones."

"Where can I find them now?"

"The one who is hidden you may find in time. As for the one in plain sight, you will find him on your way back to Baiae."

"In the woods?"

"Not in the woods."

"Then where?"

"There is a stone shelf that overlooks Lake Avernus. . . ."

"Olympias showed us the place."

"On the left side of the precipice there is a narrow path that leads down to the lake. Cover your mouth and nose with your sleeve and descend to the very mouth of the pit. He will await you there."

"What, the shade of a dead man escaping from Tartarus?"

"You will know him when you see him. He will greet you with open eyes."

It would be a clever place to hide, granted, but what sort of man could pitch his camp on the very shores of Avernus, amid the sulphur and steam and the reeking phantoms of the dead? The stone shelf was as near as I had cared to venture to the place; to descend to its edge sent a shiver through me. I could tell from the way he clutched my arm that Eco disliked the idea as much as I did.

"The boy," said the Sibyl crisply, "why does he not speak for himself?"

"He is unable to speak."

"You lie!"

"No, he cannot speak."

"Was he born dumb?"

"No. When he was very small he was stricken by a fever. The same fever killed his father; from that day Eco never spoke again. So his mother told me before she abandoned him."

"He could speak now if he tried."

How could she say such a thing? I began to object, but she interrupted.

"Let him try. Say your name, boy!"

Eco looked at her fearfully, and then with an odd glimmer of hope in his eyes. It was another strange moment in a day of strange moments, and I almost believed that the impossible would come to pass there in the Sibyl's cave. Eco must have believed as well. He opened his mouth. His throat quivered and his cheeks grew taut.

"Say your name!" the Sibyl demanded.

Eco strained. His face darkened. His lips trembled.

"Say it!"

Eco tried. But the sound that came from his throat was not human speech. It was a stifled, distorted noise, ugly and grating. I closed my eyes in shame for him, then felt him against my breast, shivering and weeping. I held him tightly, and wondered why the Sibyl should demand such a cruel price—an innocent boy's humiliation—in return for so little.

I drew a deep breath and filled my lungs with the scent of decaying flowers. I summoned my courage and opened my eyes, determined to reprimand her, vessel of the god or not, but the Sibyl was nowhere to be seen.

THIRTEEN

WE left the Sibyl's cave. The cavern of echoes and voices no longer seemed quite so mysterious—a curious enclosure, to be sure, but not the awe-inspiring place it had been when we entered. The way back to the temple was strenuous and rocky, but it hardly required that we crawl; nor was it as long on the way back as it had been on the way to the Sibyl's cave. The whole world seemed to have awakened from a strange dream. Even the fitful fog had receded, and the hillside was bright with afternoon sunshine.

The fire had died in the brazier. The blackened entrails still sputtered and popped occasionally on the hot stone, startling the swarm of flies that circled overhead. The sight was unpleasant, but the smell of charred flesh reminded me again that we had not eaten in hours. In a small recess behind the temple, the boy Damon had strung up and skinned the carcass of the lamb and was carving it with surprising expertise.

We scrambled down the ravine and untethered our horses. Bright sunshine reflected off the maze of rocks, making it as baffling a place as before, if not quite so menacing. We made our way toward the coast. At the crest of a small rise, a glittering expanse opened before us, not the circumscribed sweep of the Cup, but the true sea, an unobstructed body of water extending all the way to Sardinia and beyond to the Pillars of Hercules in the west. The ancient village of Cumae was at our feet.

We rode in silence. On our journeys I usually kept up a running conversation, even if Eco could not answer with his own voice. Now I could think of nothing to say. The silence between us was heavy with an unspoken melancholy.

A wagon driver pointed us to the house of Iaia, which stood perched on a cliff at the far end of the village, overlooking the sea. It was not impressive as villas go, but it was probably the largest house in the village, with modest wings extending to the north and south and what appeared to be another story stepping down toward the sea on the west. The wash of colors that decorated the facade was subtly original, a blending of saffron and ocher together with highlights of blue and green. The house at once stood out boldly against the backdrop of the sea, and yet seemed an essential part of the view. The hand and eye of Iaia turned everything to art.

The door slave informed us that Olympias had gone out but would return, and had left word that our needs should be attended to. He led us to a small terrace with a view of the sea, and brought food and drink. Presented with a bowl of steaming porridge, Eco began to seem more himself. He ate with relish, and I was heartened to see him shake off his sadness. After eating we rested, reclining on couches on the terrace and gazing at the sea, but I soon grew restless and began to query the slaves about Olympias's whereabouts. If they knew where she was, they would not tell. I left Eco dozing on his couch and wandered through the house.

Iaia had collected many beautiful things in the course of her career—finely crafted tables and chairs, small sculptures so delicately molded and painted they seemed almost to breathe, precious objects made of glass, ivory figurines, and the paintings of other artists as well as her own. These things were displayed about the house with a great sense of harmony and an unfailing eye for beauty. No wonder she had been so disparaging of Lucius Licinius's taste in paintings and statues.

It was my nose that led me to the room where Iaia and Olympias created their pigments. I followed a strange medley of odors down a hallway until I came to a chamber cluttered with pots, braziers, mortars and pestles. Stacked all about the room were dozens of clay jars, some large, some small, all labeled in the same hand that had signed the portrait of Gelina. I opened the lids and examined the various dried plants and powdered minerals. Some of them I recognized—brown-red sinopis made from rusted Sinopean iron; Spanish cinnabar the color of blood; dark purple sand from Puteoli; blue indigo made from a powder scraped off Egyptian reeds.

Other jars seemed to contain not pigments but medicinal herbs—black and white hellebore ground to a powder, poisonous but having many uses; the holosteon or "all-bone" plant (perversely named by the Greeks because it is entirely soft, just as they call gall "sweet") with its slender, hairlike roots, good for closing wounds and healing sprains; white lathyris seeds, good for curing dropsy and drawing away bile. I was just replacing the lid on a tiny jar full of aconitum, also called panther's-death, when someone cleared his throat behind me. The door slave watched me disapprovingly from the hallway.

"You should be careful before you stick your nose in the jars," he said. "Some of the things inside can be very poisonous."

"Yes," I agreed, "like this stuff. Aconitum—they say it sprang from the mouth foam of Cerberus when Hercules pulled him up from the Underworld. That's why it grows near openings to the Underworld, like the Jaws of Hades. Good for killing panthers, I'm told . . . or people. I wonder why your mistress keeps it."

"Scorpion stings," the slave answered curtly. "You mix it with wine to make a poultice."

"Ah, your mistress must be very wise about such things."

The slave crossed his arms and stared at me like a basilisk. I slowly replaced the jar on the shelf and left the room.

I decided to take a walk along the cliffs beyond the village. The afternoon sun was warm, the sky was crystal. A progression of clouds scudded along the blue horizon, and overhead gulls circled and shrieked. The fog that had blanketed the coast an hour before had vanished. The Sibyl of Cumae began to seem unreal, like the vapors that rose from Lake Avernus, as if all that had happened since we left Baiae that morning were a waking dream. I breathed deeply of the sea air and was suddenly weary of the villa in Baiae and its mysteries. I longed to be in Rome again, walking through the crowded streets of the Subura, watching the gangs of boys who play trigon in the squares. I longed for the secluded quiet of my own garden, the comfort of my own bed, and the smell of Bethesda's cooking.

Then I saw Olympias climbing up a narrow trail from the beach. In one hand she carried a small basket. She was still quite distant, but I could see that she was smiling—not the ambiguous smile that she wore in Gelina's villa, but a true smile, radiant and content. I also saw that the hem of her short riding stola was dark, as if she had been wading in water up to her knees.

I looked beyond her and tried to imagine where she had come from. The trail she was taking vanished from sight among a tumble of rocks, and I could see no beach at all at the water's edge. If she wanted to gather shells or sea creatures, there must surely be better and safer places in the vicinity of Cumae.

As she drew nearer I hid behind a stone. I circled behind it, trying to find a way to watch her without being seen, and noticed a movement from the corner of my eye. A hundred paces away I saw what might have been my mirror image, had I been wearing a dark hooded cloak and worn a long pointed beard. The philosopher Dionysius stood just as I did, poised behind a rock on the edge of the cliff, furtively watching Olympias climb up the hillside.

He did not see me. I moved slowly around the stone, concealing myself from Olympias and Dionysius both, and then scurried away from the cliff until I was out of sight. I hurried back to Iaia's house and rejoined Eco on the terrace.

Olympias arrived a few moments later. The door slave spoke to her in a hushed tone. Olympias stepped into another room. When she reappeared some moments later, she had changed into a dry stola and no longer carried her basket.

"Was your visit to the Sibyl fruitful?" she asked, smiling pleasantly.

Eco frowned and averted his eyes. "Perhaps," I said. "We'll find out on the way back to Baiae."

Olympias looked puzzled, but nothing could dampen her buoyant mood. She walked about the terrace, caressing the flowers that bloomed in their pots. "Shall we go back soon?" she asked.

"I think so. Eco and I still have work to do, and Gelina's house will no doubt be in much confusion, such as always occurs on the day before a great funeral."

"Ah, yes, the funeral," Olympias whispered gravely. She nodded thoughtfully, and the smile almost faded from her lovely lips as she bowed her head to smell the flowers.

"The sea air agrees with you," I said. She looked more beautiful than ever, with her eyes shining brightly and her golden hair swept back by the wind. "Did you take a walk along the beach?"

"A short walk, yes," she said, averting her eyes.

"When you came in the door a moment ago, I thought I saw you carrying a basket. Gathering sea urchins?"

"No."

"Shells?"

She looked uneasy. "Actually, I didn't go to the beach." The sparkle in her eyes became opaque. "I walked along the ridge instead. I gathered some pretty stones, if you must know. Iaia uses them to decorate the garden."

"I see."

We left shortly thereafter. As we walked through the foyer toward the door, I saw that Olympias had not bothered to conceal her basket when she entered but had left it in plain sight in the corner opposite the door slave's stool. While Olympias stepped through the door into the sunlight, I lingered behind. I stepped toward the basket and lifted the cover with my foot. There were no stones within. Except for a small knife and a few crusts of bread, the basket was empty.

The passage through the stone maze and across the bald, windy hills seemed quite different in the bright sunshine, but when we began to enter the woods around Lake Avernus I sensed the same atmosphere of uncanny seclusion that I had felt before. I looked back occasionally, but if Dionysius followed he kept himself out of sight.

It was not until we came to the precipice that I told Olympias I wanted to stop. "But I showed you the view already," she protested. "You can't want to see it again. Think what a beautiful day it must be down in Baiae."

"But I do want to see it," I insisted. While Eco found a place to tether the horses, I located the beginning of the path on the left side of the slab, just as the Sibyl had described. The opening was obscured by overgrown brush and old branches, and the path itself was faint and disused. There was no sign of fresh footsteps in the fog-dampened earth, not even the mark of a deer. I pushed through the brush with Eco behind me. Olympias protested but followed.

The path descended in sharp switchbacks over barren, rocky ground. The odor of sulphur grew ever stronger, borne on a wave of hot, rising air, until we were compelled to cover our faces with our sleeves. At last we found ourselves on a wide, shallow beach of yellow mud. The lake was not a uniform liquid surface, as it appeared from above, but a series of interconnected pools of sulphur overhung by clouds of vapor and separated by bridges of rock that might have been used to traverse to the other side, if a man cared to take the risk and could survive the heat and the smell. The stench of the bubbling pits was almost overpowering, but I thought I detected an even more unwelcome odor borne on the reek.

I looked up. We stood almost directly below the shelf of rock from which we had descended. In the face of the cliff I could see no cave or any other sign of shelter. I shook my head, more dubious than ever of the Sibyl's word.

"How can anyone possibly meet us here?" I grumbled to Eco. "I'd sooner expect to see the Minotaur come strolling up this beach than one of Gelina's escaped slaves." Eco gazed up and down the beach, as far as the obscuring mists allowed. Then he raised his eyebrows and pointed at something at the water's edge only a few feet away.

I had seen the thing already and had taken no notice of it, thinking it was only a piece of driftwood or some natural detritus thrown up by the lake. Now I looked at it more closely, and realized with a shock what it must be.

Eco and I stepped cautiously toward it, with Olympias following. At one time most of the thing had been submerged in the pit, where the greater part of it had been eaten away by the boiling, caustic sludge. The remains were drained of color, spattered with mud, and rapidly beginning to decay. We looked at what was left of a human head attached to shoulders still covered by bits of discolored cloth. The face was turned downward into the mud. On the back of the corpse's head a ring of gray hair swirled around a bald spot. Eco stepped back in fright and stared into the lake beyond, as if he thought the thing had emerged from the pit rather than fallen into it.

I found a stick and prodded at the shoulders to turn the thing over, at the same time keeping my nose covered. It was not easy; the flesh of the face seemed to have become melted somehow into the mud. When at last I succeeded, the sight was hard to bear, but enough of the features remained for Olympias to recognize him. She drew in a shuddering breath and wailed into her sleeve: "Zeno!"

Before I could think of what to do with the thing, Olympias decided for me. With a piercing shriek she stooped, picked up the head by its remaining hair and cast it into the lake. It flew through the mists, causing them to furl and flutter in its wake, and landed not with a splash but with a slap. For an eerie moment time stopped and the head remained afloat on the bubbling caldron. A hissing vent of steam opened beneath it. Through the vapor I thought I saw the eyes of the thing open and peer back at us, like a drowning man looking desperately to those on shore. Then it sank beneath the mud and vanished altogether.

"Now the Jaws of Hades claims him for good," I whispered to no one, for Olympias was running headlong back to the path, tripping and weeping, and Eco was on his knees, vomiting on the beach.

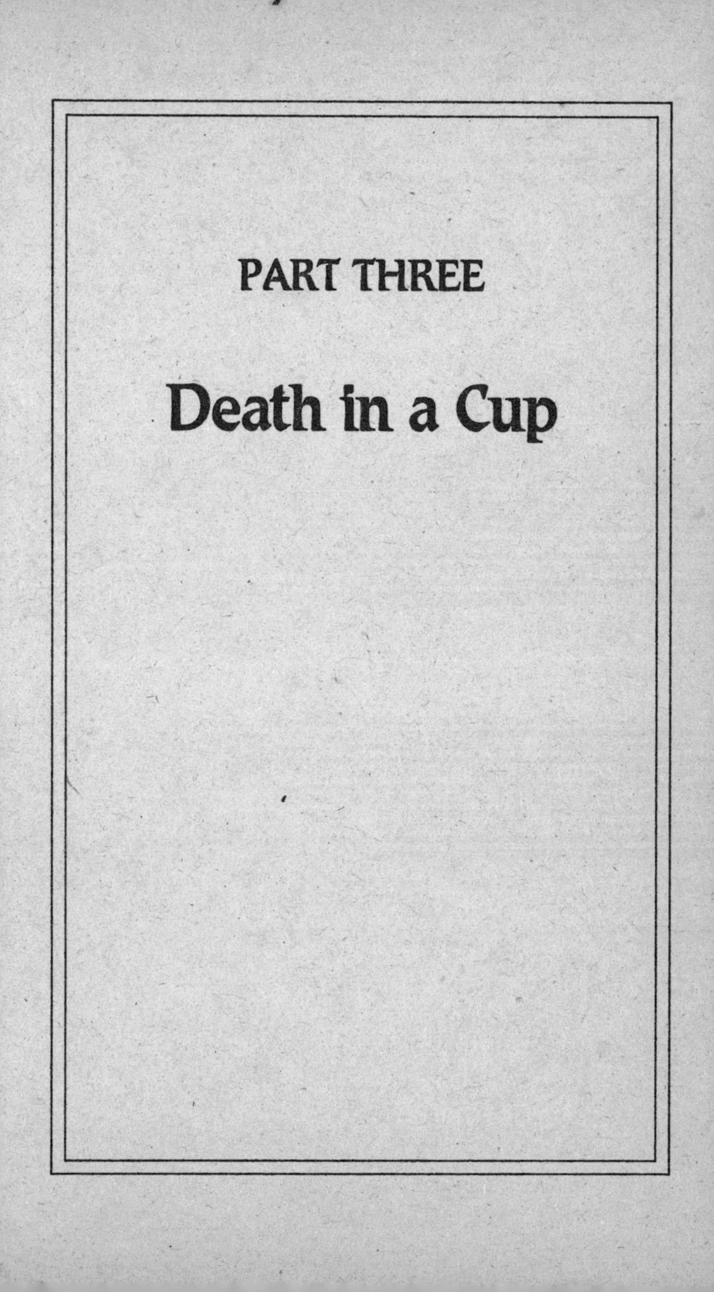

PART THREE

Death in a Cup

FOURTEEN

"WILL this day never end?" I peered at the ceiling above my bed and rubbed my face with both hands. "My backside will ache tomorrow from all this riding. Up hill and down, through the woods and across the wastes." I babbled, the way that weary men do when given a chance to rest in the course of a long day and they find themselves too overwrought to relax. It might have helped if I closed my eyes, but whenever I did I saw the horribly decayed face of Zeno staring at me from a gaping mouth of flame.

"Eco, could you pour me a cup of water from that ewer on the windowsill? Water!" I slapped my forehead. "We still have to find someone who can dive down into the shallows around the boathouse to see what was dropped from the pier last night." I sat up to accept the cup from Eco, and peered past his shoulder through the window. The sun was still up, but not for long. By the time I found Meto, assuming he was fit for the task, and trundled down to the water's edge, the shadows would be growing longer and the evening chill would have begun to settle. We needed bright sunlight piercing the water if we were to find something amid the rocks on the bottom. The task would have to wait.

I groaned and rubbed my eyes—then quickly snatched my hands away when the face of Zeno loomed up before me.

"Not enough time, Eco, not enough time. What's the point of all this scurrying about when we can never hope to get to the bottom of things before Crassus has his way? If only Olympias hadn't cast the head into the lake and then raced back to the villa alone, we would at least have had something to show Crassus—proof that we had found one of the slaves.

But what would that have served? Crassus would see it as just another proof of Zeno's guilt—what better way for the gods to show their fury at a murderous slave than for Pluto himself to swallow the miscreant feetfirst?

"For all our work, all we have are questions, Eco. Who attacked me on the pier last night? What was Olympias up to today, and why was Dionysius following her? And what part does Iaia play in all this? She seems to have some agenda of her own, but toward what end, and why does she play her part behind a veil of secrecy and magic?"

I stretched my arms and legs and suddenly felt as heavy as lead. Eco dropped onto his bed, his face turned toward the wall. "We shouldn't lie here any longer," I murmured. "We have so little time. I still haven't spoken to Sergius Orata, the businessman. Or Dionysius, for that matter. If I could catch the philosopher off his guard . . ."

I closed my eyes—for just an instant, I thought. Around me it seemed that the room itself sighed wearily. Perched atop the villa with an east-facing terrace, it captured the heat of the morning and stored it all through the day, but now the walls began to give up their warmth. A coolness seeped in from the window and pervaded the air. The back of my body, pressed into the bed, felt deliciously warm, while my hands and feet were slightly chilled. I could have used a light blanket, but I was too tired to bother. I lay on the bed, exhausted, alert to every sensation and yet beginning to doze.

The dream began in the bed on which I lay, except that I seemed to be at my house in Rome, for I lay on my side with Bethesda pressed against me, face to face. With my eyes closed I ran my hands over her warm thighs and up her belly, amazed that her flesh was still as firm and supple as when I first bought her in Alexandria. She purred catlike at my touch; her body writhed against mine and I felt myself grow achingly stiff between the legs. I moved to enter her, but she stiffened and pushed me away.

I opened my eyes and saw not Bethesda but Olympias looking back at me with aloof disdain. "What do you think I am," she whispered haughtily, "a slave, that you could ever use me so?" She pushed herself up from the bed and stood naked, bathed in the soft glowing light from the terrace. Her hair was a golden aureole about her face; the full, sleek curves and the subtle hollows of her body formed a beauty that was almost unbearable to look at. I reached for her and she started back. I thought she mocked me, but suddenly she covered her face with her hands and ran weeping from the room, slamming the door behind her.

I rose from the bed and followed. I opened the door with a sudden foreboding, and felt a breath of hot air on my face. The door opened not into a hallway, but onto the shelf of rock above Lake Avernus. I could not tell whether it was day or night; everything was lit with a harsh, blood-red glow. On the edge of the rock a man sat in a low chair, draped in a crimson military cape. He leaned forward, his chin on his hand and his elbow on his knee, as if he watched the progress of a battle far below. I looked over his shoulder and saw that the whole of the lake was a vast pool of belching flames, filled from shore to shore with the writhing bodies of men, women, and children trapped waist-deep in the burning mud. Their mouths were wrenched open in agony, but the distance muffled their screaming so that it was like the roar of the sea or the sound of a crowd in an amphitheater. They were too far away for their faces to be distinct, and yet among them I recognized the slave boy Meto and the young Apollonius.

Crassus looked over his shoulder. "Roman justice," he said with grim satisfaction, "and there is nothing you can do about it." He looked at me oddly, and I realized I was naked. I turned about to return to my room, but I could not find the door. In confusion I stepped too close to the edge. Part of the rock began to crumble and give way. Crassus seemed not to notice as I fell backward, desperately trying to scramble onto the rock even as it fell with me, plummeting into the empty void—

I woke in a cold sweat to see the boy Meto standing over me with a look of grave concern on his face. From across the room I heard the gentle sawing of Eco's snore. I blinked and wiped my hand across my forehead, surprised to find it beaded with sweat. The sky beyond the terrace was dark blue, alive with the first stars of evening. The room was lit by a lamp which Meto carried in his small hand. "They're waiting for you," he finally said, raising his eyebrows uncertainly.

"Who? For what?" I blinked in confusion and watched the lamplight flicker across the ceiling.

"Everyone is there but you," he said.

"Where?"

"In the dining room. They're waiting for you to begin the dinner. Though why they're in such a hurry I don't know," he went on, as I shook my head to clear it and struggled to rise from the bed.

"Why do you say that?"

"Because it's a dinner hardly fit for slaves!"

A great gloom seemed to have settled over the dining room. Partly it came from the gravity of the occasion, for this was the last meal before the funeral; throughout the night and all the next day, until the funeral feast that would follow Lucius Licinius's cremation and interment, everyone in the household would fast. Tradition prescribed a meal of rigorous simplicity: common bread and bowls of plain lentils, watered wine and a grain porridge. As an innovation, Gelina's cook had included a few delicacies, all black in color: black roe served on crusts of black bread, pickled eggs stained black, black olives, and fish poached in octopus ink. It was not a repast to spark clever conversation, even from Metrobius. Across the room Sergius Orata surveyed the prospect with a glum eye and filled himself up with pickled eggs, popping them whole into his mouth.

The gloominess had another source, which emanated from the couch beside Gelina. Tonight Marcus Crassus was in attendance, and his presence seemed to swallow up all spontaneity. His lieutenants Mummius and Fabius, reclining next to each other at his right hand, seemed unable to shake their taciturn military bearing, while, from their shifty glances and grim faces, it was evident that neither Metrobius nor Iaia felt at ease in the great man's presence. Olympias was understandably distracted; considering the shock she had received at Lake Avernus, I was surprised to see her in attendance. She dabbed at her food, bit her lips, and kept her eyes lowered. She wore a haunted expression that only enhanced her beauty by the muted glow of the lamps. Eco, I noticed, could not take his eyes from her.

Gelina was in a state of fretful agitation. She could not be still and was constantly waving at the slaves and then, when they scurried to her side, could not remember why she called them. Her expression shifted from haggard despair to a timorous smile for no apparent reason, and far from averting her eyes she looked from face to face around the room, fixing each of us with an intense, inscrutable gaze that was unnerving. Even Metrobius could not cope with her; he occasionally took her hand to squeeze it reassuringly, but avoided looking at her. His wit seemed to have run dry.

Crassus himself was preoccupied and aloof. Most of his conversation was reserved for Mummius and Fabius, with whom he exchanged curt observations on the state of his troops and the progress made toward completing the wooden amphitheater by Lake Lucrinus. Otherwise he might have been dining alone for all the attention he paid to his guests. He ate heartily but was pensive and withdrawn.

Only the philosopher Dionysius appeared to be in good spirits. His cheeks had a ruddy glow and his eyes sparkled. The ride to Cumae and back had invigorated him, I thought, or else he was very pleased with whatever result he had obtained by spying on Olympias that afternoon. It suddenly occurred to me that perhaps he was as stricken by her beauty as everyone else, and his purpose for following her was simply prurient. I remembered seeing him on the cliff, furtively watching Olympias from the hidden folds of his cloak, and with a shudder I imagined him secretly fondling himself. If the smile on his face that night was the afterglow of satisfying his peculiar sexual appetite, then the gods were granting me a far more intimate look into the man's soul than I cared to see.

Yet, for a man obsessed, Dionysius seemed quite capable of ignoring Olympias and her distress, even though she reclined at his right hand. Instead he focused his attentions on Crassus. As on the night before, it was Dionysius who finally picked up the reins of desultory conversation and sought to entertain us, or at least to impress us, with his erudition.

"Last night we talked a little about the history of slave revolts, Marcus Crassus. I was sorry you were not here. Perhaps some of my research would have been new to you."

Crassus took his time to finish chewing a crust of bread before replying. "I seriously doubt it, Dionysius. I've been doing my own research into the subject during the last few months, chiefly into the mistakes made by unsuccessful Roman commanders when confronting such large but undisciplined forces."

"Ah." Dionysius nodded. "The wise man takes an interest not only in his enemy, but in, shall we say, the heritage of his enemy, and the historical powers at his enemy's disposal, no matter how seamy or disreputable."

"What on earth are you talking about?" said Crassus, hardly looking up.

"I mean that Spartacus did not exactly arise from nowhere. I have a theory that among these slaves there are whispered legends about the slave revolts of the past, stories built about the likes of the doomed slave-wizard Eunus and embellished with all sorts of mock-heroic details and wishful thinking."

"Nonsense," said Faustus Fabius, pushing back a lock of unruly red hair. "Slaves do not have legends, or heroes, any more than they have wives or mothers or children they can call their own. Slaves have duties and masters. That is the way of the world as the gods have designed it." There was a general murmur of agreement around the room.

"But the way of the world can be disrupted," said Dionysius, "as we have seen all too clearly for the last two years, with Spartacus and his rabble cavorting up and down the length of Italy, wreaking havoc and inciting more and more slaves to join them. Such men thumb their noses at the natural order of things."

"And so the time has come for a strong Roman to reassert that order!" boomed Mummius.

"But surely it would be helpful," Dionysius pressed on,

"to understand the motivations and the aspirations of these rebellious slaves, all the more surely to defeat them."

Fabius curled his lip derisively and bit into an olive. "Their motivation is to escape the life of service and labor that Fortune has allotted them. Their aspiration is to be free men, though for that they lack the requisite moral character, especially those who were born slaves."

"And those who were reduced to slavery, because they were captured in war or made destitute?" The question came from Olympias, who blushed as she asked it.

"Can a man degraded to slavery every become wholly a man again, even if his master should see fit to free him?" Fabius cocked his head. "Once Fortune has turned a man into property, it is impossible for him to ever recover his dignity. He may redeem the body, but not the spirit."

"And yet, by law—" Olympias began.

"The laws vary." Fabius tossed an olive pit onto the little table before him. It bounced off the silver tray and onto the floor, where a slave hurried to retrieve it. "Yes, a slave may purchase his freedom, but only if his master allows him to do so. The very act of allowing a slave to accumulate his own price in silver is a legal fiction, since a slave can truly own nothing—anything he may possess belongs to his master. Even after emancipation, a freedman can be reduced to slavery again if he shows impertinence to his former master. He is politically restricted, socially retarded, and barred by good taste from marriage into any respectable family. A freedman may be a citizen, but he is never truly a man."

Gelina glanced over her shoulder at the slave who had retrieved the olive pit, and who now was retreating with a tray toward the kitchens. "Do you think it's wise to carry on such discussions, considering . . ."

Crassus snorted and leaned back on his couch. "Really, Gelina, if a Roman cannot discuss the nature of property in the presence of property, then we have come to a sad pass. Everything Fabius says is true. As for Dionysius and his notion about some sort of vague continuity between slave revolts, the idea is absurd. Slaves have no link with the past; how can they, when they don't even know the names of their ancestors? They're like mushrooms; they spring from the earth in vast numbers at the whim of the gods. What is their purpose? To serve as the tools of men greater than themselves, so that those men can realize their greater ambitions. Slaves are the human implements given to us by that divine will which inspires great men and enriches a great republic like our own. They have no past, and the past does not concern them. Nor do slaves have a sense of the future; otherwise Spartacus and his ilk would know that they are doomed to a fate far worse than the one they thought they were escaping when they turned on their masters."

"Hear, hear!" said Mummius tipsily, banging his cup on the table. Metrobius shot him a withering glance and started to speak, then thought better of it.

"The common slave who labors in the fields lives from day to day," Crassus continued, "conscious of very little beyond his immediate needs and the necessity of satisfying his master. Contentment, or at least resignation, is the natural condition of slavery; for such men to rise up and kill their betters is in fact unnatural, or else it would happen all the time and slavery could not exist, which means that civilization could not exist. The revolt of Spartacus, like that of the wizard Eunus and a handful of others, is an aberration, a perversion, a rent in the fabric of the cosmos woven by the Fates."

Dionysius leaned forward, gazing at Crassus with cloying admiration. "You are truly the man of the hour, Marcus Crassus. Not only a statesman and a general, but a philosopher as well. There are those who would say, however perversely, that Spartacus is the man of the hour, that he dictates the agenda of our hopes and fears, but I think that Rome will soon forget about him in the splendor of your victory. Law and order will be restored and all will be as if Spartacus never existed."

"Hear, hear!" said Mummius.

Dionysius leaned back and smiled coyly. "I wonder where the wretch Spartacus is at this very moment?"

"Holed up near Thurii," said Mummius.

"Yes, but what is he doing even as we speak? Does he

gorge himself on stolen victuals, gloating to his men about stolen victories? Or has he retired to bed already—after all, what kind of conversation can uneducated slaves enjoy to keep them up past dark? I imagine him lying awake in the darkness, restless and far from sleep, vaguely troubled by an intuition of what Fortune and Marcus Crassus have in store for him. Does he lie within a tent that reeks of his own foul smell? Or upon hard stones beneath a starry sky—no, surely not, for then he would be naked to the sight of the gods who despise him. I think such a man must sleep in a cave, burrowed into the dank earth like the wild beast he is."

Mummius laughed curtly. "There's nothing so awful about sleeping in caves. Not from the stories I've heard about a certain great man in his younger days." He cast a shrewd eye at Crassus, who grudgingly smiled.

Dionysius pursed his lips to suppress his own smile of triumph at this turn in the conversation, which he had obviously intended and in which Mummius was his unwitting accomplice. He leaned back and nodded. "Ah, yes, how could I have forgotten such a charming tale? It was in the bad old days before Sulla, when the tyrants Cinna and Marius, enemies of all the Licinii, spread terror through the Republic. They drove Crassus's father to suicide and killed his brother, and young Marcus—you must have been no more than twenty-five?—was forced to flee to Spain for his life."

"Really, Dionysius, I think that everyone here has heard the story too many times already." Crassus tried to sound bored and disapproving, but the smile at the corners of his lips betrayed him. It seemed to me that he was as aware as I that Dionysius had contrived to bring up the subject to make his own as yet unspoken point, but the memory of the story clearly pleased Crassus too much for him to resist having it told again.

Dionysius pressed on. "Surely not everyone has heard the tale—Gordianus for one, and his son Eco. The tale of the cave," he explained, looking at me.

"It sounds vaguely familiar," I admitted. "Some bit of gossip overheard in the Forum, perhaps."

"And Iaia and her young protégée—surely the story of

Crassus in the sea cave would be new to them.'' Dionysius turned toward the women with a look that was strangely like a leer. Their reaction was equally strange. Olympias blushed a deeper red while Iaia blanched and drew herself up stiffly. ''I know the story quite well,'' she protested.

''Well, then, for Gordianus's sake it should be told. When the young Crassus arrived in Spain, a fugitive from the depredations of Marius and Cinna, he might have expected to be warmly greeted. His family had old connections; his father had served as praetor in Spain, and Marcus had spent time there as a youth. Instead he found the Roman colonists and their subjects overawed by their fear of Marius; no one would speak to him, much less help him, and indeed there was considerable danger that someone would betray him and deliver his head to the partisans of Marius. So he fled the town, but not alone—you had arrived with some companions, had you not?''

''Three friends and ten slaves,'' said Crassus.

''Yes, so he fled the town with his three friends and ten slaves and journeyed down the coast, until he came to the property of an old acquaintance of his father's. The name eludes me . . .''

''Vibius Paciacus,'' said Crassus, with a wistful smile.

''Ah, yes, Vibius. Now there happened to be a large cave on the property, right on the seashore, which Crassus remembered from his boyhood. He decided to hide there with his company for a while, without telling Vibius, seeing no reason to endanger his old friend. But eventually their provisions ran out, so Crassus sent a slave to Vibius to sound him out. The old man was delighted to learn that Crassus had escaped and was safe. He inquired after the size of the company and, though he did not go himself, he ordered his bailiff to have food prepared each day and to deliver it to a secluded spot on the cliffs. Vibius threatened the bailiff with death if he poked his nose any further into the business or started spreading rumors, and promised him freedom if he carried out his orders faithfully. In time the man also brought books, leather balls for playing trigon, and other diversions, never seeing the fugitives or where they were hidden. The cave itself—''

''Oh, that cave!'' interrupted Crassus. ''I had played there as a boy, when it seemed as mysterious and haunting as the cave of the Sibyl. It's very near the sea, but safely high above the beach, surrounded by steep cliffs. The path that leads down to its mouth is steep and narrow, hard to find; inside, it opens to an amazing height, with chambers off to each side. A clear spring emerges from the base of the cliffs, so there's plenty of water. Fissures pierce the rock, so there's plenty of daylight but also protection from wind and rain. Not at all a damp or dank place, thanks to the thickness of the stone walls; the air was quite dry and pure. I felt like a child again, free from all the cares of the world, safely hidden. The months before had been a terrifying ordeal, with the death of my father and my brother, and the panic in Rome. There were melancholy days in the cave, but there was also a feeling that time had stopped, that for the moment nothing was wanted of me, neither grief nor revenge nor struggling for a place in the world. I think my friends grew quite bored and restive, and there was hardly enough for the slaves to do, but for me it was a time of rest and seclusion, sorely needed.''

''And eventually, so the tale goes, every need was met,'' said Dionysius.

''Alethea and Diona,'' said Crassus, smiling at the memory. ''One morning the slave who had been sent to fetch our daily provisions came running back, flustered and tongue-tied, saying that two goddesses, one blond and one brunette, had emerged from the sea and were strolling toward us down the beach. I crept down the path and had a look at them from behind some rocks. If they had emerged from the sea, they were curiously dry from head to toe, and if they were goddesses, it was a strange thing that they should be dressed in common gowns much less beautiful than they were themselves.

''I let them see me and they came forward without hesitation. The blonde stepped forward and announced that she was Alethea, a slave, and asked if I was her master. I realized then that Vibius had sent them, knowing that I had not been with a woman since leaving Rome and wanting to be the best host he could to a young man of twenty-five. Alethea and Diona made the rest of those eight months far more pleasurable."

"How did your sojourn end?" I asked.

"Word came that Cinna had been killed and Marius was vulnerable at last. I gathered up all the supporters I could find and went to join Sulla."

"And the slave girls?" asked Fabius.

Crassus smiled. "Some years later I bought them from Vibius. Their beauty had not yet faded, nor had my youth. We had a most amusing reunion. I found a place for them at my house in Rome, and they have served me there ever since. I have made sure they are well provided for."

"A charming episode in such a turbulent and fascinating life!" said Dionysius, clapping his hands together. "How that story has always fascinated me, especially in recent days. There is something so lovely and elusive about its incongruous elements—the idea of a cave on the sea used for a hiding place, the image of a beautiful girl bringing sustenance to the fugitive, the beguiling improbability of it all. It's almost too much like a fable to have actually happened. Do you imagine that such a thing could ever take place again? That such a strange circumstance could be twisted a bit askew and occur in another place, another time?"

Dionysius was quite full of himself, purring like a cat in the delight of his own rhetoric, but I found myself looking instead at Olympias, who was visibly trembling, and at Iaia, who reached for her protégée's hand and squeezed it, not too gently to judge by the way the girl's flesh turned white in her grip.

"Are you posing some sort of conundrum?" asked Crassus, growing bored again.

"Perhaps," said Dionysius. "Or perhaps not. There are many peculiar things afoot in the world today, the alarming sorts of things that happen when the will of the gods is distorted and the line between slave and free becomes blurred. Amid such chaos, unnatural alliances are forged and wicked betrayals flourish. Thus we come to have a man like Gordianus in our midst. Is he not here to uncover truth and melt away our distrust? Tell me, Gordianus, would you object if I decided to pose as your rival in this quest for knowledge? The philosopher versus the Finder? What would you say to that, Crassus?"

Crassus looked at him darkly, trying, as I was, to fathom his purpose. "If you mean that you can solve the mystery surrounding the murder of my cousin Lucius—"

"That is exactly what I mean. Along with Gordianus, parallel with him, you might say, I have been conducting my own investigation, though along somewhat different lines of inquiry. I have nothing to reveal at this moment, but I think that very soon I shall be able to answer all the questions that have arisen from this tragic event. I consider it my duty as a philosopher, and as your friend, Marcus Crassus." He set his jaw in a rigid, mirthless smile and looked from face to face around the room. "Ah, but the meal must now be over, for my concoction has arrived."

Dionysius took the cup from the slave who stood silently waiting beside his couch. He sipped at the green froth. Beside him Olympias and Iaia squirmed as if their couches had been stuffed with tiny nettles. They were trying very hard, I thought, to conceal the quiet panic that had slowly crept over them, and they were failing miserably.

FIFTEEN

"NOT another bite until tomorrow evening. Imagine that!" Sergius Orata stood alone on the terrace outside the dining room. He looked over his shoulder at my arrival, then gazed wistfully toward the lights of Puteoli, as if he could smell the aroma of a late dinner being served across the bay. "Fasting is bad enough, but to do it after such a dreary meal. My stomach will be growling all through the funeral orations. Lucius Licinius wouldn't have wanted it that way. With Lucius here, every night was a feast."

Around us the treetops soughed in the breeze. Within the house the slaves were quietly gathering up the remains of the evening's repast with a muffled clatter of knives and spoons. Fitting the solemnity of the occasion, there had been no entertainment following the meal. As soon as Marcus Crassus had risen and excused himself, the other guests had dispersed like anxious children dismissed by their tutor. Eco, hardly able to keep his eyes open, had gone straight to bed. Only Orata and I remained. I imagined that he lingered close by the ghost of the dinner as a frustrated lover might linger about his beloved's empty bed, brooding over the smell and the memory of what he craved but could not have.

"Was Lucius Licinius so extravagant?" I asked.

"Extravagant? Lucius?" Orata shrugged his round shoulders. "Not by Baian standards. By Roman standards I suppose he might be the sort against whom the Senate is always threatening to pass some punitive sumptuary law. Let us say he spent his money with relish."

"Or spent Crassus's money?"

Orata wrinkled his brow. "Strictly speaking. And yet . . ."

I stood beside him and leaned against the stone railing. After the first chill of evening the air seemed to have calmed and grown slightly warmer, as sometimes happens on the Cup. I studied the line of lights, as tiny as stars, that ringed the coastline. Areas of darkness alternated with clusters of muted fire, where the towns sparkled like jewels in the crystalline air.

"You were here the night Lucius was murdered, weren't you?" I said quietly. "It must have been a considerable shock to awaken the next morning and find—"

"A shock, indeed. And when I learned of the name scrawled at his feet, and the fact that his slaves were responsible—imagine, they might have murdered us all in our sleep! Such a thing actually happened only a few weeks ago down in Lucania, when Spartacus was fighting his way to Thurii. A wealthy family was massacred in the night, along with all their houseguests. The women were raped; the children were made to watch their fathers beheaded. It makes the blood run cold."

I nodded. "Your visit here—it was strictly for pleasure?"

Orata smiled faintly. "I seldom do anything strictly for pleasure. Even eating serves a vital purpose, does it not? I do a great deal of visiting around the Cup at all seasons of the year; I enjoy it immensely. But there's always time for business. To be utterly idle and to pursue pleasure for its own end is decadent. I must always be striving toward some object; I was born in Puteoli, but I think I follow the Roman virtues."

"Then you had business with Lucius Licinius?"

"There were plans afoot."

"You had already rebuilt his baths—a stunning piece of work." He smiled at the compliment. "What more was there to do? Build a fish pond?"

"To start with."

"I was joking."

"Do not joke about fish ponds here in Baiae. Here, great men weep tears of grief when their mullets die, and tears of joy when they spawn."

"In Rome they say that the Baians have developed a positive mania for pisciculture."

"They've turned it into a vice," Orata confided with a laugh, "the way the Parthians are said to turn simple horse racing into a vice. But it brings a tidy profit for the man who knows the secrets of the trade."

"It's an expensive hobby?"

"It can be."

"And Lucius was prepared to indulge in it? I don't understand. Was he wealthy or not? If he had so much money, why did he not own his own home?"

"Actually . . ." Orata paused and his face lengthened. "You must understand, Gordianus, that after my ancestors and the gods there is nothing I respect so much as the confidentiality of another man's private finances. I'm not the sort to gossip about the source or extent of someone else's wealth. But since Lucius is dead . . ."

"Yes?"

"May his shade forgive me if I tell you that there was more than met the eye when it came to Lucius's finances."

"I don't follow you."

"Lucius had all sorts of improvements in mind for this villa. Expensive renovations and additions. That was why he asked me to the house for a few days, to discuss the feasibility and expense of some projects he had in mind."

"But why would he spend so much to improve a house in which he was only a tenant?"

"Because he was planning to buy the house from Crassus, very soon."

"Did Crassus know this?"

"I think not. Lucius told me he would be approaching Crassus with an offer within a month or so, and he seemed quite confident that Crassus would accept. Do you have any idea what a villa like this costs, especially when you consider the expenses of running the place?" Orata lowered his voice. "He told me, very confidentially, that his chance to break away from Crassus had come at last. He suggested that he and I should launch a partnership; my business expertise matched with his capital, he said. He came up with some good ideas, I must admit."

"But you were wary."

"The word 'partnership' always makes me wary. I learned early on always to make my own way."

"But if Lucius was offering the money—"

"That's just it: where did he get it? When I rebuilt the baths here, it was Crassus who signed the final contract, and Crassus always saw that I received my payments on time. But occasionally there were incidental expenses, little things about which Lucius hated to bother Crassus, so Lucius would pay for them himself. He always acted as if it were a great sacrifice just to come up with a few sesterces to buy a wagonload of lime." Orata wrinkled his plump brow. "I told you earlier that Lucius always served sumptuous dinners, but that was only in the last year or two. Before that, he always pretended to be better off than he was. You could see the brass beneath the gold, so to speak—the oysters might be fresh, but you could see that the slaves kept washing the same silver spoons to serve each new course because there weren't enough silver spoons to go around."

"A subtle point, surely."

"In my line of work one learns to observe the fine distinctions between true wealth and pretense. I hate being left with a bill I can't collect."

"And in the last year or so Lucius had managed to buy all the silver spoons he needed?"

"Exactly. And he seemed to be in the market for more."

"I suppose he must have been saving his stipend from Crassus for a long time."

Orata shook his head glumly.

"Then what? Did he have some other source of income?"

"None that I know of. And there is very little that transpires on the Cup that I don't know about—very little of a legitimate, legal nature, that is."

"Do you mean—"

"I only mean that Lucius's sudden wealth was an enigma to me."

"And to Crassus?"

"I don't think Crassus knew about it."

"But what could Lucius have done, without Crassus's even knowing? Are you suggesting some clandestine—"

"I suggest nothing," Orata blandly insisted. He turned from the view of the bay and looked into the house. The last traces of the dinner had vanished; even the serving tables had been taken away. He sighed and suddenly seemed to lose all interest in our conversation. "I think I shall go to my room now."

"But, Sergius Orata, surely you have some ideas, some suspicions—"

He shrugged quite extravagantly, a well-practiced gesture good for escaping unwanted investors and clients too small to bother with. "I only know that one of Marcus Crassus's reasons for coming here was to have a careful look at Lucius's financial records, so that Crassus might assess his own resources on the Cup. If he looks long and hard enough, I suspect that Crassus may uncover some very unpleasant surprises."

On my way to the library I avoided walking through the atrium where the remains of Lucius Licinius were displayed; if a part of my mission now included uncovering some embarrassing transactions or even criminal activity on his part, I did not care to encounter his shade in the middle of the night. I took a lamp to find my way through the unfamiliar halls, but hardly needed it; moonlight poured like liquid silver through the windows and skylights, flooding the halls and open spaces with a cold luminescence.

I hoped to find the library empty, but when I turned the corner I saw the same bodyguard who had attended the door the previous night. At my approach he turned his head with military precision and fixed me with a piercing gaze. His stare softened when he recognized me. The frigid mask of his face loosened; indeed, the closer I came the more chagrined he looked. When I was close enough to hear the voices from within, I understood his embarrassment.

They must have been speaking quite loudly for the sound to pass through the heavy oak door. Crassus's voice, with its oratorical training, penetrated more clearly; the other voice had a lower, rumbling timbre that was less easy to distinguish, but the bombastic tone unmistakably belonged to Marcus Mummius.

"For the last time, there will be no exceptions!" This came from Crassus. A rumbling retort from Mummius followed, too muffled for me to catch more than a few words—"how many times . . . always loyal, even when . . . you owe me this favor . . ."

"No, Marcus, not even as a favor!" Crassus shouted. "Stop dredging up the dead past. This is a matter of policy—there's nothing personal in it. If I allow even a single sentimental exception, there will be no end to it—Gelina will have me save them all! How do you think that would look in Rome? No, I won't be made a fool of because you lack the good sense to avoid this kind of petty attachment—"

This evoked angry shouting from Mummius; I was unable to make out the words, but there was no mistaking the note of anguish amid the fury. An instant later the door abruptly opened, so violently that the bodyguard started back and drew his sword.

Mummius emerged, red-faced, his eyes bulging, his jaw set hard enough to grind stones. He turned back toward the room and clenched his fists at his sides, making the veins in his thick forearms writhe like the one that pulsed across his forehead. "If you and Lucius had allowed me to buy him for myself, this wouldn't be happening! You wouldn't be able to touch the boy! If Jupiter himself tried to harm a hair on his head, I would—"

He made a choking noise and began to shake, unable to go on. For the first time he seemed to notice that someone else was in the hall. He turned to look blankly first at the guard and then at me. His furious expression never changed, but his eyes began to glisten hotly as they filled with tears.

Farther down the hall, toward the atrium, a door opened. Gelina, her hair awry, her makeup smeared, peered toward us with a look of confusion. "Lucius?" she whispered hoarsely. Even from such a distance I could smell the wine from her pores.

Crassus emerged from the library. There was a moment of strained silence. "Gelina, go back to your bed," Crassus said sternly. She drew her eyebrows together and meekly obeyed. Crassus dilated his nostrils with a deep breath and lifted his chin. For a long moment Mummius returned his stare, then spun around and hurried down the hallway without a word. The young guard silently sheathed his sword, clenched his jaw, and stared straight ahead. I opened my mouth, searching for some way to explain my presence, but Crassus relieved me of the obligation.

"Don't stand there gaping in the hall. Come inside!"

With the typical good manners of the nobility, Crassus said nothing at all about the argument I had just witnessed. Except for a slight flush across his forehead and a sigh that escaped his lips as he shut the door behind us, it might never have happened. As on the night before, he wore a Greek chlamys rather than a cloak to ward off the chill; apparently the altercation had warmed him enough, for he stripped off the garment and tossed it onto the centaur statue. "Wine?" he offered, taking a cup from the shelf. I noticed there were two cups already on the table, one for himself and another for Mummius; both were empty.

"Are we not fasting?"

Crassus raised an eyebrow. "I have it on good authority that one need not abstain from wine while fasting for the dead. The custom can be bent either way, I am told, and in my experience it is always best to bend custom to present need."

"On good authority, you say?" I accepted the chair that Crassus offered while he turned his around and leaned against the table, which was littered with documents.

Crassus smiled and sipped his wine. He shut his eyes and ran his fingers through his thinning hair. He suddenly looked very weary. "Good authority, indeed. Dionysius tells me that wine is the metaphysical equivalent of blood, and so should not be denied to a fasting man, any more than the air he breathes."

"I suspect that Dionysius is ready to tell you anything he thinks you might want to hear."

Crassus nodded. "Exactly. A hopeless sycophant—and sycophants are not what I need at the moment. What was all that nonsense this evening, about his being your rival? Have you offended him?"

"I've hardly spoken to him."

"Ah, then he's concocted this scheme to solve Lucius's murder on his own, thinking he can use it to impress me. You see what's happening, don't you? With Lucius gone and the household about to dissolve . . . one way or another . . . he'll be needing a new patron and a new residence."

"And he would like to attach himself to you?"

Crassus laughed mirthlessly and drank more wine. "I suppose I should be flattered. Clearly he thinks I'm on my way up. Spartacus has only humiliated two Roman consuls and defeated every army that's been sent to destroy him; what do I have to worry about?"

This note of self-doubt was so unexpected that for a moment I missed it entirely. "Is it so certain then that you'll be given the command against Spartacus?"

"Who else would take it? Every politician in Rome with military experience is quaking with fear. They want Spartacus to be someone else's problem."

"What about—"

"Don't even say his name! If I never heard it again, I could die happily." Crassus slumped against the table. His expression softened. "Actually, I don't hate Pompey. We were good comrades, under Sulla. No one can say that his glory is unearned. The man is brilliant—a great tactician, a splendid leader, a superb politician. Handsome as a demigod, too. He really does look like a bust of Alexander, or used to. And rich! People say that I'm rich, but they forget that Pompey's as wealthy as I am, if not wealthier. Pompey, they say, is brilliant, Pompey is handsome, but rich is something they say only about me—'Crassus, Crassus, rich as Croesus.' " He reached for the wine and poured himself another cup. He offered more to me, but I showed him that my cup was still half full. "Besides, Pompey has his hands full in Spain, mopping up that rebel Sertorius. He can't possibly get back in time to put an end to Spartacus. Actually, he could, but he won't, because I'll have done the job already. What do you know about Spartacus, anyway?"

"No more than the merchants down at the Subura markets know, when they tell me their prices have tripled because of someone called Spartacus."

"It all comes down to that, doesn't it? They can burn a whole town in the countryside and hang the city fathers by their ankles, but the real rub comes when Spartacus and his nasty little revolt start making life uneasy for the rabble in Rome. The situation is so absurd that no one could have invented it; it's like a nightmare that won't go away. Do you know where it started?"

"Capua, wasn't it?"

Crassus nodded. "Just a short ride from here, up the Via Consularis from Puteoli. A fool named Batiatus ran a gladiator farm on the edge of town; bought his slaves wholesale, weeded out the weak, trained the strong ones and sold them to clients all over Italy. He came into a number of Thracians—good fighters, but notoriously temperamental. Batiatus decided to put them in their place from the very start, so he kept them in cages like beasts and fed them nothing but thin gruel and water, letting them out only for their exercises and training. The idiot! Why is it that men who would never think of beating a horse or salting a patch of good earth can be so reckless with their human property? Especially a piece of property that knows how to carry a weapon and kill. A slave is a tool—use it wisely and you profit, use it foolishly and your efforts are wasted.

"But I was talking about Spartacus. In the normal course of things these Thracians would have been broken to Batiatus's will, one way or another, or they might have revolted against him and been killed on the spot, putting a sorry end to a sorry episode. But among their number was a man called Spartacus. It happens sometimes that even among slaves you'll find a man of forceful character, a brute with a way of making other brutes gather around him to do his will. There's nothing mystical about it—I suppose Dionysius has babbled on to you about his history of the supposed magician Eunus and the slave revolt in Sicily sixty years ago, a thoroughly disgusting episode; at least it was contained on an island. They're already saying the same sort of rubbish about Spartacus, that before he was sold into slavery he was seen sleeping with snakes coiled around his head, and the slave he calls his wife is some sort of prophetess who goes into convulsions and speaks for the god Bacchus."

"So they say down in the Subura markets," I admitted.

Crassus wrinkled his nose. "Why anyone would live in the Subura when there are so many decent neighborhoods in Rome—"

"My father left me a house, up on the Esquiline," I explained.

"Take my advice and sell whatever sort of rattrap you've got on the Esquiline and buy a newer place outside the city walls; out on the Campus Martius beyond the Forum Holitorium there's a lot of new building going on, by the old naval yards. Close by the river, clean air, good values. More wine?"

I accepted. Crassus rubbed his eyes, but from the way he ground his jaw I could see he was not sleepy.

"But we were talking about Spartacus," he said. "In the beginning there were only seventy of them—can you imagine, just seventy miserable Thracian gladiators who decided to escape from their master. They didn't even have a plan; they were going to bide their time and look for an opportunity, but then one of their number betrayed them—slaves always betray one another—and they acted on impulse, using axes and spits from the cookhouse for weapons. The goddess Fortune must have looked down and been amused, because on their way out of town they came upon a driver with a cart full of real weapons, headed for Batiatus's gladiator farm. From then on it seemed that nothing could stop them. To be sure, the threat was badly gauged at the start; no one in Rome could take a revolt of gladiators seriously, so they sent out Clodius with a half legion of irregulars, thinking that would be the end of it. Ha! It was merely the end of Clodius's career in politics. Victory feeds on victory; every time he triumphed over Roman arms Spartacus found it easier to incite more slaves to join him. They say he now commands a movable nation of over a hundred thousand men, women, and children. And not only slaves; even freeborn herdsmen and shepherds have cast their lot with him. For one thing, they say he hands out the booty with no regard for rank or station; his foot soldiers get as great a share as his generals."

Crassus curled his lip as if his wine had gone sour. "The whole affair is perverse! To think it should come to this, that I should be scrambling for glory by pitting myself against a slave, a gladiator. The Senate won't even allow me a triumph in Rome if I win, never mind that Spartacus is a greater threat to the Republic than Mithridates or Jugurtha ever were. I'll be lucky if they give me a garland. And if I should lose . . ." A shadow crossed his face. He muttered a prayer of supplication, dabbed his fingers in his wine cup and tossed the drops over his shoulder.

It seemed a good time to change the subject. "Was it true, the story that Dionysius told this evening, about the sea cave?"

Crassus smiled, as he had at dinner. "Every word. Oh, I suppose it's become a bit embellished in the retelling over the years, given a nostalgic polish. In many ways those were terrible times for me, miserable months of anxious waiting. And grief." He swirled his cup and studied its depths. "It is a hard thing for a young man to lose his father, especially to suicide. His enemies drove him to it. And an older brother, assassinated only because Cinna and Marius were bent on destroying the best families in Rome. They would have wiped out the nobility altogether if they could have. Thank the gods, and especially Fortune, that Sulla rose up to save us."

He sighed. "Do you know, stuck in that miserable cave day after day, month after month, I made a vow to myself every morning: They won't get *me*, I said. They struck down my father, they struck down my brother, but I will not be struck down! And so far I haven't been."

He swirled his cup and blinked, squeezing his eyes shut and opening them wide, looking weary but far from sleep.

"I did the right thing, you know, the pious thing. I honored the gods and the shades of the dead. I paid my father's debts, though it left me with nothing, and I took up his cause, and when the times became more settled I married my brother's widow. I married Tertulla for piety, not love; even so, I have never regretted the choice. Not all of us can indulge ourselves in cheap sentiment, like Lucius Licinius. Or Mummius!" he snorted. "Now Lucius is dead, and I—I am either the man of the hour, as Dionysius will gladly tell you, or else a man who is marching steadily and without the slightest hesitation toward his utter ruination at the hands of a slave. I would rather see my wealth vanish than to hear them whisper behind my back in the Forum: 'He was brought low by a mere gladiator. . . .' "

While I shifted uneasily in my chair, he paused to sip from his cup. "You think I should spare the slaves, don't you, Gordianus?"

"If I can prove to you that they should not die."

He shook his head sadly. "All men are fated to die, Gordianus. Why does the idea fill them with such abhorrence? Wealth and possessions, joy and pain, even the body—especially the body—all these vanish in the well of time. Only honor matters in the end. Honor is what men remember. Or dishonor."

Such a way of thinking sums up the difference between nobles and ordinary men, I thought; it excuses the most horrifying atrocities and lets go the simplest opportunities for charity and mercy.

"But you must have come here for a reason," said Crassus, "unless you were merely eavesdropping. Do you have something to report, Gordianus?"

"Only that we found the body of one of the missing slaves."

"Yes?" He raised an eyebrow. "Which one?"

"The old secretary, Zeno."

"Where was he? My men supposedly searched every possible hiding place within a day's ride."

"He was in plain sight. Or at least what was left of him. Somehow he ended up in Lake Avernus. We found his remains on the shoreline; most of his body had been eaten away. Fortunately, enough remained of his face for Olympias to recognize him."

"Avernus! I know for a fact that before he left for Rome Mummius assigned a group of men to search the whole area around the lake, including the shore. How long had Zeno been there?"

"For days, at least."

"Then somehow they missed finding him. Probably one of them saw a bit of mist in the shape of his dead wife, or the lake spat like a baby with colic, and the whole lot of them turned and ran, then they lied when they reported there was nothing to find. They will have to be disciplined; the time to make one's authority clear is long before the fighting starts. Just another of the endless details I shall have to attend to tomorrow!" He turned wearily toward the table and rifled among the documents until he found a wax tablet and stylus. He scribbled a note and tossed the tablet back onto the table. "Where is the body of Zeno now, or what remains of it?"

"There was very little of him left, as I said. Unfortunately, my son Eco slipped in the mud while he was carrying the head along the shore; it fell into a boiling pool of water. . . ." I shrugged. I was uncertain why I lied, except that I wanted to avoid calling attention to Olympias.

"You mean you have nothing to show me?" Crassus suddenly seemed to have reached the end of his patience. "This whole business is absurd. Between you and Gelina and Mummius—really, it's been a very long day, Gordianus, and tomorrow will be even longer. I think you may go now."

"Of course." I stood and began to turn, then stopped. "One other thing, if I may impose on your patience for another moment, Marcus Crassus. I see that you've been looking over Lucius Licinius's documents."

"Yes?"

"I wonder if you've come across anything . . . untoward?"

"What do you mean?"

"I'm not sure. Sometimes a man's records can reveal unexpected things. There might be something among all those documents that might have a bearing on my own work."

"I can't imagine how. The truth is, Lucius usually kept impeccable records; I required him to do so. When I was here in the spring I looked over his ledgers and found everything accounted for, using the methods I had prescribed. Now it's all a puzzle."

"In what way?"

"Expenses have been entered with no explanation. There are contradictory indications of how often he used the *Fury*, and on what errands. Stranger still, it seems to me that some documents must be missing altogether. I thought at first that I could reconstruct and make sense of them by myself, but I think I shall be unable to. I'd have brought along my chief accountant from Rome if I'd known the state of things, but I had no idea that Lucius's affairs were in such chaos."

"And do you find any of this suggestive?"

"Suggestive of what?" He looked at me quizzically, then snorted. "With you, everything comes back to the murder. Yes, it suggests something to me—namely, that the old secretary Zeno had made such a muddle of things that Lucius decided to give him a sound beating, whereupon the hotheaded young stableman Alexandros exploded in a Thracian rage and killed his master, whereupon the two slaves fled into the night, only to find themselves swallowed up by the Jaws of Hades. There, I've done your work for you, Gordianus. Now you can go to bed content."

From the tone of his voice I knew that Crassus insisted on having the final word. I was at the door, reaching to open it, when my hand froze. Something had been not quite right from the moment I entered the room; I had felt an apprehension so vague that I had dismissed it as one blinks away a mote of dust. At that instant I knew what it was, and that I had seen it not once, but over and over as I had sat listening to Crassus and letting my eyes wander about the room.

I turned and walked to the little statue of Hercules in his lion hood.

"Marcus Crassus, was there a guard on this room during the day?"

"Of course not. My bodyguards go where I go. The room was empty, so far as I know. No one has legitimate business to come into this room except me."

"But someone might have entered?"

"I suppose. Why do you ask?"

"Marcus Crassus, you mentioned the blood on this statue to no one?"

"Not even to Morpheus," he said wearily, "with whom I have a meeting long overdue."

"And yet someone else in the house knew of it. Because since last we spoke someone has done a thorough job of removing the dried blood from the lion's mane."

"What?"

"See here, where last night there was plentiful evidence of blood trapped in the sculpted furrows, someone has since then deliberately and carefully scraped them clean. You can even see where the metal has been newly scratched."

He pursed his lips. "What of it?"

"The rest of the room isn't freshly cleaned; I see dust on the shelves, and a circle from a wine cup on the table. It seems unlikely that a slave would have given such a thorough cleaning to this particular object in this particular room, with so much other work to do in preparation for the funeral. Besides, any domestic slave fit for this house would have known how to clean a statue without scarring the metal. No, I think this was done hurriedly by someone who didn't know that the blood had already been noticed, and hoped to prevent us from seeing it. That someone was not Alexandros, and it surely was not Zeno. Whereby it follows that the murderer of Lucius Licinius, or someone who knows something about the murder, is here among us, actively concealing evidence."

"Possibly," Crassus admitted, sounding weary and cross. "It's getting chilly," he complained, plucking his chlamys from the centaur statue and wrapping it across his shoulders.

"Marcus Crassus, I think it might be a good idea to place

a guard inside this room at all times, to make sure that nothing else is taken or altered without our knowledge."

"If you wish. Now, is there anything else?"

"Nothing, Marcus Crassus," I said quietly as I left the room, walking backward and nodding my head in deference.

SIXTEEN

WHY you? asked Eco, signing skeptically the next morning when I told him of my midnight conversation with Crassus. I took the question to mean: *Why should such a great man confide so much to a man like you?*

"Why not?" I said, splashing my face with cold water. "Whom else can he talk to in this house?"

Eco squared his shoulders and mimed a beard on his face.

"Yes, Marcus Mummius is his old friend and confidant, but at the moment they're feuding about the fate of the slave, Apollonius."

Eco stuck his nose in the air and painted tendrils of hair swept back from his forehead.

"Yes, there's Faustus Fabius, but I can't imagine Crassus showing weakness to a patrician, especially a patrician who happens to be his subordinate."

Eco circled his arms in a hoop before him and puffed his cheeks. I shook my head. "Sergius Orata? No, Crassus would be even less likely to show weakness to a business associate. A philosopher would be a natural choice, but if Crassus has one, he's left him behind in Rome, and he despises Dionysius. Yet Crassus desperately needs someone, anyone, to listen to him—here and now, because the gods are too far away. He faces a great crisis; he is full of doubt. Doubt hounds him from hour to hour, moment to moment, and not just about his decision to take on Spartacus. I think he secretly doubts even his decision to massacre Gelina's slaves. He's a man used to absolute control and clear-cut decisions, counting up tangible profits and losses. The past haunts him—bloody chaos and the death of those he loved most. Now he's about to step into a dark and uncertain future—a terrible gamble, but one worth taking, because if he succeeds he may at last become so powerful that no power on earth can ever harm him again."

I shrugged. "So why not tell everything to Gordianus the Finder, from whom no one can keep a secret anyway? As for confidentiality, I'm famous for it—almost as well known for keeping my mouth shut as you are."

Eco splashed me with a handful of water.

"Stop that! Besides, there's something about me that compels others to empty their hearts." I said it jokingly, but it was true; there are those to whom others quite naturally confide their deepest secrets, and I have always been one of them. I looked at myself in the mirror. If the power to pull the truth from others resided somewhere in my face, I couldn't see it. It was a common face, I thought, with a nose that looked as if it had been broken, though it had not, common brown eyes and common black curls streaked with more and more strands of silver every year. With the passing of time it had come to remind me of my father's face, as best as I could recall it. My mother I barely remembered, but if my father told the truth when he insisted she had been beautiful, then I had not inherited her looks.

It was also a face that badly needed a shave, if I was to put in a decent appearance at the funeral of Lucius Licinius.

"Come, Eco. Surely out of ninety-nine slaves Gelina has one who's a decent barber. You shall have a shave as well." I said it just to please him, but when I glanced at his smiling face in the morning sunlight, I saw that there actually was a faint shadow across his jaw.

"Yesterday you were a boy," I whispered, under my breath.

Ironic as it sounds, there is nothing quite so alive as a Roman household on the day of a funeral. The villa was full of guests, who thronged the atrium and the hallways and spilled over into the baths. While Eco and I reclined on couches, submitting our jaws to be shaved, naked strangers loitered about the pools, refreshing themselves after hard morning rides from points as distant as Capua and the far side of Vesuvius. Others had arrived by boat, ferried across the bay from Surrentum, Stabiae, and Pompeii. After my ablutions I stood on the terrace of the baths and looked down on the boathouse, where the short pier was too small for all the arrivals; skiffs and barges were lashed to one another, so that the later arrivals had to walk to the pier over a small floating city of boats.

Metrobius, draped in a voluminous towel, joined me on the balcony. "Lucius Licinius must have been a popular man," I said.

He snorted. "Don't imagine they've all come just to see poor Lucius go up in smoke. No, all these wealthy merchants and landowners and vacationing nobility are here for quite a different reason. They want to impress you-know-who." He glanced over his shoulder toward the heated pool, where the slave Apollonius was helping an old man emerge from the water. "I had to push and shove all through the house to get here. The atrium is already so crowded I could hardly cross it. I haven't seen so much black in one place since Sulla died over in Puteoli. Though I noticed," he said, wrinkling his nose, "that most of the visitors were giving the corpse a wide berth." He laughed softly. "And they're already whispering jokes; usually that doesn't start until *after* the ceremony, when the eating begins."

"Jokes?"

"You know—stepping up to the bier, peering into the corpse's mouth, then sighing, 'The coin is still there! Imagine that, with Crassus in the house!' And don't you dare repeat that to Crassus," he quickly added. "Or at least don't tell him that you heard it from me." He stepped away with a dry smile. Apparently he had forgotten that he had told me the same joke the day before.

I peered over the balcony again, wondering how I would ever manage to discover what had been dumped off the pier with so many vessels moored there. Many of the rowers were still in their boats, or loitered about the boathouse, waiting for their masters to return.

Eventually I found Eco, who had disappeared into one of

the cubicles for a cool bath to follow his hot one. We dressed in the somber black garments that had been laid out for us that morning. The slave Apollonius assisted us with the various tucks and folds. His bearing was grave, as suited the occasion, but his eyes were a clear and dazzling blue, unclouded by the fear that haunted the eyes of the other slaves. Was it possible that Mummius had somehow kept him from knowing what the next day might bring? More likely, I thought, Mummius had secretly assured him that he himself would be spared. Did he know that Mummius had failed to sway Crassus?

As he dressed me, I took the opportunity to study him more closely. That he was beautiful was obvious at a glance, and yet the closer and longer I looked the more beautiful he seemed. His perfection was almost unreal, like the famous Discus Thrower of Myron come to life; as he moved, the shifting planes of light across his face highlighted a succession of cameos, each more striking than the last. Where many youths of his age have a stumbling gait, he moved like an athlete or a dancer, without any trace of artifice. His hands were nimble, infusing every movement with an innate and unassuming grace. When he stood close to me, I felt the heat of his hands and smelled the warm sweetness of his breath.

There are rare moments when one senses not the surface of other men and women, but the very life force which animates their being, and by extension all life. I have glimpsed it in moments of passion with Bethesda, and on a few other occasions, in the presence of men or women in great extremity, in the throes of orgasm or close to death or otherwise reduced by crisis to their very essence. It is a frightening and an awesome thing to see beyond the veils of the flesh into the soul. Somehow the force of life in Apollonius was so great that it rent through those veils, or else suffused them with the perfect physical embodiment of itself. It was hard to look at him and imagine that something so alive, so perfect could ever grow old and die, much less be snuffed out in an instant merely for the aggrandizement of a politician's career.

I suddenly felt a great pity for Marcus Mummius. On the journey from Rome, aboard the *Fury*, I had callously remarked that he had no poetry in his soul. I had spoken rashly and in ignorance. Mummius had touched the face of Eros and been stricken; no wonder he was so desperate to save the boy from a senseless death at the hands of Crassus.

Little by little the guests emptied the house and lined the road that led away from the villa. Those who had been closest to Gelina or Lucius congregated in the courtyard to become part of the procession. The Designator, a small wizened man whom Crassus had hired and brought over from Puteoli, set about arranging the participants in their places. Eco and I, having no place in the procession, walked on ahead to find a sunny spot on the crowded tree-lined road.

At length we heard the strains of mournful music. The sound grew louder as the procession came into view. The musicians led the way, blowing on horns and flutes and shaking bronze rattles. In Rome, deference to public opinion and the ancient Law of the Twelve Tables might have restricted the number of musicians to ten, but Crassus had hired at least twice that number. Clearly, he meant to impress.

Next came the hired mourners, a coterie of women who walked with a shuffling gait, wore their hair undressed and chanted a refrain that paraphrased the playwright Naevius's famous epitaph: "If the death of any mortal saddens hearts immortal, the gods above must this man's death bemoan. . . ." They stared straight ahead, oblivious of the crowd; they shivered and wept until great torrents of tears streamed down their cheeks.

There was a small gap in the procession, just long enough for the plaintive song of the mourners to recede before the buffoons and mummers arrived. Eco brightened at their approach, but I inwardly groaned; there is nothing quite so embarrassing as a funeral procession marred by incompetent clowns. These, however, were quite good; even at the end of the holiday season, there is no lack of first-rate entertainers on the Cup, and the Designator had hired the best. While some of them resorted to crude but effective slapstick, drawing polite laughter from the crowd, there was one among them with a stirring voice who recited snatches of tragic poetry. Most of the standard passages used in funeral processions are familiar to me, but these words were from some fresh and unfamiliar poet of the Epicurean school:

> What has death to frighten man,
> If souls can die as bodies can?
> When mortal frame shall be disbanded,
> This lump of flesh from life unhanded,
> From grief and pain we shall be free—
> We shall not *feel*, for we shall not *be*.
> But suppose that after meeting Fate
> The soul still feels in its divided state.
> What's that to us? For we are only *we*
> While body and soul in one frame agree.
> And if our atoms should revolve by chance
> And our cast-off matter rejoin the dance,
> What gain to us would all this bring?
> This new-made man would be a new-made thing.
> We, dead and gone, would play no part
> In all the pleasures, nor feel the smart
> Which to that new man shall accrue
> Whom of our matter Time molds anew.
> Take heart then, listen and hear:
> What is there left in death to fear?
> After the pause of life has come between,
> All's just the same had we never been.

The reciter was abruptly interrupted by one of the buffoons, who shook a finger in his face. "What a lot of nonsense. My body, my soul, my body, my soul," the buffoon parroted, rocking his head back and forth. "What a lot of Epicurean nonsense! I had an Epicurean philosopher in my house once, but I kicked him out. Give me a dull-as-dishwater Stoic like that clown Dionysius any day!"

There were some warm chuckles of recognition among the crowd. I gathered this must be the Arch Mime, employed by the Designator to present a fond parody of the deceased.

"And don't think for an instant that I'll pay you even half a copper for such pathetic poetry, either," he went on, still wagging his finger, "nor for any of this so-called entertainment. I expect true value for my money, do you understand? True value! Money doesn't fall from the sky, you know, at least not into my hands! Into the hands of my cousin Crassus, maybe, but not mine!" He abruptly pursed his lips and turned on his heel, clasped his hands behind his back and began to pace.

I overheard the man next to me whisper: "He's got Licinius down to perfection!"

"Uncanny!" the man's wife agreed.

"But don't think that just because I *won't* pay you it's because I *can't* pay you," piped the Arch Mime. "I could! I would! Only I owe debts to seven shops in Puteoli and six in Neapolis and five in Surrentum and four in Pompeii and three in Misenum and two in Herculaneum"—the Arch Mime gasped and took a deep breath—"plus a long-standing debt to a little grandmother who sells apples by the side of the road right here in Baiae! Once I have them all paid off, come back and try another poem, you Epicurean fool, and perhaps I'll sing another tune."

"Another tune—" hooted the man beside me.

"Sing another tune!" said his wife, nodding and laughing appreciatively. Apparently the Arch Mime had delivered one of Lucius Licinius's pet phrases.

"Oh, I know," he went on, crossing his arms petulantly, "you all think I'm made of money because I live like a king, but it just isn't so. At least not yet." He bobbed his eyebrows up and down. "But just you wait, because I do have a plan. Oh, yes, a plan, a plan. A plan for making more money than you Baian big boys could swallow with a serving spoon. A plan, a plan. Make way for the man with a plan!" he bleated, breaking character and running to catch up with the other buffoons.

"A plan," the man next to me murmured.

"Just as Lucius was always saying," smiled his wife. "Always going to get rich—tomorrow!" She sighed. "Only this happened instead. The will of the gods—"

"—and the ways of Fortune," the man concluded.

I remembered Sergius Orata's hints of shady dealings. A

disquieting suspicion began to form in my head, then unraveled and vanished with the arrival of the waxen masks.

Lucius's branch of the Licinii family had not been without its distinguished ancestors. Their lifelike images in wax, normally displayed within his foyer, were now paraded before his funeral bier, worn by persons especially hired for the task by the Designator and dressed in the authentic costumes of the offices they had held in service to the state. Such a presentation is part of the funeral procession of every Roman noble. The masked actors walk solemnly, slowly, turning their heads from side to side so that all may see their expressionless faces, looking like the dead come to life. Thus, even in death do the noble distinguish themselves from the ignoble, the "known" from the "unknown," proudly flaunting their lineage to those of us in the crowd who have no ancestors, only parents and forgotten forebears.

Next came Lucius Licinius himself, reposed upon his ivory couch and framed by freshly cut blossoms and boughs, redolent with powerful perfumes that could not quite conceal the scent of putrefaction. Crassus was foremost among the bearers, his face set in a stern, impassive stare.

The family followed. Not many Licinii of Lucius's branch had survived the civil wars, and most of them were of an older generation. Gelina led the group, attended by Metrobius. I have often seen women in funeral processions on the streets of Rome who stagger in a paroxysm of grief, tearing their cheeks in defiance of the laws of the Twelve Tables, but Gelina did not weep. She moved in a stupor, staring at her feet.

Conspicuously absent from the procession were the slaves of the dead man's household.

After the family passed, the onlookers who lined the road closed in behind them and joined the retinue. At length we came to an open spot beside the road, where a break in the trees afforded a glimpse of the bay. Nearby stood a stone sepulcher as tall as a man. It was newly built; the slabs were smooth and unweathered, and the earth surrounding it was worn by footsteps and dusted with chiseled stone. There was only one decoration, a simple bas-relief of a horse's head, the ancient symbol of death and departure.

In the center of the clearing, a funeral pyre had been erected of dried wood piled in the form of a square altar. Normally the ivory couch bearing the corpse might have been tilted against it, as such couches are tilted against the Rostra in the Forum at Rome, so that the spectators may look upon the dead man while the oration is delivered, but Lucius's corpse was placed directly upon the pyre, out of sight, no doubt in deference to the disfiguring wound on his head.

Slaves came forward with folding chairs for the family. As the crowd settled, Marcus Crassus stepped in front of the pyre. A hush fell over the gathering. Overhead a sea gull screamed. A slight breeze stirred the treetops. Crassus began his speech; in his voice there was no hint of the indecision and uncertainty he had shown to me the night before. His was a trained orator's voice, skilled at all the techniques of volume, tonality, and rhythm. He began in a quiet, deferential tone that gradually grew more forceful.

"Gelina, devoted wife of my beloved cousin Lucius Licinius; family members, who have come from places far and near; shades of his ancestors, represented here by their cherished images; friends and members of his household, acquaintances and people of Baiae and all the nearby towns of Campania and the Cup: We have come to entomb Lucius Licinius.

"What a simple thing that seems: A man has died, and so we consume his body with flames and entomb his ashes. It is a common event. Even the fact that he died by violence does not distinguish it; nowadays, such violence has become commonplace. Certainly, in our family, there has been so much grief and loss imposed by violence that we have become brittle and numb to the vagaries of Fortune.

"And yet the presence of so many of you here today is proof that the death of Lucius Licinius was no small thing, just as his life was no small thing. He had many dealings with many men, and who among you can say that he was ever less than honest? He was a Roman, and an embodiment of Roman virtues. He was a fine husband. That the gods had not blessed his marriage with offspring—that he leaves behind no son to carry on his name and blood, to revere him as he revered his ancestors—that is one of the accomplishments left unfulfilled by the untimely and bitter tragedy of his death.

"With no son to look after his grieving widow or to avenge his senseless murder, those duties have fallen to another, to a man tied to Lucius by bonds of blood and long years of mutual respect. Those duties fall to me.

"Word has already spread among you concerning the manner in which Lucius met his death. Have no doubt that he faced it bravely. He was not a man to flinch in the face of any adversary. Perhaps his only fault was that he placed his trust in those who did not deserve it—but what man can foresee the moment when a trusty blade long used will suddenly break, or a loyal dog will turn vicious without warning?

"The fate of Lucius Licinius is far from unique. Indeed, in some ways he is the paradigm of the good citizen, and of the state itself, for does not Rome suddenly find herself imperiled by a whole nation of trusted mastiffs gone mad with a lust for blood and thievery? Lucius was another victim of that pestilence which threatens to overturn the order of nature, to wipe out tradition and honor, to pervert the normal intercourse of affairs between men.

"That pestilence has a name. I will not whisper it, for I do not fear it: *Spartacus*. That pestilence entered even into the household of Lucius Licinius; it dissolved the bonds of obligation and loyalty; it twisted the hands of slaves against their master. What happened in his house cannot be forgotten or forgiven. The shade of Lucius Licinius is restless; it hovers near us even now, strengthened by the shades of his ancestors, who all together clamor that we, the living, must set this wickedness aright."

I looked about me, at the faces of the funeral guests. They watched Crassus with mingled admiration and sorrow, open to whatever pronouncement he was preparing. I felt a pang of dread.

"There are those who might say that Lucius Licinius was

beyond all doubt a good man, but not a great one, that he did not rise in his lifetime to high office, did not accomplish wondrous things. That is the tragic truth, I fear; he was slain before his prime, and his life was smaller than it should have been. But his death was not a small death. If there can be a great death, then the death of Lucius was that—something terrible, awful, profoundly wrong, an offense to god and man alike. Such a death demands more than sorrow and pity, more than words of praise or vows of vengeance. It demands that we all take action, if not as the vessels of vengeance, then as its witnesses."

Crassus lifted his arm. On either side of him the Designator and one of his men set about igniting their torches, which burst into flame.

"Long ago our ancestors founded the tradition of holding gladiatorial contests in honor of the dead. Normally this glorious tradition is reserved for the death of the great and powerful, but I think that the gods will not begrudge our paying honor to the shade of Lucius Licinius with a day of games. These will begin tomorrow upon the plain beside Lake Lucrinus. There are those who whimper that we should suspend the use of gladiators, saying that Spartacus was a gladiator and that no slave should bear arms so long as Spartacus runs loose. But I say it is better to honor the traditions of our ancestors than to fear a slave. I say also that the occasions of these games will give us not only the opportunity to pay our last respects to the shade of Lucius Licinius, but to begin the task of avenging his death."

Crassus stepped aside. He took one of the torches and touched it to the pyre, while opposite him the Designator did the same. The dry wood ignited and crackled, shooting up tongues of flame and fingers of gray smoke.

In time the pyre would be consumed. The embers would be soaked with wine, and the bones and ashes of Lucius Licinius would be gathered up by Crassus and Gelina, who would sprinkle them with perfumes and place them in an alabaster urn. A priest would purify the crowd, moving among them and sprinkling them with water from an olive branch. The remains of Lucius would be sealed into his sepulcher, and together the crowd would murmur, "Farewell, farewell, farewell . . ."

But I left before these things were done. I was not purified; I did not say farewell. Instead I slipped quietly away and returned to the house, taking Eco with me. So little time remained before the slaughter would begin.

SEVENTEEN

WHERE will we find the boy Meto?" I wondered aloud. The atrium, which that morning had been thronged with funeral guests and their attendant slaves, was deserted. Our footsteps echoed hollowly in the empty space. The incense and the flowers were gone, but their odor, like that of the decaying corpse of Lucius Licinius, lingered behind.

I followed my nose to the kitchens. Long before I found them I heard the din of activity. There was much preparation still to be done for the funeral feast.

We stepped through a great wooden door and found ourselves swallowed up by noise and heat. Their tunics spotted with stains and soot, the kitchen slaves scurried about. Hoarse voices cried back and forth, heavy knives chopped against blocks of wood, kettles boiled and hissed. Eco covered his ears to protest the din, then pointed at a figure across the room.

Little Meto, standing on a stool, was reaching into a deep clay pot atop a table. He looked around to see that no one was watching, then pulled out a handful of something and stuck it into his mouth. I walked across the room, dodging to avoid the hurrying slaves, and grabbed the neck of his tunic.

He gave a squawk and looked over his shoulder at me. His mouth, covered with a paste of honey, millet, and crushed nuts, opened in a cry of distress, then turned abruptly into a grin when he saw my face—and as abruptly twisted into a howl of pain when a wooden spoon came down on his head with a crack.

"Out of the kitchen! Out! Out!" screamed an old slave

whose superior dress and manner marked him as the chief cook. He seemed ready to strike me as well, then saw the iron ring I wore. "Forgive me, Citizen, but between Meto pilfering sweets, and the slaves of all these guests sneaking in to steal food, we can hardly do our work. Could you please find an errand for the little pest?"

"Precisely what I came for," I said. I gave Meto a sharp slap on the rump as he hopped off the stool and scurried across the crowded room, licking the honey from his fingers and tripping cooks and helpers in his wake. Eco caught him at the door and held him for me.

"Meto!" I cried, catching up and closing the door behind us. "Just the man I was looking for. Are you a swimmer, Meto?"

He looked up at me gravely, licking the sweet mash from the corners of his mouth. He slowly shook his head.

"No?"

"No, sir."

"You don't swim at all?"

"Not a stroke," he assured me.

I shook my head, vexed. "You disappoint me, Meto, though it's no fault of your own. I had convinced myself that you must be the offspring of a faun and a river nymph."

He was perplexed for a moment, then laughed out loud at my foolishness. "But I know who swims better than anybody!" he offered.

"Yes? Who would that be?"

"Come with me, I'll show you. He's with the others in the stables!" He began to run down the hall, until Eco caught up with him and grabbed the neck of his tunic like a leash. We followed his lead to the center of the house, through the atrium and out into the courtyard. He broke from Eco's grasp and hurried toward the stables. We came to the open doors, where the cooler air from within carried the mingled scents of hay and dung. Meto hurried on.

"Wait! You said you were leading us to the stables!" I protested.

"Not those stables!" he called over his shoulder. He pointed ahead and ran around the corner of the building. I thought he must be playing a game with us, until I turned the corner and saw the long, low wooden annex attached to the stone stables.

"Is there no end to this villa?" I muttered to Eco. Then I saw the soldiers who guarded the doorway to the annex.

The six of them sat cross-legged in a small clearing beneath the evergreens. They failed to see us, until a shrill whistle pierced the air. I looked up and saw a seventh guard atop the red tile roof of the annex, his spear in the crook of his arm and his fingers in his mouth.

The six were on their feet immediately, their swords drawn and their dice abandoned in the dust. Their chief officer—or at least the one with the most insignia—stepped toward me, brandishing his sword and scowling through his gray-streaked beard. "Who are you and what do you want?" he asked gruffly. He ignored Meto, who stepped past him and hurried to the annex door. I gathered that Meto was already known to the guards; one of them even reached down and ruffled his hair affectionately.

I held my hands at my sides, a bit away from my body, in clear sight. Eco glanced at me nervously and did the same. "My name is Gordianus. I'm a guest of Gelina and of your general, Marcus Crassus. This is my son, Eco."

The soldier narrowed his eyes suspiciously, then put his sword away. "It's all right, men," he called over his shoulder. "He's the one Marcus Mummius told us about. Calls himself the Finder. And what do you expect to find here?" He no longer seemed like a fierce warrior ready to kill, but instead appeared quite affable and polite. More than anything else, he looked like an extremely bored man glad for any interruption to break the monotony.

"The slave boy led us here," I explained. "I had forgotten that the stables had an annex."

"Yes, the stables hide it from the courtyard; you can't see it at all from the house, I'm told, not even from the upper story. Which makes it the perfect place to hide them all, nicely out of sight."

"Hide whom?" I said, forgetting what Gelina had told me regarding the whereabouts of most of the slaves.

"See for yourself. It looks like little Meto is quite eager for you to follow him. It's all right, Fronto," he called to the guard who had ruffled Meto's hair. "You can open the door."

The guard produced a large brass key and fitted it into a lock which hung on a chain. The lock opened and the door swung outward. The guards stood at a distance, their hands on their hilts and their eyes alert. Meto ran inside, waving for us to follow.

The smell that came from within was quite different from that which came from the stables. There was the sweet smell of straw, to be sure, but the odor of urine and waste came not from animals but from men. The stench of human sweat was heavy in the air as well, along with the smell of women in period and the mingled odors of rotting food and vomit. It reminded me of the smell below the deck of the *Fury*—not as acrid with the stench of men on the verge of collapse, but not relieved by fresh salt breezes, either; it had the foul, closed, musty stench of the slaughterhouse rather than the slave galley.

Eco balked at stepping within, but I took his arm. The door closed behind us. "Bang on the door and call out when you're ready to leave," yelled the guard through the wood. The chain rattled and the lock snapped shut.

It took my eyes a moment to adjust to the dimness. There were only a few barred windows near the roof, admitting beams of sunlight thick with dust. "What is this place?" I whispered.

I didn't expect an answer, but the boy Meto was nearby. "The master used it to store all sorts of things," he said, pitching his voice low to match mine. "Old bits and saddles and blankets, and broken chariot wheels and ox carts. Sometimes, even swords and spears, and shields and helmets. But it was almost empty when Master Lucius died. When Master Crassus came the next day, this is where he put the slaves, all but a few of us."

The place had fallen silent when we entered, but now voices began to murmur in the darkness. "Meto!" I heard an old woman call out. "Meto, come here and give us a hug!"

The boy disappeared into the shadows. As the room lightened, I saw the woman who embraced him. She sat on the straw-littered floor, her white hair knotted in a bun, her long, pale hands trembling in the dim light as she fondled the boy's hair. Everywhere I looked I saw more and more of them—men, women, and children, all the slaves who had been gathered up from the fields or released from unnecessary tasks in the house and locked away to await the judgment of Crassus.

They sat huddled against the walls. I passed between them, walking the length of the long, narrow room. Eco followed behind me, gazing wide-eyed from face to face and tripping against the uneven floor. The smell of urine and waste grew stronger at the farther end of the room. The slaves forced to sit nearby huddled as far as they could from the stench. Exposed to it day after day, they must have grown used to it, enough to bear it. I covered my face with a fold of my heavy funeral garb, and still I could hardly breathe.

I felt a tug at my knee. Meto gazed up at me gravely. "The best swimmer there ever was," he assured me with a whisper. "Better than Leander, and he could swim across the Hellespont. Better than Glaucus when he swam after Scylla, and Glaucus was half fish!"

No good it will do us if he's locked away here, I thought. Then I saw the young man at whom Meto pointed. The youth knelt on the straw, holding an old man's hands in his own and speaking in a low voice. The pale light gave his face a marmoreal smoothness, so that he looked more than ever like a statue come to life, or a living youth turned to stone.

"Apollonius," I said, surprised to see him here.

He gave the old man's hands a final clasp, then stood and brushed the straw from his knees. The simple motion was as elegant as a poem. There is the haughty, manmade aristocracy of patricians like Faustus Fabius, I thought, and then there is the natural aristocracy of specimens such as this, which proceeds from the gods without regard to earthly status.

"Why are you here?" I asked, thinking Crassus must have

banished him from the house simply to spite Mummius. But his explanation was simple.

"Most of the slaves have been locked away here since the day the master was found dead. A few of us have been allowed to stay at our posts, sleeping in our usual quarters between the stables and the house. Like Meto, I come here as often as I can, to see the others. The guards know me and let me pass."

"Is he your father?" I said, looking down at the old man.

Apollonius smiled, but his eyes looked sad. "I never had a father. Soterus knows herbs and poultices. He tends the other slaves when they're sick, but now he's sick himself. He craves water but can't drink, and his bowels are loose. Look, I think he's sleeping now. Once when I had a bad fever he tended to me night and day. He saved my life that summer. And all for nothing."

I could discern no bitterness in his voice, no emotion at all. It was like the voice of his namesake, dispassionate and mysterious.

I held the cloth to my face and tried to catch a breath. "Can you swim?" I asked, remembering why I had come.

Apollonius smiled a genuine smile. "Like a dolphin," he said.

There was a path which started just south of the annex and led down to the boathouse, switching back and forth down the steep hill below the southern wing and the baths. The path was largely invisible from the house, hidden by high foliage and the steep angle of the hillside. It was a cruder path than the one I had taken down from the terrace at the north wing, but it was well-trampled and in most places wide enough for two to walk abreast. The boy Meto led the way, leaping over tree roots and scrambling down rock shelves. Eco and I descended at a more careful pace, while Apollonius followed deferentially behind us.

It was the warmest, sleepiest hour of the day. As we neared the boathouse I gazed up toward the hills, thinking of the funeral congregation forced to stand for hours while the flames slowly disintegrated all that remained of Lucius

Licinius. I could see the tiny column of smoke rising above the treetops, thick and white but quickly blown into tattered streamers by the sea breeze, vanishing altogether as it dispersed into the blue above.

The little navy of boats moored at the pier knocked quietly against one another. As we stepped onto the pier, I noticed only a few dozing figures lounging in the boats, their feet dangling in the water and their faces covered by broad-brimmed sailors' hats. Most of the ferrymen and slaves had gone off scavenging for food, following the scent of roasting meats from the kitchens above, or else had slipped off to nap between the trees on the shady hillside.

"What did you lose?" asked Apollonius, peering down into the clear water in the open space between two of the boats.

"It's not exactly that I've lost something. . . ."

"But what am I to look for?"

"I don't really know. Something heavy enough to make a loud splash. Perhaps several such objects."

He looked at me dubiously, then shrugged. "The water could be clearer, but I suppose most of the silt stirred up by all these boats arriving will have settled by now. And I could use more sunlight; all these boats together cast a great shadow over the bottom. But if I see anything that shouldn't be there, I'll bring it up to you."

He unbelted and stripped off his tunic, then pulled his undertunic over his head and stood naked, his tousled hair glinting blue-black in the sunlight while lozenges of light, reflected off the water, danced across the sleek muscles of his chest and legs. Eco looked at him with a mixture of curiosity and envy. From beneath a broad-brimmed hat, one of the sailors made a crude but appreciative whistle. Apollonius lifted an eyebrow, but otherwise he ignored the sound; long ago he must have grown used to having others take note of his appearance.

He squared his shoulders and drew several deep breaths, then found a spot with room enough to dive into the water between two boats. The surface barely rippled behind him.

I strode up and down the jetty, peering into the green

depths and catching glimpses of his naked whiteness as he darted amid the mossy stones and the wooden beams. In the water he propelled himself as gracefully as he moved on land, kicking with both legs in unison and using his arms as if they were wings.

A gull flew overhead. The column of smoke from the faraway funeral pyre continued to rise above the trees. Still Apollonius remained beneath the water. At last I saw his face gazing up at me from the murky bottom, then grow larger and larger as he propelled himself upward and at last broke through the surface.

I began to ask him what he had seen, but he gasped and held up his hand. He needed to breathe, not speak. Gradually his breathing grew slower and more regular. Finally he opened his mouth—to speak, I thought, but instead he sucked in a deep breath, bent his body double, and plunged beneath the surface again. His kicking feet left a spume of tiny bubbles behind.

He dove straight down, disappearing into the darkness. I walked up and down the pier, gazing over the edge. The gull circled, the smoke rose, a cloud rolled across the sun. By now the dozing figures in the boats had all awakened and were curiously watching us from beneath their hats.

"He's been under a long time," one of them finally said.

"Very long," said another, "even for such a big-chested boy."

"Ah, it's nothing," said a third. "My brother dives for pearls, and he can stay down twice as long as this one's been under."

"Even so . . ."

I looked between the boats, trying to see if he had come up in a hidden spot, wondering if he had struck his head. It had been a bad time to demand this task of him, with so many boats moored at the dock. Apollonius himself had complained of the dark shadow covering the bottom; even dolphins must need light to swim by. No matter what the pearl diver's brother might claim, it hardly seemed possible that a man could stay underwater as long as Apollonius had been gone.

I began to fret. Eco was no swimmer, and neither was the boy Meto, by his own admission. The idea of plunging into the water myself made me think of my ordeal of the other night; I tasted seawater in my throat and felt it burn my nostrils and experienced a tremor of panic. I looked at the scattered chorus of sailors' hats and the shadowy faces beneath them.

"You men!" I said at last. "There must be a good swimmer among you! I'll pay any one of you five sesterces to take a look under the pier and tell me what's happened to the slave."

There was a commotion among the scattered hats. Feet were drawn from the water, faces appeared, hands sought for balance.

"Hurry!" I shouted, looking into the bottomless green darkness and feeling a cold fear grip my throat. "Hurry! Dive from where you are! Ten sesterces—"

But at that instant I was silenced by the bizarre apparition that emerged from the water at the end of the pier. The ferrymen froze in their places and stared as a long, gleaming blade soared straight upward into the air. Wrapped in seaweed, the sword glittered silver and green beneath the sun. A long, white, muscular arm followed it, and then the broad shoulders and gasping face of Apollonius, smiling in triumph.

EIGHTEEN

APOLLONIUS had compared himself to a dolphin—and indeed, lying naked on the pier with one arm slung over his face, his broad, clefted chest heaving for breath, his pale flesh wet and glistening, he looked to me like a young ocean god pulled from the deep. The planks all around him were dark with water, forming a rough outline of his body. Steam rose from his taut flesh, and rainbow-colored beads glinted amid the ridges of his belly. Meto fetched his undertunic, which Apollonius dropped casually onto his lap.

Beside him, the sword shone in the sunlight. I knelt and plucked away the strands of seaweed. It had not been underwater for long; there were no traces of rust about the hilt. I knew little enough about the workmanship of such weapons, but from the decoration on the handle it appeared to be of Roman manufacture.

Apollonius sat up, crossed his legs and leaned back against his arms. He brushed one hand through his scalp and sent a spray of water through the air. A few drops caught Eco in the eye. He wiped his face and looked at Apollonius with an odd, sullen fascination, then averted his gaze. They were about the same age; I could imagine how intimidated Eco must feel in the presence of another male of such superb appearance, who could display his naked perfection without the least hint of awkwardness.

"This is not the only one?" I said, picking up the sword for a closer look.

"Far from it. There are whole bundles of them, lashed together with leather straps. I tried to bring up a bundle, but it was too heavy. The straps are all knotted and bloated with water, impossible to undo; I finally managed to rub one of the straps against a blade and cut through it."

"Are swords all you saw?"

He shook his head. "Spears, too, bundled the same way. And sacks full of something else. They were tied shut so that I couldn't see inside, and they were too heavy to lift."

"I wonder what could be in those sacks," I said, and felt a glimmer of intuition. "How soon can you go down again?"

Apollonius shrugged, a gesture which upset the pools of water nestled in his collarbone and sent them streaming like quicksilver over his chest. "I've caught my breath. But I could use a knife this time."

The curious ferrymen kept their distance but had gathered close enough to overhear. One of them offered his knife, a strong blade fit for cutting leather straps, and Apollonius disappeared again beneath the water.

He was not gone long. This time he resurfaced headfirst, and when he pulled himself onto the pier it appeared that the knife was the only thing he carried. He stuck in into the wood, took his undertunic from Meto, then hurried toward the boathouse without a word. Meto ran after him. Eco and I followed. Apollonius's left hand, I noticed, was clenched tightly shut.

He walked around the boathouse and leaned against the wall, out of the ferrymen's sight. I approached him, tilting my head quizzically.

"Cup your hands together," he whispered, "like a bowl."

He extended his arm and opened his fist. The wet coins slithered into my hands like a school of tiny silver fish.

The same coins, having dried in the meantime, made a higher, more tinkling sound when I poured them onto the table in the library. Crassus had just returned from the funeral ceremony, still garbed in his black vestments and smelling of wood smoke. He raised a startled eyebrow.

"You found them where?"

"In the shallows just off the pier. The first night I arrived I saw someone dumping something from the dock. Whoever it was knocked me into the water and tried to drown me. He very nearly succeeded. It wasn't until today that I managed to send someone scavenging in the water. The slave Apollonius—yes, Mummius's favorite. This is what he found. Sacks and sacks full of silver, he says. And not just coins; there appear to be sacks full of gold and silver jewelry and trinkets as well. And weapons."

"Weapons?"

"Bundles of swords and spears. Not gladiatorial or ceremonial weapons, but true soldier's weapons. I brought one of the swords to show you, but your guard confiscated it at the door. And speaking of guards, I'd suggest that you post several at the boathouse immediately. I left Eco and Apollonius to keep an eye on the ferrymen, but an armed guard will need to be set night and day until you can recover the whole cache."

Crassus called to the guard outside the door and issued instructions, then had him bring in the sword that Apollonius had retrieved. From the open door came the noise of the funeral guests in the atrium. Crassus waited for the door to shut before he spoke.

"Curious," he said. "This was made at one of my own foundries here in Campania, from ore that came from one of my mines in Spain; you can see by this stamp on the pommel. How did it come to be here?"

"More to the point," I said, "where was it supposed to end up?"

"What do you mean?"

"If we assume that these things were being stored in the boathouse, and had been put there by Lucius Licinius, then what need did he have for so many weapons?"

"None."

"Had he gathered them for your use?"

"If I had wanted Lucius to divert weapons from one of my foundries and to bring them here, I would have told him so," said Crassus curtly.

"Then perhaps these weapons were being stored here for someone else. Who could possibly have a need for so many spears and swords?"

Crassus looked at me sternly, comprehending but unwilling to say the name aloud.

"Consider the valuables," I went on, "the coins and jewelry and metalwork all hoarded together in sacks like a pirate's booty. Assuming that Lucius didn't somehow steal it all, then perhaps it was delivered to him as payment."

"Payment for what?"

"For something he himself didn't need but could obtain—weapons."

Crassus looked at me, ashen-faced. "You dare to suggest that my cousin Lucius was smuggling weapons to an enemy of Rome?"

"What else is a reasonable man to assume when he comes upon a hoard of weapons and valuables all lumped together in a hidden place? And the boathouse may not have been the only place where such things were stored in transit. The slave boy Meto mentioned to me that he sometimes saw swords and spears stored in the annex behind the stables, the place where the slaves are now imprisoned. That annex may have been empty of such wares when you arrived here, but that doesn't mean that it hasn't housed shipments of weapons in the past. And not only weapons; Meto also mentioned seeing stacks of shields and helmets. I hear that some of the Spartacans are reduced to wearing dried melon husks for helmets. Spartacus has a desperate need for well-made armor."

Crassus glared at me and took a deep breath, but did not speak.

"I also hear that Spartacus has forbidden the use of money among his men. They're a nation without currency. The necessities of life they take from the land and the people on it, but they have no use for luxuries. Everything is shared. Spartacus believes that money will only corrupt his warriors. To what better use could he put all the pretty coins and trinkets he's accumulated than to smuggle them outside his zone of influence in return for things that he and his warriors truly need—things like swords, shields, helmets, and spears?"

Crassus considered for a long moment. "But it couldn't have been Lucius who dumped these things off the pier," he objected. "You've just told me that you heard them being dropped into the water on the night you arrived. You said that whoever was doing it then attacked and tried to drown you. It certainly wasn't Lucius, unless you believe that his shade was stalking you on the pier that night."

"No, not his shade. But perhaps his partner."

"A partner? In such a disgusting enterprise?"

"Perhaps not. Perhaps Lucius was innocent of the affair, and the whole business was being conducted right under his nose, without his knowledge. Perhaps he found out and that's why he was killed."

"My cousin's nose cast a considerable shadow, but not long enough to hide a business like this. And why do you insist on linking this discovery to his death? You know as well as I that he was murdered by those escaped slaves, Zeno and Alexandros."

"Do you honestly believe that, Marcus Crassus? Did you ever believe it? Or is it simply so convenient to your own schemes that you refuse to see any other possibility?" The words came out in a rush, louder and harsher than I intended. Crassus drew back. The door opened and the guard looked inside. I stepped back from Crassus, biting my tongue.

Crassus dismissed the guard with a wave of his hand. He crossed his arms and paced the room. At length he stopped before one of the shelves and stared at a stack of scrolls.

"There are more than a few documents missing from Lucius's record," he said in a slow, cautious voice. "The log which should account for all the trips taken by the *Fury* this summer, the inventories of her cargo . . ."

"Then summon the ship's captain, or one of her crew."

"Lucius dismissed the captain, and the crew, only a few days before I arrived. Why do you think I manned the vessel with Mummius and my own men to fetch you? I've sent messengers to look for the captain in Puteoli and Neapolis, but without success. Even so, there's evidence that Lucius sent the vessel on a number of trips which are not accounted for."

"What other documents are missing?"

"Records to account for all sorts of expenses. Without

knowing what was here before, it's impossible to know what's missing now."

"Then what I say is possible, isn't it? Lucius Licinius could have been transacting clandestine business without your knowledge. Treasonable business."

Crassus was silent for a long moment. "Yes."

"And someone knows of this besides ourselves, because someone was trying to conceal the evidence by hiding the weapons and booty underwater, just as someone cleaned the blood from the statue that killed Lucius—the same person who must have pilfered the incriminating records. Isn't it far more likely that this person was responsible for Lucius's death, rather than two harmless slaves who suddenly decided to run off and join Spartacus?"

"Prove it!" said Crassus, turning his back to me.

"And if I can't?"

"You still have a day and a night in which to do your work."

"What if I fail?"

"Justice will be done. Retribution will be swift and terrible. I announced my pledge at the funeral, and I intend to fulfill it."

"But, Marcus Crassus, the death of ninety-nine innocent slaves, to no purpose—"

"Everything I do," he said slowly, emphasizing each word, "has a purpose."

"Yes. I know." I bowed my head in defeat. I tried to think of some final argument. Crassus walked to one of the windows and gazed out at the funeral guests who milled about in the courtyard.

"The little slave boy—Meto, you call him—is running about, announcing to the guests that the banquet is about to begin," he said quietly. "It's time to trade our black garments for white. You'll excuse me while I go to my room and change, Gordianus."

"One last word, Marcus Crassus. If it comes to the crisis—if what you have determined comes to pass—I ask that you consider the honesty of the slave Apollonius. He might have kept his discovery of the silver a secret—"

"Why, when he's scheduled to die tomorrow? The silver is of no value to him."

"Still, if you could see your way to pardon him, and perhaps the boy Meto—"

"Neither of these slaves has done anything of extraordinary merit."

"But if you could show mercy—"

"Rome is in no mood for mercy. I think you will leave me now, Gordianus." While I left the room he stood stock-still, his arms crossed, his shoulders stiff, staring through the window at nothing. Just before I stepped through the door, I saw him turn and gaze at the little pile of silver coins I had left on the table. His eye glimmered and I watched the corner of his mouth quiver and bend into what might have been a smile.

The atrium was once again crowded with guests, some still in black, some already changed into white for the banquet. I made my way through the crush, ascended the steps, and walked toward my room.

The little hallway was deserted and quiet. The door to my room was slightly ajar. As I drew close I heard strange noises from within. I paused, trying to make sense of them. It might have been the sound of a small animal in pain, or the nonsensical babbling of an idiot with his tongue cut out. My first thought was that Iaia had committed some further sorcery in my room, and I approached cautiously.

I looked through the narrow opening and saw Eco seated before the mirror, contorting his face and emitting a series of uncouth noises. He stopped, scrutinized himself in the mirror, and tried again.

He was trying to speak.

I drew back. I took a deep breath. I walked halfway up the hall, then banged my elbow against the wall, to make a noise so that he would hear. I walked back to the room.

I found Eco inside, no longer before the mirror but sitting stiffly on his bed. He looked up at me as I stepped inside and smiled crookedly, then frowned and quickly looked out the window. I saw him swallow and reach up to touch his throat, as if it hurt.

"Did Crassus's guards come to take your place at the boathouse?" I said.

He nodded.

"Good. Look, here on my bed, our white garments for the banquet, neatly laid out for us. It should be a sumptuous feast."

Eco nodded. He looked out the window again. His eyes were hot and shiny. He bit his lip, blinked, and drew in a shallow breath. Something glistened wetly on his cheek, but he quickly brushed it away.

NINETEEN

THE banquet was held in three large, connected rooms along the eastern side of the house, each with a view of the bay. The guests flowed in like a tide of white sea foam. The murmur of the crowd hummed in the high-ceilinged rooms like a faint ocean roar.

As his final duty, the Designator assigned the seating and saw that a slave showed each guest to his place. Crassus, resplendent in white and gold, held court in the northernmost room, where he was joined by Fabius, Mummius, Orata, and the more important businessmen and politicians from the various towns around the Cup. Gelina presided over the central room, with Metrobius at her side, surrounded by Iaia and Olympias and the more prominent female guests.

To the third room, the biggest and the farthest from the kitchens, belonged those of us who belonged nowhere else, the junior partners and second sons, the leftovers and hangers-on. I was amused to see Dionysius assigned to our company; he balked when the slave showed him to his couch, quietly demanded to see the Designator, and was then summarily sent back to his place across the room from Eco and me, stuck away in a corner, not even beside a window. In any normal circumstance the household's resident philosopher would have been seated close to the master or mistress. I suspected it was Crassus who had instructed the Designator to stick Dionysius away in a dark corner, as a deliberate snub. He truly despised the philosopher.

Since the time was as near to midday as evening, Dionysius elected to have his green potion before rather than after the meal. To assuage his dignity, he made quite a show of demanding it immediately and was unnecessarily rude to the young slave girl who ran to the kitchens to fetch it for him. A few moments later she returned with trembling hands and set the cup on the little table in front of him.

I looked around the room, at the various couches clustered about the little tables. I saw no one I knew. Eco was pensive and withdrawn and had no appetite. I was content to nibble at the delicacies placed before me and contemplate my course of action over the remaining hours.

From where I lay, I could see straight into the farther rooms. If I rose onto my elbow I could glimpse Crassus sipping his wine and conferring with Sergius Orata. It was Orata who had first told me that Lucius Licinius had come into unexplained wealth; did he know more than he had told me? Could he indeed have been the shadowy partner involved in Lucius's smuggling scheme? With his round, blandly self-satisfied face, he hardly looked capable of murder, but I have often found that rich men are capable of anything.

Marcus Mummius, reclining close to Crassus, looked nervous and unhappy—and why not, considering that all his pleas for the salvation of Apollonius had been rebuffed by Crassus? It struck me as unlikely that Mummius could have been Lucius's shadow partner, given the bad blood between them over the matter of Apollonius. Yet it occurred to me that Mummius could have ridden up from the camp at Lake Lucrinus and back again on the night of the murder. What if he had done so, to give himself a chance to approach Lucius again about buying the slave? If Lucius was half as stubborn as his cousin, he would have refused once more to sell the slave; could that have sent Mummius into a murderous rage? If so, then by killing Lucius, Mummius would have inadvertently set in motion the destruction of the very person he desired, the young Apollonius—and the only way to save the boy would be to admit his own guilt. What a pit of misery that would plunge him into!

My eye fell on Crassus's "left arm," Faustus Fabius of the haughty jaw and the flaming hair. He had met Lucius Licinius on the same occasions as Mummius, and thus had

had the opportunity and the connections to have become Lucius's shadow partner and to embark on what must have been a fabulously lucrative, if extraordinarily dangerous, enterprise. Mummius had told me that Fabius came from a patrician family of limited means, but of his character I knew very little; such men face the world wearing masks more rigid than the waxen masks of their dead ancestors. The Fabii had been present at the birth of the Republic; they had been among the first elected consuls, the first to wear the toga trimmed with purple and to sit in the ivory chair of state wrested from the kings. It seemed presumptuous even to suspect a man of such high birth of treachery and murder, but then, such traits must run in the blood of patricians, or else how did their ancestors pull down the kings, stamp down their fellow Romans, and become patricians in the first place?

Nearer at hand, in the middle room, my eyes fell on Gelina. She seemed the least likely candidate of all. Everything indicated that her love for her husband had been genuine, and that her grief was deep. Iaia, however low her opinion of Lucius, also seemed unlikely; besides, she and Olympias had been in Cumae on the night of the murder, or so I had been told. Would any of the women in the house, even Olympias, have had the strength to smash Lucius's skull with the heavy statuette, and then to drag his body into the atrium? Or to carry the bundles of weapons from the boathouse to the pier, and to knock me into the water?

The same might be asked of Metrobius, given his age, but he bore watching. He had been a part of Sulla's inner circle, and thus could possess few scruples, even about murder. He was a man who held long and festering grudges, as I knew from his tirade against Mummius. Retired from the stage, bereft of his lifelong benefactor, deprived by the passing years of his legendary beauty, in what secret pursuits did he invest his restless energies? He was devoted to Gelina and had despised Lucius; could he have used Gelina's misery as an excuse to kill her husband? Was he the shadow partner? His hatred for Lucius wouldn't necessarily have kept him from investing a part of his accumulated fortune in Lucius's schemes. It was even possible, I thought, that he might have foreseen Crassus's decision to annihilate the slaves, including Apollonius, as a consequence of the murder; thus, by killing Lucius and letting events take their course, he could wreak a terrible revenge on Mummius. But was even his subtle and conniving mind capable of such a vicious and convoluted plot?

Of course, despite my discoveries at the boathouse and all evidence to the contrary, it could still be that—

"It was the slaves who did it! Knocked off half of Lucius's head and then ran off to Spartacus!"

For an instant I thought it was a god who spoke, reprimanding me for my lurid speculations and reminding me of the one possibility I refused to consider. Then I recognized the voice, which came from the couch behind me. It was the man I had overheard gossiping with his wife at the funeral. They were gossiping again.

"But remember Crassus's oration? The slaves won't go unpunished—and a good thing!" said the woman, smacking her lips. "One has to draw a line. Slaves of the lower sort can never be relied upon to know their place; let them witness an atrocity such as this one in their own household and they're spoiled forever—no use to anyone for anything. Once they've seen another of their kind get away with murder, from that point on you can never turn your back on them. Best to put them out of their misery, I say, and if you can turn that to setting a good example for other slaves, then all the better! That Marcus Crassus knows the right way to do things!"

"Well, he certainly knows how to run his own affairs," the man agreed. "His wealth speaks for that. They say he wants the command against Spartacus, and I hope those fools in the Senate for once have the wisdom to give the right job to the right man. He's a tough nut, no doubt about that; it takes a hard man to put a household of his own slaves to death, and that's just the sort we need right now—a stern hand to deal with the Thracian monster! My dear, could you pass me one of those green olives? And perhaps a spoonful more of the applesauce for my calf's brains? Delicious! Alas, that Crassus should have to put such splendid cooks to death, as well!"

"But he's going to do it, even so. That's what I've heard—and poor, pitiful Gelina shaking her head the whole time and wishing it wasn't so. She's always had a soft heart, just like Lucius had a soft head, and you see what's come of that! But not Marcus Crassus—hard head and an even harder heart. He allows not a single exception to Roman justice, and that's as it should be. You can't make exceptions in times like these."

"No, you certainly can't. But a man would have to be as unflinching as Cato to put to death a cook who can create a dish as exquisite as this." The man smacked his lips.

"Shhh! Don't speak the word."

"What word?"

"Death. Can't you see the serving girl is just over there?"

"So?"

"It's bad luck to say the word out loud where a doomed slave can hear."

They were quiet for a moment, then the woman spoke again. "Drafty in here, isn't it?"

"Now, woman, don't start . . ."

"The food gets cold having to come so far from the kitchens."

"I think you're eating fast enough that you needn't worry about that."

"Well, even so, that self-satisfied Designator might have put us in one of the better rooms if you'd had the nerve to ask, as I told you to."

"My dear, don't start on that again. The food's the same, I'm sure, and you can't complain about that."

"The food, maybe, but you can't say the same for the company. You're twice as rich as anybody in this room! We really should have been put closer to Crassus, or at least in the middle room with Gelina."

"There are only so many rooms and so many couches," sighed the man. "And there are more people here than I've seen at a funeral banquet in many a year. Still, you have a point about the people in this room. Not exactly the cream, are they? Look over there, at that philosopher fellow who lives here. Dionysius, I think he's called."

"Yes, like half the Greek philosophers in Italy," the woman grunted. "This one's not particularly distinguished, from what I hear."

"Strictly second-rate, they say. I can't imagine why Lucius kept him on; I suppose Gelina picked him out, and there's no accounting for her taste, except in the matter of cooks. With Lucius gone, he'll be hard-pressed to find a situation as comfortable as this one. Who needs a second-rate philosopher about the house, especially a Stoic, when there are so many good Epicureans to choose from, especially here on the Cup? A disagreeable fellow—and rather uncouth as well. Just look at him! Making faces and sticking out his tongue like that—really, you'd think he was only half-civilized!"

"Yes, I see what you mean. He's making quite a spectacle of himself, isn't he? More like a buffoon than a polymath."

Dionysius hardly seemed the type to display bad table manners, even if he was piqued at his placement. I turned my head to have a look for myself. He did indeed appear to be making faces, wrinkling his nose and pushing his tongue in and out of his mouth.

"But he does look funny," the woman admitted. "Like one of those hideous masks in a comedy!" She started to laugh, and her husband joined her.

But Dionysius was not striving for comic effect. He clutched at his throat and pitched forward on his couch with a spastic jerk. He sucked in a wheezing breath and then, with his tongue half out of his mouth, tried to speak. The garbled words were barely audible from where I sat. "My tongue," he gasped, "on fire!" And then: "Air! Air!"

By now others had begun to notice him. The slaves stopped serving and the guests turned their heads to watch as Dionysius went into convulsions. He drew his arms stiffly to his chest, as if trying to control the spasms, and kept pushing out his tongue, as if he could not bear to have it in his mouth.

"Is he choking?" asked the woman.

"I don't think so," said her husband, who then snorted in disapproval. "Really, this is too much!" he protested, as

Dionysius bent forward and began to vomit onto the little table set before his couch.

A number of guests sprang to their feet. The commotion spread gradually into the middle room, like a ripple passing through a pond. Gelina frowned anxiously and turned her head. A moment later the whispers spread to the far room, where Crassus, laughing at one of Orata's jokes, turned and peered quizzically through the doorways. I caught his eye and waved at him urgently. Gelina rose to her feet. She hurried toward me. Crassus followed with measured steps.

They both arrived in time to witness the philosopher disgorge another spume of greenish bile onto a tray of what had been calf's brains with applesauce, while a semicircle of alarmed guests looked on. I pushed my way through the crowd. Just as I stepped next to Crassus, the guests wrinkled their noses in unison and stepped back a pace. The philosopher had soiled himself.

Crassus made a face at the smell. Gelina hovered at the philosopher's side, trying to help but afraid to touch him. Dionysius suddenly convulsed and catapulted forward from his couch, falling against the little table of delicacies. The crowd drew back to avoid the flying calf's brains and bile.

The cup that had held Dionysius's herbal concoction tumbled through the air and landed at my feet with a clang. I knelt, picked it up and peered inside. There was nothing to see but a few green drops; Dionysius had drained it dry.

Crassus clutched my arm with a bruising grip. "What in Hades is happening?" he demanded, clenching his teeth.

"Murder, I think. Perhaps Zeno and Alexandros strike again?"

Crassus was not amused.

PART FOUR

Funeral Games

TWENTY

ONE disaster follows another!'' Crassus stopped pacing long enough to stare at me with one eyebrow raised, as if holding me responsible for complicating his life. ''For once I think I shall actually be glad to get back to the relative calm and security of Rome. This place is accursed!''

''I agree, Marcus Crassus. But cursed by whom?'' I glanced at the corpse of Dionysius, which lay sprawled on the library floor where Crassus had ordered his men to put it for want of a better place, simply to get it out of sight of the dinner guests. Eco stood peering down at the dead man's contorted face, apparently fascinated by the way that Dionysius's tongue refused to recede into his mouth.

Crassus pinched his nose and made a wave of dismissal. ''Take it away!'' he shouted to one of his bodyguards.

''But where shall we put him, Marcus Crassus?''

''Anywhere! Find Mummius and ask him what to do—just get the body out of here! Now that I no longer have to listen to the fool, I certainly don't intend to put up with his stench.'' He fixed his stare on me. ''Poison, Gordianus?''

''An obvious deduction, given the symptoms and circumstances.''

''Yet the rooms were full of other people eating. No one else was affected.''

''Because no one else drank from Dionysius's cup. He had a peculiar habit of drinking some herbal concoction before his midday meal and again with his dinner.''

Crassus blinked and shrugged. ''Yes, I remember hearing him extol the virtues of rue and silphium at other meals. Another of his irritating affectations.''

"And an ideal opportunity for anyone who might wish to poison him—a drink which he alone ingests, and always at a prescribed time and place. You must agree now, Marcus Crassus, that there is a murderer at large, here in this house. Quite likely it's the same person who murdered Lucius, since only last night Dionysius publicly pledged to expose that person. This could hardly have been the work of Alexandros or Zeno."

"And why not? Zeno may be dead, but we still don't know where Alexandros is, or with whom he might be in contact. No doubt he has confederates in the household, among the kitchen slaves."

"Yes, perhaps he does have friends in this house," I said, but I was not thinking of slaves.

"Obviously, it was a mistake for me to allow any of the slaves to go on serving Gelina. As soon as the dinner is finished and the overnight guests are seen to their quarters, I shall have every slave rounded up and locked into the annex. It would have to be done in the morning, anyway. Fabius!" He called to Faustus Fabius, who had been waiting in the hall, and issued instructions. Fabius nodded coolly and left the room without even looking at me.

I shook my head wearily. "Why do you think it was one of the slaves who poisoned Dionysius, Marcus Crassus?"

"Who else had access to the kitchens, where no one would notice? I suppose that's where Dionysius kept his herbs."

"All sorts of people have been in and out of the kitchens all day. People were half-starved from waiting for dinner; guests dropped by to filch food or sent slaves to do it for them long before the meal began; the kitchen slaves were rushing about and could hardly be expected to take note of everyone who stepped in their way. And you're mistaken, Crassus; Dionysius gathered his herbs himself and kept them in his room. He sent fresh batches down to the kitchens to be prepared each day; he usually bundled them up first thing in the morning and gave them to a kitchen slave, but today he didn't deliver them until after the funeral. That means the herbs could have been tampered with in Dionysius's room this morning, while everyone was busy preparing for the funeral."

"How do you know all this?"

"Because while you and your men were gathering up Dionysius's body and bringing it here, I asked a few questions of the serving girl who brought him the drink tonight. She says that he brought the herbs to the kitchen after returning from the funeral. As usual, they were already mixed and crushed and gathered up in a scrap of cloth. Apparently Dionysius made quite a ritual of measuring and preparing them in advance. She herself added the watercress and grape leaves, then boiled and strained the concoction just before the meal."

"She could have added the poison as well," Crassus insisted. "You must know something of poisons, Gordianus. What do you think it was?"

"I would guess aconitum."

"Panther's-death?"

"Some people call it that. It's said to be palatable, so he might not have noticed it in his concoction. It's the fastest of poisons. The symptoms match—a burning in the tongue, choking, convulsions, vomiting, loosening of the bowels, death. But who," I wondered aloud, "would have known enough of such things to have obtained the poison and administered a proper dose?" I glanced at Eco, who pursed his lips. He had napped while I browsed through the various herbs and extracts in the house of Iaia at Cumae, but I had told him about them later.

Crassus stretched his shoulders and grimaced. "I hate funerals. Even worse than funerals are funeral games. At least this shall all be over tomorrow."

"If only Dionysius had been able to tell us what he knew about the murder of Lucius," I said, "if indeed he knew anything at all. I should like to have a look in his rooms."

"Certainly." Crassus shrugged. His mind had already wandered to other matters.

I found the boy Meto in the atrium and instructed him to show us to the philosopher's chambers. We passed the dining rooms. The meal had abruptly ended with the death of Dionysius and the withdrawal of the host and hostess, but many of the guests still lingered among the tables and couches. I paused and searched the crowd.

"Who are you looking for?" asked Meto.

"Iaia and her assistant Olympias."

"The painter lady left already," he said. "Right after the philosopher started having his fit."

"Left the room?"

"Left the house, for her own house at Cumae. I know, because she sent me to the stables to see that their horses were ready."

"Too bad," I said. "I should very much like to talk with her."

Meto led us farther up the hall and around a corner. "Here it is," he said, indicating the door to Dionysius's rooms.

The apartment consisted of two small rooms separated by a hanging curtain. In the outer room a round table was surrounded by chairs, set beside a window that faced the low wooded hills on the west. A clay urn was set atop a small table in one corner. When I lifted the lid I smelled the mingled scents of rue, silphium, and garlic. "Dionysius's concoction. Poisoned or not, it should all be burned or emptied into the bay to be sure it harms no one else."

The inner room, furnished with a Stoic's austerity, contained only a sleeping couch, a hanging lamp, and a large trunk.

"Not much to see," I remarked to Eco, "unless something has been hidden out of sight." I started to open the trunk and found that it was clasped shut with a lock that required a key. "We could break it open, I suppose. I doubt that Crassus would object, and we can ask the shade of Dionysius to forgive us. Indeed, it looks to me as if someone has already tried to force it open, and failed. See the scratches, and this scarred strip of metal, Eco? We shall need a strong, slender bar of steel to pry it open."

"Why not use the key?" suggested Meto.

"Because we don't have it," I said.

Meto smiled mischievously, then flattened himself on the

floor, wriggled under the couch and emerged clutching a simple brass key in his tiny fist.

I threw up my hands. "Meto, you are invaluable! Every household needs a slave like you." He grinned and hovered over me as I stopped to fit the key into the lock. "Indeed, Meto, I think you shall grow up to be like those slaves in Plautus's plays, the ones who always know what's going on when their masters are too stupid or love-struck to see the truth." Whoever had tried to force the lid had jammed the lock as well, so that I had to jiggle the key. "Plautus's clever slaves always come in for a chiding from their jealous masters, but the world could never manage without them. Ah—there, it's open! What treasures did the philosopher find so valuable that he locked them safely away, I wonder?"

I pushed the lid up. Eco sucked in a breath. Meto started back.

"Blood!" he whispered.

"Yes," I agreed, "most assuredly, blood." Atop the other scrolls that had been unrolled and laid flat within the trunk was a strip of parchment covered with tiny, crabbed writing, over which had been cast a great, spattered stain of blood.

"The missing documents?" I asked.

Back in the library, Crassus pored over the flattened sheets one by one. Finally he nodded. "Yes, there are the records I was searching for, together with others I had no idea existed, full of all sorts of irregularities and cryptic references—expenditures and amounts received, itemized in some sort of secret code. I shall have to take them back to Rome with me after the funeral games. There's no way to make sense of it all without considerable time and study; perhaps my chief accountant can decode them."

"I saw that the notation 'A Friend' recurs several times, always connected to a sum of money, often a rather large sum. You don't suppose that could be a record of investments and disbursements relating to Lucius's silent partner?"

Crassus gave me a disgruntled look. "What I really want to know is what these documents were doing in Dionysius's room."

"I have a theory," I said.

"I'm sure you do."

"We know that Dionysius wanted to solve Lucius's murder, if only to impress you with his cleverness. Suppose he was ahead of us when it came to noticing the bloodstains on the statue that was used to kill Lucius, and had already concluded, even before I arrived, that Lucius was murdered in this room. Suppose also that he had some inkling of Lucius's shady dealings; after all, he lived in the house and might very well have noticed the flow of silver and arms, no matter how secretive Lucius might have been."

Crassus nodded. "Go on."

"Knowing these things, he must have purloined these documents himself, before you had a chance to find them, taking them from this room to his own where he could peruse them in secret and search for clues to the murderer's identity."

"Perhaps. But how do you account for this?" He pointed to the bloodstained scroll.

"Lucius must have been looking at it when he was killed. It must have been open, here on this table."

"And the murderer, who was so careful to drag Lucius's body into the atrium, left this document for Dionysius to find the next time he came into the library? It seems to me that the killer would have destroyed it rather than leave it for Dionysius to ferret away. This would indicate that the document has nothing to do with the murder."

Crassus stared at me grimly, then slowly smiled when he saw that I had no answer. He shook his head and laughed softly. "I will say this, Gordianus—you are tenacious! If it makes you feel better, I'll admit that I myself am not entirely satisfied with what we know of the circumstances surrounding Lucius's death. It does appear, from the evidence you found in the water and from these documents, that my dear, foolish, accursed cousin was involved in smuggling weapons to someone—yes, perhaps even to Spartacus. But that only weakens your case and strengthens mine."

"I don't see it that way, Marcus Crassus."

"Don't you? When word arrived that I was coming on short notice, Lucius panicked and tried to sever his contacts with the representatives of Spartacus, the customers who bought his stockpile of weapons. Seeing they would get no more out of Lucius, they set about taking their revenge on him. Who could these criminals, these agents of Spartacus, have been? Who else but Zeno and the Thracian Alexandros, who were nothing less than Spartacan spies in this household. Yes, I see it quite clearly now—hear me out, Gordianus!

"They confronted Lucius here in the library, in the dead of night. Zeno, who helped keep his master's books, produced these various documents exposing Lucius's perfidy, and threatened to betray him to me if he didn't continue to smuggle arms to Spartacus. But even blackmail would not sway Lucius; he had decided to sever his ties with the Spartacans, and he would not be intimidated. So Zeno and Alexandros murdered him, using the statue, just as you said. To make his death more public, they dragged his body into the atrium and began to scrape out the name of their master, Spartacus.

"Ah, but Dionysius was up late that night, mulling over whatever it is that second-rate philosophers mull over in the middle of the night. There was some scroll or other that he needed to fetch from Lucius's library. He must have made a noise, which disturbed the assassins and sent them flying, before they could finish carving the full name of their master. Dionysius enters the library and sees the bloody scroll. He goes into the atrium and finds the body. But instead of raising an alarm, he concocts a scheme to further his own career. He knows that I'll be arriving the next day; without Lucius, he has no patron, but if he could somehow attach himself to me, all would be to his benefit. He thinks he can impress me by providing a solution to the murder. He studies the bloodstained document, comprehends its import, and looks through the other scrolls for similarly incriminating evidence. He takes them all back to his room to decipher and piece together at his leisure."

"But why didn't he tell you these things sooner?" I protested.

"Perhaps he planned to reveal all he knew at the funeral

games tomorrow, thinking his eloquence could compete with the blood and drama in the arena. Or perhaps he was dissatisfied because there were still some scraps of evidence he couldn't quite piece together; after all, he wanted his presentation to me to be as impressive as possible. Or—''

Crassus's eyes lit up. ''Yes!'' he cried. ''Dionysius was on the trail of Alexandros and wanted to deliver the slave to me in person—yes, that solves everything! After all, who else would have poisoned him, except Alexandros, or another of the slaves acting to protect Alexandros? Dionysius must have discovered Alexandros's hiding place, and intended to deliver him publicly to me for the execution tomorrow, together with all the evidence he had uncovered.'' Crassus shook his head ruefully. ''I'll admit it would have been quite a coup for the old buzzard—a chance for him to show off in front of everyone gathered for the games. I'd have had a hard time begrudging him a place in my retinue after that. So the buzzard turned out to be a fox!''

''A dead fox,'' I said dully.

''Yes, and silent forever. Too bad he can't tell me where to find Alexandros. I should dearly love to have that scoundrel in my hands tomorrow. I'd lash him to a cross and burn him alive for the crowd's amusement.'' His eyes glinted cruelly, and he was suddenly angry. ''Do you see now, Gordianus, how you've wasted my time and your own, chasing after this illusion that the slaves were innocent? You should have been setting your cleverness to catching Alexandros for me and bringing him to justice, but instead you've let the fiend commit another murder in front of your very eyes!''

He began to pace furiously. ''You're a sentimental fool, Gordianus. I've met your type before, always trying to intercede between a slave and his just deserts, turning squeamish at the ugliness that's sometimes required to maintain Roman law and order. Well, you've done your best to stand in the way of justice in this case, and, by Jupiter, you've failed. Call yourself the Finder, indeed!''

He began to shout. ''We have your ineptitude to thank for Dionysius's death and for the fact that the murderer Alexandros is still at large. Get out! I have no use for such incompetence! When I get back to Rome I shall make you the laughingstock of the city. See if anyone ever comes seeking the services of the so-called Finder again!"

"Marcus Crassus—"

"Out!" In his fury he seized the documents that littered the table, crushed them in his fists and threw them at me. They missed, but one of them struck Eco in the face. "And don't show yourself to me again unless you can bring me the slave Alexandros in chains, ready to be crucified for his crimes!"

"The man is more unsure of himself than ever," I whispered to Eco as we walked toward our room. "The strain of the funeral, the bloodshed that looms tomorrow—he's become overwrought . . ."

Suddenly I realized that my face was hot and my heart was beating fast. My mouth was so dry I could hardly swallow. Was it Marcus Crassus I was talking about, or was it myself?

I took a few steps and stopped. Eco looked up at me quizzically and touched my sleeve, asking what we should do next. I bit my lip, suddenly confused and disoriented. Eco drew his brows together in an expression of concern. I couldn't meet his eyes.

What was there left to do? I had been in constant motion for days, always able to glimpse the next step, and now I suddenly found myself adrift. Perhaps Crassus was right, and my defense of the slaves had been a sentimental folly all along. Even if he was wrong, my time was almost up and I had nothing to offer him—except for the fact that I knew, or thought I knew, who had poisoned Dionysius, just as I thought I knew where the slave Alexandros was hiding. If I could do nothing else, at least I might discover the truth, for my own satisfaction.

In our room I produced the two daggers I had brought from Rome and handed one to Eco. He looked at me, wide-eyed. "Things may come to a crisis very suddenly," I said. "I think it best that we arm ourselves. The time has come to confront certain persons with *this*." I pulled out the bloodstained cloak from where I had hidden it among our things. I rolled it up tightly and tucked it under my arm. "We should bring cloaks for ourselves, as well. The night is likely to be chilly. Now, to the stables!"

We walked quickly down the hall, down the stairway, and through the atrium. We stepped through the front doorway into the courtyard. The sun had just begun to sink behind the low hills to the west.

We found Meto in the stables, attending to the horses for the night. I told him to prepare mounts for Eco and me.

"But it's getting dark," he protested.

"It will get even darker before I find my way back."

We were mounted and ready to begin, pausing in front of the stables, when Faustus Fabius and an armed cordon of guards passed through the courtyard. Between the ranks of soldiers, in single file, walked the last of the household slaves on their way to the annex.

They walked silently, meekly. Some had their heads bowed, weeping. Others looked about with wide, frightened eyes. Among them I saw Apollonius, who walked with his eyes straight ahead, his jaw tightly clenched.

It seemed to me that the villa was being drained of its lifeblood. All those who gave the great house its animation, who kept it in motion from dawn to dusk, were being emptied from its corridors—the barbers and cooks, the stokers of fires and openers of doors, the servitors and attendants.

"You there, boy!" yelled Fabius.

Meto shrank back against my mount, clutching at my leg. His hands trembled.

My mouth went dry. "The boy is with me, Faustus Fabius. I'm on an errand for Crassus, and I need him."

Faustus Fabius waved for the contingent to continue to the annex and stepped toward us. "I hardly think that's the case, Gordianus." He gave me one of his aloof, patrician smiles. "The story I hear is that you and Marcus have parted ways for good, and he'd just as soon see your head on a platter as on your shoulders. I doubt you should even be allowed to take his horses from the stables. Where are you headed, anyway—just in case Crassus should ask."

"Cumae."

"Is it as bad as that, Gordianus, that you need to ask the Sibyl for help, and with night falling? Or does your son want a last look at the beautiful Olympias?" When I made no answer, he shrugged. An odd expression crossed his face, and I realized that a bit of the bloodstained cloak, folded and concealed beneath my own cloak, had slipped into view. I moved to cover it with my elbow.

"At any rate, the boy comes with me," Fabius said.

He grabbed Meto's shoulder, but the child refused to let go of my leg. Fabius pulled harder and Meto began to squeal. Slaves and guards turned their faces toward us. Eco grew agitated; his mount began to neigh and stamp.

I whispered through my teeth, "Have mercy on the boy, Faustus Fabius! Let him come with me—I'll leave him with Iaia in Cumae. Crassus will never know!"

Fabius relaxed his grip. Meto, shivering, released my leg and reached up to wipe his eyes. Fabius smiled thinly.

"The gods will thank you, Faustus Fabius," I whispered. I reached down to scoop the child onto the horse's back, but Fabius swiftly pulled him away and stepped back, gripping him tightly.

Fabius shook his head. "The slave belongs to Crassus," he said. He turned and pushed Meto, stumbling and looking desperately back over his shoulder, toward the other slaves.

I watched dumbly until the last guard disappeared around the corner of the stables. Twilight covered the earth and the first stars glimmered above. At last I spurred my mount and set out. To any god who might happen to be listening, I said a prayer that morning would never come.

TWENTY-ONE

WE would have been wiser, I chided myself afterward, to have taken the road to Cumae rather than the shortcut through the hills that Olympias had shown us. It was on such nights, I imagine, that lemures escape from Hades, rise like vapor from Lake Avernus, and go walking through the fog, spreading the chill of death through the forest and across the barren hills. The presence of the walking dead is attenuated and weak when compared to the vivid, blood-rich fecundity of living matter, like the paleness of a candle when seen beside the sun. But in certain times and places, as on battlefields or around the entrances to the underworld, the spirits of the dead are so concentrated that they can become as palpable as living flesh—or so the phenomenon has been explained by those wiser than myself in such matters. I only know that death stalked the way to Cumae that night, and that those it claimed would not have far to go to be sucked into the mouth of Hades.

It was not hard to find our way, at first. We had no difficulty reaching the main road from the villa, and Eco's sharp eyes spotted the narrow trail that branched toward the west. Even in twilight the way looked familiar. We passed through the stand of trees onto the bald ridge. Off to the north I saw the camp fires of Crassus's soldiers clustered around Lake Lucrinus. Faint sounds of singing rose from the valley below. Beneath the rising moonlight I could make out the hulking mass of the arena. Its high wooden walls shone dully, like the hide of a slumbering behemoth; tomorrow it would awaken and devour its prey.

It was after we entered the woods and darkness fell that I

became less certain of our way. I had forgotten how faint the path became, and how quickly. Without sunlight there was no way to be certain of the direction. The full moon was still low in the sky, and the blue glow it cast through the woods created a strange, confused jumble of light and shadow. Wisps of fog coiled around us, whether sea fog or vapors rising from the damp earth, I could not tell. Perhaps the wisps were not fog at all, but the wavering, half-glimpsed spirits of the uneasy dead.

The stench of sulphur grew heavy on the dank air. Far away a wolf howled. Another joined it, and then a third, so near us that I gave a start. Three voices howling, like the three heads of Cerberus. The night was colder than I had expected. I pulled my cloak more tightly around my shoulders. I thought of the cloak I carried under my arm, and worried that the wolves could smell the blood that stained it, and that it drew them nearer. For a brief moment I thought I heard horses behind us, then decided it was only our echo.

I pressed on, less and less certain that I knew the way. At last we came to a vaguely familiar spot where the sky opened above and the horses' hooves clacked against hard stone. My horse hesitated but I urged him on. He hesitated again, then Eco grabbed my arm from behind and made a gulping noise of distress. I let out a gasp.

We stood on the verge of the precipice overlooking Lake Avernus. A gust of sulphurous heat blew against my face, like the foul breath of Pluto himself. In the stillness I heard the wheezing and belching of the fumaroles, and in my mind's eye I saw the hapless dead struggling like drowning men amid the scalding muck far below. The moon rose above the treetops and cast a sickly blue light across the waste. In that illusory glow I saw the pocked, scarred face of a monster too huge to comprehend, and then, as the light shifted imperceptibly and the fumaroles opened and closed, I saw a vast bowl teeming with maggots the size of men. From the distant woods across the lake, visible only in jagged silhouette, I heard the barking of three dogs together.

"Cerberus is loose tonight," I whispered. "Anything might happen."

Eco made an odd, stifled noise. I bit my tongue, cursing myself for frightening him. I took a deep breath, despite the stench of sulphur, and turned toward him.

The blow descended and sent me flying headfirst from my horse.

Eco's stifled noise had been a warning. The blow came from behind and landed square between my shoulder blades. Even as I fell, I wondered why the assassin chose to cudgel rather than stab me, and I could only conclude that Eco had somehow managed to deflect his blow. Perhaps it was an elbow that struck me, or the pommel of a sword.

The palms of my hands struck the hard rock and went scraping over it. Some other part of me struck next, probably my hip, to judge from the bruises I noticed later. I scrambled forward, to the very brink of the precipice.

A hard kick landed against my ribs and sent me lurching halfway over the stone lip. Then I knew why I hadn't been stabbed, as I could have been so easily, caught unawares: Why leave evidence of murder when you can simply throw a man over a cliff to his death? Or perhaps it didn't matter how they killed me; if they intended to dispose of me afterward by casting my body into the fiery lake, I would be swallowed whole by Pluto, bones and all.

I felt the breath of Pluto hot on my face, and reared back from the precipice. I was kicked square on the buttocks. I held my ground and was kicked again. From somewhere behind me came a noise like the bleating of a slaughtered sheep—Eco, crying out to me.

I rolled to the left, not knowing whether the shelf ended there or not and steeling myself to plunge into empty space. Instead I rolled onto hard stone and scrambled to my feet, spinning toward the assassin. Steel glinted in the moonlight and I dipped my head, just in time; the blade whooshed above me, and the wake of its passing blew through my hair. I reached for the assassin's arm and caught him off-balance. I never saw a face or even a body, only the forearm I gripped with both hands and twisted at a cruel angle.

He gasped and cursed. He reached with his other arm to take the blade from his useless hand. I kneed him in the groin. His free hand flailed aimlessly, clutching at the sudden pain, and I felt him weaken. There was no way for me to take his knife or to reach for my own. I lurched backwards, pulling him with me, and when I sensed that I had reached the edge of the cliff I spun about with all my strength, forcing him to spin with me, like an acrobat swinging his partner.

There was a sound of feet scuffling against bare rock, and then his forearm was jerked from my grip, as if something incredibly strong grabbed his feet and pulled him straight down. I held him almost too long, and felt myself jerked downward with him. The blade in his fist whipped by and cut my hand. I cried out and then staggered for a long, dizzy moment on the verge. I held out my arms like those of a crucified man, reaching for balance. My knees turned to water.

At that moment the barest shove would have sent me flying over the cliff, or the barest backward tug on my cloak could have pulled me to safety. Where was Eco?

I wheeled my arms wildly in the air and finally folded backwards, landing with a grunt on my backside. I twisted onto my hands and knees and sprang to my feet. My horse stood a little to one side, having backed away from the precipice, but Eco and his mount where nowhere to be seen. Nor was there any sign of another assassin.

The night fog had grown thick, diffusing the growing moonlight and obscuring everything. I stared into the gloom and whispered, "Eco?" I said his name louder, and then shouted: "Eco!" But there was no answer—neither the pitiful, half-human murmur I had heard him make in our room, nor the stifled, strangling sound he had made to warn me. There was only silence, broken by the soughing of the wind in the treetops.

"Eco!" I shouted, heedless of alerting whatever other assassins might be lurking in the darkness. "Eco!"

I thought I heard noises from far away, or else from nearby but muffled by fog and dense foliage—the clang of metal on metal, a shout, the snorting of a horse. I ran to my horse and mounted him.

I felt abruptly dizzy, so dizzy that I almost fell. My head

throbbed. I reached up to press my temple, and felt a slick wetness. Even in the thickening gloom, I could see that the stuff on my fingers was blood. From the cut on my hand, I thought, and then realized that the blade had cut my other hand. Somehow I had struck my head without realizing it—or else the assassin's blade had swung closer to my scalp than I had realized.

Blood made me remember the cloak. I had dropped it when I fell. I looked about the bare stone and saw it nowhere.

There were more noises from the forest—a whinnying horse, a man shouting. I was confused and unable to think. I rode into the woods, toward the distant noises, but all I could hear was a rushing in my head, louder than the wind in the trees. The fog closed around me like gauze draped over my face.

"Eco!" I shouted, suddenly fearful of the silence. The world seemed vast and empty around me.

I rode forward. For all my watching and listening I was as helpless as a man without sight or hearing. The rushing in my head became a roar. The moonlight grew dimmer, pierced by bright, vaporous phantoms that darted in and out of the darkness. *Death comes as the end,* I thought, remembering an old Egyptian saying Bethesda had taught me. Death came for Lucius Licinius and for Dionysius, as it came for the beloved father and brother of Marcus Crassus, as it had come for all the victims of Sulla and the victims of Sulla's enemies, as it had come for Sulla himself and for the wizard Eunus, both eaten alive by worms, and would come for Metrobius and Marcus Crassus, for Mummius and even for haughty Faustus Fabius. Death would come for beautiful Apollonius even as it had come for old Zeno, who ended up a half-eaten corpse on the shores of Lake Avernus. Death would come for little Meto, who had hardly lived—if not tomorrow, then another day. I found a curious, cold comfort in these thoughts. *Death comes as the end. . . .*

Then I remembered Eco.

I could not see or hear—I was blind and deaf, or else the night had turned black and the wind was howling. But I was not mute. I cried out his name: "Eco! Eco!" If he answered, I did not hear. But how could he answer, when he was mute? Something trickled down my cheeks—not blood, but tears.

I fell forward and clutched my horse. He stopped his pacing and stood very still. The howling of the wind died down, but the world was still dark, for I held my eyes tightly shut. At some point everything turned upside down and I found myself lying on the ground amid the drifted leaves and twigs.

Some passing god had heard my prayer, after all. This night would be unending, and morning would never come.

TWENTY-TWO

I opened my eyes to a world that was neither dark nor light. Above me, in the gentle predawn breeze, branches creaked and groaned—or was it my own head cracking open?

I slowly pulled myself upright and sat against the trunk of a tree. My horse was nearby, casually nuzzling among the leaves in search of something to eat. My stomach growled; I groaned at the flashes of pain in my head. I reached up and touched dried blood—enough to make me queasy, but not enough to alarm me. "Plenty more where that came from," my father used to say when I was a boy and came home bleeding; he was neither Stoic nor stern, but knew how to put an injury in its place.

I stood shakily and took a deep breath, grateful, and not a little surprised, simply to be alive. I called Eco's name, loud enough for the hills to call it back to me. Shouting sent a thunderclap of pain through my skull. Eco did not appear. The world began to grow lighter.

I could search the woods for him; I could return to the villa. I decided instead to press on to Cumae, without Eco, without the bloodstained cloak. The funeral games would begin in a matter of hours. There was still a slender hope that I might be able to squeeze the truth from those who knew it.

The forest seemed to dwindle and contract in the growing daylight. From where I stood I could see the precipice where the assassin had attacked me; in the opposite direction I could see beyond the trees into the rocky region that surrounded the Sibyl's cave, and even glimpse a bit of the sea. And yet it had been so easy to lose my way the night before! Night and darkness rob men not just of their sight but of their senses. A blow to the head doesn't help.

I found the path quickly enough. After a few minutes I left the woods for the rocky maze, darting uneasy glances left and right, more afraid now of finding Eco than of not finding him. Again and again I saw the stump of a tree or a gray clump of rock and imagined it was his body.

No one was yet stirring on the little road that ran through the village of Cumae, but plumes of smoke rose from the houses of the early risers. I came to Iaia's house at the far edge of the village. No smoke rose from the ovens within; no sound or light issued from the windows. I tethered my horse and walked on.

I found the narrow path that led down to the sea, the same trail from which Olympias had emerged on the afternoon of our visit to the Sibyl. I followed the way downward through the low brush. It switched back and forth along a steep grade, hemmed in by sheer stone walls. The path grew faint in places and disappeared altogether where it was interrupted by outcrops of weathered stone. A few times I slipped on loose rocks and had to struggle for balance. It was not a trail that anyone was likely to take purely for pleasure or by accident; it would have been more suitable for an adventurous goat than a man, or perhaps for a nimble young woman who had a good reason for taking it.

The trail came to an end amid a jumble of boulders at the water's edge, closely hemmed in by the sheer stone walls that towered above. The waves pounded the rocks and receded, leaving only a narrow strip of black sand for a momentary beach. I looked about and saw no sign of a cave or fissure. The stain of saltwater and the strange creatures that clung to the stones indicated that the tide could rise considerably higher, swallowing the boulders and leaving no beach at all. If the water now was at only mid tide, then at low tide the waves might ebb enough to uncover a beach a man could properly walk on, at least for a little way beyond the boulders. As it was, I saw no indication of a hidden way into the sheer walls. I had come to a dead end.

And yet, I had seen Olympias come up from this trail

carrying a basket that was empty except for a knife and some crusts of bread, and the hem of her riding stola had been wet. I had seen how she blanched when Dionysius insisted on telling the tale of Crassus's weeks of hiding in the sea cave.

I steeled myself for the cold and stepped over the boulders onto the narrow beach. A moment later the waves came splashing at my feet and swallowed me to the knees, then withdrew, tugging at my ankles. I shivered at the cold and clutched at the stones behind me to keep my balance. The waves receded and then splashed again, higher this time, wetting me to the thighs. I hissed at the cold, forced my fingers to let go of the rock, and stepped forward onto the shifting sand.

I waded outward until the water came to my waist. The ebb and flow of the waves pulled at me strongly, and the sand gave way beneath my feet as quickly as I could regain my balance. In such a narrow place, I thought, a man could easily be seized by an undertow and pulled out to deep water in the blink of an eye, disappearing beneath the surface, never to see daylight again.

What was I hoping to find? A miraculous cave that would open in the rock at my whim? There were no secrets here, nothing to see but stone and water. I took another step. The waves rose to my ribs. The water lapped against a slab of stone that peaked from the foam like a turtle's head, then splashed into my face. Sputtering and clutching myself against the cold, I took another step. The water rose to my chest and then ebbed with a powerful force that threatened to suck me into the depths. I grabbed the stone for balance and felt my feet pulled from beneath me. I clung to the rock as a leaf clings to a branch in a strong wind. The cold took my breath away. For a moment I saw spots before my eyes.

Then the spots vanished and I saw the cave.

It was visible only when the waves receded, and then only for a moment. I saw a jagged black opening cut into the jagged black rock, like the gaping maw of a toothless beast. Foam eddied and poured from the lips, then the waves filled it up again.

Until the tide had ebbed substantially, it would be impossible to enter that hole. Any reasonable man could see as much. But a reasonable man would not be immersed to his neck in cold water, clinging to a slippery stone for dear life in the pale light of early morning.

I managed to release the rock and push myself toward the fissure, and then grabbed hold of the foaming lips and pulled myself inside. The waves came rushing in from behind and I was trapped, unable to go either forward or back while the spray surged around me, whipping seaweed against my face and filling my nose with saltwater. When the waves receded I scrambled forward and hit my head against the low ceiling of rock. That must have been when the wound on my head started bleeding again.

Darkness surrounded me. My strength suddenly vanished, sucked out to sea with the tide. I steeled myself for the next wave, which came surging around me like a blast from Neptune's nostrils. My nose was flooded with saltwater and I tasted blood on my tongue. The water ebbed. I thought it would surely pull me with it, but somehow I held on.

I opened my eyes, blinking at the burning salt. The wave had pushed me deep into the fissure. I looked up and saw a ray of sunlight from a hole high above. I was within the cave.

It was not merely surprising that I should have managed such a thing; it was impossible. The stunned looks on their faces told me as much.

Even in the dim light I recognized Olympias. I had dreamed of seeing her naked. Now I saw. Her flesh was smooth and unblemished, covered with a sheen of sweat that made the paler parts of her glow like alabaster in the sepulchral light. Her arms and legs were darker than the rest of her, burned by the sun to pale gold. She was slender but hardly frail, and looked even more vital and robust naked than clothed. Her breasts were full and round, with large nipples that were surprisingly dark considering her golden mane and the patch of gold between her sleek thighs. Sadly, I was in no condition to appreciate the sight.

Her companion appeared to appreciate it very much—just how appreciative was evident when they sprang apart and I saw the proof of his arousal. He scrambled to his feet, bumped his head against a shelf of rock, and cursed. Olympias meanwhile rolled onto her side and searched among the cushions and coverlets on the stone floor. She found what she was seeking, a shiny dagger with a blade as long as a man's forearm, and swung it upward in a great arc. I suppose she meant to hand it to her defender, but in her haste and confusion she very nearly cut his arousal short. They both gasped loudly at the near miss. Alexandros staggered back, struck his head again, and cursed. I might have laughed, had I not been in so much misery from the cold and wet and the throbbing in my head.

He was a physical match for Olympias, as I would have expected; it was unlikely that a beautiful young woman of her talent and discernment would have fallen in love with a Thracian stable slave who was anything less than impressively broad-shouldered and handsome. His shaggy mane of hair glinted chestnut in the dim light; his chest and limbs were dusted with a covering of the same soft stuff. His features were starkly molded, with generous lips and bushy eyebrows that converged in a single line above his fiery eyes; his sparse beard, only a few days old, accentuated his high cheekbones and thrusting jaw. His arousal, even in its rapidly fading state, looked substantial. He was not beautiful as Apollonius was beautiful, but I could see why Olympias had chosen him. Apparently he had a brain as well as brawn, since Zeno had used him to help keep accounts, but at the moment he looked rather dull and bovine as he rubbed his head and fumbled to take the dagger from Olympias.

"Put the weapon away," I said wearily. "I haven't come to hurt you."

They stared at me, wide-eyed and dubious. There was a softening in Olympias's eyes; only in that instant did she finally recognize me. What must I have looked like, rising up from the spuming tunnel wrapped in tendrils of seaweed, with blood trickling down my face? Alexandros stared at me as if I were a sea monster, and perhaps he thought I was.

"Wait," Olympias whispered. She laid her hand on Alexandros's arm. "I know him."

"Yes? Who is he?" He spoke with a heavy Thracian accent, and there was a wild, desperate note in his voice that caused me to slide my hand nearer to where my own dagger was sheathed beneath my tunic.

"The Finder," she said. "From Rome—the man I told you about."

"Then he's found me at last." He pulled his arm free. The long blade sliced through a pale shaft of sunlight and glimmered like quicksilver. He drew back against the cave wall and stared at me like a trapped animal.

"Is that what's happened, Gordianus?" Olympias looked at me suspiciously. "You've come to take him to Crassus?"

"Put the knife away," I whispered. I began to shiver uncontrollably. I clenched my teeth to stop them from chattering. "Can you make a fire? I suddenly feel very cold, and a little faint."

Olympias studied me for a moment, then made up her mind. She reached for a woolen gown and pulled it over her head, then stepped toward me and reached for the hem of my tunic. "Out of this, first, or else you'll die from the cold more surely than you will from a dagger. No fire, I'm afraid—we can't have anyone seeing the smoke—but we can wrap you in something warm. Alexandros, you're shivering as well! Put that knife away and cover yourself."

The cave, when I had first glimpsed it, had seemed enormous, stretching away like the Sibyl's cave into unknown space. It was not as large as that, but it did rise to a considerable height and was cut into the stone at an angle that slanted sharply away from the sea, so that the floor was stepped in a number of rocky terraces. Stowed here and there in small nooks were Alexandros's comforts—dirty coverlets, bits of food, utensils, jugs of fresh water, and a plump wineskin. Olympias took me to one of the higher terraces and wrapped me in a wool blanket. When my shivering subsided she offered me some crusts of bread and cheese, and even a few delicacies that I recognized from the funeral banquet; she must have pilfered them from the table and brought them as a treat for Alexandros. I protested that I wasn't hungry, but once I began I could hardly stop eating.

Soon I felt better, though bolts of pain still shot through my head when I moved it too sharply. "How soon will the opening of the cave be passable? Without serious risk of drowning, I mean?"

Alexandros glanced at the mouth of the cave, where already the foaming tide seemed to have ebbed. "Not long now. There won't be clear beach beneath the opening for another few hours, but already you could make your way into the water and up to the path without danger."

"Good. Whatever else happens, I must be there, at the arena. No matter how terrible. And I must find Eco."

"The boy?" said Olympias. Apparently she had never cared enough to catch his name.

"Yes, the boy. My son. The one who casts such longing looks in your direction, Olympias."

Alexandros wrinkled his brow disapprovingly. "The mute boy," Olympias explained to him. "I told you about him, remember? But, Gordianus, what do you mean when you say you must find him? Where is he?"

"Last night, when we set out for Cumae, we followed the route we took with you. We were attacked, on the precipice that overlooks Lake Avernus."

"By lemures?" whispered Alexandros.

"No, by something worse: living men. Two, I think, but I can't be certain. In the confusion Eco disappeared. Afterward I went searching for him, but my head . . ."

I touched the tender spot and winced. The bleeding had stopped. Olympias studied the wound. "Iaia will know what to do for this," she said. "But what about Eco?"

"Lost. I never found him, and then I lost consciousness. When I awoke I came here. If he's gone back to Gelina's villa, he may end up at the funeral games by himself. He's seen gladiators fight to the death before, but the massacre—whatever else happens, I must get back before it starts. I don't want Eco to see it alone. The old slaves, and Apollonius . . . and little Meto . . ."

"What are you talking about?" Alexandros looked at me, puzzled. "Olympias, what does he mean by a massacre?"

She bit her lip and looked at me ruefully.

"You haven't told him?" I said.

Olympias gritted her teeth. Alexandros was alarmed. "What do you mean by a massacre? What are you saying about Meto?"

"Doomed," I answered. "All of them, doomed to die. Every slave from the fields and the stables and the kitchens will be publicly slain to satisfy the good people of the Cup. Politics, Alexandros. Don't ask me to explain Roman politics to a Thracian slave, just take my word for it. For the crime of the true killer, whom he cannot find, Crassus intends to have every slave in the household put to death. Even Meto."

"Today?"

"After the gladiator contests. Crassus's men have erected a wooden arena in the flatlands by Lake Lucrinus. It should be quite an event, the kind of thing people will talk about from here to Rome for a long time to come, even after Crassus defeats Spartacus and finally gets himself elected consul—and after that, who knows? Perhaps he'll manage to make himself dictator, like his mentor Sulla, and people will still talk about the day he put the slaves of Baiae in their place."

Alexandros leaned back, aghast. "Olympias, you never told me."

"What would have been the point? You would only have fretted and brooded—"

"And perhaps he would have made some grand gesture by returning to Baiae to face Crassus's judgment himself?" I suggested. "Is that why you didn't tell him, Olympias? Instead you let him think that he merely had to stay in hiding long enough for Crassus to leave, and then he might escape, and you never whispered a word about all the slaves fated to die in his place."

"Not in his place, but alongside him!" said Olympias angrily. "Do you think it makes any difference to Crassus whether he finds Alexandros or not? He *wants* to put the slaves to death—you said so yourself, just now, for politics, to put on a show. Better for Crassus if he never finds Alexandros—that way he can keep scaring people with stories of the murdering Thracian monster who ran off to join Spartacus."

"What you say may be true now, Olympias, but was it so at the beginning, when Alexandros first fled to Iaia's house? What if you had turned him over to Crassus then? Would Crassus ever have concocted his scheme to avenge Lucius Licinius in such a terrible way? Do you feel no guilt for what you've done, hiding your lover and letting all the other slaves be slain? The old men and women, the children—"

"But Alexandros is innocent! He never murdered anyone!"

"So you say; so he tells you, perhaps. But how do you know, Olympias? *What* do you know?"

She drew back and sucked in a breath. The lovers exchanged an odd glance. "You know as well as I that it makes no difference whether Alexandros is innocent or not," she said. "Guilty or innocent, Crassus will crucify him if he's caught."

"Not if I could prove him innocent. If I could discover who *did* kill Lucius Licinius, if I could prove it—"

"Then—most especially then—would Crassus be certain to put Alexandros to death. And you as well."

I shook my head and grimaced at the flash of pain across my forehead. "You talk in riddles, like the Sibyl."

Olympias looked at the mouth of the cave, where flashes of light were reflected from the churning water beyond. "The tide has ebbed enough," she said. "It's time for us all to go up to the house to see Iaia."

TWENTY-THREE

IAIA made a great fuss over the wound on my head. She insisted on brewing a compound of foul-smelling herbs which she slathered onto the cut, then wrapped a long strip of linen around my head. She also gave me an amber-colored infusion to drink, which I put to my lips with some trepidation, thinking of Dionysius.

"You seem to know a great deal about herbs and their uses," I said, sniffing at the steam that rose from the cup.

"Yes, I do," she said. "Over the years, learning to make my own paints—to harvest and prepare the proper plants at the proper time of year—I came to know quite a lot about such things, not only which root might provide a splendid blue pigment, but which one might cure a wart."

"Or kill a man?" I ventured.

She smiled thinly. "Perhaps. The brew you're sipping now could possibly kill a man. But not in the concentration I've given you," she added. "It's mostly an extract of willow bark, mixed with just a touch of the stuff Homer called nepenthes, made from the Egyptian poppy. It will ease the pain in your head. Drink up."

"The poet says nepenthes brings surcease to sorrow." I gazed into the cup, searching for a glimpse of death in the swirling steam.

Iaia nodded. "Which is why the queen of Egypt gave it to Helen to cure her melancholy."

"Homer says also that it brings forgetfulness, Iaia, and what I have seen and learned I do not choose to forget."

"The amount I've given you will not set you to dreaming, only ease the throbbing." When I still hesitated, she frowned and shook her head in disappointment. "Really, Gordianus, if we had wanted to do you harm, I imagine Alexandros could have done away with you down in the sea cave or on the steep hillside. Even now, I imagine, we could somehow manage to send you plummeting from this terrace onto the rocks below, if we were determined to do so; you would be swept out to sea and vanish forever." She gazed at me intently. "I've come to trust you, Gordianus. I didn't trust you at first, I'll admit, but I do now. Won't you trust me?"

I looked into her eyes. She sat stiffly upright in a backless chair, dressed in a voluminous yellow stola. The sun had not yet risen above the roof of the house and the terrace was in shadow. Far below us, beyond the terrace wall, the sea pounded against the rocky coast. Olympias and Alexandros sat nearby, watching the two of us as if we were gladiators engaged in a duel.

I lifted the cup to my lips again, but set it down untouched. Iaia sighed. "If you would only drink, the pain would vanish. You'll thank me for the gift."

"Dionysius is beyond all pain, but I don't think he would be thankful if he could be here with us now."

Her brow darkened. "What do you insinuate, Gordianus?"

"You say you trust me, Iaia. Then at least admit to me what I already know. On the day when I came to see the Sibyl, I saw Dionysius following Olympias in secret. I think he knew about the sea cave and who was hidden there, or at least he guessed; that was why he insisted on telling the tale of Crassus hiding in the cave in Spain. I saw how you and Olympias reacted that night. Dionysius was very near to giving away your secret. The very next day, at the funeral feast, Dionysius was given poison in a cup. Tell me, Iaia, was it aconitum you used? That was my guess."

She shrugged. "What were the precise symptoms?"

"His tongue was aflame. He began to choke and convulse, then to vomit; his bowels were loosened. It all happened very fast."

She nodded. "I would say that you made an excellent

guess. But I cannot say for sure. I did not poison the cup, and neither did Olympias."

"Who did?"

"How can I say? I am not the Sibyl—"

"Only the vessel and the voice of the Sibyl."

She pursed her lips and sucked at her teeth. Her face became gaunt, and she looked as old as her years. "Sometimes, Gordianus. Sometimes. Do you really want to know the secrets behind the Sibyl? It is dangerous for any man to know them. Think of foolish Pentheus, torn apart by the Bacchae. Certain mysteries can be truly comprehended only by women; to a man, such knowledge is often quite useless, and it can be very dangerous."

"Would it be any less dangerous if I didn't know? Unless some god decides to intervene, I begin to wonder if I shall ever get back to Rome alive."

"Stubborn," said Iaia, slowly shaking her head, "very stubborn. I see that you will not be satisfied until you know everything."

"It is my nature, Iaia. It is how the gods made me."

"So I see. Where shall we begin?"

"With a simple question. Are you the Sibyl?"

She made a pained expression. "I will try to answer, though I doubt you'll understand. No, I am not the Sibyl. No woman is. But there are those of us in whom the Sibyl sometimes manifests herself, just as the god manifests himself through the Sibyl. We are a circle of initiates. We maintain the temple, keep the hearth burning, explore the mysteries, pass on the secrets. Gelina is one of us. She is more dear to me than you can know, but she is too delicate a vessel to be used directly by the Sibyl; she has other duties. Olympias is also an initiate. She is as yet too young and inexperienced for the Sibyl to speak through her, but it will come to pass. There are others besides myself who act as vessels; some live here in Cumae, others come from as far as Puteoli and Neapolis and the far side of the Cup. Most are descendants of the Greek families who settled here even before Aeneas came; their understanding of these matters is passed on in the blood."

"Iaia, I cannot deny that an interview with the Sibyl is a most wondrous thing, no matter whose form she takes. I wonder, for example, what it was that you burned on the fire before you took us into the Sibyl's cave. Could it be that the smoke had some effect on my senses?"

Iaia smiled faintly. "You miss very little, Gordianus. True, certain herbs and roots, used in certain ways, are conducive to a full apprehension of the Sibyl's presence. The use of those substances is a part of the discipline which we learn and pass on."

"In my own travels I've encountered such herbs, or heard of them. Ophiusa, thalassaegle, theangelis, gelotophyllis, mesa—"

She shook her head and grimaced. "Ophiusa comes from distant Ethiopia, where they call it the snake plant; it is said to be as horrible to look at as the visions it conjures up. The Sibyl has no use for such horrors. Thalassaegle is likewise exotic and harsh; I hear it grows only along the river Indus. Alexander's men called it 'sea-glimmer' and found that it caused them to rave and suffer blinding visions. Theangelis I know of. It grows in the high places of Syria and Crete and in Persia; the Magi call it 'the gods' messenger' and drink it to divine the future. Gelotophyllis grows in Bactria where the locals call it laughter-leaves; it merely intoxicates and brings no wisdom. Believe me, it was none of these that you inhaled."

"What about the other I named, mesa? A kind of hemp, I understand, with a strong aroma—"

"You exasperate me, Gordianus. Will you waste time and breath merely to satisfy your idle curiosity?"

"You're right, Iaia. Then perhaps you can tell me why you placed that ugly statuette in my bed on my first night in the villa."

She lowered her eyes. "It was a test. Only an initiate could understand."

"But whatever the test was, I passed it?"

"Yes."

"And then you left another message, advising me to consult the Sibyl."

"Yes."

"But why?"

"The Sibyl was ready to guide you to Zeno's body."

"Because the Sibyl thought I might assume that the same fate that befell Zeno had befallen Alexandros as well, and that his body had been consumed in the lake? That possibility did cross my mind; after all, two horses returned riderless to the stable. I might have returned and told Crassus as much, advising him to call off his search for Alexandros."

"And why didn't you?"

"Because I had seen Dionysius following Olympias, and I had seen Olympias bringing an empty basket up from the sea cave. It occurred to me then that Alexandros was hidden here in Cumae. But tell me, Iaia, did you lead me to Zeno's body to throw me off the scent?"

Iaia spread her hands. "One cannot always discern the Sibyl's methods; even when the god grants a supplicant's desires, he doesn't always use the means expected to accomplish his end. You might have assumed Alexandros was dead and proceeded from that assumption. Instead, here you sit, in the same house with Alexandros. Who can say this is not what the Sibyl intended, even if it is not what I expected?"

I nodded. "You knew, then, of Zeno's fate, and where he could be found. Did Olympias know?"

"Yes."

"And yet Olympias seemed genuinely shocked when we discovered Zeno's remains."

"Olympias knew of Zeno's fate, but she had not seen his body, as I had. I never intended for her to see it; I intended for you to visit Lake Avernus without her. Instead she went with you, and in horror she cast his remains into the pit. I have no doubt that this, too, was the will of the god."

"And I suppose it was the will of the god that brought Alexandros to your door in the first place, on the night of the murder?"

"Perhaps we should let Alexandros speak for himself," said Iaia, who cast a sidelong look at the young Thracian. "Tell Gordianus what transpired on the night of your master's murder."

Alexandros reddened, either because he was unused to speaking to strangers or because of the memory of that night. Olympias drew closer to him and laid her hand on his forearm. I wondered at the casual way she displayed her intimacy with a slave in the presence of a Roman citizen. In the sea cave I had caught them unaware in the middle of coitus, and she had been unembarrassed, but fear and surprise had ruled her then and might have overridden her normal judgment. I was more impressed by the public affection and tenderness she willingly gave Alexandros before Iaia and myself. I marveled at her devotion, and at the same time despaired for her; how could such an ill-begotten love end in anything but misery?

"That night," Alexandros began, his harsh Thracian accent overshadowed by the intensity with which he spoke, "we knew that Crassus was on his way. I had never seen him, I was new in the household, but I had heard much of him, of course. Old Zeno told me that the visit was unexpected and had come about on very short notice, and that the master was unprepared, very nervous and very unhappy."

"Did you know why Lucius was unhappy?"

"Some irregularity in the accounts. I didn't really understand."

"Even though you helped Zeno sometimes with the ledgers?"

He shrugged. "I can add figures and make the proper marks, but I seldom knew what it was that I was adding. But Zeno knew, or thought he did. He said that the master had been busy with some very secret business, something very bad. Zeno said the master had done things behind Crassus's back and that Crassus would be angry. That afternoon we were all three busy in the library, going through the accounts. At last the master sent me from the room; I could tell he wanted to say things to Zeno that I shouldn't overhear. Later he sent Zeno away as well. In the stables I asked Zeno what was happening, but he only brooded and wouldn't talk. It began to grow dark. I ate and helped the other stablemen to look after the horses. Finally I went to sleep."

"In the stables?"

"Yes."

"Was that where you normally slept?"

Olympias cleared her throat. "Alexandros usually slept in my room," she said, "next to Iaia's, in the house. But that night Iaia and I were here in Cumae."

"I see. Go on, Alexandros; you were sleeping in the stables."

"Yes, and then Zeno came to wake me. He carried a lamp and poked at my nose. I told him it couldn't be morning yet; he said it was the middle of the night. I asked him what he wanted. He said that a man had ridden up from nowhere and tethered his horse by the front door, then had gone in to see the master. He said they were both in the library, talking in low voices with the door shut."

"Yes? And who was this visitor?"

Alexandros hesitated. "I never saw him myself, not really. You see, that's the strange part. But Zeno said . . . poor Zeno . . ." He furrowed his thick eyebrows and stared intently into space, caught up in the remembrance.

"Yes," I said, "go on. What did Zeno tell you? Why did you flee the house?"

"Zeno said he had gone into the library. He had rapped gently on the door and thought he heard his name spoken, so he stepped inside. Maybe he didn't hear his name at all, or maybe the master was telling him to go away; Zeno was like that, he had a habit of stepping in when he wasn't wanted, just to have a sniff at what was happening. He said the master spun around in his chair and told him to get out—yelled at first, then lowered his voice very quickly and cursed him in a whisper."

"And the visitor?"

"He was standing by the shelves, looking through some scrolls with his back to the door. Zeno didn't really see him, but he saw that he was dressed in military garb, and he saw the man's cloak thrown over one of the chairs."

"The cloak," I said.

"Yes, just a simple dark cloak—but one corner had an emblem on it, a seal pinned to the cloth like a brooch. Zeno had seen it plenty of times before; he said he'd know it anywhere."

"Yes?"

"It was the seal of Crassus."

"No," I said, shaking my head. A throb of pain passed through my skull with such power that I finally reached for the cup of willow bark and nepenthes and drank it down. "No. That makes no sense at all."

"Even so," Alexandros insisted, "Zeno said it was Crassus in the library with the master, and the master's face was as white as a senator's toga. Zeno began to pace up and down in the stables, shaking his head with worry. I told him there was nothing we could do; if the master had gotten himself into trouble, that was his problem. But Zeno said we should go stand outside the library door and listen. I told him he was mad and rolled over to go back to sleep. But he wouldn't leave me alone until I got up from the straw and put on my cloak and stepped into the courtyard with him.

"It was a clear night, but very windy. The trees thrashed overhead, like spirits shaking their heads, whispering *no, no.* I should have known then that something terrible was afoot. Zeno ran ahead to the door and opened it. I followed him." Alexandros wrinkled his brow. "I have a hard time remembering all that happened next, it happened so fast. We were in the little hallway that leads to the atrium. Suddenly Zeno backed against me, so hard he almost knocked me down. He sucked in a breath and started blubbering. Over his shoulder I saw a man dressed like a soldier down on his knees, holding a lamp, and beside him was the body of the master, his head all crushed and bloody."

"And this man was Crassus?" I said, disbelieving.

He shrugged. "I only glimpsed his face for an instant. Or perhaps I didn't see his face at all; the lamp cast strange shadows and he was mostly in darkness, I think. Even if I had seen him clearly, I wouldn't have recognized him. I told you, I had never seen Crassus. What I remember looking at was the master—his lifeless body; his broken, bleeding face. Then the man put down his lamp and sprang to his feet, and I saw his sword, leaping like a flame in the lamplight. He spoke in a low voice, not frightened, not angry, but cold, very cold. He accused *us* of killing the master! 'You'll pay for this!' he was saying. 'I shall see both of you nailed to a tree!'

"Zeno grabbed me and pulled me out the door, across the courtyard, into the stable. 'Horses!' he was saying. 'Flee! Flee!' I did what he said. We mounted and were out the door of the stables before the man could follow. Even so, Zeno rode like a madman. 'Where can we go?' he kept saying, shaking his head and weeping like a slave about to be whipped. 'Where can we go? The poor master is dead and we shall be blamed!' I thought about Olympias, and remembered Iaia's house in Cumae. I'd been here a few times before, carrying supplies back and forth. I thought I could find the way in the dark, but it wasn't as easy as I thought."

"So I myself discovered," I said.

"We were going too fast, and the wind kept getting stronger, so that we couldn't hear each other shouting, and the fog closed in. Zeno was in a mad panic. Then we took a wrong turn and came to the cliff that overhangs Lake Avernus. My mount knew me, she warned me in time, and even so I almost went tumbling over. But Zeno knew very little about horses. When the beast tried to stop he must have kicked her, and she threw him. I saw him disappear, flying head over heels into the fog. The mist swallowed him up. Then silence. Then I heard a faint, distant splash, like a man falling into shallow water and mud.

"He screamed then. His voice rose up from the darkness—a long, terrifying scream. Then silence again.

"I tried to find a way down to the shore in the darkness, but the trees and fog and shadows baffled me. I called his name, but he never answered, not even a moan. Have I said something wrong?"

"What?"

"The look on your face, Gordianus—so strange, as if you had been there yourself."

"I was only remembering last night. . . ." I thought of Eco and felt a pang of dread. "Go on. What happened next?"

"Finally I found the way to Cumae. I entered the house

without waking the slaves, found Olympias and told her what had happened. It was Iaia's idea to hide me in the cave. Cumae is a tiny village, they could never have hidden me in the house. Even so, you discovered us."

"Dionysius discovered you first. You should thank the gods that he didn't tell Crassus. Or perhaps you can thank someone else." I looked sidelong at Iaia.

"Again you insinuate!" Iaia gripped the arms of her chair.

"Credit me with having eyes and a nose, Iaia. This house is full of strange roots and herbs, and I happen to know that aconitum is among them. On the day we consulted the Sibyl I saw it in a jar in the room where you make your paints. I imagine you might also have strychnos, hyoscyamus, limeum—"

"Some of these I keep, yes, but not for murder! The same substances that kill can also cure, if used with proper knowledge. Do you insist on an oath, Gordianus? Very well! I swear to you, by the holiness of the Sibyl's shrine, by the god who speaks through the Sibyl's lips, that no one in this house committed the murder of Dionysius!"

In the vehemence of her oath, she rose halfway to her feet. As she slowly settled into her chair again, the terrace became preternaturally quiet. Even the crashing of the waves below was hushed. The sun had at last risen above the roof of the house, tracing the terrace wall with a fringe of yellow light. A lonely cloud crossed the sun and threw all into shadow again; then the cloud passed, and the heat reflected from the dazzling white stones was warm against my face. I noticed in passing that the pain in my head had vanished, and in its place I felt a pleasant lightness.

"Very well," I said quietly, "that much is settled, then. You didn't kill Dionysius. Who did, I wonder?"

"Who do you think?" said Iaia. "The same man who killed Lucius Licinius. Crassus!"

"But for what reason?"

"I can't say, but now I think it is time for you to tell me what *you* know, Gordianus. For example, yesterday you sent the slave Apollonius diving off the pier below Gelina's house. I understand you made some startling discoveries."

"Who told you? Meto?"

"Perhaps."

"No secrets, Iaia!"

"Very well, then, yes. Meto told me. I wonder if we came to the same conclusion, Gordianus."

"That Lucius was trading arms to the rebel slaves in return for plundered silver and jewels?"

"Exactly. I think Dionysius may have also suspected some such scandal; that was why he hesitated to reveal Alexandros's hiding place, because he knew that there was a greater secret to uncover. Meto also told me that you discovered certain documents in Dionysius's room—incriminating documents regarding Lucius's criminal schemes."

"Perhaps. Crassus himself couldn't fully decipher them."

"Oh, couldn't he?"

A faint tracing of pain flickered through my skull. "Iaia, do you seriously suggest . . ."

She shrugged. "Why not speak the unspeakable? Yes, Crassus himself must have been involved in the enterprise!"

"Crassus, smuggling arms to Spartacus? Impossible!"

"No, quite disgustingly possible, for a man as vain and greedy as Marcus Crassus. So greedy that he couldn't resist the opportunity to reap a huge profit by dealing with Spartacus—surreptitiously, of course, using poor, frightened Lucius as his go-between. And so vain that he thought it would ultimately make no difference to his cause when he gains the command against the slaves. He thinks himself such a brilliant strategist that it won't matter that he has armed his own enemy with Roman steel."

"Then you say he poisoned Dionysius because the philosopher was close to exposing him?"

"Perhaps. More likely Dionysius had begun to insinuate blackmail, subtle blackmail, merely asking for a handsome stipend and a place in Crassus's retinue. But men like Crassus will not put up with subordinates who hold a secret over them; Dionysius was too stupid to see that there was no profit in the knowledge he was seeking to exploit. He should have kept his secrets to himself; then he might have lived."

"But why did Crassus kill Lucius?"

Iaia looked down at her feet, where the sunlight had crept close enough to warm her toes. "Who knows? Crassus came that night in secret to discuss their secret affairs. Perhaps Lucius had begun to balk at the tasks to which Crassus set him and threatened to expose them both; it would be like Lucius to panic. Perhaps Crassus had discovered that Lucius was cheating him. For whatever reason, Crassus struck him with the statue and killed him, then saw a way to turn even that moment of madness to his advantage, by making it look as if a follower of Spartacus had committed the crime."

I stared out at the unending progression of waves that proceeded from the horizon. I shook my head. "Such supreme hypocrisy—it's almost too monstrous to be believed. But why, then, did Crassus send for me?"

"Because Gelina and Mummius insisted. He could hardly refuse to allow an honest investigation of his cousin's death."

"And how did Dionysius come to have the documents?"

"That we can't be sure of. The only thing we know for certain is that we shall never have an explanation from Dionysius's lips."

I thought of Crassus's dark moods, his unspoken doubts, his long nights of searching through the documents in Lucius's library. If all was as Iaia had concluded, then Crassus was killer, eulogist, judge, and avenger combined, beyond the power of any of us to punish.

"I see you are not entirely satisfied," Iaia said.

"Satisfied? I am most dissatisfied. What a waste, what futility, to have put myself in such danger, and not only myself—Eco! All for a bag of silver. Crassus solves all his problems with silver—and why not, when men like me will settle for mere coins. He might as well have sent me the money and allowed me to stay in Rome, instead of dragging me here to take part in his hideous deception—"

"I meant," said Iaia, "that you might not be satisfied with my explanation of events. There are certain other circumstances of which you know nothing, which might grant you a little more insight into the workings of Crassus's mind. These matters are so delicate, so personal that I hesitate even now to discuss them with you. But I think Gelina would understand. You know that she and Lucius were childless."

"Yes."

"And yet Gelina very much wanted a child. She thought the problem might lie with her, and she sought my help; I did what I could with my knowledge of medicines, but to no avail. I began to think the problem rested with Lucius. I brewed remedies which Gelina administered to him in secret, but that was of no use, either. Instead, Priapus eventually withdrew his favor from Lucius entirely. He became crippled in his sex—powerless, just as he was powerless to control his own life and destiny. Imagine being Crassus's creature, compelled to fawn over his greatness, reduced to tawdry schemes of escaping his domination—which Crassus would never allow, because it gave him a perverse pleasure to keep his cousin pressed beneath his foot.

"And yet Gelina still wanted a baby. She wouldn't be denied. You've seen her; you know that she could hardly be called demanding or domineering. In many ways she's more retiring and acquiescent than befits a woman of her station. But in this one thing she would have her way. And so, against all my advice but with the full knowledge of her husband, she asked Crassus to give her a child."

"When was this?"

"During Crassus's last visit, in the spring."

"Why did Lucius allow it?"

"Don't many husbands quietly allow themselves to be cuckolded, because to protest would only aggravate their humiliation and shame? Beyond that, Lucius had a perverse penchant for making choices that would harm him. And Gelina appealed to his family pride—Crassus would at least give them an heir with the blood of a Licinius.

"But no child resulted. The only result was the coolness that developed between Lucius and Gelina. She had done exactly the wrong thing, of course. Had she approached any man but Crassus, Lucius might have kept a shred of dignity. But for his all-powerful cousin to be invited into his wife's bed—for Crassus to be asked to bring a child into the household he already dominated—these humiliations preyed on his soul.

"You see, then, that there was more than financial deception and fraud to spark a murder between the two cousins. Crassus can be quite cold and brutal; Lucius's shame pricked at him like a crown of thorns. Who knows what whispered words passed between them that night in the library? Before it was over, one of them was dead."

I looked heavenward. "And now a whole household of slaves will die. Roman justice!"

"No!" Alexandros jumped to his feet. "There must be something we can do."

"Nothing," whispered Olympias, reaching for his arm and grasping at thin air when he drew away.

"Perhaps . . ." I squinted at the edge of sunlight that blazed along the scalloped tile roof. Time was fleeting. The games might already have begun. "If I could confront Crassus directly, with Gelina as witness. If Alexandros could see him and identify him for certain—"

"No!" Olympias interposed herself between us. "Alexandros cannot leave Cumae."

"If only we had the cloak—the bloodstained cloak from which Crassus tore his seal before he discarded it along the road! If only I hadn't lost it to the assassins last night. The assassins . . . oh, Eco!"

And then the cloak appeared, wafting out of the dark shadows of the house into the bright sunshine, held aloft by the outstretched arms of Eco himself, who smiled and blinked the sleep from his eyes.

TWENTY-FOUR

BUT I thought you knew,'' Iaia kept saying. ''I thought that Olympias must have already told you.'' She was forgetting that on the night before, before Eco had come breathlessly beating on her door, Olympias had already slipped down to sleep with Alexandros in the sea cave and so had no way of knowing, as I had no way of knowing, that all the while we debated and deduced on the terrace, Eco was fast asleep within the house, clutching the filthy, bloodstained cloak he had saved from the assassins.

''How foolish I feel, Gordianus. Here I've sat, trying to impress you with my deductions, when all along I should have been telling you what you most wanted to know—that your son was safe and sound here under my roof!''

''The important thing is that he's here,'' I said, swallowing to clear the sudden hoarseness in my voice and blinking back the tears that made Eco's beaming, dirt-smudged face swim before my eyes. I squeezed him tightly in my arms and then stepped back, sighing from a sudden shortness of breath.

''When he came to me last night I could see that he was frightened and exhausted but not hurt,'' said Iaia. ''He was frantically trying to tell me something—I had no way of understanding. I gave him a special brew to calm him. At last he mimed using a wax tablet and stylus; I went to fetch them but when I came back he was fast asleep. I roused two of the slaves to carry him to bed. I looked in on him once or twice; he slept like a stone through the night.''

Eco looked up at me. He gingerly touched the bandage around my head.

"This? Nothing at all; a little bump to remind me to be more careful in the woods."

The smile abruptly faded from his lips. He averted his eyes and looked deeply troubled. I could guess the root of his shame: he had failed to warn me of the assassins' approach, failed to rescue me last night, and instead of sending aid to me in the forest he had fallen asleep against his will.

"I fell asleep myself," I whispered to him. He shook his head gloomily, angry not at me but at himself. He grimaced and pointed to his mouth. His eyes brimmed with tears. I understood as clearly as if he had spoken: *If only I could speak as others can, I could have shouted a warning to you on the precipice. I could have told Iaia that you were hurt and alone in the woods. I could say all that I need to say at this moment!*

I put my arms around him to hide him from the others. He shivered against me. I looked over his shoulder and saw that Olympias and Alexandros were smiling warmly, seeing only the joy of our reunion. Iaia smiled, but her eyes were sad. I released him, and while Eco turned toward the empty sea to compose his face, I pulled the bloodstained cloak from his trembling fingers. "The important thing now is that we have the cloak!"

"That changes nothing," protested Olympias. "Tell him, Iaia."

Iaia looked at me sidelong and pursed her lips. "I'm not sure . . ."

Alexandros stepped forward. "If there *is* any way to stop Crassus from killing the slaves—"

"Maybe," I said, trying to think. "Maybe . . ."

"I would never have stayed in the cave all this time had I known what was happening," Alexandros said. "You shouldn't have deceived me, Olympias, even to save me."

Olympias looked from his face to mine and back again, at first desperately and then shrewdly. "You won't leave me behind," she quietly insisted. "I shall go with you. Whatever happens, I must be there."

Alexandros moved to embrace her, but now it was she who shrank back. "If it's to be done, we should move now," she said. "The sun is getting higher. The games will have already begun."

The slave who fetched our horses gave me an odd look, puzzled at the bandage around my head. When he saw Alexandros he let out a gasp and turned pale. Iaia and Olympias had managed to deceive even their household slaves. Iaia did not bother to bind the man to secrecy; soon all the Cup would know that the escaped Thracian was still among them.

"Iaia, are you coming?" Olympias asked.

"Too old, too slow," Iaia insisted. "I shall go on to the villa at my own pace and wait there for news." She stepped beside me and gestured for me to bend down from my mount, then spoke softly into my ear. "Are you sure of yourself, Gordianus? To challenge Crassus like this . . . to box the lion's ears in his own den . . ."

"I think I have no choice, Iaia. It is how the gods made me."

She nodded. "Yes, the gods give us gifts, whether we ask for them or not, and then they give us no choice but to use them. We can blame the gods for many things." She lowered her voice. "But I think you should know that the gods did not make your son a mute."

I frowned at her, puzzled.

"Last night I looked in on him a number of times, to see that he slept soundly. He kept calling for you."

"What? Calling? In words?"

"As clearly as I speak to you now," she whispered. "He said, 'Papa, Papa.' "

I sat upright and looked down at her, baffled. She had no reason to deceive me or to delude herself, and yet how could such a thing be? I turned and glanced at Eco, who looked gloomily back at me.

"What are we waiting for?" said Olympias. Having made up her mind, she was determined to begin. Alexandros, on the other hand, seemed to be having second thoughts. A shadow of doubt crossed his face, then his features resolved themselves into a mask of perfect acquiescence to the will of the gods, such as any Stoic would have envied.

With a last wave to Iaia, the four of us set off.

* * *

From the Avernine woods we emerged onto the high, windy ridge overlooking Lake Lucrinus and Crassus's camp. The plain was dotted with great plumes of smoke that rose from spit-fires and ovens; a crowd must eat. Through the haze I saw the great bowl of the wooden arena filled with spectators who had come to gawk and thrill at the funeral games. No faces were discernible at such a distance, only the mottled colors of the spectators dressed in their brightest clothing to enjoy the holiday and the perfect weather of a crisp autumn day. I heard the clash of swords against shields. The vague, general murmur of the crowd rose to roaring shouts that must have been heard across the water in Puteoli.

"The gladiators must still be fighting," I said, squinting and trying to make out what was happening within the ring.

"Alexandros has strong eyes," said Olympias. "What do you see?"

"Yes, gladiators," he said, shielding his brow from the sun. "There must have already been several matches; I see pools of blood on the sand. Now three matches are being staged at once; three Thracians against three Gauls."

"How can you tell?" asked Olympias.

"By their arms. The Gauls carry long, curved shields and short swords; they wear torques about their necks and plumed helmets. The Thracians fight with round shields and long, curved daggers, and wear round helmets with no visor."

"Spartacus is a Thracian," I said. "Crassus no doubt chose Thracians so the crowd could vent its anger against them. They can expect no mercy from the spectators if they fall."

"A Gaul is down!" Alexandros said.

"Yes, I see." I squinted through the haze.

"He's thrown his blade aside and lifts his forefinger, asking for mercy. He must have fought well; the spectators grant it—see how they pull out their handkerchiefs?" The arena was like a bowl filled with fluttering doves as the crowd waved their white handkerchiefs. The Thracian helped the Gaul to his feet and they walked toward the exit together.

"Now one of the Thracians falls! See the wound in his

leg, how it pours blood onto the sand! He stabs the ground with his dagger and holds up his forefinger." A resounding chorus of catcalls and boos rose from the arena, a noise so full of hatred and blood lust that it caused hackles to rise on my neck. Instead of waving handkerchiefs the crowd pointed upward with clenched fists. The defeated Thracian leaned back on his elbows, exposing his naked chest. The Gaul dropped to one knee, gripped his short sword with both hands and plunged it into the Thracian's heart.

Olympias turned her face away. Eco watched in glum fascination. Alexandros still wore the look of stern resolution with which he had departed Cumae.

The triumphant Gaul walked once around the perimeter of the ring, holding his sword aloft and receiving the accolades of the crowd while his opponent's body was dragged to the exit, leaving a long smear of blood across the sand.

The remaining Thracian suddenly bolted and began to run from his opponent. The crowd laughed and jeered. The Gaul chased after him, but the Thracian outdistanced him, refusing to fight. There was a commotion in the stands, then a dozen or more attendants entered the ring, some carrying whips and others wielding long, smoldering irons, so hot that I could see the glow at their tips and the little plumes of smoke that trailed after them. They poked at the Thracian, searing his arms and legs, making him jerk and clutch himself with pain. They lashed him with the whips, driving him back toward his opponent.

Olympias gripped Alexandros's bare arm, sinking her nails into the flesh. "This was a mistake!" she hissed. "These people are mad, all of them. There's nothing we can do!"

Alexandros wavered. He stared down at the sickening spectacle, his jaw clenched. He gripped the reins so tightly that his arms began to tremble.

In the arena the Thracian finally began to fight again, running toward the Gaul with a high, mad scream that rose above the murmur of the crowd. The Gaul was taken unaware and retreated, tripping over his own feet and falling on his backside. He recovered enough to protect himself with his shield, but the Thracian was relentless, banging his shield against the other's and stabbing again and again with his curved blade. The Gaul was wounded; he threw his blade aside and frantically waved his forefinger in the air, signaling for mercy.

Handkerchiefs and clenched fists filled the air, together with a thunderous roar. At last the fists began to outnumber the handkerchiefs, and the crowd began to stamp and chant: "Kill him! Kill him! Kill him!"

Instead, the Thracian threw down his dagger and shield. The attendants came after him again with their whips and irons, lashing and poking him from all directions, compelling him to perform a hideous, spastic dance. At last he picked up his dagger. They drove him back toward the Gaul, who was already covered with blood from the wounds on his arms. The Gaul rolled onto his stomach and pressed his hands to his visor, steeling himself. The Thracian dropped to his knees and drove the dagger into the Gaul's back again and again in time with the chanting of the crowd: "Kill him! Kill him! Kill him!"

The Thracian stood and held his bloody dagger aloft. He began to perform a strange parody of a victory strut, lifting his knees comically and rolling his head on his shoulders, mocking the crowd. A great chorus of hissing, catcalls, booing, and raucous laughter echoed up from the arena; within the walls the noise must have been deafening. The attendants came after the Thracian with their whips and pokers, but he seemed not to feel the pain and only grudgingly allowed them to drive him toward the exit and out of sight.

"Do you need to see more, Alexandros?" whispered Olympias hoarsely. "These people will tear you apart before you can utter a word! Crassus is giving them exactly what they want—there is nothing you can do, nothing Gordianus or anyone can do, to stop it. Come back with me to Cumae!"

I saw the fear in his eyes. I cursed my own vanity. Why drag him before Crassus, when it could only result in another needless death? What sort of fool was I, to imagine that the proof of his own guilt could humble Marcus Crassus, or that mere truth could sway him from giving the crowd the bloody entertainment they craved? I was ready to send Alexandros and Olympias fleeing back to the sea cave when the trumpets began to blare from the arena below.

A gate beneath the stands opened. The slaves trudged into the arena. In their hands they carried objects made of wood.

"What is it?" I said, squinting. "What is it they carry in their hands?"

"Little swords," Alexandros whispered. "Short wooden swords, such as gladiators use to practice. Training swords. Toys."

The crowd was quiet. There were no boos or hissing. They watched with hushed curiosity, wondering why such a sorry rabble was being paraded before them and curious to see what sort of spectacle Crassus had devised.

Gathered outside the eastern rim of the arena, where the crowd could not yet see them, a contingent of soldiers had gathered. Their armor glinted in the sun. Among them I saw trumpeters and standard bearers. They began to gather into ranks, preparing for an entrance into the arena. I suddenly understood and felt sick at heart.

"Little Meto," I whispered. "Little Meto, with only a toy sword to defend himself . . ."

My eyes met those of Alexandros. "We're too late," I said. "To take the path to the road, and the road down into the valley—" I shook my head. "It will take too long."

He bit his lip. "Straight down the slope, then?"

"Too steep," protested Olympias. "The horses will stumble and break their necks!" But Alexandros and I were already bounding over the edge and racing down the steep hillside, with Eco a heartbeat behind.

I held on for dear life. Once we were over the crest, my mount locked her forelegs and slid down the slope, her shoulders as rigid as stone while her hind legs kicked and stamped against the furrowed earth. She shook her head and whinnied, like a warrior screaming to his gods to steel himself for battle.

The desperate descent uprooted bushes and set off avalanches of pebbles and sand. Suddenly a half-buried boulder loomed directly below me. For an instant I saw the features of Pluto himself in its weathered face, grinning at me horribly; we would collide with the stone and be shattered to bits. Closer and closer we came to it, and then my mount gave a great leap and bounded over it.

She landed with a jolt that nearly snapped my neck. There was no more sliding with locked forelegs; she had no choice but to gallop full speed down the steep face of the hill. I fell forward, clutched her neck, and dug my heels into her hide. Sky became wind; the earth became a cloud of dirt. The whole world was a ball tumbling through space. All balance was gone. I shut my eyes, clutched the beast as tightly as I could, and sucked in the odor of torn earth, horse sweat, and blind panic.

Suddenly the plummet became a gradual curve. Little by little the earth became flat again. We raced with the accumulated speed of the descent, but no longer out of control. The world righted itself; sky was sky and earth was earth. I squinted into the wind and slowly asserted control, reining the beast in. I half expected her to throw me out of anger and distrust, but she seemed glad for the reassurance of my hands on the reins. She shook her head and whinnied again, and it sounded as if she were laughing. She submitted and slowed to a trot, flinging spumes of sweat from her mane.

Alexandros was far ahead of me. I turned and caught a glimpse of Eco close behind. I sped onward toward the arena.

We raced between the tents. Soldiers in tunics sat in circles gambling, or played trigon stripped to the waist, enjoying their holiday. They scattered before us and shook their fists in alarm. We raced past the spits and ovens with their plumes of white smoke, kicking dust into the flames. The cooks chased after us, screaming curses.

Alexandros waited for me outside the arena, his face confused and uncertain. I pointed to the north, where I had seen the red canopy and the pennants that decorated Crassus's private box. We set off at a gallop. Eco had fallen far behind. I waved to him to follow us.

The periphery of the arena was mostly deserted, except for a few patrons who had left the stands to relieve themselves against the wooden wall. Entrances opened onto steps that led upward to the seats, but I gestured to Alexandros that we should ride on until we found the steps that would take us directly to Crassus's box.

At the northernmost end of the circle we came to an opening smaller than the others and flanked by red pennants that bore in gold the seal of Crassus. Alexandros reined his beast and looked at me quizzically. I nodded. He leaped from his horse. I rode a few paces farther and peered as best I could around the edge of the arena; outside the eastern rim the soldiers were still forming ranks and had not yet entered.

I rode back to Alexandros. Above us, on the rim of the arena, a movement caught my eye. I looked up but saw only a face that quickly disappeared.

I dismounted, and almost fell to my knees. In the mad descent down the hill and the race through the camp I had felt no pain or dizziness, but as soon as my feet touched the earth my knees went weak and the throbbing returned to my temples. I staggered and steadied myself against my horse. Alexandros, already bounding up the steps, turned and ran back to me. I reached up to my forehead, touched the bandage, and felt a spot of warm wetness. I pulled my hand away and saw something red and viscous on my fingers. I was bleeding again.

From somewhere behind me, between the pounding drumbeats in my head, I thought I heard a boy calling, "Papa! Papa!"

Alexandros clutched my arm. "Are you all right?"

"Just a little dizzy. A little nauseous . . ."

Again I heard an unfamiliar voice calling, "Papa, Papa," louder and closer than before. I turned my head, thinking I must be in a dream, and saw Eco riding toward us, pointing to the sky. "There!" he screamed, above the trampling hooves of his mount. "A man! A spear! Watch out!"

I looked upward, over my shoulder. Alexandros did the same. An instant later he tackled me and we tumbled onto the ground. I was amazed at his strength, alarmed at the jolt of pain that ricocheted through my head, and only vaguely aware of what I had glimpsed above us—a man with a spear leaning over the arena wall. In the next instant the spear came plummeting down with a whistling noise and planted itself in the earth, missing my horse by less than a hand's width. Had Alexandros not pulled me to safety the spear would have entered the back of my neck and exited somewhere below my navel.

It took only a moment to vomit. The yellow bile left a bitter taste in my mouth and a mess all over the front of my tunic, but I felt vaguely better afterward. Alexandros impatiently grabbed one shoulder while Eco grabbed the other. Together they pulled me to my feet.

"Eco!" I whispered. "But how?"

He looked at me, but did not answer. His eyes were glassy and feverish. Had I only imagined it?

Then they were pulling me up the steps. We came to a landing and doubled back, came to another landing and doubled back again. We stepped onto thick red carpeting and emerged into bright sunlight filtered through a red canopy. I saw Crassus and Gelina seated side by side, flanked by Sergius Orata and Metrobius. I heard the slithering noise of steel unsheathed as Mummius stepped from behind Crassus and bellowed, "What in Jupiter's name!"

Gelina gasped. Metrobius grasped her arm. Orata gave a start. Faustus Fabius, standing behind Gelina's chair, gritted his teeth and stared down at us with flaring nostrils. He lifted his right hand and the rank of armed soldiers at the back of the canopy took up their spears. Crassus, looking at once unpleasantly surprised and resigned to unpleasant surprises, scowled at me and lifted a hand to keep everyone in place.

I looked dizzily around, trying to orient myself. Red draperies hung from the canopy overhead, hiding us from the spectators immediately on either side, but beyond the edge of the draperies I could see the great circling bowl of the arena, jammed with people from top to bottom. Nobles sat in the lower tiers while the common people were crowded into the seats higher up. To separate them a long white rope circled the arena, running from one side of Crassus's box back around to the other.

Directly before the canopied box, down in the arena, huddled on the sand amid pools of blood, were the slaves. Some were in filthy rags; others, the last to have been taken from the household, still wore tunics of clean white linen. They were male and female, old and young. Some stood as still as statues while others listlessly turned and turned, looking about in fear and confusion. Each held a blunt wooden sword. How must the world have looked from where they stood? Blood-soaked sand beneath their feet, a high wall surrounding them, a circle of leering, laughing, hateful faces staring down at them. They say a man cannot see the gods from the floor of an arena; he looks up and sees only the empty blue sky.

I saw Apollonius among them, his right arm encircling the old man he had comforted in the annex. I searched the crowd for Meto and did not see him; my heart skipped a beat and for an instant I thought he must somehow have escaped. Then he stepped into an open space near Apollonius, ran to him, and hugged his leg.

"What is the meaning of this?" said Crassus dryly.

"No, Marcus Crassus!" I shouted and pointed into the arena. "What is the meaning of *this*?"

Crassus glared at me, as heavy-lidded as a lizard, but his voice was steady. "You look quite terrible, Gordianus. Does he not look terrible, Gelina? Like something spat up half-chewed by the Jaws of Hades. You've hurt your head, I see—from banging it against a wall, I imagine. Is that vomit on your tunic?"

I might have answered, but my heart was beating too fast in my chest, and the throbbing in my head was like thunder.

Crassus pressed his fingers together. "You ask me, what is the meaning of this? I take it you mean: what is happening here? I will tell you, since you seem to have arrived late. The gladiators have already fought. Some have lived, some have died; the shade of Lucius is well pleased, and so is the crowd. Now the slaves have been ushered into the arena—armed, as you can see, like the ragtag army they are. In a moment I shall step out onto that little platform behind you, so that the crowd can see and hear me, and I shall announce a most splendid and sublime amusement, a public enactment of Roman justice and a living parable of divine will.

"The slaves of my household here in Baiae have been

polluted by the seditious blasphemies of Spartacus and his kind. They are complicit in the murder of their master; so all the evidence indicates, and so you have been unable to disprove. They are useless now, except to serve as an example to others. In the spectacle I have planned, they shall represent—they shall embody—that which the crowd most fears and despises: Spartacus and his rebels. Thus I have armed them, as you see."

"Why don't you give them real weapons?" I said. "Weapons like the swords and spears I found in the water off the boathouse?"

Crassus pursed his lips but otherwise ignored me. "A few of my soldiers shall represent the power and glory of Rome—ever vigilant and ever conquering under the leadership of Marcus Licinius Crassus. My soldiers are readying themselves, and as soon as I have made my announcement they shall enter through that gate opposite, with blaring of trumpets and banging of drums."

"A farce!" I hissed. "Useless and monstrously cruel! A bloody slaughter!"

"Of course a slaughter!" Crassus's voice took on an edge like flint, cutting and brittle. "What else could transpire, when the soldiers of Crassus meet a band of rebellious slaves? This is only a foretaste of the glorious battles to come, when Rome grants me supreme command of her legions and I march against the rebel slaves."

"It's an embarrassment," muttered Mummius in disgust. His face was ashen. "A disgrace! Roman soldiers against old men and women and children with wooden toys! There is no honor in it, no glory! The men are not proud, believe me, and neither am I—"

"Yes, Mummius, I know your sentiments." Crassus's voice burned like acid. "You allow yourself to be blinded by carnal lust, by decadent Greek sentimentality. You know nothing of true beauty, true poetry—the harsh, austere, unforgiving poetry of Rome. You understand even less about politics. Do you think there is no honor in avenging the death of Lucius Licinius, a Roman killed by slaves? Yes, there is honor in it, and a kind of merciless beauty, and there shall be political profit for me, both here and in the Forum at Rome.

"As for you, Gordianus—you have arrived just in time. I certainly hadn't intended to seat you in my private box, but I'm sure we can find room for you, and for the boy. Is Eco, too, unwell? He sways on his feet, and I seem to see a feverish glimmer in his eyes. And this other person—a friend of yours, Gordianus?"

"The slave Alexandros," I said. "As you must already know."

Alexandros put his mouth to my ear. "Him!" he whispered between the drumbeats in my head. "I'm certain of it! I must have seen his face more clearly than I thought; I recognize him now that I see him again—the man who killed the master—"

"Alexandros?" said Crassus, raising an eyebrow. "Taller than I expected, but the Thracians are a tall people. He certainly looks strong enough to crack a man's skull with a heavy statue. Good for you, Gordianus! It was wise of you to bring him directly to me, even at the last possible moment. I will announce his capture and send him down to die with the others. Or shall I save him for a special crucifixion, to climax the games?"

"Kill him, Crassus, and I will scream at the top of my lungs the name of the man who really murdered Lucius Licinius!"

I produced the bloodstained cloak. I threw it at his feet.

Gelina lurched forward, clutching the arms of her chair. Mummius turned pale and Fabius looked at me in alarm. Orata squinted down at the lump of cloth. Metrobius bit his lips and put a protective arm around Gelina's shoulder.

Only Crassus seemed unperturbed. He shook his head as if he were a pedagogue and I a pupil who could not keep my grammar straight, no matter how many times he corrected me.

"On the night of the murder, before he fled for his own life, Alexandros saw everything," I said. "Everything! The corpse of Lucius Licinius; the murderer who knelt beside the body, scraping the name of Spartacus in the stone to deflect suspicion from himself; the murderer's face. That man was not a slave. Oh, no, Marcus Crassus, the man who killed Lucius Licinius had no other motive than devouring greed. He traded arms for gold with Spartacus. He poisoned Dionysius when Dionysius came too close to the truth. He threw me off the pier and tried to drown me on my first night in Baiae. He dispatched assassins to kill me in the woods last night. That man is not a slave but a Roman citizen and a murderer, and there is no law on earth or in the heavens that can justify the wholesale slaughter of innocent slaves for his crimes!"

"And who would this man be?" Crassus asked mildly. He poked his toe at the crumpled, bloodstained tunic. He wrinkled his nose, then frowned with dawning recognition.

I opened my mouth to speak, but Alexandros was quicker. "It was him!" he shouted, and raised his arm. He pointed—but not at Crassus.

Mummius bared his teeth and grunted. Gelina cried out. Metrobius held her tightly. Orata looked slightly queasy. Crassus clenched his jaw and made a face like thunder.

All eyes turned toward Faustus Fabius. He blanched and took a step backward. For just an instant his imperturbable patrician mask slipped to reveal an expression of pure desperation. Then, just as quickly, he recovered his composure and stared catlike at the finger pointing toward him.

Beside me, Eco swayed and crumpled onto the red carpet.

TWENTY-FIVE

ECO fell unconscious into a burning fever. As soon as I could, I took him to the villa, where Iaia was already anxiously waiting for news. She took the matter into her hands and insisted that Eco be brought to her room, where she brooded over him, sending Olympias to the house in Cumae to fetch unguents and herbs. The air in the room was quickly filled with smoke from braziers and vapor from tiny boiling pots. She roused Eco from his uneasy sleep to pour her strange concoctions between his lips and rubbed a foul-smelling salve behind his ears and around his lips. For me she prescribed a strong dose of nepenthes ("For a few hours, at least, it will take you far away from this place, which is what you need"), but I refused to drink it.

Day turned to night without formalities to mark the hours. Dinner was never served; people slipped into the kitchens to pick at leftover portions from the previous day's feast, or nibbled at delicacies brought back from the games. Without slaves to tend to the beds and light the lamps, to indicate the hours with the unending cycle of their labor, time seemed to stop; yet darkness still descended.

That night Morpheus passed over the villa at Baiae. His spell covered all the rest of the world, but he overlooked the inhabitants of that house; there was no sleep for anyone, only the darkness and stillness of the long night. With Iaia and Gelina I kept a vigil in Eco's room, listening in amazement as he muttered a fitful stream of names and incoherent phrases. What he said made no sense, and the sounds were often crude and slurred, but there was no denying that he spoke. I asked Iaia if she had put a spell on him, but she claimed no credit.

I sat and fretted in the dim light of Iaia's room, my head spinning at all the terrible and wonderful things that could happen in a single day.

At last I wrapped a cloak around my shoulders, lit a small lamp, and wandered through the quiet house. The empty hallways were dark, illuminated only here and there where cold white moonlight poured through a window.

Done with her errands for Iaia, Olympias had retired to her own room, but not to sleep. Through her door I heard soft murmurings and sighs, and the low, hearty laugh of a young man released after long days and nights of exile in a cave, luxuriating amid soft pillows and the caresses of warm, familiar flesh. I smiled, wishing I had some excuse to stumble in on their coupling, now that the throbbing in my head had finally ceased and I could truly appreciate the sight.

I continued to wander until I made my way to the men's baths and stood beside the great pool. The waters of the mineral spring seethed and gurgled; the rising steam danced and vanished in the glow of my little lamp. I looked toward the terrace and saw two naked figures standing side by side, leaning against the balustrade and each other. They gazed out at the reflection of the moon on the shimmering bay. Pools of water marked the path of their footsteps from the bath to the balustrade, and great clouds of steam rose from their heated flesh. The moonlight shone like a fuzzy halo on Mummius's great hairy shoulders and buttocks; the same light shone on Apollonius and seemed to turn him into quicksilver and polished marble.

I covered my lamp with my hand. Silent and unseen, I found a way down from the terrace onto the path that led to the pier. I turned toward the annex instead and ascended the hill. I came to the long, low building where the captives had been held. Its door was pressed back against the wall and opened onto utter blackness. I paused for a moment and stepped inside, then recoiled at the shock of the smell. The place was filled with the odor of human misery, but tonight it was empty and silent.

From the stables farther ahead I heard the sounds of quiet conversation and laughter. I followed the path around the corner of the building to the open courtyard. Three guards were posted outside the stables, wrapped in cloaks and gathered around the warmth of an open fire. One of them recognized me and nodded. Behind them, the door to the stables stood ajar, and within I saw the slaves huddled in groups around tiny lamps. Above the low murmur of conversation I heard someone snap, "Get out of there, you pest!" and I knew that Meto must be among them.

I turned toward the villa and took a long, deep breath of cold air. There was no wind; the tall trees that surrounded the villa stood upright and silent. All the world seemed strangely alert and bemused by moonlight.

I walked across the courtyard, hearing the soft crunch of gravel beneath my feet. On the doorstep I hesitated; instead of entering the villa I lingered beneath the portico, then walked along the outer wall until I came to one of the windows that looked into the library. The draperies were only partly shut. The room was brightly lit. Within I saw Marcus Crassus wrapped in his chlamys, toiling over a stack of opened scrolls with a cup of wine in his left hand. He never appeared to look up, but after a long moment he spoke. "You need not skulk outside, Gordianus; your spying is done. Come inside. Not through the window—this is a Roman house, not a hovel."

I returned to the front door and passed through the entry hall. In the darkness the waxen faces of Lucius Licinius's ancestors gazed down on me, looking grim but satisfied. I walked through the atrium, where the odor of incense had at last covered the lingering smell of putrefaction. Moonlight poured through the open roof like a great column of liquid opal. Holding my lamp aloft, I studied the letters SPARTA on the floor. Under the wavering lamplight and moonlight the crude scratches shone gold and silver, as if some passing god, and not a mere murderous mortal, had drawn them with his fingertip.

There was no guard outside the library. The door stood open. Crassus did not turn or look up when I entered, but indicated that I should sit in the chair to his left. After a moment he pushed the scrolls away, pinched the bridge of his nose, and produced a second silver cup, which he filled to the brim from a clay bottle.

"I'm not thirsty, thank you, Marcus Crassus."

"Drink," he said, in a tone that allowed no rebuttal. I obediently put the cup to my lips. The wine was dark and rich, and spread a warm glow through my chest.

"Falernian," said Crassus. "From the last year of Sulla's dictatorship. An exceptional vintage; it was Lucius's favorite. There was only one bottle left in the cellar. Now there are none." He filled his own cup again, then poured the last drops into mine.

I sipped, breathing in the bouquet. The wine was as bemusing as the moonlight. "No one sleeps tonight," I said quietly. "Time seems to have stopped altogether."

"Time never stops," said Crassus with a bitter edge to his voice.

"You are not pleased with me, Marcus Crassus. And yet I only did what I was hired to do. Anything less would have shown contempt for the generous fee you promised me."

He looked at me sidelong. His expression was unreadable. "Don't worry," he said at last, "you'll get your fee. I didn't become the richest man in Rome by swindling petty hirelings."

I nodded and sipped the Falernian.

"Do you know," said Crassus, "for a moment, out there in the arena today, when you were rolling your eyes and making your passionate speech, I actually thought—can you believe it?—I thought that you were going to accuse *me* of killing Lucius."

"Imagine that," I said.

"Yes. If you had dared such impudence, I think I might have ordered one of the guards to put a spear through your heart then and there. No one would have questioned such an act. I would have called it self-defense; you had a knife concealed on your person, you looked like a madman, and you were ranting like Cicero on a bad day."

"You would never have done such a thing, Marcus Crassus. Had you killed me immediately after I made such a public accusation, you would only have planted a seed of doubt in everyone who was there."

"You think so, Gordianus?"

I shrugged. "Besides, the point is hypothetical. I never made such an accusation."

"And you never intended to?"

I sipped the Falernian. "It seems useless to dwell on such a question, since what you describe never occurred and the true murderer was identified—just in time to avoid a terrible miscarriage of justice, I might add, though I know you find that to be a minor point."

Crassus made a low noise in his throat, rather like a growl. It had not been easy for him to cancel the slaughter after arousing the curiosity and whetting the blood lust of the crowd. Even after the revelation of Fabius's guilt, he might have gone on with the massacre had it not been for the intervention of Gelina. Meek, mild Gelina had at last put her foot down. Armed with the truth, she was transformed before our eyes. Her jaw set, her eyes hard and glittering like glass, she had demanded that Crassus cancel his farce. Mummius, blustering and outraged, had joined her. Assaulted from both sides, Crassus had acquiesced. He had ordered his guards to escort Fabius and himself back to the villa, curtly charged Mummius with closing the games, and then had made an abrupt and unceremonious exit.

"Did you stay for the end of the games?" Crassus asked.

"No. I left only moments after you did." Why bother to explain that Alexandros and I had carried Eco back to the villa, fearing for his life? Crassus had hardly noticed Eco's collapse, and probably did not even remember it.

"Mummius tells me that all went smoothly, but he's lying, of course. I must be the laughingstock of the whole Cup tonight."

"I seriously doubt that, Marcus Crassus. You are not the sort of man at whom people would ever dare to laugh, even behind your back."

"Still, to have the slaves rounded up and herded from the ring as unceremoniously as they were herded into it, with no explanation—I could hear the murmurs of disappointment and confusion even from outside the arena walls. For a climax, Mummius tells me he hastily assembled all the surviving gladiators and forced them to fight again in simultaneous matches; not exactly an original idea, was it? Imagine what a farce that became, with the gladiators already weary and some of them wounded, hacking away at each other like clumsy amateurs. When I pressed him about it, Mummius admitted that the lower tiers quickly emptied out. The connoisseurs know a bad spectacle when they see it, and the status seekers saw no point in remaining when I was no longer there to smile back at them."

We sat in silence for a moment, sipping the wine.

"Where is Faustus Fabius tonight?" I asked.

"Here in the villa, as before. Except that tonight I've placed guards outside his room and had him stripped of any weapons, poisons, or potions, lest he do some harm to himself before I decide what I shall do with him."

"Will you bring charges against him? Will there be a trial in Rome?"

Crassus again put on the face of a disappointed tutor. "What? Go to so much trouble on account of the murder of a nobody like Lucius? Alienate the Fabii, expose an unspeakable scandal in which my own cousin was involved, embarrass myself in the process—they were using *my* ship and *my* resources to carry out their schemes, after all—do all this on the eve of the great crisis, when I stand ready to take the command against Spartacus and begin my campaign for the consulship next year? No, Gordianus, there will be no public accusation; there will be no trial."

"Then Faustus Fabius will go unpunished?"

"I never said that. There are many ways for a man to die during wartime, Gordianus. Even a high-ranking officer can be struck down by a spear accidentally cast from behind him, or receive a fatal blow which cannot afterward be accounted for. And I never said *that*, either."

"Did he confess everything to you?"

"Everything. It was just as you thought; he and Lucius had hatched their smuggling scheme together during my visit to Baiae last spring. Faustus comes from a very old, very distinguished patrician family. His branch of the Fabii retain a vestige of their old prestige, but they lost their fortune long ago. Such a man can become very bitter, especially when he serves under another man of a lower social rank whose wealth and power far exceed his own and always will. Still, to have betrayed Rome for the sake of his own aggrandizement, to have sacrificed the honor of the Fabii, to have given succor to an army of murderous slaves—these crimes are unforgivable and beneath contempt."

Crassus sighed. "The crimes of my cousin Lucius are even more painful to me. He was a weak man, too weak to make his own way in the world, neither wise enough nor patient enough to trust my generosity. I consider it a personal affront that he should have used my own organization and embezzled my own funds to engage in such a disgusting criminal enterprise. I always gave him more than he deserved, and this was how he repaid me! I'm only sorry that he died as quickly and painlessly as he did; he deserved an even crueler death."

"Why did Fabius kill him?"

"My visit was unscheduled and unexpected. Lucius had only a few days' notice before my arrival. He panicked—there are dozens of improprieties in his records; there were swords and spears hidden down in the boathouse, awaiting shipment. The night before we arrived, Fabius stole away from the camp at Lake Lucrinus after dark and came to confer with Lucius. To confuse anyone who might see him, and without my knowledge, he took my own cloak before he rode off. It was suitably dark; all the better to hide himself. He didn't foresee the use to which he would put it, and the fact that he would have to dispose of it altogether. Once it was ruined with blood he could neither leave it at the scene of the crime nor return it to me. He tore the seal from the cloak and threw both into the bay. The seal, being heavier, must have reached the water; the cloak caught on the branches.

"I missed my cloak the next day and wondered where it had gone; I mentioned it to Fabius himself and he never batted an eyelash! Why do you think I've been wearing this old chlamys of Lucius's every night? Not to conform to the Baian taste for Greek fashion, but because the cloak I brought from Rome was missing."

I stared at him, suddenly suspicious. "But on the same night that I suggested Lucius had been killed here in the library, you asked me where the blood had gone; do you remember, Marcus Crassus?"

"Perfectly well."

"And I told you then that a bloodstained cloak had been found, discarded by the road. You must have suspected that it was your cloak!"

He shook his head. "No, Gordianus. You told me that you had discovered a *cloth*, not a *cloak*. You never called it a cloak; I remember your words exactly." He breathed through his nostrils, sipped his wine, and looked at me shrewdly. "Very well, I admit that at that moment I experienced an odd quiver of apprehension; perhaps a part of me glimpsed a path that might lead to the truth. Perhaps a passing god whispered in my ear that this *cloth* might be my missing *cloak*, in which case there was far more to Lucius's murder than I had previously suspected. But one hears such vague whisperings all the time, no? And even the wisest man never knows if the gods whisper true wisdom in his ear or cruel folly."

"Still, why did Fabius murder Lucius?"

"Fabius left Rome prepared to kill Lucius, but the actual murder was spontaneous. Lucius became hysterical. What if I found him out, as I surely would if I made more than a cursory inspection of his records or located the captain of the *Fury*? He saw his own destruction loom before him. Fabius urged him to keep a cool head; together, he argued, they could keep me busy with other matters and deflect me from ever suspecting their enterprise. Who knows? They might have succeeded. But Lucius lost his wits, began to weep and insisted that a full confession was their only recourse. He intended to tell me everything and throw himself on my mercy, exposing Fabius along with himself. Fabius reached for the statue and silenced his babbling forever.

"It was a stroke of genius to incriminate the slaves, don't you think? That kind of quick-witted, cold-blooded reaction is exactly the quality I need in my officers. What a waste! When Zeno and Alexandros walked in on him, all the better—Fabius scared them off and sent them fleeing into the night to become his scapegoats. He was lucky that Zeno died, because Zeno almost certainly had recognized him. But Alexandros had never seen him before, and so couldn't tell Iaia and Olympias whom he had seen."

"That was why Fabius left the name Spartacus unfinished—because the slaves disturbed him?"

"No. He had already cleaned the visible blood in the library and wiped it from the floor of the hallway, but he had not yet gathered up the incriminating scrolls that Lucius had been poring over. Some of them had been open on the table when he killed Lucius and were spattered with blood. Fabius had simply rolled them up to get them out of the way and put them on the floor. He intended to finish scrawling the name, rearrange the corpse in a more convincing manner, and then go back to the library to gather up the incriminating documents, so that he could toss them into the sea along with the cloak, or perhaps burn them.

"Then he heard a voice from the hallway. Someone in the house had apparently heard him working or had been awakened by the clatter of the slaves departing and had gotten up to investigate. The voice called again, closer to the atrium; Fabius knew he would have to flee immediately or else commit a second murder. I don't know why he lost his nerve; of course he had no way of telling if the newcomer was armed or not, alone or with others. At any rate, he grabbed the cloak and fled."

"But no one in the house admitted to hearing anything that night."

"Oh?" Crassus said sardonically. "Then someone lied to you. Imagine! Who might that have been?"

"Dionysius."

Crassus nodded. "The old scoundrel walked into the atrium to find his patron lying dead on the floor. Instead of raising an alarm, he took his time to evaluate the situation and consider how he might profit from it. He headed for the library to do some quick snooping. He found the incriminating documents; why they were incriminating he had no way of knowing, but the blood on the parchment spoke for itself. He took them up to his room and hid them away, then presumably pored over them at his leisure, trying to connect them with the murder.

"Imagine Fabius's panic when he arrived at the villa with me the next day and, sneaking off to the library at his first opportunity, found that the documents had vanished! And yet he gave no outward sign of his agitation. What a cool, calculating countenance! What an officer Rome has lost!

"It wasn't until the night you arrived that he was able to slip down to the boathouse to throw the weapons into the water; he had attempted to do so on previous nights, but there was always some interruption, or else he was seen and couldn't risk going through with it. Actually, I think he was being overhesitant; your arrival spurred him to take the risk—and then you came upon him in the middle of the act! Stabbing you would have looked too much like a second murder, so he tried to drown you instead."

"He failed."

"Yes. From that moment, Fabius told me, he knew you were the arm of Nemesis."

"Nemesis has many arms," I said, thinking of all those who had played a part in exposing Faustus Fabius—Mummius and Gelina, Iaia and Olympias, Alexandros and Apollonius, Eco and Meto, loose-tongued Sergius Orata and the dead Dionysius, and even Crassus himself.

"So it was Fabius who later slipped into the library and cleaned the blood from the statue's head?"

Crassus nodded.

"But why did he wait so long? Was it a detail he had simply overlooked until then?"

"No, he had wanted to do a more thorough cleaning of the library before, but I was always here working, or he was busy attending to duties, or else there was someone who might see him in the hallway. But your arrival set him in furious motion to cover all his tracks."

"My arrival," I said, "and Dionysius's vanity."

"Exactly. When the old windbag bragged at dinner about beating you to the solution, he sealed his own fate. Whether he actually suspected Fabius is doubtful, but Fabius had no way of knowing what the philosopher had deduced. The next morning, amid the confusion of the funeral arrangements, he slipped into Dionysius's room and added poison to his herbal concoction. You were correct, by the way; he used aconitum. While he was in the room he also attempted to pry open Dionysius's trunk, suspecting the missing scrolls might be hidden there; the lock proved too strong and he finally fled the room, fearing that Dionysius or a slave would walk in on him."

"Where did he obtain the poison?"

"In Rome. He purchased the aconitum from some vendor in the Subura the night before we set out. Even then he realized he might have to kill Lucius, and he hoped to be able to do it in a more subtle, more secretive fashion than bashing in his skull. The poison was brought for Lucius, but it was used to silence Dionysius. I found more of the stuff in Fabius's room, and confiscated it to keep him from using it on himself. I don't intend to let him off that easily."

"And last night, on my way to Cumae, Fabius attempted to murder me."

"Not Fabius, but his agents. During your altercation in front of the stables he glimpsed the bloodstained cloak hidden under your own. He thought he had tossed it into the sea on the night of the murder; that was the first time he knew that the cloak had been found."

"Yes," I said, "I remember the odd look on his face."

"Had you bothered to show the cloak to me—had you trusted me from the outset with *all* the evidence, Gordianus—I would have recognized it immediately, and all manner of wheels would have begun to turn. But alas! Fabius could only hope that you had withheld it from me, either on purpose or through neglect, and that I hadn't yet seen it, as was the case. He had no choice but to kill you and recover the cloak and destroy it as quickly as possible.

"It was Fabius whom I had charged to obtain gladiators and organize the funeral games; usually I would have assigned Mummius, but given his weakness for the Greek slave and his distaste for the spectacle I was planning, he was unreliable. Fabius had already determined to eliminate you, one way or another. He had brought two gladiators up from the camp at Lake Lucrinus, just in case he needed them, and so had them ready to send after you immediately when you departed for Cumae. Fabius asked you where you were headed, do you remember? You made the grave error of telling him. Fabius sent the gladiators to follow you and the boy, assassinate you both, and bring him the cloak."

I nodded. "And when our bodies were found, the murders would have been blamed again on Alexandros, hiding in the woods!"

"Exactly. But you would have been no safer here at the villa. His other plan, had you spent the night here, was to steal into your room and pour a draft of hyoscyamus oil into your ear. Do you know its effects?"

A chill crept up my spine. "Pig-bean oil; I've heard of it."

"It was another poison he had purchased and brought from Rome, another option for eliminating Lucius, short of murdering him; given its effects, it would have taken care of you quite nicely. They say that if one pours an adequate dose into the ear of a sleeping man, he will wake up the next morning raving and incoherent, completely deranged. You see, Gordianus, had you spent last night here in your room, you might be a babbling idiot now."

"And had Eco not shouted a warning outside the arena today, a spear would have pierced me from neck to navel."

"Another gift from Fabius. When only one of his assassins returned to him last night with news that you had escaped with the cloak, he ordered the gladiator to act as his private watchman, to hide above the entrance to my box and watch for your arrival. Without my knowledge, Fabius discharged the guards who should have been standing before the entrance, so there would be no witnesses. It was his last desperate gambit; had the assassin succeeded in spearing you, he would have informed Fabius and you would have been carted off to rot with the dead gladiators, an anonymous and unlamented corpse."

"And tonight Faustus Fabius would be free of all suspicion."

"Yes," Crassus sighed, "and the people of the Cup would be spreading tales of the unique and glorious spectacle staged by Marcus Licinius Crassus, stories that would reverberate all the way up to Rome and down to Spartacus's camp at Thurii."

"And ninety-nine innocent slaves would be dead."

Crassus looked at me in silence, then smiled thinly. "But instead, the opposite of each of these things has happened. I think, Gordianus, that you are indeed an arm of Nemesis. Your work here has merely fulfilled the will of the gods. How else could it be, except as a jest of the gods, that tonight I should be sitting here drinking the last of my cousin's excellent Falernian wine with the only man in the world who thinks the lives of ninety-nine slaves are more important than the ambitions of the richest man in Rome?"

"What will you do with them?"

"With whom?"

"The one hundred."

He swirled the last of the wine in his cup and stared into the red vortex. "They're useless to me now. Certainly they can't be returned to this house, or to any of my properties; I could never trust any of them again, after what's happened. I considered selling them here at Puteoli, but I don't care to have them spreading their story all over the Cup. I shall ship them off to the markets at Alexandria."

"The Thracian slave, Alexandros—"

"Iaia has already approached me, asking to buy him as a gift for Olympias." He sipped his wine. "Completely out of the question, of course."

"But why?"

"Because it is just possible that someone might decide to bring a murder charge against Faustus Fabius and force a trial; I've told you that I have no desire for such a public spectacle. Any prosecutor would of course call on Alexandros to testify, but a slave cannot testify without his master's permission. Now, so long as I own Alexandros I will never allow him to speak of the matter again. He must be put out of reach. He's young and strong; probably I shall make him a galley slave or a mine worker, or send him to a slave market so far away that he will quietly vanish forever."

"But why not let Olympias have him?"

"Because if murder charges are ever brought against Faustus Fabius, she might allow him to testify."

"A slave can't testify except under torture; Olympias would never permit that."

"She might manumit him; in fact, she probably would, and a freedman can testify to his heart's content, and to my eternal embarrassment."

"You could extract a pledge—"

"No! I cannot permit the slave to stay anywhere in the region of the Cup, don't you see? So long as he's about, people will keep talking about the affair of Lucius Licinius, and wasn't Alexandros the slave everyone accused of the murder, and didn't it actually turn out that some patrician did it, or so the gossips say—you see, he simply has to vanish from the Cup, one way or another. My way is more merciful than simply killing him, don't you see?"

I clenched my jaw. The wine was suddenly bitter. "And the slave Apollonius?"

"Mummius wants to buy him, as you must already know. Again, out of the question."

"But Apollonius knows nothing!"

"Nonsense! You yourself sent him diving for the weapons that Faustus Fabius tossed into the water."

"Even so—"

"And his presence among the other ninety-nine this afternoon ruins him for any further service in any proximity to me. Mummius is my right-hand man; I can't have a slave I almost put to death living in Mummius's home, serving me wine when I come to visit and turning down my bed for me at night, slipping an asp between the coverlets. No, like Alexandros, Apollonius must vanish. I expect it won't be difficult to find a buyer for him, considering his beauty and his talents. There are agents in Alexandria who buy slaves for rich Parthians; that would be best, to sell him to a rich master beyond the edge of the world."

"You'll make an enemy of Marcus Mummius."

"Don't be absurd. Mummius is a soldier, not a sensualist. He's a Roman! His ties to me and his sense of honor far outweigh any fleeting attraction he may feel for a pretty youth."

"I think you're wrong."

Crassus shrugged. Behind the mask of hard logic on his face, I saw his smug satisfaction. How could such a great and powerful man take pleasure in exacting such petty revenge on those who had foiled him? I closed my weary eyes for a moment.

"You said earlier that I would be paid the fee I was promised, Marcus Crassus. As part of my fee . . . as a favor . . . there is a boy among the slaves, a mere child called Meto—"

Crassus shook his head grimly. His mouth was a straight line. His narrow eyes glinted in the lamplight. "Ask me for no more favors concerning the slaves, Gordianus. They are alive, and for that you may credit your own tenacity and Gelina's insistence, but your fee will be paid in silver, not in flesh, and not one of the slaves will receive special treatment. Not one! They shall be dispersed beyond the reach of anyone in this house, sold to new masters and put to good use, doing their small share to build the prosperity and maintain the eternal power of Rome."

Crassus and his retinue made ready to leave for Rome the next morning. The slaves, with Apollonius, Alexandros, and Meto among them, were herded from the stables down to the camp by Lake Lucrinus, and then to the docks at Puteoli. Olympias, weeping and refusing to be comforted, shut herself away in her room. Mummius watched the slaves depart with a grim jaw and an ashen face.

Iaia's household slaves were summoned from Cumae to tend to necessities at the villa. Eco's fever broke but he did not awaken.

That night a dinner in Crassus's honor was held at one of Orata's villas in Puteoli, where Crassus and his retinue spent the night. Gelina attended, but I was not invited. Iaia stayed with me to watch over Eco. Crassus departed the Cup the next morning. Gelina made ready to vacate the villa to spend the winter at Crassus's house in Rome.

Eco awoke the next day. He was weak but his appetite was strong, and the fever did not return. I half expected that his newly restored power of speech would vanish with his illness; if, as Crassus had said, my work in Baiae had merely been to fulfill the will of the gods, then it was reasonable to assume that the gods had granted Eco the ability to cry out merely for the purpose of saving my life outside the arena, and that now they would reclaim the gift. But when he opened his eyes that morning and looked up at me, he whispered in a hoarse, childlike voice, "Papa, where are we, Papa?"

I wept, and did not stop weeping for a long time. Iaia, even with her access to Apollo's mysteries, could not explain what had transpired.

As soon as he was well enough, Eco and I began the journey back to Rome, by land rather than sea. Mummius had left horses for our use and soldiers to act as our bodyguards on the road. I appreciated his concern, especially since I was carrying a rather substantial amount of silver on my person, my fee for finding the murderer of Lucius Licinius.

We took the Via Consularis to Capua, where Spartacus had trained to be a gladiator and had revolted against his master. Then we took the Via Appia northward, drinking in the splendid autumnal scenery, never imagining that in the spring its broad, paved width would be lined for mile after mile, all the way to Rome, with six thousand crucified bodies—unlucky survivors of the annihilated army of Spartacus, nailed on crosses and publicly displayed for the moral edification of slaves and masters alike.

EPILOGUE

YOU'LL never believe who's come to see us!'' said Eco. His voice was a bit deep and hoarse for such a young man, but to me it was more beautiful than any orator's.

''Oh, I might,'' I said. Just to hear him speak, even two years after the events at Baiae, was enough to make me believe almost anything. I had learned not to question the whims of the gods or to take them for granted.

I set down the scroll I had been perusing and took a sip of cool wine. It was a midsummer's day. The sun was hot, but a cool breeze fluttered about the flowers in my garden, causing the asters to bob their heads and the sunflowers to dance.

''Could it be . . . Marcus Mummius?'' I said.

Eco looked at me from beneath beetling brows. For a while, after he regained his speech, he had become a child again, always questioning, always curious, but speech had also made him whole and had quickened his manhood. His father's amazing deductions could no longer impress him as easily as in the old days.

''You heard his voice from the foyer,'' he said accusingly.

I laughed. ''No, I heard his voice from all the way outside the house. I couldn't place that loud bellowing at first, but then I remembered. Show him in.''

Mummius had come alone, which surprised me, given his important new rank in the city. I stood to greet him, citizen to citizen, and offered him a chair. Eco joined us. I sent one of the slave girls for more wine.

He looked different somehow. I studied him for a moment, perplexed. ''You've shaved your beard, Marcus Mummius!''

''Yes.'' He reached up and tugged self-consciously at his

naked chin. "They tell me a beard is too old-fashioned for a politician, or too radical, I can't remember which. Anyway, I shaved it off during the electioneering last fall."

"It flatters you. No, really, it does. It shows off your strong jaw. And that handsome scar on your chin—from the battle of the Colline Gate?"

"Ha! A fresh one, from fighting the Spartacans."

I laughed. "You've prospered, Marcus Mummius, and set your foot on a new career."

He shrugged and looked about the peristyle. The place was less of a mess than usual, which was as it should be, given the new slaves that Bethesda had insisted I purchase. "You've prospered, too, Gordianus."

"In my way. But to be elected Praetor Urbanus—such an honor! What are your reflections, midway through your term of office?"

He suppressed a foolish-looking grin. "It's all right, I suppose. Pretty boring, really, sitting in courts all day. Believe me, falling asleep standing upright is a small trick compared to staying awake on a hot afternoon listening to those advocates bicker and drone about some tedious lawsuit. Thank Jupiter it's only for a year! Although I will admit that organizing the Apollinarian Games this summer was amusing enough. You were there?"

I shook my head. "No, but I'm told that the Circus Maximus was filled to overflowing and the spectacles were unforgettable."

"Well, as long as the god Apollo was pleased."

The slave girl arrived with wine. We sipped in silence.

"Your son has become quite a man." Mummius smiled at Eco.

"Yes, he brings greater joy to his father every year. But tell me, Marcus Mummius, have you simply come to visit an acquaintance you haven't seen in two years, or does the Praetor Urbanus of Rome have business with Gordianus the Finder?"

"Business? No. Actually, I've been meaning to visit you for some time, but my duties are quite demanding. I don't imagine you've had much contact with Crassus since Baiae?"

"None at all, except for seeing his election graffiti everywhere last fall, and hearing him speak in the Forum from time to time. I'm a busy man myself, Marcus Mummius, and my duties don't seem to bring me in contact with the great Consul of the Roman Republic."

He nodded. "Yes, Crassus got everything he wanted, didn't he? Well, not quite everything, and not exactly as he wished. You went to the ovation they gave him last December, for defeating Spartacus?"

I shook my head.

"No? But you attended the great feast he gave this month, in honor of Hercules?"

I shook my head again.

"But how could you have missed it? They set up ten thousand tables in the streets and the thing lasted for three days! I should know, it was part of my job to keep the peace. Surely you collected the three months' worth of grain that Crassus distributed to every citizen?"

I shook my head. "Would you believe, Marcus Mummius, that I made a point of being at a friend's house up in Etruria during that time? It occurred to me that Eco might enjoy walking in the hills and fishing in a stream, and Rome does become so hot and crowded in midsummer."

He pursed his lips. "My own relations with Marcus Crassus are not exactly warm."

"Oh?"

"They're strained, actually. I suppose you know all about the slave war, the decimation, all that."

"Not from your point of view, Marcus Mummius."

He sighed and folded his hands. Clearly, he had come to unburden himself. I had said before that there is something in me that compels others to bare their secrets. I took a stiff draft of wine and tilted my chair so I could lean back against a pillar.

"It happened early in the campaign," he began. "Crassus had his six legions, raised with his own money. He assigned the Senate's two legions to my command, the ones that had already encountered Spartacus and been defeated. I thought

I could whip them into shape, but they were already badly demoralized, and there wasn't much time.

"The Spartacans were bearing down on Picentia from the south, heading for the Cup. Crassus sent me to observe and report back on their movements. It's true, he ordered me not to engage them, not even to skirmish with them, but a lieutenant in the field has to use his judgment. A group of Spartacans became separated from their fellows in a narrow valley; no reasonable military man would have failed to attack them. In the midst of the battle, word spread that Spartacus had set an ambush for us and that his whole army was closing in. It was a false rumor, but panic spread through the ranks. My men bolted and fled. Many were killed. Many were captured and tortured to death. Many threw down their weapons and ran.

"Crassus was furious. He berated me in front of his other lieutenants. He decided to make an example of my men."

"So I heard," I sighed, but Mummius was determined to tell the story anyway.

"They call it 'decimation'—the removal of one in ten. It's an old Roman tradition, though no one I know can remember it ever happening before in his lifetime. Crassus is a keen one for reviving grand old traditions, as you know. He ordered me to identify the first five hundred who had fled—not an easy task among twelve thousand soldiers. Those five hundred he divided into fifty units of ten men each. The men drew lots. One man in ten drew the black bean. That's fifty men in all who were chosen to die.

"The units were formed into circles. Each victim was stripped naked, his hands bound behind his back and his mouth gagged. The other nine in each unit were given clubs. At Crassus's signal a drumbeat commenced. It was done without honor, without glory, with no dignity at all. There are those who say that Crassus did the right thing—"

"There certainly are," I said, remembering the grunts and grave nods of approval when the story had been told in the marketplaces of Rome.

"But you'd be hard-pressed to find a soldier who believes that. Discipline had to be maintained, certainly, but it's no way for a Roman warrior to die, clubbed to death by his fellows!'' He bit his lips and shook his head. ''But I'm not telling you this story simply to brood over my own bitterness. I thought you deserved to know what became of Faustus Fabius.''

''What do you mean?''

''Did you ever hear of his fate?''

''I know that he never came back from the war. I kept my ears open in the Forum for news about him. I heard he died in combat against the Spartacans.''

Mummius shook his head. ''No. Crassus somehow arranged to have Fabius inserted among the men chosen for the decimation. Naked, bound and gagged, there was nothing to identify his rank or station. When the clubbing began, I forced myself to watch, along with Crassus and the other lieutenants. They were my men, after all; I couldn't turn my back on them. Among the victims there was one who managed to spit out his gag; he kept screaming that a mistake had been made. No one else paid any attention, but I ran over to take a closer look.

''A moment later and I would never have recognized him, not after the clubs struck his face. But I saw him clearly enough. It was Faustus Fabius. The look in his eyes! He recognized me; he called my name. Then they knocked him to the ground. They crushed his skull and beat him to a bloody pulp, until you could hardly tell he was a man at all. What a horrible way to die!''

''No more horrible than the deaths of Lucius Licinius or Dionysius; certainly no more horrible than the fate that Crassus had in mind for the slaves.''

''Even so, for a Roman patrician and officer to die such a shameful death! I stared at Crassus in horror. He wouldn't look back at me, but I saw a smile on his lips.''

''Yes, I know that smile. Here, drink more wine, Marcus Mummius. Your voice grows hoarse.''

He swallowed the wine like water and wiped his lips. ''The war didn't last long. Six months, and it was over. We trapped them like rats at the southern tip of Italy and destroyed them.

Crassus had the six thousand survivors nailed to crosses along the Via Appia."

"So I heard."

Mummius smiled faintly. "Fortune nodded to Marcus Crassus, but she smirked as well. A small band of the Spartacans escaped and made their way north, just in time to meet Pompey's army returning at last from Spain. Pompey crushed them like ants beneath his heel and then sent a letter to the Senate, claiming that while Crassus had done a worthy job, it was he, Pompey, who had finally put an end to the slave revolt!" He laughed, and some of the color returned to his cheeks.

"Why, Mummius, you sound as if you'd changed camps and become a partisan of Pompey."

"I'm no man's partisan now. I'm a war hero, didn't you know? At least that's what my family and friends told me when I came back to Rome. They're the ones who made me stand for Praetor Urbanus. I'd rather be in a tent under the stars, eating out of a wooden pot."

"I'm sure you would."

"Anyway, Pompey and Crassus have made peace with each other, for the moment. After all, there are two Consuls every year, so each of them gets to be Consul. Of course, Pompey received a full triumph for defeating Sertorius in Spain, and the Senate would only allow Crassus an ovation for defeating Spartacus; there can be only so much glory for beating a slave. So while Pompey entered the city with trumpets and a chariot, Crassus followed behind on horseback to the sound of flutes. But he did manage to talk the Senate into letting him wear a laurel crown, not just a myrtle wreath."

"And the great feast he hosted this month?"

"In honor of Hercules. Why not, since Pompey dedicated a temple and held games in honor of Hercules at the same time! They go back and forth, stealing one another's thunder. Still, Pompey can't claim to have sacrificed a tenth of his wealth to Hercules and the people of Rome, as Crassus did. It takes a very rich man to be a successful politician these days!"

I looked at him skeptically. "Somehow, Marcus Mummius, I don't think that you came to visit me after all this time just to gossip about politics, or even to tell me the fate of Faustus Fabius."

He looked back at me with equal shrewdness. "You're right, Gordianus. I can't fool you for long. Though I will say that you're one of the few men in Rome with whom it would be worth sharing gossip—I feel I can speak to you honestly. No, I came with other news, and to offer you a gift."

"A gift?"

At that moment one of the slave girls caught my eye. "More visitors," she announced.

Mummius was smiling from ear to ear.

"Yes?" I said.

"Two slaves, master. They say they belong to your guest."

"Then show them in!"

A moment later two figures appeared in the peristyle. It was Apollonius who caught my eye first. He was as striking as ever. From behind him a smaller figure came racing headlong into the garden and was upon me before I could steady myself in my chair. Meto wrapped his arms around my neck and sent me tumbling backward. Eco laughed out loud.

Mummius rose and extended his hand. Apollonius stepped forward, walking with a slight limp. Together they pulled me to my feet.

Meto stood grinning at me and shuffling from foot to foot, suddenly shy. He had grown considerably since I had seen him, but was still a boy.

"Marcus Mummius, I don't understand. Crassus told me—"

"Yes, that he would disperse the slaves to the ends of the earth, beyond recall. But Marcus Crassus isn't the cleverest Roman, you know, just the richest. My agent found Apollonius in Alexandria. His new owner was a cruel man, and not disposed to part with him. I traveled there last summer, after the war was over and before the election campaign began in the fall. To loosen the man's grasp I had to resort to Roman persuasion: a little silver, a little steel—such as a sword pulled halfway from its scabbard—and just the right tone of voice to set a fat Egyptian quivering.

"Apollonius was weak from mistreatment and fell sick on the journey to Rome. He was ill all through the autumn and winter, but he's recovered now." Mummius scratched his bare chin, and a glimmer lit his eye. "He says I look better without my beard."

"And you do!" said Apollonius, smiling affectionately.

"I suppose I'll eventually get used to it."

"Does Crassus know?" I said.

"About my beard? Ha! No, you mean about Apollonius. Maybe, maybe not. I don't see Crassus very often nowadays, except when duty demands it. He isn't likely to encounter my household slaves in the normal course of events, and if he does, I shall say to him, 'Why else did Romans fight and die against Spartacus, Marcus Crassus, except to protect the right of a citizen to own slaves as he chooses?' I don't fear Crassus. I think he's much too busy matching strokes with Pompey to fret over an old spite against me."

He reached out to tousle Meto's hair. "It took me longer to track down this one, though he was only down in Sicily. Quite a few of the other house slaves ended up there, sold as a lot. The stupid farmer who bought him ignored his training and put him to work in the fields. Isn't that right, Meto?"

"He made me play scarecrow in the orchards. I had to stand out in the hot sun all day to scare them off, and he wrapped my hands up in rags so that I couldn't eat the fruit off the trees."

"Imagine that," I said, swallowing to clear a sudden lump in my throat. "What about Alexandros, the Thracian?"

Mummius's face darkened. "Crassus sent him to work in one of his silver mines in Spain. Slaves usually don't live long in the mines, even strong, young slaves. I sent an agent to try to buy him, anonymously, but the foreman wouldn't budge. Word must have got back to Crassus; Alexandros was transferred from the mines to a galley—the *Fury*, in fact. Even so, I still hoped to save him. Then, only a few days ago—on the very day that Meto arrived in Rome—I learned that the *Fury* had been raided and burned by pirates off the coast of Sardinia. A few sailors escaped to tell the story."

"And Alexandros?"

"The *Fury* was sunk with the slaves still chained to their posts."

I sighed and gritted my teeth. I threw back my head to empty my cup and stared at the sunflowers that nodded in the breeze. "A death more terrible than that of Faustus Fabius, I should think! He might have saved himself if he had stayed hidden in that cave, if he hadn't come forward to identify Fabius. But then Apollonius and Meto would not be alive today. What a remarkable people these Thracians are! Does Olympias know?"

He shook his head. "I had hoped to surprise her with good news. Now I think I shall never tell her."

"Perhaps we should. Otherwise she may hope and hope, to no end. Iaia is wise enough to find a way to tell her."

"Perhaps."

For a long moment there was silence in the garden, except the rustling of a cat among the asters. Mummius smiled.

"You see, I waited to call on you until I had a surprise for you. Meto is my gift to you. You told Crassus that you wanted to buy the boy, didn't you? It's the least I can do, to thank you for saving Apollonius and the others."

"But I wished to buy him only to save him from Crassus . . ."

"Then take him now, please, if only to spite Crassus! You know that the boy is clever and honest; he'll be a credit to your household."

I looked at Meto, who smiled at me hopefully. I thought of him with his hands wrapped in rags, hungry and hot, chasing after crows in a dusty orchard.

"Very well," I said. "I accept your gift, Marcus Mummius. Thank you."

Mummius grinned broadly. Then an odd look passed over his face, and he rose hurriedly to his feet. I turned and saw that Bethesda had entered the peristyle from the direction of the kitchen.

I took her hand in mine. Mummius made a funny, bashful

face and shifted about nervously, as men often do in the presence of a very pregnant woman.

"My wife," I said. "Gordiana Bethesda."

Mummius nodded dumbly. Behind him, Apollonius smiled. Little Meto looked up at Bethesda's looming belly with parted lips, clearly in awe of his new mistress.

"I can't stay long in the garden," Bethesda said. "It's much too hot. I was on my way to lie down for a while, but I thought I heard voices here in the peristyle. So you are Marcus Mummius. Gordianus has spoken of you often. Welcome to our home."

Mummius only swallowed and nodded. Bethesda smiled and withdrew. "Oh, Eco," she called over her shoulder, "come along and help me for a moment."

Eco nodded to our guests and followed after her.

Mummius cocked an eyebrow. "But I thought . . ."

"Yes, Bethesda was my slave. And for years I was very careful to avoid producing another slave by her. I wanted no children of my own blood, certainly not slave children."

"But your son . . ."

"Eco came into my life unannounced. I thank the gods every day that I had the wisdom to adopt him. But I saw no reason to bring a new life into such a world." I shrugged. "After Baiae something stirred in me. Bethesda is now a freedwoman, and my wife."

Mummius grinned. "And now I see what you were busy doing nine months ago, last December, instead of going out to watch Crassus's ovation!"

I laughed and leaned toward him. "Do you know, Mummius, I believe it did occur on that very night!"

Eco suddenly appeared at the far end of the peristyle. The two slave girls flanked him. All three wore expressions of shock, dismay, confusion, and joy.

Eco opened his mouth. For a long moment he seemed to be mute again. Then the words tumbled out. "Bethesda says she's ready—she says it's beginning!"

Mummius turned pale. Apollonius smiled serenely.

Meto whirled and clapped his hands. I rolled my eyes heavenward.

"Another crisis arrives," I whispered, feeling suddenly fearful, and then impossibly elated. "Another story begins."

AUTHOR'S NOTE

ALTHOUGH he attained fabulous wealth and shared in the First Triumvirate with Caesar and Pompey, Marcus Licinius Crassus is universally regarded as one of history's biggest losers. His crucial mistake was getting killed in his ill-conceived campaign against the Parthians in 53 B.C., at the height of his power and prestige. Decapitation has a way of making even the richest man in the world irrelevant.

There are two biographies of Crassus in English. Allen Mason Ward's invaluable *Marcus Crassus and the Late Roman Republic* (University of Missouri Press, 1977) is meticulously researched and argued; F. E. Adcock's *Marcus Crassus, Millionaire* (W. Heffer & Sons, Ltd., Cambridge, 1966) is essentially a long, elegant essay. Ward is sometimes forgiving to a fault, as when he writes of Crassus's decimation of his own soldiers: "Times were desperate, and desperate measures were needed. . . . it would not be fair to criticize Crassus's behavior as unnaturally vicious." Adcock, on the other hand, may be too glib when he writes of the young Crassus: "He did not wear his heart upon his sleeve, and it might be doubted whether he had a heart to wear."

Our chief sources for the Spartacan revolt are Appian's *History* and Plutarch's *Life of Crassus*. Original source material on other slave uprisings, and on Roman slavery in general, can be found in Thomas Wiedemann's *Greek and Roman Slavery* (Routledge, London, 1988).

The most comprehensive guide to Roman painting, potions, and poisons is Pliny's *Natural History*, which also supplies our scant knowledge of Iaia and Olympias. Those interested in the mythic properties of the Sibyl of Cumae may consult Virgil's *Aeneid*. References to food are scattered through many sources (the Pythagorean comment on beans in chapter 7, for example, comes from Cicero's *On Divination*), but the richest larder of information is Apicius; adventurous cooks and armchair gourmets may consult *The Roman Cookery of Apicius* (Hartley & Marks, Inc., 1984), translated by John Edwards with recipes adapted for the modern kitchen.

Every now and then a researcher discovers a previously unknown volume that fits his needs with uncanny precision. So it was when I discovered *Romans on the Bay of Naples: A Social and Cultural History of the Villas and Their Owners from 150 B.C. to A.D. 400* (Harvard University Press, 1970), by John H. D'Arms. It was a book I longed to read even before I knew it existed.

For small details and matters of nomenclature, I consulted on an almost daily basis a massive, musty, 1300-page edition of William Smith's unsurpassed *Dictionary of Greek and Roman Antiquities* (James Walton, London; second edition, 1869), and to a lesser extent *Everyday Life of the Greeks and Romans* by Guhl and Koner, another nineteenth-century reference work (Crescent Books, reprinted 1989).

My adaptation of Lucretius's "Why Fear Death?" (following Dryden's translation) for the funeral in chapter 16 is arguably anachronistic, given that Lucretius's *On the Nature of the Universe* was not published until around 55 B.C. However, I like to imagine (and it is possible) that in 72 B.C. Lucretius, still in his twenties, might already have been working on early drafts of his great poem, bits of which might have circulated among the philosophers, poets, and performers who lived on the Cup.

I want to say thank you to some people whose personal interest in my work and professional support of my career have been unflagging: to my editor Michael Denneny and his assistant, Keith Kahla; to Terri Odom and the Odom clan; to John W. Rowberry and John Preston; to my sister Gwyn, Keeper of the Disks; and of course to Rick Solomon.

A library figures prominently in this novel—the library of Lucius Licinius is the scene of the murder. In the here and now, it is libraries which are being killed—cut back, shut down, dismantled and dispersed, book by book and dollar by dollar. Yet without them, I could hardly have done my research. I especially appreciate the San Francisco Public Library, severely shaken but not shut down by the earthquake of 1989; the Interlibrary Loan system, which allows access to volumes from collections all over the country; the Perry-Castañeda Library on the campus of the University of Texas at Austin, where I've spent whole days among the stacks in a kind of information ecstasy, uncovering material for both *Arms of Nemesis* and its sequel, *Catilina's Riddle*; and the Jennie Trent Dew Memorial Library in Goldthwaite, Texas, where in a sense all my historical research began some thirty years ago.